DARK SKIES

ALSO BY DANIELLE L. JENSEN

THE DARK SHORES SERIES
Dark Shores

THE MALEDICTION TRILOGY
Stolen Songbird
Hidden Huntress
Warrior Witch
The Broken Ones (prequel)

THE BRIDGE KINGDOM SERIES
The Bridge Kingdom
The Traitor Queen

DARK SKIES

DANIELLE L. JENSEN

A TOM DOHERTY ASSOCIATES BOOK
NEW YORK

DARK SKIES

Copyright © 2020 by Danielle L. Jensen

Map by Jennifer Hanover

A Tor Teen Book
Published by Tom Doherty Associates
120 Broadway
New York, NY 10271

www.tor-forge.com

Tor® is a registered trademark of Macmillan Publishing Group, LLC.

The Library of Congress Cataloging-in-Publication Data
is available upon request.

ISBN 978-1-250-31776-6 (hardcover)
ISBN 978-1-250-31775-9 (ebook)

Our books may be purchased in bulk for promotional,
educational, or business use. Please contact your local bookseller
or the Macmillan Corporate and Premium Sales Department
at 1-800-221-7945, extension 5442, or by email at
MacmillanSpecialMarkets@macmillan.com.

First Edition: May 2020

Printed in the United States of America

0 9 8 7 6 5 4 3 2 1

For Nick

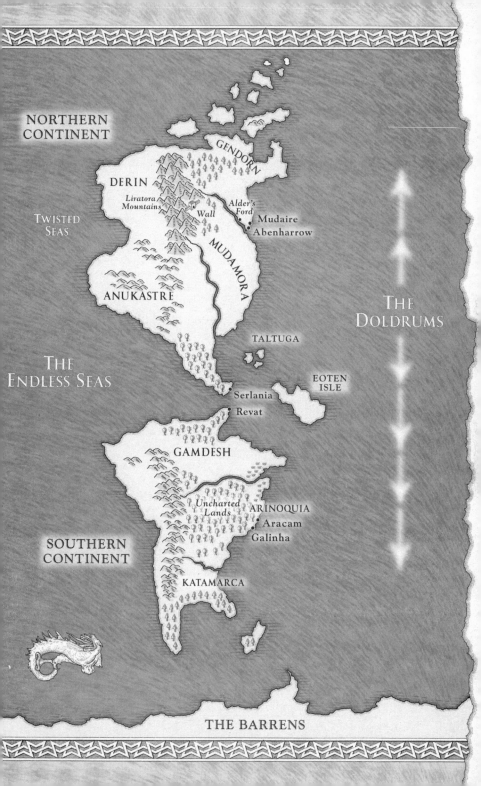

DARK SKIES

1

KILLIAN

Killian dusted sand across the report, taking care not to smear the ink of what was already lackluster penmanship.

Not that it mattered.

The correspondence was nearly identical to what he'd sent the week prior. And the week prior to that. All quiet on the wall. No sign of Derin scouts. No defections. Nothing but monotony—broken by the not-so-occasional game of cards—expected in the weeks to come.

It always took a concerted effort *not* to include the last part.

This was the first command where Killian had been left entirely to his own devices, and it was about gods-damned time. He was nineteen and had been training his entire life to inherit command of the Royal Army, never mind that he'd been marked by the god of war himself. Killian was born to lead soldiers into battle, and yet every time an opportunity arose, his father found some excuse for him to remain taking orders from someone else.

For three years, that someone else had been High Lady Dareena Falorn. It had only been when she'd sent Killian back to the capital carrying a letter stating he was as ready as he'd ever be that his father conceded on the matter. Killian had all of the space of a day to dream about glory before word arrived that the captain of the border wall's garrison had toppled off the very piece of architecture he was supposed to be defending, resulting in an opening in his position. It was, in Killian's mind, a bad bit of luck all around.

The wall blocking the pass between Derin and Mudamora hadn't seen worse than a skirmish in generations and, in his opinion (as well as that of everyone else in the kingdom), never would. The jagged peaks of the Liratora Mountains and the grace of the Six ensured that while Derin and its Seventh-worshipping inhabitants were a problem, they weren't his problem. He'd have seen more conflict guarding the entrance to a palace privy.

Killian softened a stick of wax over a candle and was in the process of smearing it across the fold of another letter when a horn blast echoed through the room, startling him.

"The Seventh take you," he muttered, glaring at the uneven glob of indigo as his good manners briefly warred with his indolence. The latter triumphed, and he pressed his signet ring against the wax, leaving behind the imprint of the galloping horse of House Calorian, less its tail.

The horn echoed a second time.

One blast of the horn meant *something* had been sighted in the pass. But two meant *someone*.

Derin scouts were occasionally seen, but not at this time of year when the snow was as deep as a man was tall. More likely, one of his men had spirited a bottle onto his watch and was seeing shapes in the swirl of snowflakes. Either way, Killian couldn't ignore it.

The horn called again.

Killian's heart slammed against his ribs and he grabbed his sword, not bothering with a cloak as he ran toward the door, the bells already ringing a call to arms.

Three blasts meant only one thing, and it was the reason the wall had been built in the first place.

Ancient and austere, the garrison fortress was built with blocks of grey stone with only arrow slits for windows, the narrow halls lit with smoking candles that cast dancing shadows on the naked floor as Killian raced down three flights of stairs, the cold air slapping him in the face as he stepped outside.

His boots sank in the muddy snow as he strode through the courtyard, noting the twang of bowstrings from above, the clatter of boots as men raced up the narrow stairs that switch-backed their way to the top of the wall. At the gate, his friend and lieutenant, Bercola, stood head and shoulders higher than the soldiers flanking her. All eyes were on what lay beyond the tunnel barred by twin portcullises, the opening of which was shadowed by high wooden scaffolding holding repair materials.

At the sound of his steps, Bercola turned, the giantess giving a grim shake of her head. "It's asking to speak to you."

It.

Killian moved through his men, his eyes drawn through the gates to the woman beyond, snowy peaks rising behind her. She was distant enough to sidestep the arrow shots with ease, her movements too swift to be wholly human. At the sight of him, she extracted a white scrap of fabric from a pocket and held it up in the air.

"Archers, hold." Killian sheathed his sword and accepted a spyglass from Bercola. "And silence all that racket."

"But Captain," one of his men protested. "She's one of the . . ."

"I know what she is." Marked by the Seventh god, the Corrupter. As deadly as a dozen armed men and twice as clever. Her kind were to be killed on sight, but this was the first time he'd seen one up close, and Killian was . . . *curious.*

"Good morning," he shouted, ignoring the exclamations of the soldiers around him. "I'd invite you in for a drink, but I'm afraid I wasn't furnished with a key to the gatehouse."

"Is that the only thing stopping you, Lord Calorian?" she called back.

Killian's jaw tightened. It was no secret he was in command, but still disconcerting to have his name on the lips of one of the corrupted. "Perhaps a certain sense of self-preservation." He raised the spyglass to his eye in time to see a smile work its way onto her face. She was lovely in the way of a poisonous flower: better from a distance.

"Likewise," she said. "You've a reputation, my lord, and I'm afraid accepting that drink might have consequences."

It was a reputation that he hadn't earned, but Killian had long since come to realize that denying it only made people more likely to believe the rumors. "*Consequences* isn't the word most people use." He stepped out of the company of his men and walked closer. "Privileges, pleasures, delights . . ."

"God-marked lunatic," someone muttered from behind him, but Killian ignored the comment. Dangerous as she was, the woman was at least fifty paces away and on the far side of a wall twelve feet thick—what harm was there in speaking to her?

"If only hubris translated into skill," she replied, half-turning her head, seemingly listening for something.

Killian caught Bercola's eye, but the giantess shook her head. No sign of anyone else in the pass. "There is only one sure way to find out," he called back.

The corrupted tucked the white fabric into her pocket. "We've no time for this. You need to let me through." She cast another glance over her shoulder and scanned the pass, snow-shoes sinking into the powder. "They're coming. There isn't much time."

Uneasy murmurs ran through the ranks, but the spyglass in Killian's hand revealed nothing but snow, rocks, and the occasional tree.

"You must think me mad," he said, resting his elbows on the thick steel bars, through with banter. "I know what you are and what you can do. And frankly, these gates haven't been opened in decades. I'm not sure if they can be." He glanced at his men. "Anyone?"

His men laughed, but there was a nervous edge to it.

"I have no intention of harming you or your men," she said. "Just the opposite—I want to help. I want to stop *her*. But I need you to help me first." Another nervous glance over her shoulder and she took two steps closer to the gate.

"Stay back," Killian shouted, sensing his archers wavering and not wanting an arrow loosed just yet.

"Please." There was more than desperation in her voice; there was fear. And it was driving her closer. "Rufina has ten thousand men with her, and that is a mere fraction of her host."

Who in the bloody underworld is Rufina?

"No closer." His heart hammered in his chest, the endless darkness of her eyes making him want to pull his sword. Or run. "I've given you fair warning."

"I know her plans." The corrupted was walking toward them now, movements smooth and predatory. "Let me through the gates and I can help you stop her."

"Why would one of the corrupted want to help *me* of all people?"

"Because if she's victorious, I'll never be free of this curse."

She was only thirty feet away. Killian's gut told him to hear her out, but logic said otherwise. His hand went to the pommel of his sword. "I don't trust you. I know what you're capable of."

Twenty feet. "I might be a monster," she said. "But I'm not a liar."

Fifteen. She was corrupted, and the King's command was to kill them on sight. But to do so didn't *feel* right. "Stop."

She kept coming. And Killian had his orders.

"Shoot!"

He saw the six shafts protruding from her chest almost before he heard the bows twang. Surprise blossomed across her face, and she stumbled forward, each step punctuated by another bowshot.

Her eyes fixed on his. "I am not a liar," she whispered, then fell face first into the snow.

No one spoke. Not a word.

You should've heard her out.

Killian's voice rasped as he said, "Get me on the other side of the wall."

You've made a mistake.

"But sir, she's—"

Something is wrong.

"Dead." *Because of him.* "Now open the gods-damned gates."

They stared at him, unmoving. Every one of them were veteran soldiers. Most had seen war countless times. Against Gendorn and Anukastre. Some, with darker skin like his own, had likely fought in the Giant Wars, which had taken place when Killian was still toddling around with a toy sword. But that woman, that *thing* lying bleeding in the snow, terrified them. "Get me a rope."

Something was coming.

2

LYDIA

The litter swayed from side to side, the motion, along with the oppressive heat, causing Lydia's eyelids to hang heavy, the cushion beneath her elbow inviting her to rest her head. Outside, the voices of the citizens filling Celendrial's streets faded to a dull drone, and her mind grew sluggish as sleep beckoned.

Adjusting the angle of her book so that the light shining through the curtains illuminated the script, Lydia read, wishing she were in her library with its doors open to the cool sea breeze.

But she cared more for her father's well-being than she did for her own comfort, and left to his own devices, he'd have insisted on walking the distance between their home and the Curia, never mind the consequences to his health.

Her eyes flicked to where he sat across from her, a letter held in one hand and several more scattered on the cushions between them, his distraction allowing her to examine his features.

Unlike her own, Senator Appius Valerius's skin was the golden hue ubiquitous to those with Cel heritage. But in recent months that gold had turned puffy and jaundiced, and over breakfast she'd noticed that the whites of his grey eyes had yellowed as well.

An affliction of the liver, the physicians had said while giving her bottles of tonics with which to dose him.

Terminal, they'd said once they'd believed her out of earshot.

"Ease your mind," her father murmured, not taking his eyes from the page. "I'm quite fine."

As though *easing her mind* were possible. Her foster father was her only family, and even if they'd been bound by blood, she didn't think it possible to love him more.

Desperate for distraction, Lydia twitched open the curtain, taking in the comings and goings of the city through the narrow gap in the fabric. They were heading to the heart of Celendrial, the men carrying the litter keeping to the shadow of the aqueduct high above them, her father's guards striding to either side. As they walked beneath a place where the system branched, the litter bearer closest to her lifted his face to the sky, opening his mouth to catch the water streaming from a crack in the masonry.

When he lowered his head, his eyes widened as he caught her watching. "Apologies."

Lydia smiled and waved her hand to dispel his embarrassment. And her own. "It's a wonder the aqueducts haven't run dry in this heat. What misery should we have to rely on the river Savio."

"As you say, Domina," the litter bearer replied, but instead of turning his attention back to the street, he eyed her brazenly. She tried to ignore the unwelcome scrutiny, knowing it was her appearance that provoked his curiosity. With her black hair, upturned green eyes, and ivory complexion, she was obviously *not* Cel, which made her rights to the honorific questionable at best.

"Do not gape at your betters, you idiot," the man next to him snapped, kicking him in the ankle. No mean feat given the weight they carried, but Lydia pretended not to notice the exchange, directing her gaze to the Great Library.

It contained the largest collection of literature on Reath: works from every province, on every subject, and in every language, living or dead. Lydia lived and breathed the place. Her greatest wish was to join the ranks of scholars studying in its hallowed halls, for her days to be filled with the smell of parchment and ink, her most precious dream of all for her work to be considered for inclusion into the collection.

Never mind that she'd been inside only three times in her entire life.

Women weren't precisely forbidden from the library, but

their presence was strongly discouraged and the idea of one being allowed to *study* would likely render those who controlled the institution either mute with horror or consumed by laughter at the audacity of such a thought. Lydia dreamed about it anyway.

They rounded a corner, the towering arch of the entrance to the Forum coming into view. But it wasn't the glittering gold of the dragon sculpture perched on top of it that caught Lydia's attention, but rather raucous male laughter.

Two men with buckets full of soapy water were engaged with trying to wash some graffiti from the walls, and the passersby were all pointing and laughing at the subject matter. Opening the curtain farther, Lydia pushed her spectacles up her nose and squinted against the bright sun.

The crudely drawn image was of a naked man tossing male infants onto a sea of spears, the enormous phallus that the artist had given the man the subject of the passersby's comedy rather than the serious nature of the scene. Unsurprisingly, the man pictured was Senator Lucius Cassius. Even without his name scrawled messily above, Lydia would've known that much.

The curtain snapped shut, blocking her view of the scene.

"Blasted plebeians and their crude drawings," her father muttered, settling back down among the cushions. "What are you on the hunt for in the markets that can't be brought to you at the house?"

"Something for Teriana, I think."

"Oh? Have you heard from her then?"

Lydia twisted the ring on her finger around and around, smiling as she thought of her friend. "No, but I rarely do until the *Quincense* sails into Celendrial's harbors."

"Serves you right for befriending one of the Maarin. They go where the winds—and the profits—take them."

The litter came to a stop before the steps of the Curia, ending their conversation, and Lydia accepted the arm of her father's guard, Spurius, to help her stand, then turned to assist her father.

"Now, now, my dear. Please, allow me."

Lydia's skin crawled, and twisting around, she found Senator Lucius Cassius standing behind her, along with a pair of servants holding sunshades over his head.

Perhaps in his midforties, Lucius was a man unremarkable in face and form, his golden skin loose around the jowls, which emphasized his weak chin. He wore the same white toga as her father, his dark blonde hair clinging to his neck, which appeared oily, as though his masseur had not toweled him thoroughly after a recent massage.

All of those were secondary impressions, however, for it was his eyes that commanded one's attention. And they were eyes one would never forget. Small and deep-set, they possessed a depth of cunning and a dearth of empathy, and having them fixed on her made Lydia want to recoil.

Lucius pressed a hand against the small of Lydia's back to ease her out of the way, leaving a sodden mark on the silk of her dress. "My friend, my friend!" he said to her father, taking his arm. "This heat is the purest form of misery."

"Truly, it is." Her father steadied himself against the other man, the servants with the sunshades pressing forward to keep both protected from the glare. "We'll have drought again if the weather continues as it has."

A shout of dismay stole Lydia's attention from the conversation, and her eyes went up the Curia steps to see soapy water spilling down the marble, one man berating another for his clumsiness. The column next to them had been defaced with more graffiti, and Lucius's name was only slightly faded from their efforts.

"Nasty business," her father said. "Have the perpetrators been caught?"

"Not yet. Though I do intend to have strong words with the legatus of the Twenty-Seventh. The policing of our fair city is a position of privilege, but his men appear to be treating it as an opportunity for leisure."

Her father gave a slow nod. "Policing Celendrial requires a

certain temperament of men. A legion that has seen combat, but not endured the trauma of heavy casualties. A legion with experience dealing with the peregrini. And one with an appropriate reputation. The Twenty-Seventh is a good fit."

Unlike the other two legions currently camped outside the city, Lydia thought, though it would explain the as yet unexplained presence of the Thirty-Seventh and Forty-First.

"As always, Valerius, your counsel is good," Lucius answered. "Perhaps I let my emotions get in the way of my good sense. In my heart, I know that it was the peregrini's relentless abuse of my character that drove my late wife to her grave, so the sight of these baseless criticisms sparks anger in my blood. Makes me desire to take action."

He pumped his fist in the air as though he might personally hunt down the perpetrators, and Lydia had to bite the insides of her cheeks to keep from laughing at the very idea of it.

Then a shout cut the air, driving away her amusement.

"Thieves!" A tall man raced across the Forum in their direction. His pale freckled complexion and the cut of his red hair suggested he was from Sibern Province, though he wore Cel garments.

"You give me back my son, you Cel vermin!" He jerked the knife belted at his waist free, lifting the blade. "You give him back or I'll kill you both!"

"Take cover, Domina!" Spurius pushed Lydia into the litter with such force that she rolled out the other side, landing on her knees in a soapy puddle.

Heart in her throat, she peered through the curtains, seeing both her father and Cassius had their backs against the litter, while Spurius had his weapon out, moving to intercept the attacker.

At the sight of the retired legionnaire, the Sibernese man slid to a halt, his eyes wild.

"Put the knife down." Spurius's voice was calm, and he cautiously set his own weapon on the ground. "We can all still part ways peacefully."

"Peacefully?" The Sibernese man screamed the word, sweat and tears rolling down his freckled cheeks. "You golden-skinned demons don't know the meaning of the word! You stole my boy away! Stole his freedom and his life!"

His speach was garbled with grief, but Lydia understood— as would anyone in the Empire. His child had been taken as part of the child tithes to the legions. Gone to Campus Lescendor where he'd be forged into a weapon and then used to enforce the Senate's authority.

"It is not theft." Lucius's voice was frigid. "It is the law. All must abide. I myself gave up my second son and I bore my grief with honor, not by groveling like a woman in the middle of the Forum."

Spurius's jaw tightened, and he held up a hand, trying to silence Lucius.

But the damage was done.

"You *stole* him!" The grieving father lifted his knife. "And once you demons have beaten all that he is out of his veins, you will send him to slaughter his own people!"

The legionnaires guarding the Forum sprinted their direction, gladius blades gleaming in the sun, their expressions grim. Lydia clenched her teeth, not wanting to watch but unable to look away.

"Calm yourself, man," Spurius said, and Lydia knew he saw the other soldiers coming. Knew that he had only moments to diffuse the situation. "That is not the way of it. You may yet see him again, but not if you carry forward with this ill-thought plan."

"He will no longer be my son!" The man lunged, his eyes bright and fixed on Lucius and her father, and Lydia screamed.

And then a blade sliced through the air.

Lydia clapped a hand over her mouth, watching the Sibernese man's head roll across the stones, coming to rest against the steps to the Curia. The legionnaire who'd decapitated him frowned, then bent to wipe his weapon on the dead man's tunic.

"Blasted fools!" Cassius shouted at them. "While you sat on your laurels, we were nearly killed!"

"Apologies, Senator," one of them—a centurion, judging from his armor—said. "We came as soon as we saw his weapon."

"Spare me your excuses! The Twenty-Seventh is *done* in Celendrial—time you were sent somewhere that will sharpen you back into the weapons we trained you to be!"

Spittle flew from Lucius's mouth, but Lydia's father placed a calming hand on his shoulder before addressing the soldier who'd murdered the poor man. "You need not have killed him. It was poorly done."

"Apologies, Senator," the man answered, but to Lydia, he didn't seem at all repentant. Likely because he knew the punishment for allowing harm to befall two senators would have been far worse than harsh words.

Rising on weak knees, Lydia held on to the side of the litter for balance, then circled around to the front. Blood pooled around the dead man, streams of it trailing away, following the straight lines between paving stones. One of the legionnaires picked up the dead man's feet, dragging him across the Forum, leaving red streaks across the stone, while another caught hold of the head by the hair, tossing it after his comrade. "You forgot a part!"

"Show some decency!" The words tore from her lips, and the legionnaires turned to regard her with cold eyes.

"Apologies, Domina," the centurion finally said. "I'll have him whipped as punishment for adding to your distress."

Lydia's eyes widened and she opened to mouth to argue, but her father caught hold of her shoulders, gently pushing her into the litter. "Today is not a good day for the markets, my dear. Spurius will escort you home and then rejoin me."

"Peregrini violence grows worse by the day." Lucius gave a grim shake of his head. "What state our fair city that law abiding citizens and those of the gentler persuasion cannot go out for fear of being accosted? It is unconscionable. We must show a firmer hand."

"A matter for discussion," her father answered, but then the litter rose, carrying Lydia away from the conversation.

"An unnecessary tragedy," she said, looking up at Spurius where he walked within arm's reach, his steady presence a comfort. "You did well in your attempts to avert it."

"Not well enough."

"Is the Twenty-Seventh to blame for the violence?" Spurius had been a centurion prior to his retirement; of a surety, he'd have his own opinions on the matter. "Is Lucius right to want to replace them?"

"They are not the cause, Domina. Only a consequence," he replied, face revealing nothing. "But the Senate knows better what Celendrial's future holds and what sort of legion it will need to keep its peace."

Something was happening, Lydia thought; then her eyes landed on the graffiti of Lucius throwing babies onto spears.

Or perhaps it already had.

3

KILLIAN

The wall dividing Mudamora from Derin was sixty feet high, but it wasn't the drop that concerned Killian. It was the bloody cold.

The wind buffeted him from side to side, ripping at his cloak as he descended, his gloved fingers growing more numb with each passing second. Gods, he wished he were back in the South. Or even on the coast, where at least he was in no danger of actually freezing his balls off. Anywhere but here.

"It's still not moving," Bercola shouted from above. "We'll set you down now."

Killian's boots sank into the snow, no longer in Mudamora, but in the enemy kingdom of Derin. Forbidden ground, and yet here he was.

He pulled the snowshoes off his back, donned them, and then started toward the dark shape in the red-stained snow.

They are coming.

She wasn't moving. Which was no damned surprise given that six arrows were embedded in her chest and her back was riddled with at least that many, but Killian still hesitated several paces back from her corpse, drawing his sword. Watching for any sign of motion.

Nothing. And yet he didn't move.

There was rumor that those marked by the god of war felt no fear. That *Killian* felt no fear. But the dull throb of blood in his ears and the thundering beat of his heart belied that rumor. Killian knew fear. He just didn't run from it.

The wind caught in the corrupted's blond hair, strands of it whipping this way and that, her skin nearly as pale as the snow she rested upon. Her cheek had been scored by an arrow, a long bloody wound across an otherwise lovely face. A lovely face marked by the Seventh god. Marked to take lives. Marked for evil.

And yet she'd said that she was here to warn them.

Feeling the eyes of his men watching him from atop the wall and through the twin portcullises, Killian took a step closer, watching the corrupted for any sign of life.

Not listening to her was a mistake.

Shoving aside the thought, he took another step closer, about to nudge her with his blade when the wound on her cheek caught his attention.

Killian froze.

The deep cut had started bleeding again and slowly, almost imperceptibly, the edges were closing. Healing.

"Shit," Killian muttered, and the corrupted's eyes snapped open.

What she said stopped his blade a hairsbreadth from her neck.

"They're coming," she whispered. "From behind."

"Rufina?" His voice was hoarse. "Who is she?"

"She's queen. She's one of *his*."

"His?"

"The Corrupter." The wound on her face had faded to a thin line. "I don't want to be like this. I try to fight it, but it's so hard. He stole me and now he won't let me go."

"Such is the downside of making a pact with a god." There was no reneging. No changing your mind. Killian knew that better than most.

"You think I agreed to be like this?" Her laugh was pained and bitter. "He's far more insidious than that."

The arrows embedded in her body were rising, her healing flesh forcing them out of her body. She whispered, "His eye is on me. I can feel it."

Killian lifted his head, giving his surroundings a quick scan, but there was only snow and rock. The whistle of wind.

A guttural growl.

His attention snapped down to see that the corrupted's eyes had pooled black, bloody flames circling the irises. Then she attacked.

A blur of motion. Reaching white hands.

Killian was faster.

His blade sang through the air, slicing through flesh and bone, and the corrupted's head landed with a soft thud in the blood-soaked snow. As the body toppled to join it, Killian turned and strode toward the gate.

"Send three riders on our fastest horses to the garrisons at Blackbriar, Harid, and Tarn," he ordered. "Inform them the wall is in need of reinforcements, no delays. Tell them to bring their healers."

"Reinforcements against what, sir? She's dead."

Killian turned back to the mountain range, the fiery orb of the setting sun casting long shadows through the empty pass. Nothing moved, but his skin crawled as though he were being watched. "I think we're about to find out."

4

LYDIA

Lydia sipped from a glass of well-watered wine, listening to the Bardenese musicians playing softly in the corner of the room while she attempted to calm her still rattled nerves by reading a book.

Within the hour, six of her father's friends would descend on her home, along with their families, and the servants were still rushing about ensuring the night would be perfection. Every surface was laden with vases of flowers from the gardens, the mosaic floors were polished to a high shine, the pillows on the couches had been fluffed, and the marble sculptures resting in the wall niches were devoid of even a speck of dust.

Now that the sun was setting, the doors to the gardens were cast open, but the trees blocked the breeze from the sea, the air between the columns stagnant. Lydia had checked thrice to ensure all was in order, but in truth her duties wouldn't truly begin until the guests arrived and the gossiping ensued.

Pressing her damp palms against the red-and-gold-striped upholstery, she smoothed the thin silk of her dress, admiring the brilliant green. High-waisted, it was ruched at the bodice to give volume to her bust, the singular shoulder strap a mesh of golden wire woven through with silk. On her feet were delicate sandals with thin leather straps that wrapped around her calves up to her knees. Her wrists and throat were encircled with emerald, her fingers gleaming with tiny bands of gold, the large black diamond she habitually wore gracing her right hand.

Her black hair had been styled in ringlets by the servants at the very last minute. It was the fashion, but her hair was not suited to it. Already it was losing its curl, her locks fighting their way toward their natural poker-straight state. Lydia glared at a limp curl in frustration, but there was no time to do anything about it.

The thud of sandals against tile filled the air, and Lydia's father entered the room with one hand behind his back. He looked healthier than he had earlier, no longer dripping with sweat from the pain of his illness. Even still, Lydia gestured to the servant with the fan to put more vigor into his motions, the crimson plumage sending gusts of air across the room.

"I trust the jeweler I had dispatched to the house departed with fewer wares," her father said, perching on the couch next to her, arm still behind his back. "It was the least I could do after what you endured today."

Lydia's jaw tightened at mention of the tragedy in the Forum. "I'm afraid I was a disappointment to them."

"I sent you the finest jeweler in Celendrial, yet within his chests you were unable to find a single hair ornament you liked?"

"Not one worthy of Teriana's hair. It needs to be something special."

She expected her father to make some jest about her grasping for an excuse to have her accounts increased, but instead he sighed, his gaze fixed on the floor. "Perhaps you might consider spending more time with your other friends."

He meant the daughters of his fellow senators, though it had been years since Lydia had thought of any of them as *friends*. When they'd all been children, no one had cared much about her questionable heritage. That had changed when her *friends* began to heed the deeply classist nature of patrician society, where friendship had little to do with affection and everything to do with the advantages the relationship might bring. And while a relationship with her father's name was of enormous value to anyone in the Empire, Lydia's less than perfect pedigree ensured that she'd marry far below her current station, if she married at all. And none of her *friends* saw any advantage in fostering a relationship with the future wife of a wealthy plebian, and even less a spinster. "I prefer Teriana's company."

"It is improper how much you favor her."

Lydia sat up straight with such violence that the wine in her glass sloshed over the rim. "How so? She is my *friend*."

"A friendship that is itself improper. The daughters of senators don't fraternize with the lower classes. It looks ill."

"Lower classes?" Lydia stared at him, horrified to hear such words coming from his mouth. "You speak as though she were some pleb sweeping the streets. Her mother is both captain and owner of her own ship—one of the most influential Maarin ships there is." Never mind that Teriana and her family were richer and more educated than half the Senate.

"Don't play the fool, Lydia. You know well what I mean."

"I do not." A lie, because she did. But if he intended to espouse these views, then Lydia would be damned if she'd let him hide behind innuendo. "Explain yourself."

Her father gestured angrily at the musicians and servants, all of them promptly exiting the room, leaving him and Lydia alone. Then he rounded on her. "As you like. Teriana is not patrician. And she is not Cel."

Rising to her full height, Lydia stared him down. "Neither. Am. I."

And no amount of pretense would make it otherwise. Not when every blasted person in Celendrial *knew* Senator Valerius had found her clutched in her dead mother's arms outside the gates to this very home. Had taken her in and, being the man he was, had given her not just a home but *his* home, adopting her as his daughter.

His eyes clouded. "It's different."

"How?" Lydia was shaking, barely in control of her anger. "How is it different?"

"Because I make it so! My name! My power! My influence!" her father shouted. "And when I am gone, you will lose all of it unless you are wed to someone willing to provide the same. Because rest assured, Vibius will not allow you to remain in this house."

Lydia knew that her father's nephew despised her, though

she didn't understand the intensity of his hate. She was careful never to cross him, yet Vibius's animosity toward her had grown with an alarming ferocity over the last year to the point Lydia was afraid to be alone with him. "It's uncharacteristic of you to speak this way, Father. I don't care for it."

Tension thickened the space between them, not vanquished until her father conceded with an exhaled breath of defeat.

"I'm sorry, my dear girl." He rested his elbows on his knees, head in his hands, an unfamiliar fruit, which was what he'd been hiding behind his back, now abandoned on a cushion. "My fear makes me speak to you in a way I should not. Please sit."

Lydia didn't move.

"Lydia, you are nearly eighteen years old and it was past time you were wed. For there to be a chance of a man with a good name taking you for a wife, you must perform the part of a patrician girl to perfection, which is perhaps something I should've been training you to do all along." He sighed. "Instead, I raised you within the framework of my own beliefs and notions, which are not shared by most. Created an unsustainable world for you, never thinking that there would be a moment in which you'd have to step outside of it. And yet that moment is now staring me in the face. The moment when I'll no longer be able to protect you."

Terminal. The physicians' prognosis echoed through her thoughts. *Terminal.* "Yet you wish me to cut ties with the only other person in the world who cares for me?"

Her father was silent for a long moment, as though he was considering his words. Then he spoke. "I know Teriana is like a sister to you, but know also that her mother is not warm to your friendship. Why else does the *Quincense* avoid the most profitable harbor on Reath like it is infested with plague? The Maarin keep to themselves, for reasons they keep to themselves, and to have a girl of Teriana's importance doing otherwise looks ill upon *her.* It may be the case that she has come to realize that fact, which is why you've not heard from her in so long."

It *had* been six months since she'd seen Teriana. A whole half a year without so much as a letter. Was it possible that Teriana, too, had decided Lydia not worth her time and trouble?

"I have some prospects in mind for you, Lydia, but it would help if you made an effort to increase your desirability. Foster relationships with other patrician girls, for if they look upon you with favor, so shall their fathers and brothers and husbands. Which will make you an asset."

An asset—as though she were a commodity to be used rather than a person with her own thoughts and hopes and dreams . . .

"Why can't you just arrange for me to leave Celendrial? Surely Vibius would be happy enough to see the back of me and would leave me to my own devices?"

Silence fell across the room, making the overheated air feel thick and unbreathable.

"Perhaps he might have," her father finally answered, staring at the tiles. "But I'm afraid I erred in my ambition for your future."

"How so?" This was the first she'd heard of it.

"A little over a year ago, I began to make discreet inquiries into whether Cel law might be changed in your favor. Whether there was a chance of creating a circumstance where you could be freed from my name upon my death and for you to inherit a portion of the Valerius fortune. Not the majority of it, of course, but enough to set you up for life."

Lydia pressed a hand to her chest, scarcely able to believe what she was hearing.

"It became clear quite quickly that such a thing was too revolutionary—that there would be no chance of pushing it through. So I let the idea go. I know not how, but Vibius became aware of my inquiries, as did some of his fellows. They took it as me attempting to disinherit him in your favor." Her father shook his head. "He was incensed, of course, and despite my protests that my inquiries were not of that nature, he took my actions quite to heart. So whereas before he might have allowed you to remain part of his household in some fashion, now I fear he will make an example of you in order to ease the embarrassment he endured."

Vibius's hate of her made so much sense now. In trying to secure her future, her father might well have destroyed it.

"Marriage is your only option, Lydia. Please do what you can to assist me in making the best match possible."

She was trapped.

Giving him a stiff nod, she gestured to the discarded fruit, needing to change the subject. "What is that?"

Passing a weary hand over his face, her father picked up the green and red oval thing. "It's called a mango. They're native to Timia Province and ship poorly, but with the newly discovered xenthier path delivering, we can have them—and other Timian goods—in Celendrial in less than a day's time." He handed her the fruit. "I thought you might wish to try one."

"I see you beat me to it, Uncle."

Lydia whipped her head around in time to watch Vibius enter the room, his wife, Ulpia, teetering along behind him. In one hand, he held one of the fruits, which he bounced up and down before tossing it at one of the servants who'd just entered, nearly hitting the poor man in the face.

"Ran across Gaius Domitius lugging a crate of the things about like some sort of pleb merchantman—he told me the xenthier's been secured and trade is flowing. That's where his father is—their holdings in Timia—but no doubt you knew that." Vibius tapped his temple while at the same time gesturing for Lydia to move. "Always the first to know, aren't you, Uncle."

Her father eyed him coolly. "I'm glad I still have the capacity to impress you, Vibius."

Able to transport man or beast countless miles in a heartbeat, the xenthier paths were much studied but little understood. Crisscrossing the Empire, they were veins of crystal that ran through the earth, the genesis and terminus the only portions visible above ground. Anything that touched the genesis was instantly delivered to the terminus, though a reverse trip was impossible; the crystal flowed in only one direction. Countless routes had been mapped, but there were still many xenthier stems where the destination or origin was unknown. Path-hunters frequently ventured through unmapped genesis stems, because if they returned to Celendrial with proof of where the path went, the Senate rewarded them with a fortune worth of gold. Most who ventured onto the unmapped paths were never seen again.

Lydia joined Ulpia on another couch, smiling at the girl who had the misfortune of being married to Vibius, kissing both her cheeks. Then she held up the fruit. "Would you like to try it?"

Ulpia beamed, her blond hair in perfect ringlets that framed her round, golden-skinned face. "Of course! I do so love exotic things."

Lydia rather doubted that was the case but allowed one of the servants to pluck the fruit from her hand, one ear for Ulpia's chatter, the other for the conversation between her father and Vibius, an effort made more difficult by the return of the Bardenese musicians.

"It's where the coin is, Uncle," Vibius said, accepting a glass of wine and drinking deeply. "Now that the legions aren't muddying up so many of the xenthier paths, we can turn them to their true purpose—commerce! Where once we transported armies a thousand miles in a heartbeat, now we transport mangos!"

The feel of Ulpia toying with the bracelet on her wrist stole Lydia's attention from the conversation. "You wear green so well!" the other girl said. "That shade always makes my complexion sallow and every woman I know complains of the same. You're so fortunate."

Lydia gritted her teeth at the veiled barb and smiled. "You flatter me. Is that a new necklace?"

More guests entered, her father's fellow senators and their families. Greetings and pleasantries filled the air, Lydia's cheeks growing sticky from the kisses of lacquered lips. Despite the servants vigorously waving fans, the heat of the room grew stifling, not even a whiff of a breeze flowing through the doors. The air became heavy with the scent of perfume and sweat and wine, made worse by the waft of cooking food coming down the corridor from the kitchens. A familiar scene, but tonight it was more suffocating than usual.

"Try it, Uncle." Vibius's voice cut through the noise. "It's from Cassius's vineyards. At the rate he's going, he'll run the Atlians out of business."

Lydia twisted on her elbow to see Vibius pushing a glass into her father's hand. Rising, she swiftly crossed the room. "The physicians said no wine."

Vibius made a face. "It's well watered, Lydia. Calm your nerves."

"They said no amount of wine." Lydia clenched her fingers, trying to curb the desire to snatch the glass out of her father's hand.

"It's true," her father said, setting aside the glass. "It seems my final days are to be so devoid of pleasure that I'll soon be begging for the end."

Clapping a hand to his chest, Vibius staggered sideways as though he'd been struck a great blow. "Do you hear him, my friends? Are those not words to break the heart?" Then he lifted his own glass. "I say defy the bastards! Pleasure unto the end!" Then he drained his wine to the roaring approval of the other guests.

"Father," Lydia tried to interject, but no one was listening to her.

"Physicians are such miserly sorts," Senator Basilius said, casting his eyes skyward. "They'd have us eating lettuce leaves and dry bread with only water to wash it down if they had their way. What sense is there to living a hundred years if it means living like that?"

"Hear, hear!" several of the men shouted, lifting their own cups.

"Perhaps Vibius speaks some sense for once." Her father retrieved the wine and lifted it in toast. "Pleasure unto the end!"

Lydia ground her teeth as he took a sip, reaching out to try to take the glass lest he drink the rest, but Vibius got in her way.

"You're a blasted mother hen, Lydia!" He flapped his arms, making noises like an angry chicken. Laughter filled the room. "Quit pecking at him."

Her father waved a hand at Vibius. "Enough. Let her be. She acts out of love. Unlike you."

Everyone laughed, no one seeming uncomfortable with the fact that it was the truth.

"Lydia knows it's all in jest." Vibius's arm slipped around her waist, fingers digging painfully into her flesh. "Don't you, *Cousin*?"

"Of course," she murmured, concern filling her as her father took another sip. But short of knocking it out of his hand, what could she do?

"Go back to your flock, little hen." Vibius patted at her hip, pushing her in the direction of the other women. "You can all cluck at one another."

He was drunk and performing for the other guests, but Lydia's cheeks still burned as she retreated, helplessness souring the wine in her own stomach. What would it be like to live with Vibius without her father to intervene when he got out of hand? Just how badly would he treat her as punishment for her father's inquiries?

Was marriage the better option?

"Lydia, is this comedic?"

She lifted her head to find Ulpia holding her book up for all to see. "Pardon?"

"Is it funny? I do adore a good comedy."

It was a linguistics text. "I'm afraid not."

Ulpia scrunched her face in a parody of disappointment mirrored by the other girls around her. "Do you have anything comedic in that library? You could read for us."

That was the *last* thing Lydia wanted to do. Already her skin was flushed hot, her heart beating too rapidly in her chest, stomach twisting with humiliation and anger and distress. "I'm afraid I have nothing that would suit."

"Of a surety, that will be one of the first things I remedy," Ulpia said, and laughter spilled out of the lips of the other young women in earshot. Laughter that was like pokers in Lydia's ears, because that was *her* library. Hers and her father's. And Ulpia would take it. Change it. Fill it with nonsense and then likely never even step inside. A room visited by servants to keep the dust in check, nothing more.

Fury burned in her chest, and Lydia snapped, "Perhaps refrain from making plans to redecorate my father's house until he's actually dead."

Ulpia's eyes widened and she pressed a hand to her glossy lips. "It was a jest, Lydia. Truly, you mistake me. Vibius and I wish nothing more than for Uncle to overcome his illness."

"I'm sure."

"Peace, peace," several of the other young women murmured, and Lydia leaned back into a cushion, allowing the conversation to carry on without her.

The noise in the room ratcheted up, dancers wearing cheap silk and plumes of feathers swaying between the couches, bare feet moving to the rhythm of pipes the Bardenese women played. Lydia could barely hear herself think, but she saw the way the other girls pressed together, mouths next to one another's ears as they gossiped.

Then above the cacophony, she heard: "Are you well, Valerius?"

Lydia turned in time to see her father double over, clutching his stomach in pain, but though she lunged to try to catch him, her fingers only grazed the fabric of his clothes as her father slumped to the floor.

5

KILLIAN

As the sun set, the first drumbeats rippled down the pass.

Boom.

Boom.

Boom.

There was no music to it, only a steady, familiar rhythm. The beat of men on the march.

A glow appeared on the horizon, as though the sun had reversed its cycle around the world, rising up like fire. Only Killian knew the light was a flame of a different sort. Torches. Thousands of them marching closer with every passing second.

The wall was thick with soldiers, the reinforcements from Blackbriar and Harid having arrived, and those from Tarn due within the hour. The men huddled next to smoking braziers, trying to keep warm in the howling wind that froze exposed skin in a matter of minutes, their heavy fur cloaks making them appear more animal than human.

There was no conversation. No banter. Only whispered words and Killian's occasional order, punctuated by the snap and pop of the wood burning beneath the vats of boiling water.

Ten thousand men. That's what the corrupted woman had said was coming. To bring such a host through these mountains was impossible, and yet there was no denying the numbers as they poured over the lip of the pass, a tide of darkness and fire flowing toward the ancient wall.

Boom.

Boom.

Boom.

Lifting his spyglass, Killian panned the approaching enemy, their faces barely visible beneath heavy hoods, glistening steel held in their hands and, where it was not, wooden poles bearing a black banner emblazoned with a burning red circle.

The sign of the Seventh.

"The Six protect us," several of his men muttered, but they held their positions, hands concealed against the wind until it was time to fight.

Boom.

Boom.

Boom.

A horn sounded, long and mournful, and the enemy host stopped just out of range of longbowmen.

"Archers," Killian shouted, marking the flashes of motion among the masses of enemy. *Corrupted.* "Target those who move too quickly. We don't want them up here with us."

"There are thousands of them," Bercola muttered. "We're outnumbered ten to one."

"The wall puts the odds in our favor," Killian replied. Even with ten thousand men, this enemy force couldn't win. The Derin army had no siege equipment and was exposed to the frigid wind surging down from the mountain peaks.

And yet Killian's skin crawled like he was covered with spiders, his gaze drawn over his shoulder to the courtyard below. The fortress was protected by a half circle of curtain wall, thirty feet tall and six feet thick, with a gate made of steel-banded oak held shut by a beam that required two men to lift. The stables and outbuildings were made of equally sturdy construction as the fortress, soldiers moving among them as they prepared their defenses, the three white-robed healers standing at the ready. But his gaze drifted beyond them, past the clear-cut at the base of the fortress's wall to the dark expanses of forest behind them. To the kingdom they defended.

The horn sounded again, tearing his attention back to the enemy host as they hammered their weapons against their shields, the noise deafening.

Then abruptly the thunder ceased.

The army parted, a lone figure carrying the standard of the

Seventh striding down the path they'd formed. The individual moved with the awful grace of one of the corrupted, the soldiers cringing away with fear that was obvious even from this distance.

Lifting his spyglass, Killian focused on the woman, the snug leather she wore making it no question *it* was a *she*, his eyes fixing on the black mask rendering her face featureless. *Rufina,* instinct told him, and Killian handed off his spyglass in favor of his bow, pulling an arrow and nocking it without taking his attention from the enemy queen. *They fight out of fear,* a voice whispered in his head. *Kill her and this ends here.*

Narrowing his gaze, Killian tracked Rufina's progress to the front of her host, torchlight illuminating her long black hair, which gusted sideways with the wind. *You'll only get one chance,* he warned himself, aiming at her heart. *Only one chance to catch her unaware. One chance to kill her.*

Rufina stopped, planting her standard deep in the snow. Far out of range of most men.

But Killian wasn't most men.

He shot the arrow, the twang of his bow loud in the silence.

It was impossible to see the trajectory in the darkness, and Killian held his breath, waiting to see if his aim was true.

Yet it was impossible *not* to see Rufina's hand move with sudden speed, stopping his arrow inches from her breast. Lifting the arrow, she regarded it, head tilting to one side in amusement that radiated across the distance. Like it was nothing more than a child's toy.

Several of his men made the sign of the Six against their chest even as Killian shot three more arrows in swift succession, but Rufina snatched them all from the air, her shoulders shaking with laughter that caught on the wind, filling Killian's ears. The ears of his soldiers.

Then she shouted, "One thousand gold coins to the one who brings me Killian Calorian's head." Her host shifted restlessly around her, and she laughed again. "Five thousand to the one who brings him to me alive."

Shit.

Killian's heart hammered against his ribs. *Thud thud. Thud thud. Thud thud.* Then he felt something *shift.* "Here they come."

Rufina snatched hold of her standard and lifted it into the air. With a roar, the enemy army charged past their queen, tripping and stumbling over one another in the deep snow, those who fell crushed beneath the snowshoes of the thousands who followed. An inky tide crossing the white snow.

"Steady!" Killian bellowed over the noise, watching the approach. Waiting for the right moment. "Shoot!"

The air filled with the twang of longbows, and a heartbeat later the front ranks of the enemy fell, screams echoing up to the top of the wall.

"Shoot!"

Volley after volley, and then the enemy hit the wall, grappling hooks launching upward, indiscriminately catching against flesh and rock, men screaming as the ropes dragged them down even as the enemy began to climb those that held true.

The Mudamorian soldiers drew their blades, cutting through ropes, dozens of enemy dropping to their deaths on the ranks clustered below even as more of Killian's men poured the vats of boiling water down on their heads.

Screams.

Screams.

But they kept coming, the archers among them firing up, arrows striking true. Killian sidestepped a blur of black fletching, but even as he killed the archer with an arrow of his own he was turning, his gaze on the darkness outside the fortress's wall. *They're coming from behind.*

"The reinforcements from Tarn are here!" The shout came from below, several of his men running toward the gate.

From behind her?

Or from behind him?

"Don't open the gate!" Killian stumbled toward the steps, heedless of the arrows flying past him. "It's a ruse! Don't open the gods-damned gate!"

He was too late.

His soldiers lifted the heavy beam, and as they set it aside, the gate swung open and a man wearing the uniform of a Mudamorian officer stepped inside. In a blur of motion, he caught hold of one of Killian's soldiers, hand around his throat, lifting him up like a shield.

"Close the gate!" Killian screamed, halfway down the steps and too far away to help. "Kill it!"

Life drained from the struggling soldier's face, years compounding on years until all the corrupted held in its grip was the desiccated corpse of an ancient man. With a wild laugh, the corrupted tossed the body aside.

Lifting his bow, Killian shot an arrow, the metal tip punching through one of the corrupted's flame-rimmed eyes, the creature dropping like a stone. Leaping off the side of the stairs, Killian hit the slush and mud of the courtyard, rolling to his feet. "It's the enemy! Close the gods-damned gate!"

His men were moving, but it seemed at a snail's pace, the only soldier near enough to close the gate staring in horror at the corpse of his fallen comrade.

The cold air burned his face as Killian ran, closing the distance.

You aren't going to make it.

He pulled his sword as the gate flew the rest of the way open, disguised Derin soldiers surging through, corrupted in their midst.

Killian carved into the first, nearly cutting the man in half before turning on the next, parrying twice before running the man through.

It was a blur of blood and steel, the air filled with screams and smoke, the stables aflame. Men and horses careened around the courtyard as Killian rallied his soldiers, but for every enemy he killed, another sprang up in his place.

The corrupted lost themselves in the madness, most bent over victims, stealing life, their faces wild with ecstasy.

But not all.

Three hemmed Killian in, swords in hand, backing him

step by step against the twin portcullises that were all that held out the horde of enemy beyond the wall.

Exhaustion bit at Killian as he fought, blood running down his face, freezing in his hair. There was snow falling now, and it whirled and gusted as he twisted and parried, trying to take the corrupted down. Trying to get past them.

He pulled a knife and threw it, catching one in the chest, but the creature only plucked the blade out and laughed, not even feeling the pain. "You've lost," it hissed, even as Killian gutted one of its companions, the thing shrieking as it tried to stuff its innards back inside the healing wound.

"I don't lose," Killian replied between his teeth.

But his men were.

One by one, they were dropping. And if they lost the gatehouse, it was over.

"Things change." The corrupted leapt backward as Killian swung. "The Six grow weak. Their Marked Ones grow weak." It lunged with preternatural speed, its blade slicing against Killian's ribs, his chain mail all that kept him from being cut in two. "You grow weak."

Fire enveloped the scaffolding that ran up the inside of the wall, building materials raining down as the wood gave way.

Killian coughed, trying to catch his breath, and then there was a sharp crack. Blocks of stone fell from the sky, one smashing the skull of the corrupted as Killian stumbled against the inner portcullis, the overhang all that saved him from the same fate.

Swiping at his stinging eyes, he blinked back tears from the smoke and heat, his vision clearing in time for him to see the last of the men defending the gatehouse fall and the enemy force their way inside. Behind him, the inner portcullis rattled upward.

"No!" Leaping over burning timber, Killian staggered as an arrow punched through his chain mail, embedding deep in his right shoulder. Switching sword hands, he ignored the hot flow of blood running down his back and broke into a run.

The broken door to the gatehouse fell aside with one blow of his boot. In the dim light, the Derin soldiers struggled with the ancient winch of the outer gate. He killed one and was about to turn on the other when a blow caught him in the side, his ribs cracking beneath the force.

Clenching his teeth against the pain, Killian rolled, then struggled to his feet. His sword was nowhere in sight.

"Looking for this, Lord Calorian?" A corrupted stood in the doorway, Killian's sword held in her hand.

Fumbling, hands slick with blood, Killian searched for another knife. But they were all gone. All lost in the fight.

"Mudamora will fall," the corrupted whispered through the smoke, her eyes burning with the Seventh god's fire. "And it will only be the first."

"The wall is not the kingdom." Killian coughed. "And one battle is not the war."

Then he lunged.

His shoulder took the corrupted in the stomach, and they rolled out of the gatehouse. He could feel her hands searching for exposed skin, and he pinned her against the ground, his body screaming with the effort.

She writhed and struggled, stronger than him but unskilled. Except his shoulder was giving out and his ribs burned.

With a snarl, she jerked her arm free of his grip, her bare hand slapping against his face, her eyes burning with triumph—

Right as the outer portcullis rattled skyward.

Derin soldiers surged through the opening, fighting with one another to get to the other side. They rolled over Killian and the corrupted like a wave, snowshoes twisting and tripping them up until it was nothing but a churn of bodies and limbs.

Then a hand caught hold of his wrist, dragging him out from under the surge of men. Killian looked up to see Bercola above him, the giantess's face streaked with soot and blood. "We need to retreat!" she bellowed. "We're overrun!"

On the wall, his surviving men were trying to flee, but they were caught in an ocean of enemy. There was no way out.

Bercola hauled him away, cracking skulls with her staff as she went, but Killian slipped her grip. Snatching up a fallen blade as he ran, he sliced at the burning scaffolding. Over and over, his body wavering and shaking with pain until the leg of the structure splintered and cracked.

In a roar of flame and ash, it collapsed over the gate, blocking the opening.

But not for long.

There were hundreds of enemy in the courtyard. As many on the wall. And a least a dozen corrupted were hunting both friend and foe.

"Retreat!" Killian's scorched throat could barely get the word from his lips, but the men nearest to him heard. They picked up the call, the survivors fighting their way down the stairs, flinging themselves off the wall.

They rallied around him and Bercola, fighting toward the fortress gate and then out into the forest beyond where the horses circled in panic. Above them, strange shrieks filled the air. The sound of wings.

Catching hold of his horse's mane, Killian hauled himself onto its bare back, the dozen men with him catching mounts to do the same. "Ride," he gasped, dispatching them in opposite directions to warn the undefended towns.

"Killian!" Bercola shouted. "Let's go!"

He needed to go back. Needed to fight. Needed to stop this.

But the giantess stepped between him and the fortress. "Going back will be suicide, even for you," she said. "I haven't watched your back all these years to stand aside now."

"Let me go!"

She caught hold of his mount's reins. "You're no good to us if you're dead."

He'd been no good to them alive.

Shaking his head to clear it, Killian dug his heels into his horse's side. "We ride for Mudaire."

And when he returned it would be with an army at his back.

But as they fled toward the tree line, Killian couldn't help a backward glance at the fortress. At the wall that had never fallen.

All he saw were flames.

6

LYDIA

Lydia stared at the pages on her desk, the words blurring together no matter how hard she tried to focus.

The physician had come straightaway, attempting to dose her father for pain, but he'd only waved the man away. "It clouds my mind and my mind is all that I have left." Then he'd motioned to Lydia. "Go see the rest of our guests out. Make my apologies for me."

She'd gone but lingered in the hallway, listening.

Six months, Senator, the physician had said. *Perhaps less. It would be well for you to ready your affairs.*

Six months and then she'd lose him. Six months and she'd be alone. A singular hot tear dribbled down her cheek, and Lydia wiped it aside furiously, then shoved her spectacles back into place, intent on losing herself in her work despite her failure to do so over the last two hours.

Dipping her pen in the inkpot, she wrote a line pertaining to an issue with pestilence afflicting poultry. Then a loud voice made her jump. "You spelled *chicken* wrong. And your Bardenese grammar is shit."

Indignation flooded her, and Lydia snapped, "It's not—" before recognition hit her. Twisting in the chair, she grinned at the girl standing behind her with an expression of amusement on her dark-skinned face. "Teriana!"

They went down in a heap of arms and legs, hugging and shrieking in complete disregard of propriety. "I wasn't expecting you," Lydia finally said after their enthusiasm had settled, not mentioning that she'd feared Teriana had abandoned her for good.

"There's a lot of that going around." Teriana pulled off her boots, tossing them aside before crossing her legs, her toes glittering with a multitude of rings. Her countless waist-length braids with their wealth of ornaments clicked and rattled together as she moved, the sound as comforting as a song. "Your father keeps poor company tonight."

Her father was supposed to be abed, *not* receiving guests. "Oh?"

"A young one who's drunk on both righteous indignation and your father's good wine. And the other . . ." A frown creased Teriana's brow. "Older. Weak chin. Eyes like a pig. He seemed . . ." She trailed off and then gave a shrug. "Seemed not your father's sort."

Lydia scrunched up her face, unnerved. "The younger is my father's nephew, Vibius." Who was supposed to have departed with Ulpia.

"Mmm-hmm." Teriana pulled a ring off Lydia's finger, examining the gemstone. She was easily the prettiest girl Lydia had ever met with her rounded cheeks, arched eyebrows, and wide smile, her smooth black skin completely flawless. Half a head shorter than Lydia, Teriana was the perfect blend of muscle and curve, her long-fingered hands calloused from a lifetime of working on her mother's ship. But it was Teriana's eyes that captured the attention.

Like all Maarin, Teriana's eyes appeared to be windows to the sea, the irises moving with waves and swells. And like the sea, they changed color with her temperament. Lydia had seen them shift from indigo to azure to emerald to graphite all in the space of a conversation.

Handing back the ring, Teriana asked, "Who was the other man?"

Lydia twisted the band around her finger. Once. Twice. Three times. "Lucius Cassius."

Teriana lifted both dark eyebrows in surprise. The Maarin were well acquainted with the ins and outs of Cel politics, and Lucius's reputation was far-reaching.

"Elections." Lydia said the word as an explanation, though

it wasn't. Nothing explained why her father had that man in this house. "Let's go out into the gardens. It's cold in here."

Taking Teriana by the hand, she led her friend out of the library and down the curving stairs, their bare feet making no noise on the tile. Except as she rounded the corner, Lydia found herself face-to-face with both her father and Vibius.

Vibius gave Teriana a scornful once-over and then turned his scowl on Lydia, eyes clouded with wine and distaste, as though a pair of rats had interrupted his evening stroll. Lydia instinctively recoiled.

Which was a mistake.

Teriana's hand snapped to her knife hilt, and Lydia was certain that if she hadn't grabbed hold of her friend's wrist Teriana would've stuck the blade into Vibius's guts.

Mercifully, Vibius didn't seem to notice, and he swayed on his feet as he said, "As if you aren't embarrassment enough, you have to fraternize with a sailor." Then he wheeled on her father. "You indulge her."

Her father straightened, anger seeming to wipe away the effects of his illness. "And I'll continue to indulge her while it is within my power to do so." Then he gave Lydia a warning nod that had her dragging Teriana around the corner before the situation could devolve further.

"That pompous prick," Teriana snarled once they were outside. "He better watch his back, because I'm of a mind to cut off his—"

Lydia held up a hand, wary of Vibius still being in earshot. "While that's a delightful visual, I really need you to curb your tongue in his presence."

Teriana stared at her as though she was a stranger. "Not like you to be a shrinking violet."

"Yes, well . . ." The situation felt too monumental to explain, a sudden weariness stealing over her. "He's my father's heir."

Realization dawned on Teriana's face, the color of her eyes shifting and darkening into stormy seas. "You'll be his property when he inherits."

Property. It was true, but Lydia hated the blasted word. Hated how it made her feel less than human.

"Any way around that?" her friend asked, though she had to know the answer.

"If I were to be married."

Silence filled the space between them, telling Lydia *exactly* what her friend thought of such a solution.

Finally, Teriana said, "Surely there are men falling over themselves to gain a connection with your family?" Her voice was light, but the turbulent waves in her eyes belied her tone.

"Perhaps they would be if everyone didn't know my father was ill. It would be a short-lived union."

"What about someone who isn't a patrician? A financial incentive might—"

"Enough, Teriana!"

Instantly she regretted the heat in her voice. Other than her father, Teriana was the only person who cared for her well-being, and she could hardly begrudge her friend for trying to find a solution to her problems. That she liked none of the solutions was not Teriana's fault.

Taking a measured breath, Lydia said, "This conversation makes me feel like a broodmare. Let's discuss something else." She motioned to the servant waiting with a tray of refreshments to bring them forth. "Tell me of your travels. Where have you been? What have you seen? How is your family? How is Bait?"

Teriana's jaw worked from side to side as though she was considering pressing the issue. Then she shrugged, falling back on one of the couches and pulling Lydia with her. "Bait's probably in the *Quincense*'s galley crying into his cup to Polin about not being invited along with me. I swear he was half-hoping my mum wouldn't let me visit tonight so that he'd have the chance to see you under the guise of sneaking me off the ship. In another hour or so, he'll probably be filling the whole damned harbor with his sad poetry about your pretty face."

Lydia's cheeks flushed at the thought of Teriana's *very* handsome crewmember doing any such thing, and she picked up a glass from the tray, trying and failing to hide her reaction. "You're making that up. Bait would do no such thing."

Teriana smirked, picking up the other glass and smelling the contents. "I *never* tell you anything but the unvarnished truth. And speaking of true stories, about a month ago we sailed into Madrascus's harbor just ahead of a storm. Each drop of rain was large enough to drown a man. . . ."

Resting her head against Teriana's shoulder, Lydia allowed herself to be swept away by her friend's adventures on the high seas, losing herself in tales of the *Quincence*'s crew's hijinks in provincial ports and the endless pranks that Teriana and Bait played in idle moments. Stories that made her forget the terror she'd felt when her father had collapsed and her helplessness over what was to come.

For hours, she and Teriana talked, and only when it was growing dangerously close to morning did they crawl into Lydia's bed, nose to nose, the sheets pulled over their heads. But in the darkness Lydia's fears reared their heads, and as though sensing her mood, Teriana asked, "How unwell is your father?"

A pair of tears escaped her eyes. "The physicians say his liver is failing." The words stuck in her throat. "They have given him six months, if he's lucky."

"I'm so sorry." Teriana pulled her close. "It's not fair. It's never the awful men who are taken before their time, and there is a great injustice to that."

Lydia wiped her face with the sheet. "It felt like one day he was well and the next he was not, and I know his concern for me is only making it worse."

Teriana's grip on her tightened, silence falling over both of them. And then her friend asked, "Are you afraid?"

The air beneath the sheet turned stifling, and it was only when Teriana pushed it back that Lydia was able to let out a gusting exhale and say, "Yes. I think the day after my father passes, Vibius will sell me to the highest bidder. And if no one will pay, he'll have me killed."

"What if you left? What if you ran away?"

Lydia choked out a laugh, because it had been tried many times by many women. And always they were dragged back, broken and shamed, eventually married off to some minor patrician family living in the provinces. Somewhere out of sight. "To where? There is nowhere the Senate doesn't control. Nowhere that its legions couldn't find me."

She heard Teriana inhale as though to speak, but then she seemed to hesitate. And with her hesitation, Lydia felt something she hadn't expected surge in her chest: hope.

Hope that flared brightly when Teriana finally whispered, "There is."

Lydia's heart fluttered, and for a moment she couldn't speak. "Where?" she finally breathed out.

"Across the Endless Seas."

"What do you mean? There's nothing but water."

"There's a whole other world."

Her breath caught in her throat, for what Teriana spoke of was nothing more than myth. "Do you mean the Dark Shores? They exist?"

Lydia felt Teriana press her forehead against hers. Felt her slow nod in the darkness. "If you decide you want to leave or if you're ever in desperate need to reach me, this is how it's done. . . ."

Teriana left at dawn, leaving Lydia standing alone at the gates to the property, one hand resting against the stone wall to keep her balance. Necessary, because it felt as though the whole world had been tipped on its side.

The existence of the Dark Shores. Immortal guardians of ships. Gods, which the Maarin—and apparently whole other nations of people on the far side of the world—worshipped. All things that would cause serious trouble for the Maarin if they were ever to be discovered by the Empire, but that concerned

Lydia far less than the sense that she didn't know her best friend as well as she'd thought.

Walking slowly down the path past the pool full of koi, Lydia entered the house, accepting a glass of iced lemon water from the waiting servant before climbing the stairs to the library. Her fingers trailed along the spines of the carefully organized volumes as she made her way through the room to her desk.

Sitting down, she worked for a time, but her mind kept drifting. Eyes kept going to the globe of Reath sitting on the corner of her desk. Setting down her pen, Lydia pulled the globe in front of her, watching it rotate.

One half depicted the Empire in blues, greens, golds, and whites, but the other half was lacquered black. The Dark Shores. *What would it be like,* she wondered, *to pull back the shadow and see what lay beneath?*

What would it be like to escape?

Then a hand pressed down on the rotating globe, stopping it so that Lydia's gaze was centered on Celendor itself.

"Lydia, some decisions have been made that you need to be aware of."

A chill ran down her spine at the tone of her father's voice, and she couldn't find the courage to lift her face to meet his gaze. Because she knew.

She knew.

"Who will it be?" Her voice quivered, and she clenched her teeth, furious that she was losing her composure already.

"You know that this is a matter of blood. Of breeding. If you were my child in truth, Domitius himself would have been banging on our door begging for your hand for his son."

But she wasn't patrician. Wasn't Cel at all. "Who?" she repeated.

"I know it's no love match and never will be, but you'll have status and wealth and he'll treat you well. He has children from a prior marriage, so you need not worry yourself with those particular concerns. He's already said that he's happy for you to carry on with your studies, which is no small thing. And he's running for consul; if he is victorious, you'll be the most influential woman in—"

"Who?" Lydia shrieked, cutting him off. Because she *knew*.

Silence filled the room. Thick and sticky and choking.

"Lucius Cassius has offered to marry you," her father finally answered, taking hold of her wrist and sliding a heavy bracelet over her hand. "And I've accepted on your behalf. You'll be wed after the elections."

7

KILLIAN

Killian galloped through the night and into the morning, switching his stallion for a fresh mount at a farm he passed, a few gold coins and a promise ensuring he'd get his animal back.

It was there he left Bercola behind. To rest. And to deliver warnings.

As such, he was alone when he encountered the first of the Royal Army scouts.

"My lord!" The man's eyes went wide at the sight of Killian's injuries. "What's happened?"

"Derin has invaded." His borrowed horse bucked, sensing Killian's agitation at the delay. "Have a pigeon sent to Mudaire warning them. I can't delay—I need to reach my father."

"But High Lord Calorian is here." The scout gestured back in the direction he'd come from. "Resting the men at High Lord Damashere's castle. He'd intended to travel to the wall to visit *you,* my lord."

Killian's stomach flipped, for while his father being close was a stroke of good fortune that might save the kingdom, Killian had thought he'd have another two days to figure out how he was going to break the news.

But apparently the gods had other plans.

Wincing at the pain in his shoulder, Killian dug in his heels, and galloped toward High Lord Damashere's castle.

He found his father already in the process of organizing the Royal Army to march.

"We received a bird from Blackbriar less than an hour past," High Lord Calorian said, not looking up from his map. "But I'd like to hear an explanation from you, Killian."

Killian swallowed, wishing for a glass of something strong. Perhaps an entire bottle of something strong. As he considered his words, blood from his injuries dripped from his fingers.

Splat.

A droplet struck the floor and, finally, his father looked up. "Gods, Killian," he snapped. "You could have seen the healers first."

Striding to the door, he leaned out, muttering to the men standing guard, and a few moments later, two white-robed healers appeared.

"Take care not to overexpend yourselves," Killian's father warned. "That he's standing doesn't mean he's not half dead."

Killian said nothing as the pair struggled to remove his chainmail and the blood-soaked garments beneath, but as they began their work erasing the injuries, he said, "One of the corrupted approached the wall yesterday claiming she desired to assist us."

High Lord Calorian stood in silence as Killian explained what had happened. Both healers were grey and faded when they finished, departing the room right as Killian completed his description of the enemy forces. "You'll need to call in reinforcements from the North and South," he said. "Rufina has at least ten thousand men, and her ranks are peppered with corrupted."

"Stop. Talking."

Killian's teeth clicked shut.

"That wall," his father growled, "hasn't been breached since it was built a *thousand* years ago, and yet within three months of you taking command of the fortress defending it we have a Derin army marching across the kingdom. And not because they laid an impressive siege to it. Not because of their manpower. No, the wall fell because they caught *you* with your trousers down."

"The fortress's wall was well manned," Killian replied, eyeing his father warily. "I'm not stupid enough to leave my rear undefended."

"And yet the enemy walked in entirely uncontested."

"It was a ruse."

"A ruse that shouldn't have worked! Not on *you*!" High Lord Calorian snarled the words in Killian's face, dusky skin red with anger. "Were you drunk? In bed with some girl?"

"No!" Killian scrambled for words. "I was on the wall when—"

"I don't need to hear it." His father turned away, resting his hands on a table covered with maps, the indigo wool of his coat straining over his shoulders. Of all High Lord Calorian's sons, Killian knew he favored his father the most. A head taller than most men and built for combat, the only differences between them that his father's dark brown hair was laced with grey and his olive skin creased around his eyes.

"You were marked by Tremon himself, Killian." His father's voice was low. "Haven't you realized by now that such a gift came with obligations? Doubly more so, given that you are *my* son. The god of war gave you the gifts needed to defend Mudamora, but what have you done but squander them?" He turned around. "Gambling, drinking, and chasing girls—those are the only things you use your talents for. This one time you had a chance to use your mark toward its intended purpose and you *failed*. And our people are dying as a result." High Lord Calorian shook his head. "Tremon chose poorly when he chose *you*."

The blood drained from Killian's face, his father's words cutting deeper than a sword. He'd been reprimanded countless times before, but this . . . this was different.

And perhaps not undeserved.

"You should've stayed on the wall and fought until the end," his father spit. "You should've *died* defending that wall."

The room felt cold and still. Killian's pulse roared in his ears. "I'll march with you, Father. I'll fight. We'll push them back—"

"You'll go to Mudaire." High Lord Calorian's voice was frigid. "The King is there and you will hear his judgment on your actions. And in the meantime, *I* will march west, and you had best pray to all the gods that I'm able to rectify your mistakes."

High Lord Calorian strode toward the door.

"Father, please!"

Fingers gripping the handle, his father turned, brown eyes fixing on Killian. "You were meant to be my greatest achievement. Instead, you've been my greatest disappointment."

8

LYDIA

If you're ever in desperate need to reach me, this is how it's done. . . . Teriana's words echoed in Lydia's ears as she tore down the narrow path toward the sea, casting backward glances at the villa to see if anyone was in pursuit. Her father believed she was brooding in the library, but it wouldn't be long before he came knocking and found an empty room.

Brambles caught at the silk of her skirts and tiny pebbles worked their way through the mesh of her sandals, digging into her feet. She tried to check her pace but slid, only a decorative railing keeping her from falling off the path into the bushes below.

Reaching the beach, she kicked off her sandals and sprinted down the sand to the water, the ocean blissfully cool against her feet. Removing her small knife from where it was tucked in the gold mesh of her belt, Lydia unfolded the blade. She stepped deeper into the water and watched as a wave rolled forward to slam against her thighs. As it retreated, she traced a circle in the water with her finger. "Hear me," she whispered, looking up at the summit of the hill and praying the heat would keep any watching eyes indoors.

The waves surged, and again as they fell back she traced a circle. "Hear me." She said it a little louder this time.

The water withdrew until only her feet were submerged. Then it gathered strength, froth and foam flying toward her. Squeezing the knife handle, Lydia sliced the blade across her fingertip. The wave retreated, and with the bloody finger she traced a final circle. "Hear me, Magnius, guardian of the deep," she shouted, the bite of pain making her brave. "Hear my call!"

The blood from her cut dripped into the water, the red

droplets staining the foam pink before fading into the vastness of the sea.

Heart thumping wildly, she waited, watching the sea expectantly. And waited. And waited.

But nothing happened.

Anger and frustration rose in her heart and, jerking the betrothal bracelet off her arm, she tried to fling it away. Except the bracelet slipped from her wet fingers, landing only a few paces ahead of her, lapis lazuli bright against the seafloor.

"Drat!" Lydia slapped her hands against the water, her spectacles slipping off with a splash. Vision blurred, she felt around in the sand for them, sighing with relief when her fingers closed over the metal frames.

Her relief didn't last.

As she straightened, motion caught her eye, whatever it was blurry until she slipped her spectacles back on her face.

Lydia's blood chilled.

A dark serpentine form slid through the clear water. A row of spikes cut through the waves.

Lydia tried to turn, tried to run, but her feet were anchored to the ground. She opened her mouth to scream, but only a faint whisper emerged. A tremble started in her hands, moving to the rest of her body, and she willed herself to move, but her toes only dug deeper into the sand. The sea monster approached, its greenish tail drifting from side to side, propelling it forward.

A wave crashed into the beach, the water rising up to her chin, where it remained, surface smooth as glass. Deep enough that the frills on the creature's head brushed her arms as it circled. Lydia's breath came in ragged gasps, her pulse roaring in her ears, and she clutched her tiny knife. For all the good it would do her.

The predator ceased its circling, lying motionless in the water. Lydia struggled against the invisible force holding her still, desperate to reach the safety of the shore, but all her body did was shiver and twitch. "Help," she tried to scream, but it came out as an exhalation. "Help me."

The creature lifted its massive reptilian head out of the water, jaws opening to reveal rows of sharp teeth. And it *looked* at her.

This . . . this was no mere serpent.

Black eyes stared at her, not with the blank glassiness of a snake, but with the endless depths of something that possessed a *mind*. A wisdom stretching beyond that of mankind. It had seen a thousand years and would see a thousand more. Its dark gaze swallowed her, and Lydia's heart slowed, her panic fading.

The logical part of her howled that only a lunatic would converse with something capable of biting her in half. Yet as whatever force binding her voice released, instead of screaming, she whispered, "Are you Magnius?"

The monster dipped its head into the water, then lifted it again. *Who summons me?*

"I do." She took a deep breath. "My name is Lydia. Lydia Valerius."

The guardian hesitated. *Why have you called me here?*

Lydia opened her mouth, only the words stuck in her throat, her problems seeming small and trivial—unworthy of summoning this creature only to turn him into her errand boy.

The guardian shifted in the still waters. *Ask.*

Lydia swallowed the lump in her throat. "Will you tell Teriana that I need her help? Tell her . . . Tell her I need to escape the Empire. Please."

The guardian stared at her for what seemed an eternity. Then he lowered his head under the water.

The surf rushed out, shoving past until not even Lydia's feet remained submerged. The strange power binding her released its hold, and she staggered, landing on her bottom in time for the next wave to splash her in the face.

Magnius was gone, and only the sand soaked far beyond the tide line gave her any comfort that it hadn't been a delusion.

Retreating up the beach, Lydia sat with her violet skirts spread around her to dry, staring blindly at the ocean while she waited. Time passed, though whether it was a matter of minutes or hours Lydia couldn't have said. It wasn't until she heard her name coming from the ocean that she snapped out of her reverie.

"Lydia! Lydia!"

A longboat flew toward shore, Teriana standing in the prow with Bait behind her holding the oars.

Once they reached the shallows, Teriana jumped out of the boat, holding a wrapped package high above her head until she was on dry sand. Then she trotted up the beach. Tossing the package on the ground, she turned eyes filled with stormy seas on Lydia. "The only thing it appears you need help with is escaping the sun. You look like a boiled lobster." Pulling off her battered hat, she plunked it down on Lydia's head. "There."

Lydia's jaw trembled. "You might have mentioned Magnius was a sea monster."

"He isn't." Teriana grinned. "He just looks like one. What did you think he was? Some sort of handsome merman who'd swim up to the beach and give you a kiss?"

The corners of Lydia's mouth crept up. "I thought he was going to eat me."

"Why would he do that?" Teriana punched Lydia gently on the shoulder. "You've got less meat on you than the half-eaten wing of a scrawny chicken. Besides . . ." Teriana hesitated, licking her lips and glancing out to sea. "Magnius is a demi-god. A scion of Madoria, Goddess of the Seas. He isn't ruled by hunger."

That had been easy to believe last night with the haze of wine and the darkness blanketing their conversation, but now Lydia found her mind recoiling from her friend's words. Recoiling from the very idea that Teriana and her people put their faith in myths and fables—practices that the Maarin had kept secret from the Celendor Empire. Practices that, until last night, Teriana had kept from *her.* "There is no such thing as gods," Lydia muttered. "All can be explained by logic and reason."

Teriana rolled her eyes. "Well, aren't we just a good little parrot today. Though if I do say so myself, you'd be a lot more convincing if you hadn't just confessed to speaking with an overgrown sea snake."

"True." Lydia stared at the sea, not sure what she believed anymore.

"What's wrong? Tell me what's happened to keep you from walking down to the harbor yourself?"

"My father has forbidden me to go to the harbor."

"That so?" Teriana frowned. "Hate agreeing with a senator, but you were well to stay away today. Whole city's in an uproar since Lucius Cassius announced he's running for consul. If he wins, all Maarin ships will be giving harbors under the Empire's control wide berth."

"Did you hear as well that Lucius Cassius has decided to take a new wife?"

"Hadn't." Teriana huffed out a breath. "Though I pity the poor girl he's chosen."

Lydia grabbed fistfuls of sand, squeezing them hard in an attempt to maintain her self-control, but Teriana wasn't fooled. "No . . ." her friend whispered.

Lydia nodded slowly. "My father signed the contract. A week after the elections, I will be the property of Lucius Cassius." Lydia lifted her face, hoping against hope that Teriana would be her salvation. "I need you to take me with you when you set sail."

But the look of misery on Teriana's face dashed those hopes to pieces.

Resting her chin on her knees, Teriana said, "If it were my ship, I would, but my mum refuses to even consider the idea. It's forbidden for us to take passengers, and she's . . . rigid."

Lydia remembered what her father had told her yesterday: *her mother is not warm to your friendship.* "I know she is." Pressing her fingers to her forehead to try to steady her chaos of emotion, Lydia was rewarded with a jolt of pain as her sunburned skin rebelled from the touch. "I know it's not your decision."

"I'm sorry—"

Lydia held up a hand to forestall her friend, giving her head a weary shake. She didn't want to hear Teriana's apologies. Poking the package sitting on the sand, she said, "Did you bring me a gift to soften the blow?"

Instead of answering, Teriana furrowed her brow and slowly pulled the wax covering off the thick tome before passing it to Lydia.

"*Treatise of the Seven.*" Lydia traced a finger over the embossed cover, the leather warm beneath her hands. "The seven what?"

"The Seven Harem Girls." Teriana's voice sounded strange, and as Lydia watched, her friend swallowed hard and shook her head. "The Seven Gods of the West—the Dark Shores."

Even now, mention of gods and the Dark Shores rang like forbidden fiction in Lydia's ears. Like something to be denied. Something that *should* be denied, given the punishment associated with such beliefs. "I'll be in all sorts of trouble if I'm caught with this."

"So you don't want it?" Teriana reached for the book, but Lydia hugged it to her chest, unwilling to let it go without at least reading it cover to cover. "I didn't say *that*. Almost no one reads Trader's Tongue, anyway. I could tell them it was a cookbook and they wouldn't know the difference."

Which wasn't entirely the case. Her father read the language well enough, but it would be easy to hide the book from him.

Teriana rolled her eyes and flopped back on the sand, one hand held above her eyes to block the sun. "The Six preserve me from crazy Cel girls and scholars. Do you even know how to cook?"

"Of course I don't." Lydia flipped through the pages, eyes dancing over the illustrations of people of many different races, all wearing unfamiliar clothing. "What about the seventh god?"

"The Corrupter." Teriana's voice was uncharacteristically toneless. "Only a select few invoke his name, and they aren't the sort you'd care to cross paths with."

Teriana's discomfort was palpable, and out of the corner of her eye Lydia could see her friend's fingers twitching as though she'd like nothing better than to rip the book out of her hands and toss it in the sea. Which made her ask, "Why are you giving me this?"

Silence sat heavily between them; then finally Teriana muttered, "You said you needed help."

And you promised me last night that you'd give it.

Resentment flooded through Lydia's core, her knuckles whitening where she gripped the cover of the book. "And your suggestion is that I ask your gods for it?" Because that was *not* the sort of help Lydia needed. Not unless Teriana was proposing Lydia escape marriage by getting herself tossed in prison.

"There are as many paths as there are travelers," Teriana said. "You must find the right one."

"What does that mean?" It was a struggle not to shout the words. A struggle to keep her anger in check. Because it would've been better for Teriana to have not come to the beach at all than to come and try to placate Lydia with this . . . this *nonsense.*

But before she could say as much, Bait approached, his clothes and skin damp. "Captain wants to sail with the next tide."

"I need to go," Teriana said, and it seemed to Lydia that she was looking anywhere but at her.

"I think this is yours." Bait held out the betrothal bracelet she'd tossed in the water, the sight of it pulling a scowl onto Lydia's face. She'd thrown it away thinking she had a way out, but leaving it behind now would cause her more problems later, so she shoved it back on her wrist.

Teriana pulled Lydia to her feet, then embraced her tightly. "I'm sorry. I wish—"

"It's fine." Lydia wished she could force away the ugly emotions rising in her chest. Teriana could walk away from all of this. Could go back to her life as it had always been. It wasn't fair. "Vibius is apparently thrilled about the union, so even after my father passes, I'll be of value to Lucius. I'm sure he'll treat me well enough."

"Right," Teriana muttered, her jaw working from side to side as though she might say more. But when Bait took her arm, Lydia noticed that Teriana didn't resist as he drew her away, leading her down to the boat, where they pushed it into the water.

Lydia stood on the beach, watching. Waiting. Hoping.

But her best friend never looked back.

Climbing the curved iron staircase leading to a small balcony off the library, Lydia slipped inside, adjusting her salt-stained dress with one hand, the other maintaining a death grip on the book Teriana had given her.

The stupid *book* and useless advice that her best friend had given her in lieu of rescue. Her blood turned to liquid fire, and with a shriek Lydia threw the volume across the room.

Where it landed, open, at Vibius's feet.

"You stupid little sow," her father's nephew snarled. "Bad enough that you tried to steal what is rightfully mine, now you try to destroy it all out of spite!"

"It's not yours. It was a gift from a friend," Lydia blurted out, then bit down on her tongue.

But rather than angering him, her words pulled a malicious grin onto his face, his gaze fixing briefly on the open page. "Not mine *yet*. But soon."

Stepping over the book, he strode toward her, a miasma of sweat and wine preceding him. Fear drove Lydia back a step, her hip smacking against the corner of her desk. But the pain was nothing compared to the way her skin crawled as he took hold of her chin, his palm warm and greasy.

"Have you enjoyed it, Lydia?" he whispered. "Have you enjoyed living on top of the hill with all that wealth and power have to offer you? Have you enjoyed living beyond your *breeding*?"

Lydia's pulse roared in her ears, but she said nothing, only jerked her chin out of his grip and glared down at him.

"I hope you've enjoyed it," he said, laughing. "Because it will make my taking it away all the more enjoyable." He looked her up and down. "How well do you think you'll enjoy serving where you were once served? For what labor do you suggest I use you?"

"You'll use me for nothing," Lydia replied, and though it disgusted her to do so, she lifted the wrist bearing her betrothal bracelet.

Vibius cackled. "Oh, it's armor now, is it?" His voice lifted into a high-pitched pantomime of her own. "'I will not marry him! I'd rather die than be wed to that loathsome man!'"

Goading him was foolish. But for years Lydia's submissiveness had earned her no respite from his taunts, and her pride would bear it no longer. "What I want matters little, Vibius. And while you seem more than willing to take advantage of my father's benevolence, I think you'll find Lucius Cassius far less tolerant of your poor behavior." Then she leaned down so they were nose to nose. "Or is your head so far up his ass that you've been deafened to his reputation?"

Vibius's face purpled. "Valerius is *not* your father." Before she could react, he slapped her sunburned cheek with a resounding crack.

Lydia rocked back on her heels, cupping one hand against her face more from shock than the pain. Never in her life had she been struck. Never . . . "Get out. Get out, or I'll call the guards."

Vibius smirked, but rather than holding his ground, he turned and strode from the room.

Lydia's weak legs finally betrayed her, and she dropped to her knees, squeezing her eyes shut. When she finally opened them, they focused of their own accord on the book that still rested on the floor, pages bent. The volume was beautifully illuminated, which normally mattered less to her than the words on the page. But not in this case.

Because on the exposed page was an illustration of a woman dressed in strange armor, her dark hair twisted into a knot atop her head, a few pieces falling loose to frame her pale face. She held a sword in one hand, her expression defiant.

Crawling on her hands and knees, Lydia picked up the volume, smoothing the bent page. "'High Lady Dareena Falorn,'" she muttered, tracing a finger under the words. "'Marked by Tremon, the god of war.'"

Lydia stared for a long time at the woman. Then she flipped to the beginning and began to read.

9

KILLIAN

It had been a fortnight since the wall had fallen. A fortnight since the Derin army carrying the banners of the Seventh god had invaded Mudamora. A fortnight since that army had unleashed all manner of creatures to terrorize the countryside.

And the majority of that time Killian had spent pacing the halls of his family's home in Mudaire waiting to hear the King's judgement.

"Would you care to break your fast in the dining room or in here, my lord?" Garrem asked. The man had been High Lord Calorian's manservant for longer than Killian had been alive, his dusky skin creased and sagging, the two tufts of white above his ears all that remained of his hair. Old enough that the only work he should be doing was shouting at youngsters from his doorstep, but the last time Killian had suggested he retire, Garrem had smacked him upside the head and told him to mind his own business.

"Not hungry," Killian muttered, striding for the hundredth time past the long row of bookshelves in the library. Not because he had any interest in reading, but because the room had the best view of the city.

Bercola, on the other hand, was ensconced in a large chair in the corner, face buried in a book. "I am," she said. "And you'll eat even if I have to force the food down your throat, you damned fool."

"Breakfast in here, then," Garrem replied. "Your tea, my lord."

Out of the corner of his eye, he saw the manservant set a steaming cup on the table, despite *knowing* that Killian despised the gods-damned stuff. "I haven't run off yet, Garrem," he said. "And I don't intend to, so feel free to ease up on your watchdog duties."

"As you say, my lord." Garrem proceeded to putter about the library, straightening books and organizing coasters and doing countless other unnecessary tasks. The man typically followed High Lord Calorian everywhere he went; that he'd instead returned to Mudaire with Killian meant that he'd been instructed to keep him in line.

Snapping the curtain shut, Killian strode past the steaming tea in the direction of the sideboard. Pouring a splash of whiskey into a cup, he stared at the amber liquid, the smell turning his stomach as he remembered his father's parting words: *You've been my greatest disappointment.*

"Breakfast is served."

Killian jumped. Setting aside the whiskey, he turned to find Garrem standing next to a tray of food, none of it appealing.

"This just came for you, my lord." The manservant held out a letter sealed with red wax, the insignia that of the striking scorpion of House Rowenes. The King's seal.

"There are soldiers waiting downstairs," Garrem continued as Killian read the few lines summoning him to attend the King and the rest of the Council of Twelve. "They say they are here to escort you to the palace."

Bercola had risen, her head nearly brushing the ceiling. She had a blade in her hand. "I'll hold them off," she said. "You get on a horse and run."

"No."

"Killian, you know what this means."

He should never have abandoned the wall. He should've died there. Clasping her shoulder, he said, "It's been an honor." Then without another word, he went down the stairs to meet his escort.

The council chambers were on the main floor of the palace, windowless, with the one entrance flanked by a dozen armored guards.

A dribble of sweat ran between Killian's shoulder blades as he waited, staring at the striking scorpion of House Rowenes gilded onto the door. It was a new addition. And a strange one. In this chamber all the great houses were supposed to be equals. A humbling reminder that a majority vote could pull the crown from the King's head as easily as it had placed it there.

For King Serrick to put his crest here smacked of something beyond a lack of humility—it suggested he believed his rule untouchable.

The door opened, and Killian waited for his titles to be announced before stepping inside. The room was dominated by a massive circular table inlaid with a map of Mudamora, surrounded by twelve high-backed chairs, each bearing the crest of one of the twelve houses. Killian's gaze went immediately to that bearing the galloping white horse of House Calorian. His eldest brother, Hacken, sat in their father's place between Houses Damashere and Falorn. The lord of the former sat ramrod straight, wineglass clutched in a white-knuckled hand, while the lady of the latter had her chair pushed back, muddy riding boots propped on the table, glass balanced on one knee. The same chair her brother had sat in while he was king. Before he'd been murdered and his family had disappeared. She looked relaxed, but Killian knew Dareena well enough to recognize unease when he saw it.

Killian took in the expressions of all the High Lords before his eyes landed on a face he hadn't seen in well over a year: Princess Malahi. The blond Rowenes heir was beautiful, with skin the color of desert sand and eyes a rich amber hue. But she was not, he thought, the sort of girl one kissed in dark corners. At least not without paying a steep price for the privilege. And given she stood to inherit the largest gold mines on the continent, the Rowenes heir couldn't be bought.

A soft voice from behind made Killian's skin prickle. "Young Lord Calorian. It has been some time since we saw you last."

Killian turned. King Serrick Rowenes stood behind him, hands clasped at the small of his back. The ruler of Mudamora was a short, fragile man, his dark blond hair braided in a single plait down his back, his skin the light brown typical of those from the arid region near the border with Anukastre. He wore heavy red robes, the collar embroidered with the symbols of each of the six gods, and the scorpion of his house was picked out in gold across his chest. His pale amber eyes had always possessed an intensity greater than his physical stature, but now they burned with a fervor that caused Killian's skin to crawl.

"Your Majesty," he said, taking a long step back so he'd have room to bow.

Serrick inclined his head. "Marked One."

Killian despised that particular honorific, which was thankfully considered old-fashioned and rarely used. But the King was known to be deeply pious, and he held to the old traditions in more ways than one. In the early days of his reign, he'd once again made it law that anyone marked by one of the Six dedicate their life to serving the realm. All Killian had ever wanted was to be a soldier, so the law was no burden to him, but more than once he'd wondered what, precisely, would happen if he decided he no longer wanted to fight.

"You are here, Marked One, so that we might determine your fate," the King continued, stepping around Killian and moving toward the Rowenes seat, where he gingerly perched. "But before we begin, let us give tribute to the Six, for their strength is the strength of our belief. Lord Damashere, would you please lead us in our prayer. Lord Calorian, would you stand next to me to lend the strength of your mark to our circle? And you, Malahi, join us as well."

Reluctantly, Killian moved next to the King's seat, noticing that the Princess appeared equally unhappy about the request as her father took her hand. Then he grasped Killian's. The man's skin was cold and unyielding and felt as dry as old paper. Like holding the hand of a corpse, and just about as appealing.

High Lord Damashere began, "By the grace of the Six does Mudamora remain mighty, and by the belief of its people do the Six remain strong. Let us acknowledge each so that they might be strengthened by our faith." He proceeded to run through each of the Six, his voice clipped and toneless.

The words came easily to Killian's lips. His own mother was known for her piety, and he'd spoken this prayer before every meal in his family home in the South. But there the words were warming and unifying. Not like . . . *this*. The air teemed with tension, the prayer forced and unwelcome despite everyone here being faithful followers of the Six.

Casting his eyes left, Killian frowned. Serrick's head was bowed, but his lips did not stir as he listened to Damashere speak. Beyond, Malahi's head was also bowed, but as Killian watched, her jaw clenched.

Something here isn't right.

"And let us put our thoughts to our ruler, King Serrick Rowenes, his reign ordained by the gods themselves."

Killian faltered; this was *not* part of the prayer he knew. Yet everyone around him parroted Damashere. Unbidden, the image of the scorpion emblazoned on the council room door rose in his mind.

"Our king alone possesses the strength to lead the faithful followers of the Six away from the dark temptations of corruptions by guiding the hands of those the gods have marked."

Disgust flared through Killian like wildfire, and with a muttered oath he jerked his hand out of Serrick's grip. Malahi had done the same, and she clutched her palm to her chest.

The King's eyes fixed upon him. "You, Killian Calorian, were marked by Tremon to protect Mudamora. Yet in our darkest hour, you failed, suffering a defeat that could well cost everyone in Mudamora their souls. That you were defeated tells us that Tremon has turned his back on you. That the Six have turned their backs on you. And to show our faith, we fear we must do the same."

A dull roar filled Killian's ears. The King's words were eerily reminiscent of those his father had spoken. And of the fears lurking in his own heart.

"This is difficult, of course. We have known you since you were a child, and your family has served our kingdom well. Harder still to deny the request of a dying man we once counted a dear friend. But even your father would've seen the necessity of our decision if he'd lived to see the results of your failure."

"Dying?" The word croaked its way out of Killian's throat, shock making him ignore his gut's warning that a reaction was precisely what the King wanted from him.

"Your father passed on. You didn't know?"

My father is dead.

White-hot pain sliced through his gut, and he found himself searching the faces of the High Lords for answers, but with the exception of Dareena's, all he found were blank expressions. And all hers contained was sympathy. "How?"

"Cyntha?" Serrick gestured to an older woman standing in the shadows of the room. She wore the white robes of a marked healer, the pale skin of her forehead tattooed with the half circle representing those trained at Hegeria's temple in Mudaire, her long black braid laced with grey and upturned eyes creased at the corners.

"Heart," the woman said impassively. "My fellows reached him too late, and not even a god-marked healer can bring back the dead."

She had no reason to lie, but the words rang false. His father was not young, but he'd been as fit as a man half his age. If he'd been killed in combat, Killian would've accepted it, but this . . .

"It was the shock, we expect," Serrick said, his fingers laced together, elbows resting on the table.

"Shock?"

"Yes. Shock." The King's face was full of sympathy. "To have his favored son—his god-marked child—fail so spectacularly and with such enormous consequences . . . Even the most stalwart of hearts can only bear so much. And yet that you be spared was his dying request. Here, you can read it for yourself."

Riffling around on the table, the King plucked up a piece of paper and handed it to Killian. It was stained with a circle of wine, someone having carelessly set a glass atop the news that his father had passed. Killian read the brief message, which was from one of High Lord Calorian's lieutenants:

> I regret to inform you that High Lord Calorian succumbed to a weak heart this morning, the healers reaching him too late to save his life. His final words, which he asked me to relay to Your Royal Majesty, were a request that Your Grace have mercy upon his beloved youngest son, Killian, and not hold him to blame for the events at the wall. All men are fallible, High Lord Calorian said, even those marked by the Six, and he begged that Your Grace allow his son the opportunity to redeem himself on the battlefield.

Killian read and reread the words, his eyes stinging with unshed tears. Then he lifted his face.

Serrick's smile had disappeared. "We've no doubt Tremon has claimed High Lord Calorian's soul. He was faithful, even if with you, it was a misguided faith."

Killian clenched his teeth, it taking all his willpower to keep from wringing the man's neck. The only person in the room capable of stopping him was Dareena, and she was on the far side of the table. Yet even as the thought crossed his mind, High Lady Falorn shifted, the boot that had been resting on her knee dropping to the floor in anticipation. Killian wouldn't get the jump on her.

Serrick pressed his palms flat against the table. "Unfortunately, we cannot make decisions based on sentiment, Lord Calorian. Derin breached the wall because of your dereliction of duty, and—"

"Your Majesty," Dareena interjected. "Derin's attack from the rear was a plan months, if not longer, in the making. They had to have been sneaking soldiers in through Mudamora's border with Anukastre and then traveling north, where they took over the Tarn garrison with no one the wiser. To punish Killian alone is unfair. *Many* had to have failed in their duties in order for such an attack to have been even possible."

"But he is not *just* anyone," the King responded. "He is one of the Marked Ones. And we must show our faith by punishing those on whom the gods have turned their backs." He bowed his head for a long moment, then said, "At dawn tomorrow you, Lord Killian Calorian, will be—"

"Father." Malahi's voice rang clear as a bell across the chamber, and Killian's heart skipped. "Is it not possible that the failing was not Lord Calorian's, but ours?"

Serrick turned his head, eyes fixing on his daughter.

"The story of his marking, after all, is well known—it happened on the eve of the day he was supposed to be named the sworn sword of the Falorn princess."

"What of it, Daughter?" Serrick's voice was cold, but to her credit, Malahi didn't flinch. And Killian said nothing. If Malahi had a plan to get him out of this, the last thing he intended to do was interfere.

"That event never transpired," she continued, "but that does not negate Tremon's intent. Perhaps Killian wasn't marked to defend the kingdom, but rather to defend its heir?"

There were nods of agreement among the High Lords. Dareena said, "She makes a valid point, Your Majesty."

The King's eyes narrowed before smoothing into an expression of serene benevolence. "Derin invaded Mudamora because of this young man's failings, Daughter. Is that the sort of sword you wish guarding your back?"

"I know all about Killian's failings." Malahi rested her delicate hands on the table, the expression in her amber eyes at odds with her smile. "Yet as you say, Father, it is ill luck to deny a dying man's request. Worse luck still to execute one marked by the god of war while we are in the midst of one."

Hacken cleared his throat, and Killian silently girded himself, certain his brother would take the opportunity to condemn him. Which perhaps, given what had happened to their father, he deserved. "The fact that he's my brother aside, I'm inclined to agree with Malahi. As you yourself have said, Your Majesty, the Corrupter gains strength when we lose our faith. What is executing one of the Marked Ones out of a belief he is incapable but a demonstration of a lack of faith? As you wisely remind us, the Twelve must lead by example."

"Indeed, indeed," Lord Damashere agreed, eyeing the Princess. "Malahi is heir to the throne, and in these troubled times she needs the greatest protection we can provide her. Who better than a god-marked sworn sword?"

Nothing about this felt right. If the High Lords didn't agree with Serrick, they were within their right to say so. Yet they were dancing around the issue as though they were . . . *afraid*.

Serrick said nothing, and tension sang through the room as everyone waited for his verdict.

"What say you to this proposition, Lord Calorian?" the King finally asked. "The plunge from commander to nursemaid is a punishment itself."

Malahi's gaze darkened with a brief flash of hate; then she blinked and it was gone. But it was enough to make Killian wonder whether she was doing this for his sake or her own. Or if her agenda went beyond that. Not that it really mattered.

"Do I have a choice?" he asked.

Serrick bared his teeth in a smile that didn't reach his eyes. "Of course, Lord Calorian. If you don't believe Malahi worth your time, I'm sure the headsman would be glad to offer you an alternative."

10

LYDIA

Lydia chewed an orange segment without tasting the fruit, her mind all for the book hidden in a section of linguistic texts. Since her engagement to Lucius had been announced, she'd spent her time closeted in the library with Teriana's book, it providing some small escape from the reality of her looming nuptials.

She lost herself in stories where the six gods stepped onto the mortal plane; where they marked individuals with gifts and powers beyond Lydia's imagination; where evil was not a greedy-minded senator, but a dark god who desired chaos and destruction. Each of the gods had dominion over certain things. Hegeria had power over the human body and spirit; Lern over animals and creatures; Yara over the earth and all that grew on it; Gespurn over the elements; Madoria over the sea; Tremon over conflict and war. The Corrupter endlessly sought control over them all.

The gods' power, she learned, came from the belief of their followers, without which they'd dwindle and cease to exist. And yet they rarely interfered directly, relying on those individuals they marked to do their works and foster the belief of the people. Most of *Treatise* detailed the deeds of famous marked individuals, their faces rendered in detail by the artists who'd illuminated this edition. As she read, the gods became real to her, but what faith she gained was cold comfort. Even if the gods of the Dark Shores were real, they'd long since abandoned Celendor. She'd find no help from them.

There are as many paths as there are travelers.

What had Teriana meant by that?

"Lydia?"

She blinked, focusing on the young woman draped over the couch next to her and watching her expectantly. All the young women present were, and she realized a question had been posed to her. Perhaps more than once. "Pardon?"

Cordelia smiled and said, "I asked if you'd decided on your dresses for your wedding?"

The gorgeous blond was four years Lydia's senior, and by virtue of being Senator Domitius's eldest daughter and of her marriage to a rising star of the Senate, Cordelia was considered one of the most influential women in Celendrial. She was, in Lydia's opinion, certainly the most meddlesome.

Averting her gaze, Lydia replied, "Lucius intends to select them."

"Ugh!" Cordelia's face scrunched up in horror. "He has garish taste. You must take over the task."

The last thing Lydia wanted was to waste her time on dresses she had no interest in wearing, but she couldn't very well say *that*. Especially not with Lucius sitting with the group of men only a dozen paces away, the glass in his hand shaking as he laughed at something another senator had said. "I have other matters that demand too much of my time, I'm afraid." She waved a hand at one of the servants to refill the women's glasses, hoping the topic of conversation would change.

"Such as?"

No such luck.

"My studies," she said. "I'm writing a paper—"

Cordelia interrupted her with a very unladylike snort. "You are so delightfully self-involved."

Lydia sat up straight, less for the insult and more for Cordelia's tone. There was anger in it, but for the life of her, Lydia couldn't understand what she'd done to provoke the young woman. "Excuse me?" she demanded, but Ulpia leaned in. "Let her be, Cordelia. Lydia is a scholar—she's above things like dresses and wedding planning."

It was difficult not to wince. Since the announcement of her engagement, Ulpia had been pestering Lydia with invitations and calling cards. But old habits died hard, and it seemed like Ulpia couldn't help getting her barbs in when she could.

"Let's talk about something different," Ulpia said. "*I* heard that the Thirty-Seventh Legion will be taking a turn policing Celendrial. I don't know about the rest of you, but *I* consider that a fortuitous turn of events."

One of the other girls made an aggrieved noise. "How can you say such a thing, Ulpia? Might as well wish for a legion of wild dogs to maintain order."

Ulpia laughed and waved a hand at the girl. "I've seen them up close, and rest assured, they are *not* dogs." Leaning in conspiratorially, she said, "They're all nineteen. Old enough to be men, unlike the Forty-First"—she named the younger legion camped outside the city—"but not old and weathered and sour like the Twenty-Seventh. Something fine to look at for the next two years, if you ask me."

"The Senate won't allow a legion like the Thirty-Seventh control over Celendrial," Cordelia snapped. "Not with their reputation."

Lydia was inclined to agree. The Thirty-Seventh was responsible for the conquest of Chersome, the southern island having been the last nation to hold out against the Empire's might. Chersome had resisted hard and paid a steep price for it, for it was said the fires the Thirty-Seventh Legion had set still burned across the island nation.

"If they aren't here to police the city," Ulpia said, interrupting Lydia's thoughts, "then why *are* they here? Hmm?"

"How should I know?" Cordelia sipped from her glass. "The better question is: What were *you* doing in a legion camp, Ulpia?"

Several of the girls covered their mouths and giggled, and Ulpia's cheeks reddened. "I heard tours of their camp were possible and Vibius obliged my curiosity."

"A camp full of stinking soldiers. Sounds delightful." Cordelia shifted her weight, holding her glass out for a servant to refill. "Tell me, Ulpia. While you were on this tour, did you happen to get an introduction to the Thirty-Seventh's legatus?"

It wasn't precisely an unexpected question given the infamy of the legion's young commander, but there was something about Cordelia's tone that made Lydia turn to look at her. Something that made her think the question was more than idle curiosity.

"No, I didn't meet him. But I've heard he's a fine thing to look upon." Ulpia flicked her hair over her shoulder; then her eyes turned sly. "Marital bed grown cool and you need a bit of soldier blood to heat it up again? How very like a Domitius to set her eyes on the man at the very top."

It wasn't like Cordelia to rise to any form of bait, but Lydia found the older girl's blue-grey eyes decidedly frigid as she said, "I think it fair to point out that I wasn't the one asking my husband for a tour of the legion's camp."

"Peace, peace," Lydia murmured, but the words were hardly necessary, as a commotion from the group of men caught the attention of the young women around her.

"You can't be serious?" a senator barked, rising to his feet. The man had long been a close associate of Lydia's father, but he was staring at her father like he'd never seen him before. "Fourth sons as well? The cost will be incredible, never mind the damage it would do to the population."

"Now, now." Her father made soothing gestures, glancing quickly at Lucius, who remained silent. "Don't be so swift to condemn the proposal. Cassius is not suggesting a blanket conscription policy as we have for second sons. This would be more . . . targeted."

"What do you mean, targeted?" Cordelia's husband asked.

"The boys would come from poorer families. From those who already struggle to feed all their children, and whose sons are unlikely to grow into contributing members of society," Lucius answered. "We can turn those who would be a burden into assets."

Several of the men's faces darkened, and Lydia's own stomach soured at how Lucius coldly reduced children to commodities. Cordelia shifted on the couch, and though her gaze was fixed on the glass in her hand, Lydia could tell she was listening intently.

"What Cassius means," Lydia's father said carefully, "is that we can provide those less fortunate boys with skills and opportunities that they would not otherwise have. At Campus Lescendor, they'd be given an education and provided with marketable skills."

Lydia couldn't believe what she was hearing. All her life, her father had fought against the legion conscriptions, had fought against war, but this . . . this was the exact opposite.

"Campus Lescendor raises soldiers, not farmers," one of the men said flatly. "Something the Empire hardly needs more of. And you still have not addressed how it will be paid for."

"It's an investment that will repay itself within a generation, if not sooner," Lucius replied, sipping at his wine. "Those schools you proposed the Empire build will no longer be necessary, and the Empire will no longer bear the burden of caring for young men who leech off society and contribute nothing in return. As to your other point, the Empire will always need its legions. Our footprint is large, and we never know when we might need an army of size."

Cordelia's husband's eyes flicked to his wife, but the young woman only drank deeply from her glass, shifting so that she was right next to Lydia.

"Cassius's passion for his proposal makes him careless in his phrasing." Lydia's father laughed, patting Lucius on the arm as though they were old friends. "Do not think of his proposal as a way to mass an enormous military machine, but as a way to improve opportunities for all our young people. Training more boys at Lescendor will allow us to release older legions from duty earlier. Imagine the benefit of having thousands of men trained not just as soldiers but as physicians, engineers, craftsman, and administrators being introduced into society right at the age best suited for them to start families."

"Precisely," Lucius said with a smile.

"Liar," Cordelia muttered, and Lydia was inclined to agree.

She held her breath, waiting for the men to spit and scoff at Lucius's proposal. Yet as her father continued to talk, spinning Lucius's plan to appeal to their way of thinking, she realized what was happening and had to clench her teeth to keep her stomach from emptying itself on the floor.

"Didn't you realize there would be a cost?" Cordelia asked under her breath. "Cassius hardly needs coin and he certainly doesn't need a new wife. What he needs is someone to sway votes."

There was no one in Celendrial more suited to that task than Lydia's father. "He did it to protect me." The words sounded strangled in her own ears.

"I know." Cordelia's voice was toneless. "All of this is for you. And I hope you remember that when Cassius begins stealing tens of thousands more boys from their families. And when he sends them off to die."

Then Cordelia scratched meaningfully at her cheek, and a servant appeared at her elbow, bending low to whisper in her mistress's ear. Sighing, Cordelia rose. "Excuse me." She approached her husband, resting her hand on his elbow. "I'm terribly sorry to interrupt, but we must retire early. Our eldest is ill, and he is asking for his father."

It was an excuse, and everyone present knew it. A subtle way of the pair indicating that despite Lydia's father's endorsement, they would not support Lucius in the elections. But rather than appearing annoyed, Lucius only smiled at the young woman and said, "Nothing serious, I hope? We really do need to be mindful of the health of our heirs. Would you like me to send over my personal physician?"

Cordelia stiffened almost imperceptibly, then shook her head. "That won't be necessary." She closed her hand tightly on her husband's arm, all but dragging him from the room, pausing only for a heartbeat to meet Lydia's gaze, her eyes full of condemnation. "Thank you for your hospitality, Lydia."

But Lydia heard what the young woman really meant: *if Lucius wins, it will be because of you.*

11

KILLIAN

Killian followed the Princess silently through the palace, trusting neither his temper nor his tongue until they were alone. Up the stairs and down the corridor and into a room full of ladies, all who stood at the sight of the Princess, their eyebrows rising with interest as Killian followed her inside.

"Lord Calorian is sworn to me now," Malahi announced. "So you can expect to see much more of him, as my safety will be his first priority."

"And our safety, by extension?" one of them—High Lord Torrington's daughter—quipped with a smirk. The way she looked him up and down made Killian feel like he was a horse at auction, and the giggles of the other young women did not improve the situation. "I'll rest ever so much easier knowing a god-marked warrior is within reach."

She said the last with a slow wink and Killian's cheeks heated, which only added to his foul temper. Gods, but he hated being at court.

Expression unreadable, Malahi gestured to the door. "If you ladies would allow us some privacy, Lord Calorian and I have much to discuss."

They all departed without a word, but the knowing looks and sly smiles frayed the remains of his self-control.

"Why have you done this?" he demanded, slamming the door with enough force that the picture hanging next to it fell from the wall with a clatter. "What are you playing at, Malahi? This is no joke. Not for me. I'm now sworn to *you* for life."

"You wouldn't have a life left to live if I hadn't done it, you ungrateful idiot," she said, crossing the room and taking a seat on a velvet-upholstered sofa, "so perhaps enough with the complaints."

Glaring at her, Killian went to stare out the glass doors leading to the expansive balcony. The sea beyond was grey and storm tossed, and he watched a Maarin vessel fly across the waves, blue sails straining against the wind.

They'd made him do it right then and there. Get down on his knees and swear to protect Malahi with his sword and his life until the gods took one of them. Dareena had supplied the proper words, but in truth, Killian hadn't needed them, because he remembered. Remembered his father sitting with him as a child, helping Killian memorize the oath to repeat to the Falorn princess, just as he himself had decades before to the girl's father. She'd died before Killian had ever had the chance to say them to her, but they still felt burned into his soul.

The thought of his father sent a slice of pain through his gut. Dead when Mudamora needed him most, and Killian might as well have stabbed him in the heart himself. Shoving aside the hurt, he muttered, "It's like being married. But worse. At least I wouldn't have to spend every waking minute with a wife."

"Would sharing my bed help ease the pain?"

Twisting around, he gaped at her. Malahi chuckled before reaching down to pick up a deck of cards, shuffling them without intent to play. "I'm joking, Killian. I've no intention of taking up with you."

"Not far enough up the chain of succession for your tastes?" He shrugged. "Your loss."

Malahi rolled her eyes. "I'm interested in your martial prowess, Killian, not your other rumored talents."

There was something easy about slipping into banter with her—certainly far easier than thinking about every gods-damned thing that had gone wrong. Losing the wall. Losing his father. Losing what semblance of freedom he'd ever had. "So you *have* heard those rumors." Never mind that most of them were total bullshit.

"Hearing isn't the same as believing."

"I couldn't agree more." He came back across the room and took the seat opposite her. "Always best to discover the truth for one's self."

Malahi gave him a pitying look. "And it's always good to have aspirations."

Laughing, he took the deck from her and dealt out the cards before splashing a generous measure of brandy into two glasses. He wanted answers from her, and in his experience nothing loosened tongues quite like a few drinks and a deck of cards. Eyeing his hand, Killian dug out a handful of gold and tossed it on the table. Malahi's brow furrowed; then she eased a ring off one finger and added it to the pile. "You've changed," he said.

"It's been over a year since you last saw me."

Killian put down a card and drew another. *A bloody two.* Not what he wanted, but he added to his bet, nonetheless. "Time itself doesn't change people, Highness. What happens to them while it passes does."

"Wise words from the dashing Killian Calorian." Malahi added an earring to the pile, the amber the same shade as her eyes. "Employing you as my bodyguard is paying dividends already."

He didn't answer, only drew another card. *Cursed seven.* His luck wasn't normally this bad.

"Does the kingdom change to fit the ruler or the ruler to fit the kingdom?" she finally asked.

Killian shrugged. "I've spent all my wisdom for the day, Highness. Your turn."

The corner of Malahi's mouth turned up, and she arranged and rearranged the cards in her hand. "I don't know the answer, only that everything is different." Toying with the corner of one card with a polished nail, she said, "You've been gone. At the wall, and before that, with Dareena in the North. So you weren't here to see."

"To see what?" He'd heard things. Rumors. Whispers. But what Killian was after was the truth, because he rather thought the truth was the reason he wasn't on his way to the headsman's block.

Malahi gave a slow shake of her head. "It's like the wilting of a flower. An incremental decay that is seen only by comparing what is before one's eye with the bloom in one's memory."

Killian's skin prickled. Exhaling a long breath, he leaned back to listen.

"Failing crops. Dying livestock. Drought. Disease. At first it was isolated to pockets in the center of the kingdom, but it's been spreading, and with it has come a loss of faith. A belief that the Six are abandoning us."

"That's nonsense. A few years of bad weather, that's all," Killian replied, though he'd heard from his own family that dozens of foals in the Calorian horse herds had been stillborn. Fruit rotting overnight on the trees. Springs drying up. Ill omens.

"Maybe so. But the weather doesn't explain why the gods have stopped bestowing marks."

"Even Hegeria?"

Malahi nodded.

Killian's hands chilled, and he splashed more brandy into both their glasses, despite the Princess not having touched hers. Hegeria was the kindest of the gods, and she was also the most generous with her healer's mark. The last count he'd heard, there had been close to three thousand healers in Mudamora alone.

"Not a single healer marked in over a year in Mudamora. Neither Yara nor Lern have marked tenders or shifters in at least two. And the last Mudamorian to be marked by Tremon was *you*. That was fifteen years ago. I can't say as to whether Madoria and Gespurn have also ceased giving marks, as neither the Maarin nor the giants are forthcoming, but that something is wrong in Mudamora is certain."

Something rotten. The thought crossed through Killian's mind, then faded away. "Gods . . . I didn't know."

"No one outside the Council of Twelve and certain individuals within the temples does. It's been kept quiet lest it further erode faith in the Six."

"I think you're underestimating the intelligence of our people. This isn't a secret that can be kept. Not for long. Nor should it be."

"I don't disagree," Malahi replied. "You know my father has always been . . . devout. He believes marks are a gift from the gods as a reward for our faith. But he also believes that those marks are often squandered."

Such had been the impetus of requiring all Mudamorians blessed with marks to come to the capital for training, most especially the healers. Killian himself had been subjected to intense schooling in the art of war, including three years of tutelage under Dareena in the North, she being the only other individual marked by Tremon in the entire kingdom. Yet his father's parting words echoed through Killian's thoughts: *The god of war gave you the gifts needed to defend Mudamora, but what have you done but squander them?*

Malahi's voice pulled him back into the present. "Your defeat at the wall . . . it was the culmination of my father's fears that the Marked Ones aren't as devoted as they should be and, with that loss of devotion, are not as strong. You didn't just lose a battle—you lost to one of the corrupted. A queen who, if the rumors are true, was placed on the throne of Derin by the Seventh himself. You might not have seen it, but my father is furious with you."

"He was ready to take my head off," Killian replied. "His sentiments were clear enough."

"It's not your fault."

Killian wasn't interested in her absolution. It *was* his fault. But the information she'd revealed about the gods no longer bestowing marks and of the rot settling into the heart of Mudamora made him certain that the odds stacked against him had been higher than he'd realized. That perhaps it had been no coincidence that the prior commander of the wall had died an *accidental* death right when Killian had been pushing his father for a position of greater authority.

"Rufina called me out," he said, staring at the contents of his glass. "Right before the battle began. She came to the front of her army and shouted that there'd be a reward for my head."

"If you were close enough to hear her, why didn't you shoot her?"

"I tried." Blood roared in his ears, realization settling into his core. *Another mistake.* "Four arrows straight at her heart. She caught them all and laughed." And his men had seen. Had heard.

Malahi's face was expressionless. She knew the story already—it must have traveled with one of the handful who had survived the battle. "Rufina wanted you to try to kill her."

Because she'd needed him to fail. Killian's hands turned to ice and he downed his drink in one swallow. The strength of his mark came from the gods. The strength of the gods came from the faith of the people. The faith of the people depended on their belief that the Marked were what stood between them and the Corrupter.

His men had watched him fail to kill Rufina. Killian cringed at the thought that their faith in the Six had been rattled by that failure, but Rufina's subsequent ruse was precisely the sort of thing his mark always predicted. Killian wasn't fool enough to brush it off as coincidence. And now . . . "All of Mudamora knows that I couldn't stop the invasion." It seemed arrogant to believe that people would think his failings were the failings of the gods, but . . .

Malahi gave a slow nod as though reading his mind. "And my father is only reinforcing their fears by keeping you from leading the Royal Army against Rufina's forces, especially given the role is your birthright. He might as well scream to all of Mudamora that he doesn't trust the Six to protect us. But he's so blinded by his fear that his own mistake caused this that he doesn't see through to the truth."

Killian narrowed his gaze. "Which mistake is that?"

Picking up her glass, Malahi swirled the contents, then set it back down. "The one pertaining to me." She broke off, her throat convulsing as if it hurt to swallow. "I'm the one he truly hates. The one he truly blames for all of this. The one he really wants dead."

The rest of the room fell away, Killian's focus entirely on her. On the slight dampening of the hair at her temples. The flutter of her pulse in the slender column of her neck.

Fear.

"Do you have any secrets, Killian?"

"Everyone has secrets."

"Any that might be the death of you if they were to be revealed?"

Killian hesitated, then shook his head.

"Can I trust you?"

"I'm sworn to protect you, Malahi." His heart was beating rapidly in his chest, like the steady throb of a war drum. "But the decision of who to trust is yours."

She rested her cards facedown on the table, then stood abruptly. Going to a potted plant that sat next to the sofa, the Princess ran a gentle finger across one of the leaves.

The leafy branches shivered; then buds formed, growing and shifting and then bursting open into pink blooms. A process that should've taken weeks, condensed to a moment. A god's power.

Killian exhaled a long breath. "You're a tender." Marked by Yara, the goddess of the earth and all that grew upon it.

"Yes." Malahi curled her hand lovingly around one of the blooms. "Yara chose me when I was ten. I was so happy—the idea that I could help to feed my people seemed such a blessing." She shook her head sharply. "Children are fools."

Killian didn't agree, but he remained silent.

"My mother was horrified, of course. This was after my father had made the enforced service of Marked Ones law. The revelation that I'd been marked would've meant me being taken from her, sent for training at Yara's temple and then to work the fields day after day until the gods took me. For my father to make an exception for me . . ." She dragged in a ragged breath. "Impossible. So she begged him to keep my mark a secret. And he agreed."

Gods . . . If it were discovered that the man who'd forced hundreds of families to give up their marked children into servitude had protected his own from such a fate, Serrick's reign would be over. His *life* might be over given that it was his law that mandated that helping a marked individual avoid service was punishable by death.

"Everything that's happening," Malahi continued, breaking Killian from his thoughts, "the invasion, the lack of new marks, the failing of the land—my father believes to be the result of a lack of devotion in the Marked. And to him, I epitomize this lack of devotion—he sees me as blasphemous. But to reveal my secret would see him lose what he sees as his gods-given duty to lead the Marked, and more than once since my mother died he's told me that if I am not able to serve I'm better off dead."

Killian didn't need to ask whether she believed that threat was real. Every instinct raging through him said that it was.

"I want to protect our people. To help keep them fed. To use my gift for their benefit." Malahi withdrew her hand from the plant. "But not under my father's terms. Not as a slave to the Crown. Service should be a choice, and I believe that in taking that autonomy away from the Marked he has weakened rather than strengthened our devotion to the gods."

Though he was far from cold, Killian shivered, feeling the weight of six sets of divine eyes upon him. *Upon both of us,* he silently amended as Malahi rubbed her arms, casting a glance over her shoulder.

Retrieving her cards, Malahi hid their faces in the folds of her silken skirts. "What is it that you want most, Killian?"

Not that long ago, he'd have struggled with the answer to the question. Now the words came straight to his lips. "To push Rufina and her damned army back across that wall and make them regret ever coming near it."

"If we work together, we might both get our wishes. We could save Mudamora."

Killian narrowed his eyes, considering both her words and his cards. With the way she was clutching hers, he wasn't going to win with a pair of sevens, so he folded. "How?"

"By putting the crown on my head."

Succession was no simple thing in Mudamora. While the right of primogeniture determined inheritance within the twelve houses, simply being heir to the ruling house did not ensure a rise to the throne when the High Lord of said house met his end. The heir needed the support of a majority of the twelve great houses—seven votes from High Lords or Ladies—in order to assume the crown. But never in the history of Mudamora had a woman been allowed to inherit the throne. That had been the reason House Falorn had lost the crown when King Derrick and his family were assassinated. His younger sister, the then fifteen-year-old Dareena, had inherited control of House Falorn, but despite Killian's father's best attempts, the other High Lords had been unwilling to stand behind the young High Lady as queen, their weak excuse that she was not of age.

The result was two years of civil war while the great houses jockeyed for control of the kingdom. Serrick Rowenes eventually won the majority under the condition that command of the Royal Army remain with High Lord Calorian.

All that aside, there was a larger obstacle to Malahi's ambitions. "Your father is still alive."

"There is precedent to the Twelve voting to move the crown to an heir's head prior to the death of the King."

Killian huffed out a breath. "Yes, when the King is on his deathbed or consumed by dementia or in some other way unable to perform his duties. Fanatic he might be, but your father is still sound of body and mind. And even if they desired to take the crown from him, it would be to be put it on one of *their* heads, not yours."

If Malahi was put off by his words, she didn't show it, her voice smooth as she said, "Mudamora is faltering under my father's rule. Faith in the Six has been faltering under his rule. Do you imagine it will do any better under any of the High Lords?"

He didn't, but neither could he imagine any of them accepting an alternative.

"Everyone was willing to let my father execute you. Was willing to let *you* take the fall. Everyone but *me*. Help me claim the throne and I'll put you at the front of the Royal Army. And I have nothing but confidence that this time you'll defeat Rufina."

"You need the majority vote, Malahi. Just how do you hope to achieve that?"

"By offering myself—and my house—up as bait."

"What do you mean?"

Instead of answering, the Princess laid her cards down on the table, and Killian's focus snapped to the faces of the cards, a slow grin working onto his face, despite the gravity of the moment. It was rare anyone outbluffed him. "You have no hand."

Malahi returned his smile, though hers was all teeth. "Let's hope the gods think otherwise."

12

LYDIA

If Lucius wins, it will be because of you.

The veracity of that fact haunted Lydia as days turned into weeks. Not once did she look to the book Teriana had given her, allowing it to languish in its hiding space in the library, unwilling to tempt herself with the thought of escape.

Instead, she turned to trying to undermine Lucius's campaign, digging deep into the facts and figures behind his proposed policies and hounding her father at every turn with how damaging it would be for Lucius to take power.

"Do you think I don't know all of this, Lydia?" her father had shouted at her after a dinner she'd spent berating him with facts. "It's too late to counter him! What's done cannot be undone, so for once, would you curb your tongue!"

Except she knew that wasn't the reason: It was his ailing health. It was Vibius, lurking in the wings and waiting to inherit. It was her tenuous future. For it seemed her father would allow the Empire to burn itself to the ground as long as the man doing the burning protected *her.*

For that reason, despite all of her efforts, all of her pleas, her father remained Lucius's stalwart supporter as Election Day came to Celendrial.

It was dreadfully hot, even in the shade, but Lydia waved away the sweating glass of wine a servant offered in favor of keeping her arms crossed under her breasts and a glare on her face. For hours now, she'd had to stand beneath the portico of the Curia, the shadows of the twenty-four towering columns that held up the roof showing the passage of time like sundials. All because it provided the best view of the Forum, and all because Lucius apparently wished to watch every last citizen cast their vote.

The only thing that made it endurable was that Lucius was losing.

Not by a large margin, but if things continued as they had, Basilius would win. Which was as it should be. Basilius was a good man and, until recently, had been one of her father's closest friends. Though no longer. Not with Senator Valerius standing in Lucius's camp, his face drawn and sweating as he listened to the other man wax superior.

As though sensing her scrutiny, Lucius turned his head. "Lydia, darling. Join us. Regale us with conversation."

"I have nothing to say."

"Lydia, please," her father said, his voice cajoling. It only fueled her temper.

Pointedly eyeing the cisterns filled with tokens, she said, "It seems you'll be using the wine you imported from Atlia to drown your sorrows rather than to toast your victory, Lucius. How fortunate that you ordered so much of it. I understand the sting of loss lingers far longer than the glow of victory."

There were several snorts of laughter from Basilius's camp, who lingered nearby, but rather than frowning, Lucius only smiled. "The polls are not closed, darling. You might yet come to thank me for my foresight in the matter of libations."

"I applaud your optimism."

"Not optimism, my love. Pragmatism. You aren't my first wife, after all. I've learned to keep my cellars stocked."

Before Lydia could retort, Lucius's head shifted as something caught his attention. A heartbeat later, she heard it. A rhythmic beat, growing louder with every passing moment.

"What is that?" someone demanded.

No one spoke; then Spurius, her father's guard, said, "It's marching men." His head cocked as he listened. "A whole legion, by the sound of it."

No one spoke, all eyes going to the entrance to the Forum. The noise grew louder, thousands of feet striking the ground in unison, the crash of drums and blaring of horns barely audible over the thunder. Lydia's skin turned cold despite the heat, some instinct deep in her core recognizing the threat of that noise.

A legionnaire on a white horse was the first to enter the Forum, crimson cloak with Celendor's dragon picked out in gold falling over his mount's hindquarters. His face was partially concealed by a helmet, which bore the red crest marking him as an officer, but she didn't need to see his face to know who he was. The 37 stamped on the steel over his chest answered that question.

This was Legatus Marcus of the Thirty-Seventh Legion.

"Who gave them leave to enter the city?" Basilius demanded.

Her father coughed, drinking deeply from his glass before he said, "They don't need leave on Election Day. They're citizens, and they are of age now. It's their right to vote."

The Thirty-Seventh Legion had the *right* to vote, but more important—and what Lydia was certain everyone was thinking—was that in having been recalled to Celendrial, the legion had been given the *opportunity* to vote.

Two more officers on horses entered behind the infamous legatus, and then the legion itself poured into the Forum, the tread of their feet making Lydia want to cover her ears. Making her, in some base and primal way, want to run for her life. Which was utter lunacy given that these young men were blades of the Empire. And yet as her eyes passed over their ranks, steel and hard muscle, scars and grim faces, she could well imagine the terror these men instilled in those they fought against.

The officers reined in their horses in front of the rostrum, faces expressionless as they watched the legion fill the Forum with neat rows until it was at capacity. Then the legatus lifted his arm and silence fell across the enormous space. Music silenced. Feet stilled. No one even seemed to breathe, not even the senators standing beneath the portico, who were masters and commanders of these men.

The legatus dismounted and pulled off his helmet, revealing a face that was as attractive as was rumored. The legions were made up of young men from every province of the Empire, but his golden skin was that of someone with Cel heritage. His fair hair was shorn nearly down to the scalp, his cheekbones high, and his mouth set in an unsmiling line. He strode toward the steps, the steel tread of his sandals making sharp clacks that echoed over the Forum. Taking a token, he ascended the platform and entered the voting pavilion.

The sharp smell of male sweat filled Lydia's nose as Lucius and the rest stepped out onto the steps of the Curia, her father tugging her along by her elbow. There they stood, she and everyone else watching. Waiting for the legatus of the Empire's most notorious legion to exit.

Seconds passed.

Minutes.

"Perhaps no one explained the process," someone joked from behind her. No one laughed. Not about the young man in question.

The names of all the commanders of Celendor's legions were much discussed, famous by virtue of the Empire's dependence on their martial prowess.

None living were more famous than *him*.

He'd been the subject of extensive conversation even prior to his graduation, a child prodigy who'd scored higher than anyone else in Campus Lescendor's history. That fame had grown after his legion had taken the field. Campaign after campaign. Victory after victory. But that fame had turned to infamy after the conquest of Chersome. *A gifted mind turned to a dark purpose,* Lydia had once heard her father say, and her fingers turned icy as it dawned on her that it was *these* men who had set the island nation on fire.

Legatus Marcus emerged, his eyes immediately going to the senators standing on the Curia steps. He said something to the enormous officer who'd voted after him, an Atlian, judging from his brown skin, who shrugged once before barking an order at the waiting legion. Then the legatus walked around the ranks of his men, crossing the Forum toward the watching senators.

"Legatus," Lucius said as he drew close. The familiarity in his voice made Lydia's stomach drop. They knew each other. Knew each other, and . . . Her eyes flicked to the cisterns. Perhaps only twenty soldiers had voted—not enough to move the mark—but as she watched, the tokens in Lucius's cistern shifted. And she *knew*.

"Lydia, darling," Lucius said, and she cringed as his hand closed around her elbow, drawing her against him. "This is Legatus Marcus of the Thirty-Seventh Legion. Legatus, Lydia is my intended, and I'm sure you know of her father, Senator Valerius."

"Senator," the legatus said, inclining his head to Lydia's father. Then his gaze turned on her. "Domina."

His voice was cool. Polished. The product of officer training at Campus Lescendor. But all the manners in the world would not make up for what he had done. What he was *doing* even as they spoke.

"It appears your legion favors Lucius, Legatus," she said. "Though I suppose that's unsurprising given that he favors the legions."

The young man's blue-grey eyes seemed to measure her words, and then he said, "In my experience, men vote for the individual they perceive will act in their best interest. Only a few vote for the good of society, altruism being a rare quality."

"Which sort of man are you, Legatus?" she asked, not caring when Lucius's grip tightened painfully on her arm. "The sort who desires to save the world? Or to save himself?"

Something shifted in the soldier's gaze, but before he could respond, Lydia's father hauled on her arm, pulling her out of Lucius's grip. "That's enough, Lydia. Perhaps we might go inside out of the heat. Excuse us."

"I am not overheated," she hissed, trying to extract herself from her father's grip but afraid if she pulled too hard he might topple over.

"Your temper certainly is."

"And what of your temper, Father? Don't you see what's happening out there? They're all voting for *him*."

Dropping Lydia's arm, her father wiped sweat from his brow before resting a hand against a column. "It's their right, Lydia."

"I know it's their right." Her words came out louder than she intended, and the men conversing in the cool hallways frowned. "But they're *all* voting for him. Something about this is off. Why are they here at all? He's tricked them or forced them. Lied to them. He's—"

"Mind your tongue." Her father's voice was flat, a sure sign he was angry. "In the space of minutes, you insulted the future consul as well as the legatus of the blasted Thirty-Seventh Legion. Did you stop to consider there might be consequences to that?"

"I hardly think the legatus is going to order his men to burn me alive on the steps to the Curia," she replied, her tone withering.

But her father only gave her a weary shake of his head. "You will stand here and remain silent," he said. "Or you will be sent home."

Scowling, she gave a sharp nod, though she knew it would take all her willpower to keep her tongue in check.

A veritable crowd of senators and their hangers-on had grown in the shade of the building, all of them drawn by the sound of the marching soldiers and the rumor that the most infamous legion in service was turning the tide of the election. There had long been speculation as to why the Thirty-Seventh had been recalled from Chersome. No one seemed to know exactly who had arranged for them to return to Celendrial, but the answer to that question seemed abundantly obvious.

Now speculation turned to what Lucius would *do* with his apparent alliance with Legatus Marcus, what it meant for his policies and plans. Such alliances between influential commanders and consuls had occurred in the past, but they were typically tied to a military campaign. Except there was no-where left *to* conquer. No one left to subdue. Which begged the question of what the legatus had to gain from putting Lucius in power.

In numb silence, Lydia listened to a dozen or more theories, but as the sun began to set in the west she eased back outside, keeping to the shadow of a column as she watched the lines of legionnaires efficiently trooping through the voting pavilion, Lucius's cistern filling while those of the other candidates remained unchanged. No other voters entered the Forum, not with *this* legion's ranks filling it, and with the polls closing at sundown, any citizen in the city who'd yet to vote would have lost the opportunity. Lucius had won the consulship. Lucius now controlled the Empire.

And the two men who'd orchestrated it stood together, elbow to elbow.

A simmering fury filled Lydia as she watched them, a slow smirk forming on Lucius's face, while the legatus's remained cold and impassive as any statue. The last legionnaire voted right as the burning edge of the sun disappeared from sight, and a horn blasted, signaling the polls had closed.

"It's finished," the legatus said. "We'll excuse ourselves from the city and return to camp. Consul." He inclined his head, the movement rigid, as though he'd had to force himself to do it. As though, improbable as it might be, the young man wasn't entirely happy about the outcome.

"Indeed," Lucius said, wiping sweat from his head with one hand, then drying it on his clothing. "Send them back, but I want you to stay. We've business to discuss."

The legatus's hands flexed, the tendons standing out against his golden skin. "With the Senate?"

"No," Lucius replied. "You and I. Attend me at my villa within the hour."

Lydia circled around the column so that Lucius wouldn't see her as he ambled inside, but her attention went immediately back to Marcus. He stood stock-still, staring out over his men but not even seeming to see them. It wasn't until the big Atlian officer whistled, the sound cutting through the silence of the Forum, that the legatus jerked out of his thoughts. He strode down the steps, pushing his helmet on his head before mounting the waiting horse.

"Back to camp," he ordered, voice carrying across the lines of men.

Except he wasn't going back to camp. He was going to meet Lucius alone, and on the assumption that whatever they planned to discuss related to why this legion had helped put Lucius in power, Lydia intended to hear every word.

13

KILLIAN

It had only taken days in his role as captain of Princess Malahi's bodyguard before Killian began questioning his decision *not* to take the King up on an engagement with the headsman.

Malahi's plan was ambitious—to convince the High Lords that Serrick's rule was not favored by the Six and to vote to put her on the throne in his place, using her hand in marriage as the prize. And it was an incentive that none of them would ignore. Even without the crown in play, Rowenes was the wealthiest of the twelve houses courtesy of large gold mines on the western edges of their territory. To marry the future High Lady Rowenes would mean eventually gaining access to all that wealth, and the High Lords of the land were nothing if not predictable in their greed. That it would be the easiest route for one of them to take the throne only sweetened the pot.

But the plan had moved beyond ambitious when Serrick announced to the Council of Twelve his intention to conscript all men of fighting age to the Royal Army. With the exception of Damashere and Keshmorn, whose lands had fallen to Rufina's armies, every one of the High Lords had abruptly discovered that their presence was sorely required back on their lands, all of them fleeing on ships hours before the law was enacted, limiting Malahi's ability to win them over to her plan. Nothing short of an act of the gods would drive those cowards of men to step foot in Mudaire—not when it meant Serrick subsequently dragging them to the front lines with him to fight.

Especially given it was a fight Mudamora was losing.

Rufina's army was moving east from the Liratora Mountains like a dark tide, driving Mudamora's Royal Army slowly backward. Refugees fled in droves toward the safety of Mudaire's walls. Though that safety was relative. Fell things had crossed the mountains with the Seventh's armies beyond even the corrupted. Strange creatures prowled the land and skies, hunting in the darkness, and stories came with the refugees of farms and villages found empty of life and drenched in blood, half-consumed corpses left abandoned for the crows. Fields and forests were crisscrossed with blight, the smell of rot riding the wind all the way to the coast.

Already the city struggled beneath the burden of feeding its people, and with those with means fleeing south in droves, soon merchant ships would have no incentive to transport food and supplies to Mudaire, because there would be no one left in the gods-damned city able to pay for them. And with escape on foot bordering on suicidal given the creatures that prowled the night, Mudaire was more prison than city. It was a matter of weeks before famine set in, and that was only if the inevitable surge of disease didn't kill everyone first.

But instead of using his gods-damned-given mark to protect his people, Killian was currently dragging a drunk palace guard down the hallway by his ankles, the useless bastard snoring as his head slid across the plush carpet. Reaching the top of the stairs, Killian balanced the man on the edge, then gave him a nudge with one booted foot.

The guard rolled down the carpeted steps and landed with a thud at the bottom. Swaying, he sat up, eyes fixing on Killian. "Wha's goin' on?"

"You're fired." Killian bounced a silver coin off the man's forehead. "This should cover a night's worth of entertainment before you march off to the front lines. Enjoy."

Turning on his heel, he started back toward Malahi's suite only to find Bercola standing behind him, the giantess's head nearly brushing the ceiling. "That wasn't very nice, Killian," she said, cocking one brow.

"Drunks bounce," he replied flatly.

"You'd know."

He glared at the giantess who'd watched his back since

he was a child. "I fight better drunk than any of this lot does stone-cold sober." Then he skirted around her and strode down the hall.

She only fell into step with him. "You're supposed to be the captain of the Princess's guard, but currently, you're captain of nothing. That one was the last."

"She's better off with nothing than the lot her father assigned to guard her. Useless conscription dodgers and cowards. Not a one of them would put himself between Malahi and an angry kitten."

And cowardice was the least of their sins. Killian had dug into the backgrounds of the men Serrick had selected to protect his daughter, and far too many had dark pasts full of violence and worse. A handful had clean records, but Killian swiftly determined that that was only because they'd never been caught, which made them doubly dangerous. The looks in their eyes—the way they looked at Malahi . . . He'd fired the lot of them the moment Serrick had marched off to take command of the Royal Army.

And there were no better guards in the city to be had. Every man capable of wielding a blade either had fled south or north beyond the King's reach or was already fighting with the Royal Army. Killian covered his anger at the situation with a smirk. "Bercola, I don't need other guards—I have you."

"Reluctantly." Bercola ducked her head under the frame of the newly installed oak door protecting the wing that contained Malahi's suite. "I spent over a decade ensuring you didn't get yourself killed, Killian, and I spent most of it alternating between wanting to drink myself to the bottom of a wine cask and wanting to fall on my own sword. You are overestimating my desire for this role."

"How much more gold will it take to compensate for that lack of desire?"

"I've no need of gold. And I'm not interested in spending day and night guarding a Rowenes princess. Make it worth my while, or I'm going home to Eoten Isle."

That stopped Killian in his tracks. His father had saved Bercola's life during the Giant Wars, earning a life debt from her. High Lord Calorian had spent that debt ensuring his god-marked son's recklessness didn't overwhelm the gifts the god of war had bestowed upon him—or, in Bercola's words, protecting Killian from his own stupidity—but his father was dead. Bercola owed Killian nothing. Yet it had never occurred to him that his friend might leave once her debt was paid. Convincing Bercola to stay would be much easier if he could tell her the truth about Malahi's mark and her plans and the threat to her life, but the Princess had sworn him to secrecy. And Killian was not one to give his word lightly.

Stopping outside the door to Malahi's sitting room, the faint sound of ladies laughing filtering through the stone walls, Killian rested his head against the wood. "I'm not suited for this." Not suited to following after a princess while she secretly played at politics. He was a warrior, not a gods-damned courtier.

Bercola exhaled a long breath. "When was the last time you slept?"

Killian couldn't remember, which meant it had been too long. His mark gifted him greater endurance, but there were limits. Limits that were being tested as he trailed after Malahi all day, then stood guard in her room through the night, but despite Serrick being leagues away and all the *guards* he'd left behind now without employment, Killian still couldn't stand down. Couldn't relax. Couldn't shake the feeling that danger crept in the Princess's direction.

Bercola shook her head when he didn't answer. "No one man can do this job alone, Killian. Not even you. Hire new men. Pull from the city guard."

"None of them are suitable. They aren't . . ." He struggled to find an explanation for *why,* but that was the trouble with being ruled by instinct, by a mark bestowed on him by a god. Some things he just *knew.*

A grimace stretched across Bercola's large face, her colorless eyes casting upward. "You're intolerable when you're tired. Worse when you're being a defeatist. Go and get some sleep. I'll watch over Her Highness until morning."

Tension flowed out of Killian's shoulders, and he gave his friend a wink. "She likes you better than me anyway."

"Only because I don't cheat at cards." She shoved him between the shoulder blades hard enough that he staggered. "Go. Sleep."

He had rooms at the palace, but rather than retreating to them, Killian made his way into the city. The skies of Mudaire were dark with cloud cover, and he pulled his hood up so that his face was mostly concealed. Partially to protect himself from the heavy wet snow falling from the sky and partially to avoid recognition among the throngs of civilians filling the streets of Mudamora's capital.

Men, women, and children of every race, from nearly every nation. Mudaire was a port city eclipsed in status only by Serlania on the southern shores of the kingdom and Revat, the mighty capital of Gamdesh on the Southern Continent. Killian wove his way through them, heading in the direction of his family's manor house in the gated quarter of the city. His *brother's* manor, given that Hacken was now High Lord Calorian. Hacken had fled for Serlania by ship, and other than Garrem and a handful of caretakers, the residence was likely to be empty. Peaceful. Quiet.

Killian avoided the god circle at the center of the city, the distinct towers dedicated to each of the seven rising several stories higher than any other structure in Mudaire. The towers seemed to shift and move, the carved reliefs of the gods' faces watching him no matter how he kept to the shadows. It was always the way, even with the rough shrines found in smaller villages. Bercola told him it was his imagination, but when one had stood face-to-face with a god—as Killian had—one never forgot what it felt like to be subjected to their scrutiny.

Killian started down the central boulevard leading to the south gate, which was lined with taverns, inns, and brothels, when a loud crash split the air. The man he'd just fired toppled out the door of a tavern, rolling backward down the steps to land with a splash in a puddle. The spectacle, Killian decided, was made far more entertaining by the fact that the idiot's trousers were around his knees. The man struggled to his feet, trying to hitch the sodden fabric back over his bare ass. "She wasn't worth it anyway!" he shouted, shaking his free hand at the door.

A blond blur shot down the steps, tackling the man back into the mud. "If you ever hurt one of my friends again," she shouted, "I'll break your bloody neck."

Killian's skin prickled, a familiar awareness that what he was seeing was important drawing his attention to the girl's face.

She continued to shout threats, emphasizing every other word with a punch, and Killian watched with interest as she broke the man's nose. Split his lip. Cracked his cheekbone. But it wasn't until she flipped the man facedown in the puddle with the apparent intent of drowning him that Killian intervened. Reaching down, he caught the girl by the belt and heaved her off, dodging as she swung her fists in his direction.

"Admirable bit of work," he said, sidestepping another swing of her fists. "But you'll be of no use to me if you're in prison for murder."

"I'm of no use to you at all." The girl cast a dark glare at the man she'd been pummeling as he scuttled bare-assed down the street. "If you're wanting to spend your last bit of coin before you're conscripted by the King, head inside. You cause trouble, I'll be the one to toss you out."

"I've no doubt." Killian pushed back the hood of his cloak, the sleet melting as it touched his forehead, running in cold dribbles down his cheeks.

The girl's eyes widened with recognition. "You're the Dark Horse!" she blurted out, then blanched and executed an awkward combination of curtsy and bow. "I'm sorry, my lord. Didn't realize it was you. It's my job, you see, to—"

"I know what your job is," Killian interrupted, ignoring his recently earned moniker. "And you clearly have a passion for it. I hope you're well paid."

Snorting loudly, the girl spit into the puddle. "Hardly."

"You come work for me and I'll double whatever it is this place pays."

"Work for you?" Her eyes widened.

Killian nodded. "What's your name?"

"Gwendolyn."

"Think about it, Gwendolyn. I'm sure you know where to find me." Pulling his hood back into place, Killian started down the street. He barely managed a half-dozen strides when the girl's voice stopped him. "I'll take the job."

Killian smiled.

"I'll take the job," she repeated. "But only if you get my friend out of prison."

Exhaling a breath of annoyance, he asked, "What's his name? And what did he do?"

"*Her* name. It's Lena."

Another wave of prickles passed over his skin.

"She . . . She's been charged with assault. But it was self-defense, my lord. Truly, it was."

The prickles intensified, as though fire ants marched across his skin. The sensation faded the moment Killian made his decision.

"I'll see you tomorrow morning, Gwendolyn," he said, reversing his path back to the palace. "Don't be late."

14

LYDIA

The air was heady with the scent of flowers, the drone of insects and the tinkle of fountains loud as Lydia crept out onto the library balcony and down the iron stairs under the cover of darkness. A faint breeze blew in off the blackness of the sea, whispering through the trees and catching at a lock of her hair. But it wasn't toward the sea that she ventured, but toward the senatorial homes overlooking the sprawl of the city.

Through the trees, Lydia could make out the gleaming lights filling Celendrial, the echoes of drums and shouts reaching the heights. Supporters of Lucius celebrating a great victory, while those who favored other candidates drowned their sorrows in cheap liquor. Fights would break out soon enough, if they hadn't already, and the Twenty-Seventh Legion would be kept busy through the night maintaining the peace. The senatorial homes would be filled with a similar behavior, albeit with expensive wine and brawls fought with words.

Lydia made her way down the narrow paths between homes, her sandaled feet silent on the paving stones, though her breath was deafening in her ears. She knew these pathways well, but tonight they felt strange and unfamiliar. Dangerous.

But there was no helping it. Lucius and the legatus were up to something, and if there was a chance it could discredit Lucius, perhaps even disqualify his victory in the elections, then she needed to discover their plans.

She had very nearly reached the entrance to Lucius's property when the sound of hooves caught her attention. Scuttling into the shadows next to the towering walls Lucius had built along the front of his property, Lydia caught sight of the white coat of a horse and the glint of light on armor as the legatus passed through the gate. The metal clanged shut behind him, and a tall, slender servant padlocked the gate.

Pulse racing, Lydia retreated up the path, pulling her skirts to her waist to climb the wall of the neighboring villa—a wall that was thankfully more for show than security. Trotting through the pathways of the garden, she heaved herself over the similarly ancient wall dividing the two properties, landing in a fountain with a splash.

Lydia held her breath, sitting motionless in the water until she was certain no one intended to investigate, and then she approached Lucius's home, her sandals squelching with each step. All the villas were laid out in a similar fashion, and Lydia made a swift guess as to where Lucius might be entertaining the soldier. Making her way along the foundation of the villa, she was soon rewarded by the sound of Lucius's voice.

"What would you say if I offered you the opportunity to lead an army on the most ambitious mission undertaken in the history of the Celendor Empire?"

"I'm listening," the legatus responded, and then there was a pause before he asked, "How did you come by this? Any Maarin captain would rather lose a hand than give up a map."

"Let's just say the captain in question lost more than his hand."

The blood drained from Lydia's face, as much from the vicious delight in Lucius's voice as the words themselves. A dull fear pulsed through her veins as he added, "Legatus, it is long past time the Maarin were brought to heel."

Lydia's hands turned to ice, her breath catching in her throat. Teriana, her mother, and the rest of the crew of the *Quincense* were in danger, and they needed to be warned.

Then the rustle of paper caught her attention, and Lucius said loudly, "Behold, the Dark Shores of Reath."

No. Impossible.

Lydia inched slowly upward until she was peering over the lip of the window frame. The two men had their backs to her, slightly obscured by the gauzy curtain. Carefully, she eased the curtain open a crack, her stomach plummeting as she took in the expansive map laid out on the table in front of them. The eastern half containing the Empire was deeply familiar, but the other half . . . the other half was entirely new to her. Yet there was no denying what it represented. Lucius had found proof of the Dark Shores' existence. The Maarin were not his primary target: they were merely the means to a far greater end.

Dropping back to her hands and knees, Lydia listened to the two men speculate as to how, precisely, the Maarin traversed the seas, bile rising in her throat as Lucius chuckled about information that had allowed him to charge the Maarin with paganism, which had enabled him to search their ships. Which had allowed him to detain them. And to torture them.

"Even as we speak," Lucius said, "our navy is moving to intercept several influential Maarin ships. They have the information we need; it's merely a matter of extracting it."

The *Quincense* was an influential ship.

Panic snapped at Lydia's heels like a whip, and she crawled toward the wall, barely feeling the bits of rock that dug into her palms and knees. Clambering over the wall, she sprinted through the neighboring property, past caring about stealth. She needed to get home. Needed to tell her father what she'd learned, because he'd have the power to stop this.

Her dress was glued to her back with sweat as she shoved through the front doors to the Valerius villa. "Father!" she shouted. "Where are you?"

There was a flurry of steps; then her father appeared, his eyes widening at the sight of her, sweaty and scratched, her dress torn and soaked, her hair disheveled. "What's happened?" he demanded. "Who's done this to you?"

"Nothing's happened to me." Grasping his arms, she said, "It's Teriana. The *Quincense*. They're in danger. Lucius has sent the navy to capture Maarin ships because he thinks they have information he wants."

Her father stared at her, silent, then finally asked, "How is it that you came in possession of this information?"

"I went to Lucius's home," she said. "I overheard a conversation between him and the Thirty-Seventh Legion's legatus. He's bribed them. That's why they voted for him."

"Have you lost your mind, Lydia? You *trespassed* on Cassius's property? Eavesdropped on a private conversation? What if you'd been caught?"

It was her turn to gape. "How is that your concern? He bribed nearly five thousand men for their votes! Surely that invalidates his victory?"

"It's not that simple," her father said slowly. "It would need to be proven in the courts, and it would be your word against theirs—"

"There's no time for that," she snapped. "Teriana's in danger. He's already captured other Maarin crews. Tortured them for information."

"He's done *what*?" Her father turned away from her, wiping sweat from his brow. "The Maarin have an agreement with the Senate, and such behavior is in flagrant violation of the terms. For him to do this, he'd need the Senate vote, and I can't imagine a circumstance where such a thing would be forthcoming. He's broken the law."

Vibius's voice cut across the room. "No, he hasn't. But the Maarin certainly have."

Lydia whirled, watching as her father's nephew sauntered toward them, his arms crossed behind his back. "The Empire's agreement with the Maarin specifically states that if a Maarin ship is found in violation of the Empire's laws they forfeit the autonomy and protections ceded to them by the agreement."

"One ship's misstep does not invalidate the agreement with the entire Maarin nation," her father responded, his tone icy. "And from your words, Vibius, it would appear that you are complicit in Lucius's crimes."

"If I'm complicit in anything it is in the protection and enforcement of the Empire's laws." The smile on Vibius's face grew, revealing teeth stained by wine. "This crime was not perpetrated by a singular individual. Or even a singular ship. It is a crime perpetrated by the Maarin people."

"And what crime would that be?"

Uncrossing his arms from behind his back, Vibius tossed a book on the table. "Paganism."

Lydia stared down at the book, a sour taste filling her mouth as she recognized the cover: *Treatise of the Seven*. A slow horror took hold of her, the memory of Vibius catching her sneaking back into the library after her meeting with Teriana on the beach. Of her inadvertently tossing it at his feet. Of her hiding it on the shelves in her library, foolishly certain that no one would have cause to look for it.

"Recognize this, Lydia?" Vibius's expression was feral. "I brought it to Cassius's attention, feeling that he should be aware of your entanglements. Imagine my shock when he was able to translate enough of it to reveal that your possession of this book was more than just a social infraction."

"Lydia?" Her father turned toward her. "Who gave you this?"

Her throat tightened. There was no explanation that would win her free of this.

"Cassius was willing to forgive Lydia's eccentricities," Vibius said. "But I suspect his forgiveness might disappear should you choose to interfere with his plans, Uncle." He shook his head, tsking softly. "Please consider Lydia's future before you make any . . . *rash* decisions."

The spark disappeared from her father's eyes, his shoulders slumping. As fond as he was of Teriana, as much as he admired the Maarin, Lydia knew he'd do nothing that would jeopardize her safety.

Which meant it was up to her.

Snatching up the book, Lydia slammed into Vibius hard enough that he staggered, and then bolted to the back of the house. She needed to reach the ocean so that she could contact Magnius. He'd be able to warn Teriana and her mother—warn them to sail as far away from Empire waters as they possibly could.

Her feet slapped against the tiles, as did those of the men her father ordered after her. Shouldering open a door, she ran into the dark gardens, focused on reaching the gate leading to the path down to the beach.

Then a hand latched on her arm, jerking her back so she landed on her bottom, her spectacles flying off into the foliage. Spurius stared down at her, his expression grim. "I'm sorry, Domina."

She lashed out at him, trying to pull from his grip, but he only caught her other wrist, pinning her to the ground. Seconds later the rest of the household was on her. "She's hysterical!" her father shouted. "She needs to be sedated!"

"No, I need to warn them!" She kicked and struggled, but Spurius's grip was relentless. Someone took hold of her face and poured a foul-tasting liquid in her mouth. She spit it out, but they only did it again, pinching her nose so that she was forced to swallow.

The drug took immediate effect, her vision doubling. Still, she tried to crawl toward the gate. If she could just get a little bit closer. "Magnius," she tried to scream, but it came out as a whisper. "Magnius, the Cel are coming for them. You have to warn Teriana. You have to warn . . ."

Spurius picked her up. Carried her toward the villa. It was possible Magnius had heard her, but even in her drugged state, Lydia knew it was wasted hope.

She had done too little, and she had done it far, far too late.

15

KILLIAN

The crystal dining room had vaulted ceilings from which hung three enormous crystal chandeliers that glittered with candlelight. The walls were papered in muted silver stripes, the floors a polished white oak imported from Katamarca. The tables were covered with silvery-white linen, the plates made of frosted glass, and the silverware polished to a shine. It made Killian feel as though he sat in the midst of a very balmy snowstorm, for Malahi insisted the twin fireplaces be kept roaring with flames.

He helped the Princess into her chair, then sat at her right, glancing over the primarily female guests seated around the large table, before scanning the room to ensure all the young women who formed Malahi's bodyguard were where they should be.

Gwendolyn and Lena had been the first girls he'd hired, but once word spread that Killian Calorian was training young women to serve as Princess Malahi's bodyguard more had followed. Farm girls and tavern wenches. Seamstresses and prostitutes. Merchants' daughters and soldiers' orphans. Most of those who came to him seeking employment Killian declined, for while they were fine fighters, they hadn't triggered the sense of *rightness* he required to allow them into Malahi's presence.

There were certain qualities he searched for. The protectiveness Gwen had exhibited when he'd seen her fight on the street. Or the defiance Lena had radiated staring out at him from behind her cell's bars. Loyalty. Determination. Honesty. Intelligence. Devotion. Few had formal military training, but *all* he'd trust to fight at his back to protect Malahi's life. And with Bercola taking to the task of training them like a fish to water, they were swiftly becoming a force to be reckoned with.

His right hand among them was Sonia, the young woman a former member of the Gamdeshian army as well as the former lover of General Kaira, the Sultan of Gamdesh's marked daughter. It was the dissolution of that relationship that had sent Sonia fleeing north to Mudamora, though as Sonia was fond of telling Killian when she was deep in her cups, one couldn't outrun heartbreak. Be that as it may, Kaira's loss was his gain, for Sonia was one of the finest soldiers he'd ever come across, as well as a born leader. That she had a sharp tongue and wit to match had swiftly earned Malahi's favor, which in turn had allowed Killian more freedom in his comings and goings.

A freedom he took more advantage of than he should.

Next to him, Malahi lifted a hand, calling silence to the room. "Let us give thanks to the Six and to the Marked who protect us in these dark hours."

Killian dutifully made the sign of the Six against his chest, then picked up a glass of wine and drank deeply. The conversation grew in volume as glasses were drained, then bottles. Plates of food soon followed, the air filling with scents that made Killian's stomach rumble: the tang of citrus dressings on salads, the spice of fried duck hearts, the savory waft of roasted beef. The table groaned beneath the weight of the food, all of it sailed in from the South at great expense.

We feast while the city starves.

The food he'd eaten abruptly felt heavy in Killian's stomach, and he pushed away the plate in front of him.

"You should eat your fill," Malahi said. "Shame for any of it to go to waste, all things considered."

"It doesn't go to waste. Your staff eats our *scraps*." This was a bone of contention between them.

"Lord Calorian," said Lady Helene Torrington from where she sat at his right, "I helped at the soup lines yesterday distributing food to the poor."

She stared at him expectantly, but Killian was in no mood to give accolades to the pampered daughter of a High Lord who'd never had to ration anything in her life. As the silence between them stretched, Helene's smile grew increasingly forced until she said, "It truly is as you say, my lord: the people suffer. I tasted the soup to ensure it was properly seasoned and"—she leaned closer to him—"it was *awful*. The worst thing I've ever tasted."

"That's because it's made with rats."

Her olive skin blanched, her dark eyes widening. *"What?"*

"You didn't think it was *beef,* did you?"

"Killian," Malahi hissed, but he ignored her.

"All the livestock in the city was slaughtered within a month of the invasion, my lady, and imports such as you see before you cost more than most earn in a year. What do you suppose the *poor* have been eating?"

"I—"

"When was the last time you saw a cat or a dog other than your own?" he demanded. "I have to keep my own dog locked up inside because he'd be roasting on a spit within moments of being let out the front door. And with the dogs and cats gone, they've moved on to the vermin. Pigeons. Mice. *Rats.* What do you suppose the *poor* will turn to when those have all been eaten?"

"Killian, enough!"

He turned to glare at Malahi. "What? Is the truth so hard for all of you to hear? Or is it only that you wished for me to applaud Lady Torrington for sparing an hour of her precious time to ladle soup, her effort surely making all the difference to our fair city?" The last he directed at the young woman in question.

Helene recoiled, her nostrils flaring with anger. "I didn't cause *any* of this, Lord Calorian. For that we have *you* to blame. Every single Mudamorian who starves should be laid at your feet so that you never forget that it was *you* who let the enemy in."

As if that knowledge didn't haunt his every waking moment. "Noted," he snapped, then shoved back his chair.

"Killian, sit down." Malahi's cheeks were flushed with anger. "Finish your dinner."

He knew he should listen. Knew that he should curb his temper and play nice with his peers. Watch over Malahi like he was supposed to. But he found he couldn't take another night of *this*. "I'm not hungry."

Turning, he caught Sonia's eye, and she gave a nod of understanding, and without another word Killian strode out of the room.

His boots made soft thuds against the floor as he strode through the halls, making his way to the kitchen, which was still in an uproar of activity when he entered. The head chef, Esme, jumped with a start at the sight of him. "My lord!" she said, fanning herself with a tea towel. "We weren't expecting you until later, after Her Highness had retired for the night."

"Thought I might give them something warm for once."

"Oh, that is a fine idea, my lord! Especially on a cool night like this." She cracked the towel at the heels of her assistants. "Well? Get him what he needs. Be quick about it, for once!"

Killian leaned against the counter watching the two young girls scurrying about, loading a sack full of what hadn't been put on the table tonight. Then Esme approached, a steaming tart in one hand. She carefully wrapped it in her tea towel. "For your young friend. I know how fond he is of sweets."

"Thank you." He kissed the woman's cheek, pretending not to hear the giggles of the kitchen girls. The heavy sack of food over one shoulder and the towel-wrapped tart held carefully in his free hand, Killian ventured out into the night.

It was long past curfew, and beyond the crash of the ocean against the cliffs the city seemed almost devoid of sound. Almost devoid of life. No one in his right mind would be out in the streets now, not with the deimos prowling the night skies.

But Killian had never been one to hide.

Easing out of a side door, he eyed the moon above him. The deimos were warier on well-lit nights, swiftly having grown wise to Killian's aim with a bow, staying high and out of range unless something worthwhile lured them in. The cursed things were far too canny for his liking, and his skin crawled with apprehension as he skirted around the shadows of the nearly empty stables before sprinting over to the cover of the wall.

The palace was walled and gated from the rest of the city, a fortress within a fortress, and to that end it had a separate sewer system that drained directly into the sea. Ideal for keeping people out, but given the gates weren't to be opened for any reason after sunset, the palace's design was also damnably good at keeping most people in.

Killian was not most people.

Using a rope to tie both ends of the sack, he looped it over his shoulder, gripping the tea towel holding the pastry with his teeth so it wouldn't be crushed. Then he dug his fingers into the narrow grooves between blocks of rock and climbed.

The muscles of his shoulders strained against the fabric of his coat, and he grimaced as a seam split. Reaching the top, he gripped the edge, keeping still within the shadows. The deimos had good eyesight, excellent hearing, and they had their hearts set on him.

Taking one final scan of the night sky, Killian flung the sack over the edge, then swiftly followed suit. Air whistled in his ears as he dropped the fifteen feet, rolling to lessen the impact of the fall, tea towel still clutched in his teeth.

A scream split the night sky, along with the flap of wings.

Snatching up the sack, Killian sprinted across the cobbled span of space between the palace wall and the city, eyes fixed on the opening in the ground ahead.

Fifteen paces.

Another scream.

Ten.

He could feel the damned things converging on him. Death on wings dropping from the sky.

Five.

The air around him stirred, and his skin prickled. Killian threw his legs forward into a slide, skidding across the cobbles even as a shape passed over his head. Twisting, he threw a knife at the shadow; then the ground fell out from underneath him.

He landed on his ass in a river of wet garbage and worse, the sack of food flopping down next to him.

"My Lord Calorian, are you quite certain that you're marked?" a high-pitched voice inquired. "Because from my vantage, that dramatic entry of yours had all the grace and style of a sea lion flopping about on a beach."

Finn sat on a ledge out of the worst of the filth, bright red coat buttoned up around his skinny frame, the stub of a candle clutched in one hand. Both his trousers and his boots had holes in them, and Killian wondered where the last pair he'd given him had walked off to. Finn's dark hair was a cap of wild curls that was badly in need of a wash, as was the tawny skin of his face, which was dulled with a film of dirt. But his brown eyes were bright with good humor, none of the city's plight ever seeming to touch him.

Climbing to his feet, Killian curbed the urge to rub his bruised backside and instead pulled the tea towel from between his teeth, handing it over. "Here. Should be still warm."

Finn accepted the gift, holding the tart, which was miraculously still intact, up to the candlelight. "This is a thing of beauty, my lord. A true thing of beauty." Then he took a bite, his eyes rolling up with delight as he slowly chewed. "Fit for a king."

"A princess, at any rate." Killian picked up the sack before the food inside got wet. "It was intended for her table."

"Speaking of Her Highness's table, what are you doing here so early? Dinner not up to your lofty standards?"

Killian snorted. "Didn't care for the company."

"Why would you when those with the true charm and wit are waiting for you in our fair city's under-kingdom?"

"My thoughts exactly." Killian gave a last upward glance, noting the shadows moving overhead. "Shall we?"

Together, they made their way through the maze of tunnels making up the sewer system, Finn's nonstop prattle echoing off the walls as he regaled Killian with his various escapades. Killian wasn't exactly certain how old Finn was, for the answer seemed to depend on who was doing the asking. He'd told Esme he was ten while staring up at her with wide, innocent eyes, but he'd told Killian that he was sixteen. Killian's best guess was somewhere in the middle. Finn's mother had been Gamdeshian, his father a Mudamorian sailor, and he'd told Killian that he'd been born in Revat, the capital of Gamdesh, providing enough detail about the city that it was likely the truth.

When his mother had died, his father had brought him back to Mudaire, where they had lived until the start of the war. Finn's father had been conscripted and marched off to join the battle, leaving Finn with a distant relative who wanted nothing to do with another mouth to feed. Finn hadn't heard from his father since.

A story all too common these days.

"Home sweet home," Finn declared, and they stepped into a small chamber off the side of the main tunnel. At the center was a sewer grate that allowed in a fair bit of moonlight, and it reflected off the dozens of faces of the children huddled together in the small space. At the sight of him, their expressions brightened, some of them smiling and saying his name.

"A feast!" Finn shouted. "A feast for my subjects!"

The children extracted themselves from their nest of filthy blankets, forming a line as they'd been taught to do. Killian stepped back as Finn carefully dispersed the food, noting the ragged coughs and crusted eyes on several of them. Grand Master Quindor opened the healing temple for two hours each day to treat the public, but most of these children feared to come out of the tunnels, and it wasn't the deimos that terrified them during the days.

There was a tiny girl in the line with long black hair tied in a loose braid. Finn handed her a piece of roasted beef, but she was coughing and shivering so hard, she could barely chew. Shrugging off his torn coat, Killian wrapped it around her shoulders, the fabric covering her from her neck to her bare feet.

"My lord, I'll get your fine coat dirty," she said, looking up at him. The moonlight caught in her upturned eyes. A northern girl.

"Don't you worry about that," he said. "The Princess gave me this coat, and you see, I've already ruined it." He ran a finger along the split seam. "She'll be angry if she sees it, so perhaps you might help me hide the evidence."

She smiled, her teeth bright white. One dirty hand reached out of the folds of the coat to touch the jet and gold of his cuff links. "Is this your horse?"

His black war-horse was built like a brick shithouse, not at all like the delicate things Malahi had the jeweler design, but Killian nodded.

Malahi.

He'd been gone long enough, and she'd be wondering where he was, especially after how he'd left things at dinner. Leaning down, he said to Finn, "I should go."

The words no sooner exited his lips than clouds passed over the moon, plunging the city into darkness. And with the darkness, the deimos descended. Shrieks filled the night sky, wings pounding the air, and on the cobbles above them hooves clattered. Several of the children started to cry, all of them scuttling to the edges of the chamber, hiding themselves in their nests of blankets. The little girl pressed against his leg, her bottom lip trembling as she watched a shadow pass over the grate above.

"They can't get down here," Killian said. "You're safe."

"But what if they can?" she asked. "What if they do?"

He met Finn's gaze, but his friend only shrugged.

Exhaling a long breath, Killian said, "Well then, I suppose I'll fight them off for you."

"You can't fight them if you're not here."

Malahi was already angry with him. If he stayed out all night, it would be twice as bad come morning. But the thought of leaving made him feel sick, so he said, "Then I suppose I'll have to stay, fair lady."

Killian ensconced himself against one wall, the little girl curling up against him for warmth. At Finn's behest, he told story after story about his time in the North training with Dareena. Funny stories, like the time he got caught in one of the border traps and was stuck hanging upside down from a tree until the High Lady finally cut him down. Or of the time she'd decided his wrestling skills were lackluster and made him spend an afternoon in a muddy pen catching greased pigs.

The children started laughing and stopped flinching every time the deimos screamed overhead. His voice grew hoarse, but Killian kept talking, hearing their breathing deepen as they fell asleep. Only then did he stop, listening to the soft noises they made as they stirred in their blankets. Children who needed their parents. Needed their families. Needed proper homes. But most of them would never have that again.

Helene's voice echoed through his thoughts: *Every single Mudamorian who starves should be laid at your feet so that you never forget that it was you who let the enemy in.*

She was right. It was his fault. Everything that had happened to these children was his fault.

The chamber grew brighter with the dawn light, and Killian's hands balled into fists as the sun illuminated the faces around him. How many of them would die? His eyes burned and he rubbed at them before gently moving the girl onto a pile of blankets, her small form still wrapped in his coat. Pulling loose one of his cuff links, he pressed the black horse into her hand, then bent to shake Finn's shoulder. "I have to go. I'll be back again tonight."

16

LYDIA

Rolling over in her bed for the hundredth time, Lydia ground her teeth in frustration, knowing sleep wouldn't come. Nights of fitful rest plagued by dreams and equally fitful days spent trying to escape to warn Teriana had left her exhausted, but with each day seeing a new Maarin ship hauled into Celendrial's harbor, her fear and guilt would give her no respite.

Climbing to her feet, Lydia donned her spectacles and, turning up her lamp, she ventured down the hallway toward the library. A faint glow was visible beneath the door, which made her pause. No one spent much time in the room but her, and it was highly unlikely that one of the servants was cleaning in the wee hours of the morning. Cracking the door, she peered inside, a frown creasing her brow at the sight of her father bent over her desk, stacks of books sitting next to him. "Father?"

He turned, and at the sight of his drawn face, a dull ache of sorrow filled her core. "What are you doing?" she asked. "You should be resting."

"I find myself not wishing to waste time abed," he said, turning back to the open book before him.

As Lydia approached, she saw it was a law text from the extensive collection on the library shelves. Her eyes skipped across the lines. He was referencing the law against pagan worship, along with its punishments. To his right were several sheets of paper—the agreement between the Maarin people and the Empire. "What are you doing?" she repeated.

"Trying to find a loophole." Reaching for a glass of water, he drank deeply and then shook his head. "There's nothing. Of course there's nothing, or he would've seen it closed before beginning this fell quest of his."

He. Lucius.

Every day, Lucius had been convicting Maarin sailors in the Forum, all of them charged with the same crime, his supporters screaming their support even as they demanded more blood. And her father had done nothing, said nothing, unwilling to do anything that he perceived might risk Lydia's future. "Why now?"

The glass in his hand trembled. "The *Quincense* has been taken. She suffered damage, but wasn't sunk, which is more than I can say for some. She's being towed into the harbor—should be here this morning."

"No." Lydia sank to the floor, her skin growing cold. "You should've let me go. Should've let me warn them. He's going to kill them because of—" A sob choked off the last word. *Me.* It was her fault.

"Cassius is after information. If they give it to him, it's possible he'll be lenient."

"Like he's been lenient with the rest?" she whispered.

"None of them have given him what he wants."

Which meant none of them would. Tears leaked down her cheeks.

"He wishes to see you."

It was the last thing she'd expected him to say. "Pardon?"

"Cassius pulled me aside after we adjourned tonight, and he asked that you attend him first thing this morning at the baths."

The library was sweltering, but Lydia pulled her wrap tighter around her shoulders, hugging herself. "Did he say why?"

"The usual reasons, I suspect." Her father's tone was flat. "You need not go. I can tell him that you wish to wait until after the wedding."

Lydia closed her eyes, focusing inward in an attempt to steady her breathing. It was so tempting to say yes, to spare herself—even if it was only for a few days. But if she went through with it, gave Lucius what he wanted, perhaps she might be able to sway him to be lenient toward Teriana and her crew. If it meant saving them from the noose, she'd sacrifice herself a thousand times over. "I'll go."

"Lydia—"

"It's fine." She rose to her feet. "I'm going to dress."

Stepping out of the litter, Lydia climbed the white steps of the baths. The frescoed portico was all yellows and blues and pinks, and she stared at it for a heartbeat before pushing in the golden doors to the women's entrance. The halls were quiet at such an early hour, the patricians of Celendrial preferring to gather late in the evening in the lounges and lecture halls, then sleep late, so the faint click of her heels against the tile and the splash of fountains were the only sounds as she made her way into the dressing room.

There was a single servant present, a tall girl with the fair skin and reddish hair of those from Sibern Province, her nose lightly dusted with freckles. She silently took Lydia's garments, supplying her with a blue silken robe that belted with a woven cord. The servant gestured for Lydia's spectacles, but she felt unnerved enough as it was without wandering about half-blind and waved the girl off.

Steeling herself, Lydia abandoned the room and walked barefoot down the hall to the first pool. It was open to the sky above but shaded by the tall walls surrounding it.

It was empty.

Lydia's skin crawled with apprehension, the sensation intensifying as she skirted the pool and went inside, the high vaulted ceiling supported with columns, the floor covered with tiny red and white tiles. The still pools she passed reflected her face like glass, and no sounds emanated from the gymnasiums to either side. Entirely empty. Entirely devoid of life. And not even the early hour could account for that. No, this was a display of Lucius's power that he was able to commandeer a facility used by all the patricians for his own personal use.

Do what he wants, she told herself, ignoring the sour burn in her throat. *Apologize for your behavior. Do whatever it takes*

*to learn where Teriana is being kept. Then do whatever it takes
to get her free.*

Heart pounding, Lydia eyed the long hallway leading to the
golden doors of the last pool. The room itself was built into
the side of the hill, entirely subterranean, and the thought of
going in there made her suddenly claustrophobic. But she had
no choice. It was in there, a room testament to the Empire's
wealth, where she knew she would find him.

The heavy doors swung easily on greased hinges, and a
great cloud of steam rushed over Lydia as she stepped inside,
causing her robe to cling to her skin and her spectacles to fog.
Pulling them off, she walked several paces before her nearsighted eyes adjusted to the dim light, leaving the doors open
though she knew she wasn't supposed to let out the heat.

The room was vast and circular, the tiles beneath her feet
like polished onyx and the walls made of the same. In the
center was a rectangular pool formed of tiny golden tiles that
reflected the flames of the oil burning in the dozens of dragon
sconces on the walls, making the water appear molten.

The pool itself was fed by a natural hot spring. It flowed
from the mouth of an enormous golden dragon at one end of
the room, running like a river through the pool to drain out
the large tunnel at the opposite end. The tunnel was usually
covered by metal mesh to prevent anyone from inadvertently
exploring where the underground stream went, yet it was currently unbarred.

Next to the pool was a small table, on which was set a tray
of gold holding two glasses and a dripping decanter of yellow
wine.

Every instinct told her to run. To retreat from this situation.
To hide back in her library.

But her carelessness was what had gotten Teriana and the
rest of the Maarin into this situation, and Lydia refused to allow her cowardice to be the reason they remained imprisoned.

Crossing the room, she filled both glasses. She took one,
though she didn't drink from it, only set her spectacles next to

the decanter, suspecting her poor eyesight might be an advantage when Lucius arrived.

The doors thudded shut behind her. Taking a large mouthful of wine, Lydia steeled herself and turned.

"Good morning, Lydia. Enjoying the wine? It's a bottle of the vintage I purchased to celebrate my victory." It was Lucius who spoke, but it wasn't to him her eyes went. It was to the young man standing at his right. He wore the garments of a bathhouse servant, but even without her glasses, Lydia recognized him.

Legatus Marcus of the Thirty-Seventh Legion.

His face was emotionless, eyes fixed on the tiles between them. He wore no weapons that she could see, but then again, a man trained at Lescendor was a weapon himself.

Hugging the flimsy robe tighter around her body, Lydia asked, "What's going on, Lucius?"

An unnecessary question. There was only one reason Lucius would bring one of the Empire's killers here with him, and it wasn't one she would walk away from. Lydia's heart thundered against her chest wall, her hands turning to ice despite the intense heat.

Lucius chuckled. "Oh, I suspect you know very well what's going on, darling. You have many, many failings, but stupidity isn't one of them."

"You give me too much credit." It was a struggle to keep the tremble from her voice. "I was foolish enough to believe you had the honor to at least follow through on your agreement with my father."

"Interestingly enough, I had intended to. Even after your father succumbs to the poison his nephew is slowly dosing him with, it would be good for appearances' sake to keep you on as a wife for a time. Unfortunately, your behavior of late has rendered that an impossibility." Lucius's expression darkened. "You would have been better served to stay hidden in that library of yours."

The legatus lifted his face at the last, his brow furrowing as he stared at her. Then he shook his head and returned to gazing at the tile.

"Then don't marry me at all," Lydia whispered, searching for a way out. But beyond the doors behind them, there was none. "You've won the consulship—you don't need my father anymore. Let me go. I won't say anything."

Lucius tilted his head from side to side as though considering her words. "An interesting idea, but as my friend here knows"—he gestured to the legatus—"secrets have a way of coming out. Better that you disappear, leaving me to comfort your father in his grief with all my heartfelt sympathies."

"My father's no fool. He'll suspect you. He knows I was supposed to meet you here."

"That might've been the case if you hadn't paved the path to your own murder with such smooth stones."

Murder. Lydia's heart hitched, and it was all she could do not to fall to her knees to beg for her life.

"You've made it so easy." Lucius clapped his hands like a child. "Almost since the moment we were betrothed, you've been maligning me." His smile fell away. "I've heard the words you use to describe me, darling. Reprehensible. Loathsome. *Disgusting.*"

The seething burn of hate filled his eyes, and Lydia took an involuntary step back toward the pool.

"Very shortly, I shall send word of concern to your father explaining that you never arrived for the little romantic interlude I had planned."

"He knows that I did." Lydia shook her head violently. "His own personal guard escorted me. The servant girl in the dressing room saw me . . ." She trailed off as a smirk grew on his face.

"Ah yes. The servant girl who is even now leaving through the side gate wearing your dress and a long dark wig. At least a half dozen of the staff working in the gardens will attest to having seen her—to having seen *you*—sneaking away from our meeting. And just as many will attest to having seen you board a ship leaving for Sibern."

Lydia opened her mouth to protest, but all that came out was a soft whine of fear. Lucius's confidence was deserved. He'd used her own actions against her. Everyone would believe she'd fled.

"The shame alone might be enough to kill your father," Lucius said. "However, Vibius is eager to claim his birthright, and his hand isn't particularly steady when he's in his cups. A bit too much poison and a weak heart flutters its last. I will, of course, ensure Senator Valerius is granted a funeral befitting a prior consul and a man of his station."

Something in Lydia snapped. She flung herself at Lucius, clawing at him. "You will not hurt my father, you disgusting wretch! I will not let you!"

But Lucius moved with surprising speed, the back of his hand connecting with Lydia's cheek.

Stars burst in her eyes; then she found herself staring at the black tile of the floor, her mouth full of blood. A blow from Lucius's foot struck her in the side, flipping her onto her back. Then another as he screamed, "You think you have a say, you little bitch? You are worth nothing! What you think is worth nothing! What you say is worth nothing!"

Abruptly the legatus dragged him off, slamming him against the golden doors. "This wasn't what we agreed to, Cassius. You had your moment to gloat. Now get out."

Curled around herself and barely able to breathe against the pain, Lydia watched as Lucius glared at the soldier before straightening his toga. "I'll avail myself of the baths. Be quick about it, Marcus, and mind you don't make a mess. I wouldn't want anything to take away from the enjoyment of my soak."

His cruel laugh echoed even after the golden doors thudded shut behind him, leaving Lydia alone with the legatus.

"Are you all right?" he asked, reaching down to help her up, but Lydia recoiled from his hand, scrambling backward.

"What difference does it make if I'm all right given that you intend to kill me?"

The legatus didn't answer, only scanned the room, the flickering flames in the sconces casting shadows across his face. Then he shook his head. "It seems he has us both trapped."

Pressing a hand to her battered ribs, Lydia climbed to her feet. "I struggle to understand how you equate our circumstances, Legatus." Maybe if she could keep him talking long enough, someone, anyone, could come. "You will walk out of here. I won't."

"Only if I do what Cassius wants, which is something I'd hoped to avoid. But it seems Cassius's choice of location was not merely theatrical." His voice was as steady as though they were discussing a change in dinner plans, not her murder. Which made a certain sort of sense. His whole life was dedicated to killing. He was a murderer of the first order.

But that didn't mean he was infallible.

"Why are you helping him? Why are you doing this?" Lydia demanded, mind racing as she tried to think of a way around him. A way out. But without a weapon, she had no chance. "Do you desire conquest so badly that this is what you'll do to have him send you to the Dark Shores?"

"*Conquest?*" The legatus's voice was incredulous. "Conquest is the last thing I want. What I need is escape, and the Dark Shores is that."

"Escape from what?" Lydia retreated, step by step, toward the pool. And the table with the decanter sitting on it.

"Everyone has secrets. Cassius has a talent for collecting them. And an even greater talent for using them to his advantage."

Her elbow rapped against the table, and Lydia stopped. "He's blackmailing you?"

"Something like that."

Keep him talking.

"My father," she said, reaching up to take hold of her spectacles, which she placed on her face. "He's a powerful man. He can help you. He can make Lucius pay for what he's done."

The legatus shook his head. "No one has the power to make Cassius pay. Not me. Not you. Not even your father."

His voice was bitter. "We are all his little puppets, made to play the role he chooses for us."

The decanter was inches from her hand, but she'd have to be fast. He was only a few paces away. There would be only one chance.

"It doesn't have to be this way." Her voice was pleading, and she hated it. "You have a choice."

"I know I have a choice. There is always a choice. But if protecting those I care about means sacrificing your life—" He broke off with a cough, then gave a quick shake of his head. "I'm sorry, because—"

Lydia moved. Her fingers closed around the neck of the decanter, arm moving in a wide arc as she swung it toward his head.

But the legatus was faster. He caught her wrist, twisting it. Pain lanced up her arm, her fingers opening, and the decanter fell to the tile with a crash, bits of glass slicing her feet.

"He'll kill my family if I don't do this and I have to protect them."

Lydia screamed, the sound piercing and shrill, primal terror racing through her veins. She fought him, twisting this way and that, but he was stronger. More skilled.

He pinned her arms. But as his ankle hooked hers, pulling her weight out from underneath her, Lydia flung herself back.

The legatus cursed, feet sliding on the slick floor, and they plunged into the steaming pool.

The water burned Lydia's skin as she struggled to get her feet under her. Jerking hard, she freed one hand from his grip, then clawed at him, her nails digging deep before he caught hold of her again.

They broke the surface, Lydia gasping for breath, the water up to her chest.

"Quit fighting." His face was inches from hers, so she saw the panic flare in his eyes as a loud knock sounded at the door.

Lucius's voice echoed through: "I don't have all day, Marcus. Please don't cause me to take this up with your father."

The legatus squeezed his eyes shut, the muscles in his jaw standing out against his skin. But without a word, he pushed Lydia down the pool toward the open drain.

"Please!" Lydia fought against him, trying to brace her feet against the pool floor, but he only lifted her, not seeming to care as she kicked at his legs. "Kill Lucius instead!" The plea tore from her lips. "He can't blackmail you if he's dead!"

"Do you think I wouldn't slit his throat in a heartbeat if I thought it would make a difference?" He shouted the words in her face, his grip on her arms tightening. "Do you think I haven't thought this through? Do you think I haven't looked for any possible way out? There is none! We are both damned."

Her shoulders hit the drain, the current tugging at her hips as the warm water flowed into the dark tunnel beyond.

"I can make this quick." His hands trembled where they gripped her. "It doesn't have to hurt."

Lydia contained her sobs long enough to speak. "For my benefit or the benefit of your conscience?"

Instead of answering, he twisted one arm behind her back, then reached up with one hand to grip the side of her jaw. Ready to break her neck.

"Please," she sobbed. "You can't do this. I haven't done anything to you. You don't even know me!"

His voice sounded strangled as he said, "I do know you."

She fought to free her wrist from his grip, her body screaming as her muscles strained beyond their limits.

"I didn't remember until Cassius mentioned your library." His breathing was ragged. "Though I remember it as your father's library."

She met his gaze, and memory made blurry by years and youth stole over her. Of a friend who went away and then came back changed. Became someone who wasn't her friend at all.

"I'm sorry, Lydia."

The muscles of his arms tensed, and she sucked in a deep breath and screamed, "Help me! Someone help me!"

With a roar, the current surged, slamming against them with incredible force.

His hand slipped from her chin to grasp the edge of the drain, but Lydia fell backward, only his grip on her other wrist keeping the water from sucking her down the tunnel. Her body twisted, her arm crying out in agony.

She reached desperately with her other hand, trying to catch hold of the edge of the drain, but it was too far. Straining her neck to get her head above the flow, she gasped in a breath and at the same time, she saw his lips move, and she swore they formed the words, "*Hold on.*"

He pulled and hope flooded through her veins. But her wrist was slipping through his grasp, his grip failing even as she caught hold of his arm with her other hand, feeling his muscles strain beneath her fingers as he struggled against the current.

Then the water twisted and surged, wrapping around her ankles like a pair of liquid hands, and with a violent tug Lydia was torn into blackness.

She clawed at the sides of the tunnel, searching for an opening and for air.

Then she was falling.

The impact drove what air remained in her lungs out in a stream of bubbles. The current dragged her back under, flipped her around and around before spewing her free. Her head broke the surface, and she gasped, steamy air filling her chest.

The blackness surrounding her was absolute, but her hand still drifted up to right her lost spectacles as though they could've pierced the darkness. The current pulled her away from the thunder of falling water, and around her was nothing but empty air. A void.

It didn't last.

The pool flowed into a tunnel and her feet banged against rocks on the river floor, her arms soon battered and bleeding from guarding her head against the unseen obstacles hanging from the increasingly low ceiling. Lydia dug her nails into the slimy surface of the rock, and she screamed.

The sound reverberated through the tunnels, bouncing off rock and water. It was all for naught. No one could hear her. And even if they could, there was no way to reach her. She thrashed, furious and afraid.

The current ripped her free, and water closed over her head. *One deep breath, and it will be over. One breath . . .*

She opened her mouth, but air rather than water filled her lungs, light bursting bright in her eyes, illuminating a cavern. The underground river poured into it, creating a circular flow that she was powerless to evade. Circular, because there was no tunnel from which it could drain.

Yet it would never fill.

Round and round the water went, dragging her toward the center of the pool where a reverse vortex rose toward the faintly glowing stem of crystal suspended from the ceiling, the water disappearing into it.

A xenthier genesis.

Lydia fought the flow, trying to reach the walls of the cavern. There was no way to know where the crystal would take her. How far it would take her. And as much as she knew that to stay here would mean her death, the unknown terrified her.

Around the water whipped her, and she thought of Lucius's cruel laughter as he walked through those golden doors.

Around, and she remembered the feel of the legatus's hand gripping her jaw, about to break her neck.

Around, and her heart twisted with the knowledge that Teriana was imprisoned, her father being slowly poisoned.

The xenthier might lead to the unknown, but the unknown was somewhere, and from somewhere she could find her way back. To voice the truth. To save her friend. To take her revenge.

Lydia stopped fighting the current and, with the last of her strength, surged up out of the water and closed her fingers around the crystal's tip.

17

KILLIAN

Groaning, Killian flopped back on Malahi's bed, feeling the feather mattress sink beneath his weight. The silken pillows moved against each other with a soft rasp and, reaching sideways, he plucked one up and pressed it to his eyes to block out the lamplight, wishing nothing more than to fall asleep.

"You could at least pretend to be paying attention, Lord Calorian."

Malahi's muffled voice filled his ears, and despite his exhaustion, Killian smiled into the pillow.

"What degree of protection can you possibly provide from across the room buried in a pile of my pillows? Are you even awake?"

"Quite awake," he replied with a yawn. "Do let me know if one of the servants attempts to stab you with a brush and I'll be at your defense in an instant."

She made a decidedly unladylike snort, and through the pillow he heard her murmur at the servants to depart. Seconds later, the pillow lifted upward only to fly back down with blinding speed to strike him in the face.

Killian gave her a lazy smile. "Is that a new dress?"

He barely managed to get his arm up in time to prevent another blow from the pillow.

"You could at least pretend," she said, then dropped a letter on his chest. "Read this."

Even without opening his eyes, he knew what it was: correspondence between her and the absent High Lords. Initially, her letters' purpose had been twofold: to convey Malahi's desire to replace her father on the throne and to suggest that her hand in marriage would be the reward given to one of the men who helped make it so. With that achieved, her letters now dripped with flattery and innuendo, all designed to make the High Lord receiving them certain that he, or his son, would be the one Malahi chose to stand in the god circle with and swear herself to.

Sighing, Killian opened his eyes and glanced at the salutation, recognized the handwriting, and tossed it aside. "I told you, I'm not helping you with your correspondence with my brother. The rest, yes, but not Hacken. I have to draw the line somewhere."

"But he's the cleverest and I can't tell if he's being genuine." Malahi picked up the letter. "You understand him."

It was Killian's turn to snort. "That I do *not*. We can barely stand to be in the same room together."

Malahi huffed out a breath. "Why don't you understand that half the reason he dislikes you so much is that he's jealous of you?"

"Hacken thinks I'm an idiot. He's told me so on several occasions."

"And he's not wrong. You most certainly are an idiot. But neither am I wrong about him being jealous—he's no better than the rest of them."

"You're talking about the wealthiest, most powerful men in the realm, Highness. I'm nothing more than a glorified soldier. Albeit one with deep pockets and the right name."

The pillow descended again with violent force.

"You," Malahi said, once she was through beating him, "are the handsome, god-marked warrior with at least a dozen songs written about him. All my ladies swoon when you walk into the room. You're the one they imagine riding in on a white horse—"

"My horse is black," he interrupted, which she rewarded with another smack of the pillow.

"On a *black* horse to save them when they are in distress."

"Why can't anyone ride in to save me when *I'm* in distress?"

"*Killian.*" She leaned over the bed to meet his gaze. "My

point is, you can do things that they cannot, despite all their power and wealth and privilege. Don't think for a heartbeat they don't resent that fact, or that their resentment didn't factor into them standing by when my father planned to execute you."

"They didn't act because they were afraid, Highness. You're braver than the lot of them."

Her cheeks colored, and she looked away. "I hate it when you're sentimental. It irritates me."

"So sorry." Reaching up, Killian caught hold of her waist and lifted, flipping her upside down and ignoring her shrieks of protest as her skirts tangled around her face before dropping her on her back on the bed next to him.

"You messed up my hair," she said, fumbling to get her skirts back around her ankles. She was quiet for a moment, and then she said, "You must hold your tongue around Helene. I know you don't like her, but she's High Lord Torrington's heir. One day she'll be High Lady, and I'd like to be assured of her support."

"That support is hardly predicated on her opinion of your bodyguard."

Malahi's jaw flexed, and she opened her mouth, then closed it again before saying, "You'll be the commander of the Royal Army, which is something she *will* care about."

Killian shrugged, turning his head to stare up at the ceiling. "Have you decided which one of them you'd prefer to marry, assuming they allow you the choice?"

"I'll choose no one until after the war is won," she answered. "And then I'll choose the man I feel is best for Mudamora. The man the people will *want* as their king."

The bed shook as he laughed. "Then you best prepare yourself for a life of spinsterhood."

"Thank you for your wisdom and insight, Killian. As always, it is so *very* helpful."

He smirked; then prickles rushed across his skin, the sensation so intense, it hurt. Rolling off the bed, he strode to the window, shoving aside the curtains to look out over the ocean, eyes drawn east to the dark horizon. Blood roared through his veins, his heart beating like a battering ram inside his chest.

"It will be you who wins this war, Killian. It has to be you. The Marked need to lead, not to be led. It's what the gods want. It's why they chose us."

Killian only vaguely heard Malahi's voice, twitching as her hand caught hold of his forearm. "I need to go into the city."

Her fingers tightened. "Send one of the guards."

"It's getting dark, so it's better I go. Besides"—he forced a grin onto his face—"if I'm not at the dinner table, you won't have to worry about me squabbling with Helene."

Malahi didn't laugh, only looked up at him, her eyes searching his before she finally looked away, shoulders bowing. "Fine. Go."

"I won't be long."

Retrieving his sword, Killian abandoned Malahi to her courtiers and allowed the compulsion guiding his steps to drag him out into the rapidly approaching night.

18

LYDIA

A blast of pressure hit Lydia in the chest, tossing her backward. The impact knocked the wind out of her lungs, warm water closing over her head, and she thrashed for several painful seconds trying to gain her footing. Then spent several more seconds coming to terms with the fact that she was no longer underground.

Mud oozed between her toes as she stood, body shaking. A blast of wind hit her wet torso, the air stinking like a fetid swamp, and she hunched down in the warm water, taking in her blurry surroundings but struggling to process them. She was alive. But where was she?

Keeping low in the water, Lydia turned in a circle, searching the trees surrounding the spring for any signs of life, but she could see nothing in the shadows. Nothing that gave her even the slightest clue to where the xenthier had taken her. So she looked up. The sunlight was faint: dusk or dawn.

It had been an hour past dawn in Celendrial, which meant if the sun was rising here, she had to be on the western coast of Sibern—it was the only place in the Empire that wouldn't be in full daylight. And Sibern wasn't the worst place to be. All she would need to do was find her way to one of the port towns and secure passage on a ship back to Celendrial, which she should be able to do on credit using her father's name. Then it was only a matter of getting to her father before Vibius murdered him.

Lucius would pay. And blackmail or not, so would his henchman of a legatus.

I do know you. Marcus's words echoed in her thoughts, and

she dug deep into her mind, the memories of playing among the library shelves with a young boy so faded as to be nearly useless.

And she had more pressing concerns. Sibern was a wild place full of wolves and bears and mountain lions, with nights that would turn cold even in the summer. And she was barefoot wearing only a silken bathrobe.

"It will be fine," she muttered. "You just need to follow the spring down to the coast. It can't be that far. Just wait for the sun to come up and start walking."

Lydia stared at the faint glow of the sun, waiting for it to brighten. Waiting for it to illuminate whatever place the xenthier had deposited her.

Waiting.

But around her, the forest grew almost imperceptibly darker, and a tremor stole over her body.

It was not dawn. She was not facing east. The spring was *not* flowing to the western coast of Sibern.

It was dusk.

Which meant she was on the far side of the world.

The Dark Shores.

The forest around Lydia spun, her knees trembling beneath her, and she lowered herself into the water, gripping the slimy stones for balance.

Her chest tightened painfully, her breath coming in fast little gasps that didn't give her enough air. She'd never been outside Celendor. Never traveled with anything less than a full escort. And now she was in an entirely foreign place with no clothing. No coin. No knowledge of who or *what* she might encounter.

The Maarin will be here. You just need to find them. They will help you.

But finding them meant finding the coast. Pushing herself upright, Lydia climbed to her feet and walked down the bank of the stream, wincing as rocks and the roots of trees bit into the soles of her feet. It didn't take her long to reach the edge of what was not a forest but a lone copse of dying trees. Her eyes went to the setting sun, blazing bright and orange over a vast range of tall and jagged peaks. Yet the mountains paled in comparison to what lay in the other direction.

A vast fortress city rose grey and menacing out of the bare plains. At the center stood seven towers in a circle, the likes of which she'd never seen before.

Seven towers. Her pulse raced, the significance of that number in this place not lost on her. *Seven gods.*

Abandoning the stream, Lydia limped toward the city, grimacing as her foot sank into a soggy patch of earth. The smell of rot rose to assault her nose, and she jerked her foot free, wiping the black sludge off on the dry grass. Peering at the ground, she noticed the rotten earth ran like a stream toward the city, narrowing before fading into nothing. And it wasn't the only stretch of it. There were others, reaching out like fingers toward the grey walls, the smell worse than that of a midden heap.

Giving her foot another wipe, she resumed her approach. The city was eerily quiet, and at first she thought it was empty, the ghost of a bygone era. But at the gate, the shadows shifted, and a soldier stepped away from the arch. His breastplate shone in the fading light, yet as she drew close to overcome her myopia she saw he was old and stooped. A strange sentry for such a vast city.

"Stop where you are, miss."

Trader's Tongue. Her heart skipped.

Two more old men stepped out, both of them extracting swords, which they leveled at her.

"Need to pass inspection, miss," the first guard said. He tossed a torch in her direction. "Pick it up so we can see your eyes."

Hands shaking, Lydia reached down and picked up the torch, holding it up so that her face was illuminated. The old man frowned, approaching slowly with his weapon in hand. When he was close enough that she could smell the foulness of his breath, he finally gave a grunt and nodded. "Get yourself inside, miss. Night is nearly upon us."

Handing back the torch, Lydia passed through the thick walls, the flapping of banners that featured a striking scorpion the only sound.

Inside, the wide cobbled street ran straight toward the center of the city and its looming towers. Grey stone buildings rose on either side, but their windows were boarded over, wind that smelled of the sea tugging at the planks. A pair of cloaked women scuttled through the shadows, but before Lydia could say anything to them they entered a house and slammed the heavy door shut behind them. The sound of several bolts falling into place suggested that knocking would be futile.

Ignoring her aching body, Lydia increased her pace, searching the empty streets for an open door. For someone to acknowledge her. For some clue that would explain this strange city. But other than an intoxicated man missing a leg, who was meandering in circles around a fountain, she saw no one.

"Excuse me," she called to the man, but he only snarled at the sky, "Fifteen years I fought and this is how you repay me?" He swung his crutch at the base of the fountain. "Curse the King! And curse the Six!"

Wary of his temper, Lydia took a step toward the crippled man, then yelped as the ground disappeared from under her foot, her elbows rapping against the metal frame of a sewer grate as she fell. Pain lanced through her ankle, and she sat back gingerly, trying to pull her leg free of the bars.

It was stuck.

"Blast," Lydia muttered, tugging harder, but her ankle was already swelling. Shifting, she tried to pull it up in a different spot and from different angles, but it was useless. She needed help.

"Excuse me," she called again to the man, but he didn't seem to hear her, his crutch tapping against the cobbles as he circled the fountain again. "Could you help?" she called a little louder, squinting in an attempt to see him better.

His head slowly tracked in her direction, eventually landing on her. "'S after dark, miss. You shouldn't be out of doors. Ain't safe with . . ." Then he trailed off and fell backward to land with a splash in the fountain, his crutch landing a few paces away.

"Of course," she said, then grumbled a few choice curses she'd heard the household guards use. With her luck, she was going to be trapped here until morning. "Help! Someone help me!"

A hand clamped over her mouth.

Fiery panic rushed through her, and Lydia lashed out, flinging her body from side to side, but both the sewer grate and the arms holding her were implacable. A low voice said in her ear, "For the love of the Six, girl, shut your bloody mouth before you get us both killed."

Lydia quit trying to scream, instinct stilling her. A second later, a young man's face appeared in her line of sight, his gloved hand still covering her mouth, the other braced against the back of her head. "I'll help you," he said. "But you need to stay silent. I don't aim to end my days in the stomach of the spawn of Derin."

She had no idea what he was talking about but nodded anyway. He released her, and as he straightened she noticed the sword belted at his waist.

"I'm fine," she said to him, knowing this was a dangerous situation that could turn out very badly for her. "I don't need any help."

"Of course you don't." The moon peeked out from behind a cloud, revealing a smile that even a blind woman, which she practically was without her spectacles, would find charming. "Though allowing me to do so would be *you* doing *me* a tremendous favor. My self-confidence has been dreadfully low of late and rescuing a damsel in distress"—he held up one hand to forestall protest—"even if she is only *pretending* to be in distress, has bolstered it tremendously."

"You're mocking me."

"Yes, but don't take it personally. I mock everyone. My brothers consider it my worst character flaw."

"You've many then?"

"Brothers or flaws?"

She couldn't help but smile. "Both."

"Two brothers and flaws beyond counting," he replied, but his attention had drifted to the sky. "Are you lodged nearby?" He bent to gently tug on her leg, his gloved hand warm against her bare skin. "I'll take you back to wherever it is you're staying. Not," he added, "because you *need* an escort, but rather for the good of my own conscience."

Lydia bit her lip. Did she lie about having a place to stay and send him on his way, or did she confess the truth?

"You've nowhere to go, do you?"

She shook her head.

"I'll put you up for the night then," he said. "Clearly we can't have you wandering the streets, and the crown shelters aren't fit for rats, much less a girl on her own. Especially one wearing"—he frowned at her—"a dressing gown."

"I didn't plan to be running about outside when I put it on," she said, her cheeks burning. "And while I appreciate the offer, I have no way to pay."

"There are many things in life I need, but coin isn't one of them. Put in a good word for me the next time you pray to the Six and I'll count us even."

A shiver ran through her at his casual reference to the gods. If she'd needed further confirmation that she had reached the Dark Shores, that was it.

Grabbing hold of the bars of the grate, he heaved, the fabric of his dark coat straining over the muscles in his arms. "This is quite the predicament."

"Who are you?" she asked, using the opportunity to examine his face. He was young—perhaps a year or two older than she was—with skin several hues darker than her own. His strong jaw was clean-shaven, his nose slightly crooked from being broken, but rather than detracting from his rather exceptional good looks, it only gave him a roguish sort of appeal.

"You must be new to the city if you have to ask." Letting go of the grate, he turned her leg in various angles. "Killian Calorian," he said. Then he heaved on her leg.

Her ankle screamed in pain, and Lydia thrashed, trying to get out of his grip.

The crippled man chose that moment to sit up out of the fountain and start singing. He only managed two lines of his song before being drowned out by a piercing scream.

The air filled with a steady *thump-thump,* like beating drums. Another scream tore through the streets. This time it was closer.

"Stay still, soldier," Killian hissed, his eyes on the man. "Shut up, shut up, shut up."

Lydia froze, but the crippled soldier had pulled a knife and was waving it at the sky. "Come and get me, you bastards! I still have some fight left in me!"

Killian jerked the sword belted at his waist free of its scabbard, pressing Lydia as close to the wall as her trapped leg would allow. She could feel the tension running through him. Tension and fear.

"What is it?" she whispered.

"Deimos." He held one finger against his lips. "And this fool is going to get himself killed."

No sooner were the words out of his mouth then a massive black shape fell from the sky and slammed into the soldier's back, sending him tumbling across the road. He screamed and tried to rise, but his spine was broken. The black shape dropped from the sky again, but before Lydia could get a good glimpse of it Killian had his sword between the bars, arms straining as he tried to bend them. "Pull," he said between his teeth, and Lydia heaved, fear chasing away the pain.

"Harder!"

The bars groaned as they bent, and then she was free.

Killian hauled her to her feet, arm supporting her as he

pulled her back into a courtyard, then under the shadowed overhang of a doorway.

The soldier's screams had ceased, replaced by the clatter of hooves against the cobbles and the sharp sound of tearing fabric. Fear coursed through Lydia, her hands cold and pulse a rapid flutter in her throat. Knowing she might need to run, she put weight on her injured leg. It ached, but not badly enough to be broken or sprained.

"Is the door open?" Killian whispered.

She tried the handle, but it was bolted. "No."

Two more screams sounded from above and more hooves clattered against the street. Peering around Killian's shoulder, she stared at the opening to the courtyard. The dead soldier's remaining leg was visible, and she recoiled as it twitched. A long tail whipped across the opening to the yard, and the body jerked out of view.

The stink of blood and offal drifted in their direction along with the distinct sound of teeth rending flesh. Lydia thought there must be three deimos on the ground, but there could be more circling above.

The bulky shadow of one of the creatures appeared in the entrance of the courtyard. It walked inside, the clip-clop of its hooves identical to that of a horse. But what stepped into the moonlight and turned its head to look at them was no horse: it was the stuff of nightmares.

19

LYDIA

The deimos turned its head toward the doorway, saucer-sized eyes piercing the darkness. It was shaped much like a spindly horse, except it had leathery wings that stretched out a dozen feet to either side, a fleshy tail that whipped back and forth across the ground, and dark grey skin that was devoid of fur. Lydia stared at it in horror as it opened its maw and filled the air with a piercing call, cruel fangs white in the moonlight.

One foreleg reached out, pawing a cloven hoof across the ground.

"I'm going to need you to get that door open," Killian muttered.

"It's locked!" she hissed.

"Unless you want to wind up in this thing's stomach, I suggest you put some muscle into it." Not waiting for a response, he raised his sword and stepped into the open.

Lydia flung herself at the door, pounding her fists against the solid wood and screaming for help in every language she knew before clamping her teeth together. No one in their right mind would open the door. Behind her, a battle waged, but she didn't turn. The deimos was Killian's problem. Getting inside was hers.

She could not break it.

She could not push it in.

She *could* force the lock, but the bolts on the door suggested another latch on the inside.

"Don't just stand there, woman!"

Thinking was *not* just standing there.

Then a solution presented itself. Whirling, she shouted, "I

need a knife! A . . ." The specifics died on her lips. There was blood everywhere. Was it his? Was it the creature's?

Something metallic whistled past her ear and embedded with a thud in the wood of the door. Lydia jerked the knife free and snatched up a loose cobble. Shoving the weapon's tip into one of the hinges, she hammered on the hilt, driving up the pin. "Come on, come on."

It gave, and she pried at it with knife and fingers, cutting herself and scarcely feeling the pain. Then it was out.

Lydia set to work on the other hinge, sweat and blood making her fingers slick. Her skin crawled with the desire to turn, to defend herself from the danger at her back.

Focus.

The hinge pin slid free. Jamming the blade into the narrow gap in the frame, she levered it against the door, slamming her weight against the hilt, praying it wouldn't break. The door shifted, a black space appearing, taunting her with the safety beyond. Shoving in one shoulder, she pushed, her feet struggling for traction.

Then she was inside.

Killian's voice came through the door, muffled but clear. "Gods-damn it, woman! You are causing me to question my commitment to chivalry!"

Fumbling in the darkness, Lydia unfastened both bolt and lock. "Behind you," she cried, then took a few running steps and threw her weight against the door. The heavy wood tipped, falling with wicked speed.

Killian danced out of the way. The deimos did not.

The door hit the creature's head with a sickening crunch, driving it to the ground where it lay motionless.

What relief Lydia felt was short-lived as a second deimos appeared. It took one look at them and screamed, the sound piercing deep into Lydia's skull.

"Run!" Killian scooped her up and they stumbled into the home, tripping blindly down the midnight hall until his fumbling hands found a door. Pulling her inside, he pressed a gloved finger that tasted like sweat and blood to her lips. *Silence.*

The house shuddered and wood splintered.

Clip-clop. The creature's hooves reverberated against the wooden floor as it walked down the hall, the claws on its wingtips scratching the plaster.

Then Killian shoved her hard.

The wall erupted in a spray of plaster and snapping teeth, the stench of the creature rolling over her as Lydia crawled, trying to get away. Her forehead smacked a chair, and she shoved it aside, clambering under a table, flinching as the tassels on the tablecloth brushed her face.

"Get upstairs," Killian shouted. "I'll lure it onto the street."

The floor shook beneath her, wood splintering. The deimos hissed, its wings rustling like a tarp, knocking against shelves and sending glass smashing against the floor. A decanter rolled across the floor and collided with her leg. Lydia snatched it up, the heavy crystal cold against her sweating palms. Shards of wood rained down around her hiding spot as Killian hurled pieces of furniture at the creature to little effect. In the darkness he was fighting blind, but the deimos suffered no such limitation.

She needed to even the odds.

Decanter in hand, Lydia grabbed hold of the tablecloth, pulling down the yards of fabric. Prying loose the decanter's plug, she sloshed the contents over the cloth, then crawled from under the table.

The deimos and Killian were on the far side of the room, but the blackness made it hard to judge the distance. Something fleshy smacked against her heels, but she kept inching forward. Then before she could lose her nerve, Lydia snapped the tablecloth out high and rushed forward blindly, pulling it down over what she hoped was the animal's head.

The deimos screamed, its hooves scrabbling against the floor as it stumbled back.

"This way!" she shouted. "It's tangled in the cloth."

Boots pounded and Killian half-collided with her, knocking them both against the wall.

"We have to get out!"

Holding on to the fabric of his coat, she dragged him with her, fingers brushing plaster as she searched for the door, finding the opening smashed in the wall instead. The deimos careened around the room, senses blinded by cloth and liquor. Any second it could get free. Upstairs would be no safer—they needed to find somewhere the animal couldn't break inside.

"There is an open sewer grate just up the street," Killian whispered. "It's too small for them to follow us down there."

The deimos that had been hit by the falling door was gone, and they eased across the wreckage of wood before peering around the corner of the courtyard at the street. Two were feasting on the corpse of the soldier, but another stood watching them. Its wing was dragging, obviously the one she'd struck with the door. At the sight of them, its nostrils flared, and it turned to snort at the other two.

One flapped its wings and took to the air, but the other trotted up the street, stopping next to a black opening in the cobbles, and Lydia could just barely make out a grate resting on the ground nearby.

"You bastards *have* been watching me." Killian shook his head, eyes tracking the direction the other deimos was flying. "They know my ways into the sewer. Which grates I've pried open."

"Can we make it to the guard post?" she asked, her attention shifting to him. Killian leaned against the wall, a streak of blood smeared across one cheek. The right shoulder of his coat was torn open, revealing ragged flesh, and his arm hung uselessly as droplets of blood rained onto the cobbles.

The decision was stolen from them as the deimos exploded out the front door of the house, the tablecloth wound around one wing. Its eyes fixed on them, and then it shrieked and broke into a gallop.

"Run!"

Lydia dashed after him, barely feeling the stones beneath her battered feet.

Ahead, the wall and the gates came into view, but her heart sank at the sight of the portcullis barring the opening.

The guards stood frozen, gaping at the monster careening toward them. They were safe, locked between bars of heavy steel and thick blocks of stone, showing no intention of allowing her and Killian in.

Lydia slammed against the metal bars. "Help us," she pleaded. "Open the gate. Let us in." The words came out in a garbled mix of languages. "Please!" She reached through a gap toward one of the old men, but he shrank away.

"Sorry, miss," he said. "We've got our orders."

"The Seventh take you!" Killian snarled, slamming the hilt of his sword against the bars, the motion splattering droplets of blood across the ground.

Scrape.

Lydia shrank into the corner of the gateway. The deimos stood a few dozen paces away from them, teeth bared.

Scrape. Its hoof pawed across the cobbles.

A hand closed around her forearm, drawing her up. "I'll distract it," Killian said. "You'll run."

Her legs felt too stiff to move, knees locked into place. "Where? Who will let me in?"

"On my mark, you'll go left," he said. "Keep to the shadows of the wall so the others don't see you, then take your first right. Third house down with the blue door. They'll let you in. Not everyone in this blasted city is a coward."

His voice was as steady as though he were giving her directions to a party. "What about you?" she asked.

He smiled and pulled a knife out of his sleeve. "Run."

In the second it took her to react, the blade flashed through the air, embedding itself in the deimos's shoulder. She stood frozen, watching as Killian stepped away from the shadow of the wall even as the creature shrieked, jaws clamping down on the knife, jerking it free.

"Run, girl!" Hands shoved at her from between the bars, but Lydia held her ground, watching the young man approach the deimos, sword raised.

She knew how this would end.

Whirling around, she reached through the bars. "Give me a weapon," she shouted. "Something. Anything."

The guards stared at her, the flicker of their torches illuminating the fear in their eyes.

Fire.

"Give me your torch!" she screamed.

When one of them finally moved, it seemed at a snail's pace. The butt end of a torch slipped through the bars, flames flaring bright in the darkness. "The gods be with you, miss," the guard said, but Lydia only jerked the torch out of his grip and stepped away from the gate.

She walked toward the deimos, waving the torch from side to side. Its attention veered from Killian to her, and it snorted and retreated, wings flapping in an attempt to dislodge the tablecloth.

"Run, you idiot," Killian snapped, moving to cut her off. She dodged him, driving the creature back as she brandished the torch. It recoiled several paces, then jerked its wings tight and charged.

Every instinct screamed, *Run.*

Lydia held her ground.

She waited until it was almost upon her, then lunged sideways, shoving the torch into the tangled folds of the tablecloth. For a heartbeat, she thought her plan had failed, but then the liquor-soaked cloth burst into flame.

The deimos shrieked and reared, hooves lashing out at her head, trying to kill her even as it burned.

"Move!" Killian slammed into her, pulling them both into a roll that didn't stop until they hit the side of a building. Extracting herself from his grip, Lydia watched the deimos run down a side street, wings burning like paper until it collapsed in a shuddering heap.

Except it wasn't dead. Not yet.

Shaking, Lydia climbed to her feet and retrieved Killian's sword from where he'd dropped it, the hilt still warm from his grip. Knees bent like springs ready to launch her back, she approached, sourness filling her mouth as she noted the labored rise and fall of its flank. The way its pulse throbbed in its throat. Before she could lose her nerve, she shoved the tip of the blade into the creature's flesh, allowing the sword to rest against the ground as blood pooled around her feet and the creature went still.

"Are you all right?"

Instead of answering, Lydia dropped the sword and threw up. Over and over her stomach heaved, the vomit burning. Twisting away from the mess, she pressed her forehead against the cobbles.

"If you're finished, we need to go." Killian reached down to retrieve his weapon. "I've already lost a chunk of flesh to one of these bastards, and I don't aim to lose any more."

He started walking, then swayed, catching his balance against the wall of a building.

Wiping her mouth, Lydia hurried to his side, noting that the sleeve of his coat was soaked with blood, a constant stream of droplets falling to splat against the cobbles. "Let me help you."

"I'm fine."

"You're not. And if your ego is so delicate that you insist on arguing otherwise, you deserve to be eaten."

His laugh turned into a growl of pain, but he didn't resist as she pulled his uninjured arm around her shoulder, staggering as his weight pressed against her.

Their progress was nerve-rackingly slow as they shifted from shadow to shadow. Lydia kept an eye on the dark skies, muscles twitching at every sound, certain they were being watched. That the deimos were waiting for them to falter and then would attack. When they reached a blue door centered in the front of a large building, Killian extracted a key, trying three times to insert it into the lock before Lydia took it from him. She had just turned the key when the door swung open, revealing the tallest woman Lydia had ever seen.

The woman's eyes widened at the sight of them. Reaching down, she grabbed Lydia's arm and jerked, sending her toppling across the floor into the house.

"Don't you dare!" Killian's strangled protest followed her in as the enormous woman picked him up like a child.

Ignoring Lydia, she kicked the door shut and hurried up the stairs. "Garrem," she shouted. "Get your arse upstairs."

An old man shuffled across the front entrance and up the stairs, past where Lydia huddled in the shadows. Trailing him was a group of girls, none appearing past twenty. All six of them wore dark trousers, knee-high boots, and dark blouses held tight to their bodies by leather corsets.

"Someone's hurt," a girl with a thick blond braid said, crouching to touch one of the many droplets of blood splattered across the floor.

"I'm sure I heard the captain's voice," another with copper-colored hair said, and the lot of them exchanged glances. Lydia debated extracting herself from her hiding place but decided she was happy enough where she was.

"Not him, surely. He's . . ." the blond trailed off, and the girl with the copper hair took her hand.

There was a heavy thud, and the large woman's voice boomed from above. "Gwen, have the cook put water on to boil and tell her I need more bandages. The rest of you get back to your dinner. There's little enough in this cursed city without you letting it go to waste."

The blond disappeared into the hallway, but the copper-haired girl asked, "Who's hurt? Is it the captain?"

The enormous woman hesitated long enough that a denial would obviously be a lie. "He ran afoul of a deimos."

The girl's hands balled into fists. "Is he . . . ?"

"He'll be fine. Go eat your dinner, Lena."

"I can go get a healer," the girl—Lena—protested. "I know the sewer tunnels—"

"No." The woman's voice was not unkind. "You will stay here unless I say otherwise, do you understand?"

The girl-soldier reluctantly nodded, then disappeared after her fellows. Lydia leaned her head against the staircase, inhaling the smell of wood polish. Everything hurt. Her feet were a raw mess, and she bled from countless small injuries on her arms and legs.

She did not know what to do.

She did not know where she was.

She did not know how she was going to get back home.

What she did know was that Killian was bleeding to death from injuries gained saving her life. And for that reason, even if the night were safe, she couldn't walk away.

Taking the steps two at a time, Lydia followed the woman's voice until she found the room where they'd taken him.

On silent feet, Lydia stopped at the doorway, taking in the sight of Killian stripped to the waist and lying on a bed. The old man—Garrem—was inspecting Killian's ruined shoulder, the skin lacerated down to the bone from the deimos's fangs.

"You need a healer," the large woman said, pounding a fist against one of the bedposts. "I'll send two of the girls to the temple."

"No." Killian's voice was weak but adamant. "The deimos aren't normal beasts, Bercola. They'll be watching this house, and I'll not have anyone risk their lives by leaving it."

"It's their job to risk their lives!"

He shook his head. "For Malahi, not for me."

"Then let me go. You are *my* responsibility."

"Bercola, I said no," he said. "Even if you made it to the temple, Quindor wouldn't allow any of his healers to go out into the night. Not for me. You'll have to wait until dawn."

"Dawn will be too late."

"We'll see about that." He turned his head and caught sight of Lydia standing in the doorway. His face was ashen except for the smear of blood across one cheek, but he still managed a crooked smile. "Not a damsel in distress, after all."

Pretending she didn't see Bercola's glare, Lydia made her way to the side of the bed. "That's kind of you to say." She tried to smile while taking in all the blood. "My confidence has taken quite a beating lately, and your gratitude has bolstered it immensely."

He laughed and then ground his teeth. "Gods, that hurts."

"Apologies." Lydia glanced nervously at the woman looming over her.

"Leave her alone, Bercola," Killian said. "Better yet, go make sure no one is thinking of doing anything stupid."

A thousand arguments were written across the enormous woman's face, but she only shook her head and left.

With the aid of a monocle, Garrem had finally managed to thread a needle and set to stitching up Killian's shoulder. "Your field dressing skills have not improved, I see," Killian said through clenched teeth.

The old man sniffed and bent lower over the injury, which had already soaked the sheets with blood.

As he winced, Killian's gaze shifted back to Lydia. "I don't even know your name."

Garrem stopped his stitching. "Lord Calorian! That's appalling, even for you."

"It isn't like that," they both said at the same time.

The old man eyed Lydia, grunted, and then returned to his work, which Lydia watched with fascination. She'd never seen an injury so severe before, and she mentally catalogued how the old man drew the bleeding muscle together, the type of stitch he used, and how swiftly the bandages soaked with blood. Killian winced with each pass of the needle, but he never once cried out.

"Are you going to tell me your name or do I have to guess?"

The question dragged her attention from the injury back to his face. "It's Lydia."

"Unusual name."

It wasn't. Not in the Empire. "I'm from somewhere else."

"Should've stayed." His jaw clenched again, and to her

surprise, he grabbed hold of her hand. His fingers were like ice. Then he sighed, eyelids slipping closed and fingers going limp in hers.

"Blast!" Garrem rose swiftly to his feet. "This is for naught—he won't last another hour much less the night without a healer. I'm going to find Bercola to see what can be done. Try to rouse him, if you can." Then he shuffled out of the room, leaving her alone with Killian.

"My . . . lord." She stumbled on the unfamiliar honorific, then gently shook his arm when he didn't respond. "My lord, you must wake up." His eyelids fluttered, but he didn't move. "Killian, please!"

"Poor boy is in a bad state."

Lydia's head snapped up so fast her neck cracked. A stooped woman with wrinkles layered on top of wrinkles stood on the opposite side of the bed, seemingly having appeared from nowhere. She wore a brown dress, and a long white braid hung down her back. "Who are you?" Lydia demanded, glancing over her shoulder to find the door still closed. "Are you a physician . . . a healer?"

The woman chuckled and rested a hand against Killian's forehead, stroking back his hair fondly. "Not as such, Lydia."

"How do you know my name?"

"I haven't seen you in a very long time," the woman said, clasping her hands in front of her. "Only my sister sees clearly through the haze of the East, and she is rarely forthcoming. Though it is her I must thank for bringing you back."

"Who are you?" Lydia demanded again. "What do you know of Celendor?"

The woman grimaced. "More and less than I would like. However, that is a distant threat for another day. I'm afraid we've more pressing concerns, my dearest girl. This boy was chosen years ago, and my brother does not wish to see him lost just yet. Nor do I—I've always been fond of this one."

Killian's breathing had grown ragged. Lydia took his hand, but his fingers remained unmoving. "Can you help him?"

The old woman shook her head. "That is not my way."

Lydia sank her front teeth into her lip to silence a nasty retort. At the best of times, she despised vagaries. This was not the best of times. "Then he's going to die."

"Not if you help him."

"I'm not a physician. I don't know how."

The woman smiled. "It's more a matter of will than knowledge. The question is, are you ready to take all the hardship that will come along with it?"

"Tell me what to do." Lydia squeezed Killian's hand, feeling the callus across his palm from what must be endless hours of holding a weapon. He was dying on the bed between them and the woman was talking prophetic nonsense. Lydia could deal with the gore; all she needed were the appropriate instructions. What to stitch and how.

"If you help him, you'll be starting down a hard and lonely road—"

"I've walked a lonely road all my life," Lydia interrupted, tired of the unnecessary chatter. "Tell me how to help him or get out."

"Oh, there is no mistaking you. You are just like your father." The woman beamed, and Lydia barely had the chance to register the woman's words before she reached out, fingers brushing Lydia's forehead.

A shock ran through her, and she staggered back, momentarily blinded by bright light. When the stars receded from her vision, the woman was gone.

And everything was different.

The air was filled with a shifting, swirling mist. It drifted toward her, clinging and absorbing into her skin. Panicked, Lydia tried to brush it away, but it only latched on to her hands. More and more of it floated toward her, like iron filings to a magnet, and the dying man was its source. It poured out of his injuries like blood, but the flow was diminishing.

It was *life*.

And he was running out.

20

LYDIA

The sun shone through the open window and Lydia blinked blearily, strange scents filling her nose, the fabric of the pillow beneath her cheek not the familiar silk of those in her own bedroom.

"Good morning."

Lydia sat upright, yanking the blankets around her bare shoulders. Killian sat in a chair, looking remarkably hale and healthy for someone who'd been on his deathbed. He had a half-finished plate of food balanced on one knee, indicating he'd been watching her for an uncomfortable length of time.

"You're alive," she stuttered.

"I noticed." He took a bite from a strip of bacon and leaned back in his chair. His shirt sleeves were pushed up to his elbows, revealing a multitude of faded scars on his olive-hued skin. "Shoulder's as good as new, though you should show more caution when healing someone who's marked. We take a fair bit more to kill, and therefore take a fair bit more to heal."

An image of her face, aged nearly beyond recognition, flashed across Lydia's mind, and she jerked her gaze to her own hand. Fingers straight and slender, skin unmarked. The hand of a young woman, not an aged hag.

Had she imagined it?

No, she decided, noting that her own minor injuries had entirely healed. As improbable—as impossible—as it seemed, none of it had been a dream.

Which meant that had been no mere old woman she'd been speaking to—it had been the goddess Hegeria; Lydia was certain of it. *Treatise of the Seven* gave no physical description to the gods, but it did describe their nature and what aspects

Stumbling forward, Lydia clapped her hands down on one stitched wound to stop the flow.

The moment their skin touched, her fingertips burned as life seared out of them, leaving behind a growing void deep in her chest. Lydia's heart labored, her lungs wheezing, each breath a greater struggle than the next. Exhaustion swept over her, and with a strangled cry she jerked backward and fell, joints rattling with the impact against the floor.

Lydia lifted her hand, terror clawing through her like a beast as she took in the gnarled fingers with paper-thin, age-spotted skin. Climbing to her feet, she stumbled toward a mirror on the wall, barely able to see through her clouded vision. Her outline sharpened as she approached, her image clarifying even as her stomach twisted, bitter and foul. The face that looked back was hers.

Hers, fifty years from now.

Lydia screamed.

of the world they had dominion over. Hegeria was said to be the most serene and kind of the gods with power over the body and spirit. She was whom the people of the Dark Shores prayed to for good health, for fertility, and for wisdom. But more important, the mark she bestowed on her chosen was the ability to heal even the most catastrophic of injuries, though doing so required the healer giving up some of themselves. *Treatise* had page after page of stories of famous healers making great sacrifices to save others, and it was not lost on Lydia now that said sacrifices were often their very lives.

The gods were real.

Their marks were real.

And Lydia had been saddled with the worst of them.

Killian set the plate aside and pulled down his sleeves, dragging her attention back to him. "You know I have to turn you in."

For what and to whom Lydia had no idea, but *being turned in* was never a good thing. And from the tone of his voice, he was in agreement. She stared at him, unwilling to speak lest she unwittingly condemn herself further.

"I don't *want* to," he continued, resting his elbows on his knees and meeting her stare. "I'm not in favor of how Serrick treats the Marked—healers especially—but I'm in no position to cross him on this. I'm not in his good graces, and my head is only tenuously attached these days." He drew a finger across his throat. "There's only so much I'm willing to do for a girl I just met. Even one who saved my life."

Lydia swallowed the dryness in her throat, thinking fast. "Your chivalry is commendable."

Killian winced, his pride pricked as she had intended. "You would've been caught anyway," he muttered. "Quindor investigates every whisper of a rumor of a healer across all corners of the kingdom. I have no notion how you managed to elude him this long."

Lydia considered his words, marking the way he avoided her eyes, his jaw working back and forth. Highborn he might be, but this young man was no politician—not with the way every emotion played across his face, most especially his guilt. "I eluded him," she said carefully, "because until last night, he'd have had no reason to be looking for me. Before last night, I wasn't . . . marked." The word stuck in her throat, the admission somehow making it *real*.

Killian went very still.

"I'm not from here. I'm from Celendor, but circumstances drove me to escape using an unmapped"—she broke off, unsure of the translation—"xenthier stem. Xenthier's a sort of crystal—"

"I know what xenthier is."

The same word in both languages. That was interesting. Pushing away the thought, she continued. "It deposited me in a stream just outside the city, and I came looking for shelter. I'd been inside the gates only a matter of minutes before I fell and you came upon me."

"I see."

"When Bercola left me alone with you, an old woman came into your chamber. I'd never seen her before in my life, but she knew my name." *Knew who I was. Said she knew my father.* "She told me that you'd been chosen years ago and her brother did not wish to see you lost. That she'd give me the chance to save your life if I was willing to take the hardship that came with it." She leveled him with a glare. "Little did I know that this hardship would be visited upon me so swiftly. Or by the man whose life I saved."

His color rose. "You're telling me that Hegeria marked *you* to save *my* life because Tremon asked her to?"

Lydia nodded, silently cursing herself for taking the woman's—no, the *goddess's*—offer without thought of the consequences. If she'd declined, she wouldn't be in this predicament—she'd be on her way to finding a route back to Celendor to help Teriana, to stop Vibius from poisoning her father, and to make Lucius pay for his actions. Back to a place where gods and their marks didn't exist.

"None of this matters anyway. As soon as I can find a Maarin ship, I'll be on my way back to Celendor." She'd smelled the ocean in the air last night, and there was little chance a city of this size wouldn't have a port. And the Maarin went everywhere.

"That's quite the tale." He leaned back in his chair. "But you have a set of problems. One, the Maarin don't take passengers—"

"They'll take me."

He huffed out an amused breath. "*Two*, since the invasion and the deimos began fouling the skies, the Maarin have been bypassing Mudaire's harbor. And three, even if the Maarin were taking passengers, Quindor is testing every person who boards a ship to ensure they aren't marked healers trying to evade conscription."

Lydia's stomach soured, and she viciously plucked at a loose thread on the coverlet, fighting back tears. "I'll go by land to wherever the Maarin are making port then. I don't care if I have to walk. I need to get home."

"Do you think this city would be filled to bursting with people if walking south was an option? The deimos aren't the limit of what crossed the wall. Every town and village between here and Abenharrow has been massacred and anyone caught outside after dark with less than a fully armed escort suffers the same. Only a good rider on a fast horse has even a chance of making it, and given only a dozen—"

Before he could finish, the door to the room swung open and Bercola stepped inside, bending her head low so she wouldn't hit the frame. "They've left. If you're going to take her to the temple, now's the time to do it."

She glanced curiously at Lydia and then tossed a folded dress in her direction. Lydia let it drop to the floor, both hands occupied with keeping the blanket wrapped around her naked body. In the light of day, she was able to get a better look at the woman. A good foot taller than Killian, Bercola's head was shaved to her ruddy scalp, but her eyebrows suggested her hair would be white if allowed to grow. Her eyes were devoid of color, only black pupils in seas of white, and Lydia found she had a hard time meeting the woman's gaze.

"Get dressed," Killian said; then he followed the giantess out of the room, shutting the door behind him.

Lydia snatched up the woolen dress and pulled it over her head before tiptoeing across the floor to press an ear against the door.

". . . says she's from some place called Celendor."

"Never heard of it."

"Neither have I, but that isn't the interesting part. She says she was marked last night to save my life."

The giantess whistled. "She isn't inked, but that's still a bold claim. You don't believe her, do you? She's too old to receive a mark. Hegeria takes them young."

"Of course I don't believe her. She's desperate to avoid conscription, is all. Healing me was likely an accident—that mark has a mind of its own."

The giantess was quiet for a minute. "It's not impossible. You *are* marked yourself, and the gods do ask favors of each other—"

"Why would Tremon incur a debt on my behalf? He gave me every skill I needed to keep this kingdom safe, and yet here we are." Killian's voice was bitter. "The gods don't give second chances. The girl's a liar."

Bercola's sigh was audible through the door. "Even if she's telling the truth, we need to turn her over to the temple and Grand Master Quindor. The last thing you need is to be caught harboring a rogue healer."

The floor creaked, and Lydia could all but see Killian pacing up and down the hall.

"You don't have a choice," Bercola said. "The King is desperate for her kind. And you know he's looking for any excuse to have you executed."

The wall shook with the sound of a fist slamming against plaster.

"You think I don't know that?" Killian's voice was dark. "But turning her in is worse than cutting her throat myself. The healers are all that's keeping the army on its feet, and they're dropping like flies. Serrick isn't even sending their bodies back for proper rites anymore; he's burning them with the rest of the corpses. Quindor won't take the time to train her—he'll send her straightaway, and she won't last a month."

Lydia didn't hear how Bercola responded. Staggering back from the door, she sat on the bed, her body numb.

The moment she'd been trying hardest to forget—when her fingers had touched Killian and all the years of her life had drained away to bolster his. The slow march toward death accelerated. If she was sent to the battlefield, it would be the same thing, but over and over again. She'd rather die permanently than be subjected to that sort of torture, and it seemed no amount of guilt was going to keep Killian from turning her in. She had to escape.

Silently, Lydia propped the chair under the door handle. Going to the window, she unlatched it and swung the glass outwards. The room was on the second story above a narrow alley, and the ground below was terrifyingly far away. But not as terrifying as what she'd face if she stayed.

Shoving the crusts of bread and scraps of gristle from Killian's plate into her pocket, she tied the edge of the blanket to the bed frame and dangled the end out the window. It came nowhere near the ground, but it might get her close enough that she wouldn't break an ankle in the fall. Standing on the bed, she eased herself onto the frame. One hand on the sill and the other gripping the fabric, she lowered herself until she was dangling in the air.

The door handle rattled. "Gods-damn it, girl!"

Heart pounding, Lydia let go of the frame and slid down the blanket, hands burning from the friction. Then the knot holding the blanket to the bed gave way and she was falling.

Her heels slammed against the ground and she toppled onto her bottom, spine shuddering. Wood cracked and splintered, and a second later Killian was looking down at her.

"I'm not a liar!" she shouted at him.

Inexplicably, his face blanched, but then he disappeared back into the room, boot steps thundering against the wooden floor, clearly intent on chasing her down.

Leaping to her feet, Lydia bolted down the alley and out onto the street. It was crowded, and she resisted the urge to push—that would only draw more attention. Turning into another alley, she broke into a sprint, dodging stacked baskets and crates, feet sliding in the slick refuse. She ran through the twisting route, pausing only when crossing a roadway where she would walk sedately and then pick up speed when she was once again out of sight. She ran until she couldn't breathe; then she collapsed onto an overturned crate, chest heaving, listening for sounds of pursuit. But there was only the hum of people going about their business.

Leaning against the cool stone of a building, Lydia took a deep breath, watching as the fresh abrasions on her feet sealed over, fading from red to pink to white until the only signs they'd been there at all were the still-drying smears of blood. It made her skin crawl, and she turned her face to the sky, trying to maintain control of the panic bubbling up in her veins.

Focus.

Lodging had to be her first priority—after last night, Lydia had no interest in being on the streets when darkness fell. Except that required coin and she had none. Extracting a crust of toast from her pocket, she nibbled on it while considering her options. She could try to steal, but given her nonexistent pickpocketing experience, that was unlikely to go well. With her luck, she'd end up in prison.

"Or you could open your eyes, you idiot," she said aloud, the solution to her problem glittering in the black diamond on one of her fingers. The ring had been a gift from her father when she'd turned fifteen. It was deeply precious to her, especially now that it was the last link she had to him. Her father who might well already be dead from Vibius's poison.

The thought stole the breath from her chest, especially knowing that he would've died believing she'd fled. Parting with the ring would hurt, but he'd want her to do it. Especially if it meant getting herself home to help those she'd left behind.

"I'm coming, Teriana," she muttered. "Don't give up yet."

21

KILLIAN

Killian shouldered past Bercola, sprinting to the staircase. He grabbed hold of the twin newel-posts, but rather than launching himself downwards, he rested his weight on his arms, letting his legs swing back and forth as he reconsidered the chase. Making a decision, he lowered his feet onto the top step.

"What in the fiery depths of the underworld do you think you're doing?" Bercola demanded from behind him.

"Did any of the girls see her last night?" Killian asked, ignoring Bercola's question even as he pondered whether the guards at the gate had gotten a good look at her. *Too dark,* he decided. Never mind that half of them had cataracts.

"No, so if you don't catch her now, she's lost." Bercola gave him a shove, nearly sending him tumbling down the stairs.

"Better lost than found," he said, recovering his balance.

"You're a block-brained idiot!" Bercola's face was purpling. "There is no way we can keep this quiet. I haven't any doubt that half the city already knows about your late-night adventure and the mystery healer who saved your life. Quindor is going to find out, and he *will* hold you accountable for letting her go."

"I didn't let her go—she escaped. I chased her as far as I could, but unfortunately, the side effects of last night's . . . *adventures* kept me from catching her." He pressed a hand to his chest and grinned. "I feel quite winded. Perhaps I should sit down."

Bercola's face tightened and she crossed her thick arms. "So you're going to just let her go? No matter the consequences?"

"I'm going to let her go for *now*. It isn't as though she'll get far."

"Why let her go at all?"

He shrugged. "You know I'm a sucker for a pretty face, Bercola." Then he waved a hand at her. "Head to the palace. Tell Malahi I'll be there shortly."

The giantess gave an exasperated shake of her head but departed without argument, leaving Killian standing at the top of the stairs.

It was true, the girl had been strikingly beautiful, but that was only a convenient excuse. It was what she had said that was making him hesitate.

I'm not a liar.

The words were a haunting echo of what the corrupted woman at the wall had said just before his men shot her down. That damnable moment when he'd ignored his instincts in favor of the King's laws. He didn't intend to make the same mistake again.

Who are you?

Celendor, that had been where Lydia had said she was from. A name that didn't ring any bells of recognition in him, despite the fact that he'd been north and south, east and west, across the entire kingdom and beyond. She had the look of the North about her, but her unusual accent said otherwise, and even that he couldn't place.

No healers marked in over a year.

And yet Lydia had been, or at least claimed to have been, which would mean that Hegeria had returned to the mortal plane after a year's absence to mark this girl so that she might save his life. And if that was true . . .

You need to get back to the palace.

Malahi is waiting for you.

You're shirking your duties.

Killian ignored all the thoughts spinning through his head, instead striding down the hallway to his study, bypassing his sleeping dog and the shelves of books on his way to a cabinet. Inside were dozens of maps, which he extracted, laying them flat on the table. For the next hour, he scanned through them, searching for the name. Nothing.

Sitting back in his chair, Killian unrolled an enormous map that showed all the known world. The Northern and Southern Continents, plus all the islands, big and small. Derin was a blank space, as were the Uncharted Lands in the center of the Southern Continent, but otherwise, this was the sum of the world.

It was possible, he supposed, that she was a Derin spy, but nothing about that felt right. She was too unprepared and the deimos had been just as keen to kill her. Never mind that it seemed unlikely that Hegeria would be marking a girl who paid tribute to the Seventh. Frowning at the map, Killian idly traced a finger over the angry-looking sea serpent in the corner, the symbol of the Maarin people. The map had been a gift to his father from Triumvir Tesya of the *Quincense* years ago. One from her personal collection, he recalled her daughter Teriana telling him, though they'd filched a bottle of rum, so his memory of the conversation was blurry.

As soon as I can find a Maarin ship . . .

The Maarin don't take passengers—

They'll take me.

What was Lydia's connection to the Maarin? Obviously they knew where this Celendor was, which meant it was likely coastal, as the Maarin were never off the water for long. Perhaps an island in the middle of nowhere?

An island with a xenthier stem that terminated right outside Mudaire's gates.

He grimaced at that. It was common practice to encase known stems in tombs of stone, and a morbid part of him had always wondered how many corpses would be found if the tombs of the terminuses were ever opened.

Most of his questions could easily be answered if any Maarin ships were in the harbor, but they were both too wise and too gods-damned wealthy to be incented to risk their ships and crew to Mudaire's dark skies. Huffing out a breath at the time wasted, Killian rolled up the map, only to pause as his eyes landed on the edges of the paper. Three sides were worn with much handling, but one . . . one was sliced smooth, as though freshly cut.

Half a map.

The thought settled on his mind, but then he brushed it away. There was nothing but ocean, or so said the Maarin. And no ship that had ventured east or west into the Endless Seas had ever returned to contradict them.

Leaving the map spread out on the table, Killian pulled on his coat and pocketed an assortment of weapons before heading out into the cool morning air. He strode through the streets and made his way to the west gate. There was a convoy passing slowly through, the wagons laden with supplies for the Royal Army from whatever ships had arrived at dawn, only that which could not be transported left for purchase at the harbor market. The crowds of civilians on the streets eyed the wagons hungrily, but the fifty armed soldiers flanking them were enough deterrence to hold them back.

Recognizing one of the men, Killian fell into step next to him, the soldier inclining his head. "Lord Calorian."

"News?"

"Time it takes to run supplies gets shorter with every passing week." The soldier shook his head. "The Seventh must have spies in our camp, for the Derin army predicts His Majesty's every strategy, and with every skirmish we lose men by the hundreds."

"Morale?"

"Bad. The corrupted pick off our scouts and leave their corpses staked out for us to find at dawn. Deimos overhead all night with their cursed racket make it near impossible to sleep, and a man can't step outside of camp to take a shit for fear of the packs of creatures that roam the dark."

"Have you ever seen them?"

The soldier shook his head. "Just their eyes. And their leavings."

Serrick needed to commit to a battle while he still had the

numbers to win it, but Killian knew from the messages Malahi received that the King still believed he could whittle down the Derin army's numbers through skirmishes and hunger, confident that the Royal Army's healers and tenders would keep it from suffering the same. Yet the enemy remained inexplicably well supplied and it was Rufina who came out ahead in every skirmish.

"Despite what happened at the wall, it would be well for morale if you or High Lady Falorn rode with us." The man pulled off his helmet to wipe sweat from his brow. "If there was ever a time we needed the strength of the Six, it is now."

They'd reached the gate, and instead of answering, Killian thumped the soldier on his shoulder. "May the Six guide your steps."

"And yours, my lord."

Stopping next to one of guards who'd been at the gate the prior night, Killian said, "Finally rustled up the nerve to open them, did you?"

The old soldiers turned, eyes widening at the sight of him. "My lord," one of them blurted out. "You're alive!"

"No thanks to you sorry cowards." He waved aside their stammered explanations of rules and protocol. "That's not why I'm here. The woman that was with me, had you seen her before?"

"Not an hour prior to the deimos attack, my lord," one answered. He was old enough to be Killian's grandfather, his nose red and bulbous, suggesting a lifetime of drowning himself in drink. "Came through the gate soaking wet and barefoot, wearing something fit for a lady's bedroom, not walking the countryside."

"Spend much time in ladies' bedrooms, soldier?"

The man's cheeks flushed. "Not in recent years, my lord."

"Which way did she come from?"

Pointing across the barren fields laced with blight, the man said, "From the trees. Wasn't another cursed thing moving out there, so we caught sight of her straightaway."

"Checked her eyes like we do everyone," another chimed in. "She wasn't corrupted."

The idea of these men doing much of anything if they did cross paths with one of the corrupted was laughable, but Killian only nodded at them before starting down the road, the mud from previous rains already drying into ruts. His eyes drifted over the ground, catching sight of a footprint in the drying earth, the size and shape matching the girl's.

Stepping off the road, he tracked her back toward the trees, noting a spot where she'd stepped in the blight and attempted to wipe the slime off on the dead grass. The fetid stench of rotten eggs was thick on the air. His boots made soft crunches in the dead grass with each step as he approached the copse of pines, many of them diseased, their needles browning. The branches should've been full of birdsong, the undergrowth rustling with rabbits and squirrels, but the only sound was the whistle of the wind and, in the distance, the gurgle of water.

Killian's skin prickled and he extracted a knife, following Lydia's trail until he reached the banks of the stream, where he paused. The mud was marked with footprints and handprints from her clambering up the slight incline, but there were no similar markings on the opposite bank. Frowning, he followed the water upstream to the rocky outcropping where it originated. Circling the hill, he searched for her trail, for any clue as to where she'd come from, but there was nothing. It was as though she'd sprung from the water itself.

Perched on top of the outcropping, Killian stared at the turbulent flow of water, knowing he needed to get back to Malahi, but *something* kept his feet frozen in place. Then he caught sight of the glitter of metal beneath the surface of the water.

One jump had him back down on the bank, and there he pulled off his boots and coat, along with his shirt, and waded out into the water. He had been vaguely aware that this stream was warm, but this close to the source it was the temperature of bathwater, with a surprisingly intense current. Picking his way out to where he'd seen the glint of metal, Killian stuck his knife between his teeth, squinting against the spray as he reached down between two rocks.

And extracted a pair of spectacles.

The lenses were miraculously intact, albeit slightly scratched, the frames delicate but well made. Turning them over in his hands, he remembered how the girl had squinted at anything distant, clearly nearsighted. *These were hers.*

The spectacles placed safely on a rock, Killian eyed the opening in the hill from which the water flowed.

Taking a deep breath, Killian grabbed the edge of the rock and pulled himself against the current. The pressure was incredible; his body shook with effort as he searched for handholds in the cave wall, his bare feet slipping on the slick stones of the stream bed.

He was considering allowing the water to push him back out when his grasping fingers found a pocket of air. Pulling himself into it, he took several deep breaths, then braced himself against the cave wall and turned.

It was a small cavern, but despite being entirely enclosed, Killian found that he could see. Glimmering faintly was the source of the flow. Not an underground stream, but a black stem of xenthier crystal.

The girl had been telling the truth.

22

LYDIA

Lydia walked through the streets, a shawl she'd found in the gutter wrapped around her head to obscure her face. The city—Mudaire—was laid out like a pinwheel, curved streets bisected by broad boulevards that ran between the towers at the center and the four main gates, all of which she was able to blearily make out with her flawed vision.

Not having her spectacles made her edgy and uneasy. Up close, she was fine, but the faces of anyone more than a dozen paces away were foggy and unrecognizable, meaning she wouldn't see a threat until it was far too late. There was no helping it, though. Even if she'd been able to find a lens maker, she couldn't spare the coin to purchase them. She'd have to make do without.

The city was overfull, and Lydia hardly took two steps without being jostled by women with their children in tow or having to step over soldiers who'd lost arms or legs in battle, the limbs apparently irreplaceable even with a healer's touch. The situation was made worse by the fact that everyone was dragging all their worldly possessions with them, on their backs or in rickety carts. The smell of unwashed bodies rivaled the stench of rot in the air, and far too many appeared to be walking aimlessly, uprooted and with no place to go. It was impossible that they could all find shelter by nightfall.

And if she had been blind to all the sights and numb to the smells, she would've needed to be deaf as well not to realize that this was a kingdom at war. Talk of battles past and battles to come was on everyone's lips, names of commanders and places where skirmishes had been won or lost. Whispers of an enemy that seemed barely human and of creatures so terrible, they defied description. But one name was whispered more than all the rest.

Rufina.

They called her the Queen of Derin. The High Priestess of the Seventh god. Mostly, they called her the Corrupted One.

It wasn't long before Lydia felt a chill in her own spine when the enemy queen's name was mentioned, and she tried to fight away the unease by listening to the sounds of their voices rather than to what they were saying. Keeping her head down, she quietly mimicked their accent. She had landed herself in a hornet's nest, but if there was an advantage to the chaos, it was that it gave her opportunity to blend in.

Following the salty breeze of the sea and the stink of fish led Lydia to a gate in the city wall leading to the harbor, where she picked her way through the crowd and down into the market. There were only two vessels in port—hardly any relative to the size of the harbor, and neither of them possessed the distinctive blue sails of a Maarin ship.

"Excuse me," she said, tapping a sailor on the arm. His skin was a dark mahogany shade, his ears pierced with a dozen golden rings, brown hair curly and thick. "Do the Maarin trade out of this harbor?"

He shook his head. "Not seen one of their ships here in more than a month." His voice carried a heavy accent different from any she'd heard before, lilting and beautiful. "The Crown has been seizing all cargos and paying below market rates, and the Maarin don't have any time for such behavior." He eyed her. "Why you looking for the Maarin?"

"I've friends among them."

The sailor shrugged. "They're still trading out of Serlania, if you can get there. Most captains are avoiding Mudaire for fear of losing their crews to conscription, never mind the vermin that haunt the skies. High Lord Hacken Calorian's ships are constantly coming and going, but passage is more than most can afford. He's touted as a hero for risking his ships and crews, but the filthy rich bastard is making a small fortune off others' misery. Yet he pays my wage, so I can't complain."

Lydia's throat tightened at the familiar surname, and she glanced around at the blurry crowds, half-expecting to see Killian's tall form striding in her direction. Booking passage on a vessel associated with him seemed like a risk, but she had to find a Maarin ship. It was the only chance she had of making it back to Celendrial, and that made it worth the gamble. "How much?" she asked.

The price the sailor named in silver made her ill, but her ring was worth a small fortune in gold. "Where do I go to book passage?"

"Ships sailing today are full to the brim," he said. "But you come back in the morning at first light with coin in hand"—he eyed her dubiously—"then like as much someone will find a place for you."

The thought of remaining another night made Lydia's stomach sink, so she ventured down to the docks, intent on finding a captain who could squeeze her aboard. But before each of the ships was a choke point, a lineup of people passing some sort of inspection before they were allowed to board.

Unable to make out what was happening, Lydia crept closer, her heart beating violently in her chest. But she needed to see. Creeping up next to a stack of empty crates, she peered around them, watching as person after person rested their hands against the bare arm of a boy whose face was marred with a livid burn. Only after a nod from an official-looking woman in white robes were the individuals allowed to proceed down the docks.

"Volunteer a broken bone or a bad burn for inspections, and one of the temple healers will fix everything that ails you as compensation at the end of the day."

The sailor had come up behind her, and she asked, "Have they caught anyone?"

"Four, last I heard. So desperate to avoid their fate they cut off their own tattoos to try to sneak past, but Quindor's nets are too fine and his rewards too lucrative. For their troubles, he rebranded them and then sent them off to join the King." He spit on the ground. "It's blasphemy, if you ask me. Mudamora treats its Marked Ones like chattel."

"Where are you from?"

"Gamdesh, miss." He grinned. "If you find yourself a ship, bypass Serlania and head to Revat. It is a better place." Then he strode past the lineup and up the gangplank of the ship.

Lydia chewed on the inside of her cheeks, her fear demanding she focus on the prospect of being caught out as a healer, though she knew that was not her greatest obstacle. Testing aside, passage required coin, and if she had to remain in the city she would require the same. She needed to sell her ring so that she'd be prepared for either circumstance.

Selling a ring, unfortunately, proved to be a far greater challenge than she'd anticipated.

No one in the city was buying luxury goods. No one was willing to even trade for it, recognizing instinctively what she hadn't—that it was worth too much to be easily sold for currency. After hours of trying and failing, Lydia found a wall to lean against and slid down until she was seated at its base.

"Blast it all," she said, staring at the black grime caked under her lacquered toenails.

"Listen all, and listen well!" A shrill voice reached her ears, demanding her attention. A young boy with tawny brown skin and a wild mop of dark curls stood on the edge of a public fountain, a small crowd gathered around him. "The sun sets tonight at half past the ninth hour. Those who linger on the streets past twilight do so at their own risk. For those who have no home of their own, the Crown offers shelter in all four quadrants of the city."

"They're filthy and filled with vermin and plague," someone shouted.

The boy shrugged one shoulder. "If you'd rather risk the deimos than bed down with a few fleas, be my guest. I merely tell it as it has been told to me."

The crowd grumbled, but before any more comments were made the boy held up one hand to silence the noise. "Before you lot go making any rash decisions, let me tell you a tale that came to my ears this very morning. There were two casualties last night. Two!" he shouted. "A sorry fellow who dared to tarry on the streets after dark fell victim to the deimos. The creatures stripped the flesh from his body and gnawed his bones until all that remained was the echo of his screams on the wind."

Lydia raised one eyebrow at the boy's dramatics, only then catching sight of two women dressed in elaborate gowns and fur-trimmed cloaks who'd stopped to watch the proceedings. Both of them wore them their hair up in elaborate coifs, and though their faces were a blur, Lydia caught a glint of jewels on their ears. An idea formed in her mind.

The boy continued. "There was a second death." He paused for a long moment, surveying his audience before shouting, "The death of a deimos!"

The crowd gasped, many leaning closer to the boy, but Lydia immediately abandoned her plan in favor of retreat. She knew this story, and if the boy described her well enough she'd be recognized.

"A man," he stage-whispered. "A lone man, caught out past sunset. He walks swiftly, keeping to the shadows even as the skies fill with the shrieks of deimos on the hunt."

Lydia eased around a woman, stepping over the children sitting at her feet.

"He reaches the door to his home—safety! The sweetest nectar to be had in the dark of night. The door handle is in his grasp, but he hesitates."

"Idiot," the woman muttered, meeting Lydia's gaze.

"Clearly," she replied, stepping over another pair of children.

"Help! Help! Help!" The boy jumped from foot to foot, shouting in falsetto. Lydia's heart sped faster.

"He hears a crone's voice split the air, begging for salvation from death on wings!"

Crone's voice? Lydia froze in her tracks, turning back to the performance.

"With no regard for his own safety, he sprints through the streets, finding the crone hemmed in by a deimos. A lesser man would run, but not this warrior. Not Lord Killian Calorian."

The crowd stirred, but the boy ignored them, climbing to the top of the fountain, heedless of the spray. "He attacks, but not even the sharpest steel can pierce the creature's hide, so he tears a door from a home with his bare hands, pummeling the creature until it flees. But more descend, circling, teeth snapping and wings flapping, so he leaps onto the back of the leader, riding it through the streets with the others on his heels."

"What?" Lydia muttered.

"He herds them toward the gate, but the cowards on guard only hide behind the steel bars, watching on as he fights five, no, ten! deimos, never faltering despite the injuries they inflict upon him. One by one, he drives them off, until only the largest remains. Not content to allow the creature to flee into the sky, Lord Calorian wrests a torch from the gate and stabs the flaming brand into the creature's heart!

"Yet even as the deimos burns at his feet, Lord Calorian knows he is mortally wounded and his only chance of salvation rests in the hands of the crone—a healer so ancient that even in these desperate times Hegeria's temple"—the boy gestured to one of the towers in the distance—"closed their doors in her face."

"You can't be serious," Lydia muttered to herself. Mistaking the source of her ire, several of the women near her nodded in agreement.

"Old or not, she should have let him die!" one of the women in the fancy dresses called out. "It would've been no less than he deserved. This plight we all suffer—it is *his* doing."

The boy ignored the comments. "Woe to those who risk the shadows of our war-torn night," he said, voice trembling loud and dramatic. "But greater woe to those who dare cross paths with the Dark Horse of House Calorian."

"Woe indeed," Lydia grumbled, uncertain why she cared that the boy had gotten the story horridly wrong.

Circling the crowd, she approached the two women who walked as though they were alone in the square, everyone else tripping over themselves to get out of their way. Lydia stepped directly in their path, and they nearly collided with her before stopping.

"A moment of your time, my ladies." Lydia dropped into the awkward dip of the knees she'd seen other women doing.

Their eyes focused on her, and one of them—a girl about Lydia's age with brown hair and the same dusky olive skin as Killian—said, "I've no time for street urchins."

She motioned for Lydia to move, but Lydia held her ground, one eye on the guards with them. Thankfully the ancient men looked too bored to intervene.

"Not even for the opportunity to own a jewel from across the Endless Seas?" Lydia held up her ring, balanced on the palm of her hand. The black diamond caught the sun, sending bits of light dancing across her skin.

"What nonsense is this? And why would someone like you have something of any value in your possession?"

"It was a gift from my father," Lydia replied, trying to imitate Teriana's voice when she was telling a tale. "Given to him by a Maarin sea captain who found his way to lands unknown and only barely managed to find his way back. Having lost his wealth on the voyage, this was the only thing he had left, and even then, he was loath to part with it."

Which was all a lie. The stone was from mines in Celendor, and her father had bought it from a renowned jeweler in Celendrial who'd been more than happy to sell it to a senator.

Eyes narrowing, the girl plucked up the ring, holding the diamond to the sun to examine the quality.

"It's probably just tin and glass, Helene," the other girl said. "She's swindling you."

"It's not glass," the girl—Helene—said. "You know I have an eye for these things."

"As you can see," Lydia said, allowing her accent to grow thick, "I've fallen on hard times, and this is all I have to remember my father by." That part was true. So painfully true. "But it would ease my parting with it to know it graced a finger as lovely as yours."

The girl gave a soft snort of amusement. "I'm sure the coins I'd pay you would ease it more."

"Only the pain in my stomach."

Helene's eyes flicked from the diamond to Lydia. "All right. If nothing else, it's a story to amuse Her Highness."

Lifting a jingling purse that matched her gown, the girl took out a handful of coins, eyeing them thoughtfully before plucking out the gold and offering Lydia the silver. "There's only so much I'm willing to pay for a story. Take it or leave it."

It was a fraction of what the ring was worth, but what choice did she have? Lydia nodded, and the girl dropped the coins onto her palm before sliding the ring on one of her fingers. Without even a parting word, both girls walked away. Lydia's heart twisted at the loss.

"You must be either very brave or very stupid to have approached that harpy."

Lydia lifted her head to see the storytelling boy.

"She swindled you," he said. "I swear she's a minion of the Seventh, but it looks like the other Six were watching out for you, because she's been known to do far worse."

Lydia bristled. "I watch out for myself."

The boy held up two grubby hands. "If you say so."

She pushed past him, heading in the direction of one of the main roads, which held many of the city's inns.

"What you going to spend it on?" the boy asked, skipping along after her.

"I need to get to Serlania."

He laughed. "You and everyone else."

"I'll make it happen," she muttered. "I have to. For now, I'm going to find something to eat and a place to stay."

"Bit late for either." The boy squinted up at the sky. "Won't be naught left but stinking fish at the harbor market, and you'll be paying a fortune for a bowl of rat soup at any common room. And you clearly aren't a talented negotiator, so it's going to cost you all you have for a space in an inn."

"I'll manage." She threw as much confidence into her voice as she could.

"No you won't." He jumped up on a low wall, walking nimbly along it as though he hadn't a care in the world.

"What do you know?" she snapped, hating that he seemed so unconcerned while all she felt was fear eating at her gut.

"It's my business to know all the comings and goings-on," he said. "It's my job."

And then create wild stories that have nothing to do with the truth, she thought. He'd been playing with the crowd—who was to say he wasn't playing with her now?

"I can help you find a place to stay. I know people." He stuck out his hand. "I'm Finn, by the way. You?"

She didn't want to give her name. Killian was still looking for her. He had likely reported her, and they would know her name. "Nothing I care to share."

Finn shrugged. "Have it your way, girl-with-no-name. But trust me, no one's going to find you a better place to stay than I am." He held up a handful of shiny coins. "I can tell already that you're going to need all the help you can get."

Lydia's eyes fixed on the silver. Then she shoved her hand in the pocket of her dress, finding it empty. "You little thief!" She grabbed his wrist and scraped her coins off his palm. "Is this what you're up to? Getting me alone so you can steal everything I have?"

He gaped at her. "That isn't what I meant!"

Lydia wasn't listening. Shoving him hard, she snatched up her skirts and ran, ignoring people's curses as she pushed them aside. When she was far away and out of breath, she stopped, pressing her cheek against the stone of a building while she waited for her racing heart to slow.

It was true that she was alone and could trust no one, but that didn't mean her situation was hopeless. If she started looking for a room to rent now, she was certain something could be found before dark. Food could wait. A day of hunger wouldn't kill her, but a night on the streets with the deimos would.

23

KILLIAN

Killian took the steps two at a time, his boots thudding against the plush carpet of the staircase, his father's parting words echoing through his thoughts.

The god of war gave you the gifts needed to defend Mudamora, but what have you done but squander them?

The servants moved out of his way as he passed, dropping into deep curtsies.

This one time you had a chance to use your mark toward its intended purpose and you failed.

Helene's poodle bolted down the hallway, stopping to piss on a potted plant before continuing in his escape.

Tremon chose poorly when he chose you.

Killian had believed him. And he'd believed the King when he'd said that Killian's failure was a result of the gods turning their backs on him.

But Lydia had been telling the truth. The truth about where she came from. The truth about being marked last night to save his life. Which meant the gods hadn't turned their backs on him just yet.

And he wouldn't turn his back on her.

Even now, he had Finn and his friends searching the streets for Lydia, trusting that they'd move faster than Quindor's lackeys, who'd only have the description the guards at the gate had provided. He also had them telling a false tale, hoping that the promise of a reward would have the populace of Mudaire dragging in every old woman in the city for the healers to test. For now, there wasn't much else he could do.

Gwen stood at the heavy door blocking off the wing belonging to the Princess.

"Find the healer?" she asked, shoving her blond braid over one muscled shoulder.

"No sign of her," he lied, not because he didn't trust Gwen, but because knowing the truth would only put her in danger.

"I'm going to go out on a limb and say that's unfortunate for you," she said. "Here. This came first thing, but no one knew where you were."

She handed him a sealed letter, and Killian suppressed a sigh as he recognized Quindor's spidery script. He cracked the wax, reading, *We need to talk. Immediately.* He should've known the Grand Master wouldn't leave it alone. Killian tapped the letter against his trousers, briefly entertaining the idea of getting the meeting over with before rejecting the notion. If the Grand Master wanted to grill him, then he could damn well find Killian himself. "Get someone to go catch Helene's dog," he said, then knocked, waiting for Brin to open the inner bolt of the door.

Malahi possessed the second level of the north wing, and the walls were decorated floor to ceiling with ornately framed watercolors, each alcove graced with a bust depicting one of the Six. Sun filtered in through skylights, winking off the crystal of the chandeliers hanging above and casting rainbows across the ivory walls. Through the open doors of the rooms he passed, balconies stretched over the sea, which was steely grey and frosted with whitecapped waves. There was not another soul in sight until he rounded the curved corridor. Two more guards, Sara and Felicity, stood outside a sitting room, and they saluted before swinging open the heavy door.

"Lord Captain Calorian, Your Highness," Sara announced, stepping out of his way to reveal a dozen ladies-in-waiting lounging across overstuffed sofas, their faces a study in boredom. Malahi sat in their midst, with Bercola across from her, both with playing cards in hand and stacks of coin on the table before them.

"Your Highness." He bowed. When he straightened, Malahi

was already halfway across the room, heading toward the balcony.

Helene cackled. "You've been measured and found lacking, Lord Calorian. Seems to be a common problem for you."

Killian cast a sideways glance at her. "Your poodle is making a break for it, Lady Torrington. He probably decided that being stuffed in a soup pot was a better fate than another hour listening to your voice."

She blanched and bolted from the room, and Killian followed Malahi outside.

An icy wind flew in from the ocean, and with the afternoon sun already behind the palace, Malahi was shivering in the shade. Pulling off his coat, Killian draped it over her shoulders, then stared down the hundred-foot cliff on which they perched, watching the waves slam against the rocks below.

"Learn your lesson yet?" Malahi asked, staring out to sea, toying absently with the hole in the elbow of his coat. "If not for that healer, you'd be dead and our plans would be in shambles."

If not for that healer, the deimos wouldn't have caught him out in the open in the first place, but Killian decided admitting that part wouldn't improve this conversation.

"And then you had to let her go." Malahi's voice dripped with irritation. "You know assisting a rogue healer is a crime, yes? One punishable by hanging. Honestly, Killian, it sometimes feels like you're *trying* to get yourself killed."

It was tempting to point out that he was committing the same crime by keeping *Malahi's* secret, but instead he said, "I didn't let her go; she escaped out of the window while I was talking to Bercola in the hallway. I've spent all day looking for her."

"Just how stupid do you think I am? Bercola comes in spouting drivel about how she didn't get a good look at her, while your little network on the streets is apparently spreading word that she was an ancient crone, and you think I don't see exactly what you're doing?"

He shrugged.

"This is the problem with you, Killian! You only see the problem right in front of you, not the bigger picture. You might have saved her life by letting her go, but how many will die from injuries gained defending our kingdom that might otherwise have been saved? Sparing her won't make a difference, just like delivering sacks of palace leftovers to the sewer children won't make a difference."

Sewer children? His skin burned hot as his temper flared. "At least I'm doing something more than writing letters. You're so focused on your *big picture*, which is really just your *quest for the crown*, that every damned person in Mudaire could die around you and you wouldn't notice."

"Is that what you think?" Her knuckles turned white from her grip on the granite balustrade.

"It's what I know."

She dug into the pocket of her skirts and slammed something against his chest. "Perhaps this will change your mind."

"What is this?"

"*This* is my excuse for gathering the High Lords in Mudaire."

Frowning at the invitation, he cracked the red wax sealing it, read, then swore before tossing the heavy paper over the balustrade.

"Have you lost your mind?" he snapped. "You plan to throw a ball in the middle of a city full of starving civilians, on the edge of a war zone, with skies full of beasts hunting anything that moves?"

Her eyes narrowed. "The ball is happening. I sent the invitations weeks ago, which you would know if you didn't spend your nights wading around in the sewers."

"You're plotting to overthrow your father, Malahi. Something a bit more subversive than a gods-damned ball would be ideal. The High Lords will never agree to it."

Reaching back into her pocket, she extracted a package of letters, handing them over. Killian flipped through them, recognizing the seals of seven houses, including his own: indigo wax stamped neatly with a galloping horse. Opening the folded paper, he read his brother's elegant script.

I am happy to accept your invitation, and I look forward to discussing your proposition in more intimate circumstances.

Killian made a face and handed the letters back.

"They're coming," she said. "And they, unlike you, know that a party is a perfect cover for them to bring soldiers and supplies without raising my father's suspicions."

"As soon as the King gets word, he's going to order you to cancel it."

"He already knows and has applauded my genius. I've promised to conscript the soldiers the High Lords bring and send them to him the day after the party. Never mind that they'll be riding behind *you* with the news that *I* am now queen."

Killian shook his head. "We haven't anywhere close to the numbers required to provide adequate security. One corrupted finds its way into the palace and most of the twelve houses, plus countless smaller ones, could be wiped out in the space of the night. It would be far less risky to do it all in Serlania, then for me to return to Mudaire with those same soldiers."

"With how much time wasted? How many lives lost? This is the best route. And you have my word that I'll sail south with the High Lords after the party. I'm not staying here without you to watch my back."

Everything she said was logical, but his gut told him this plan was a mistake. "It's not the best route if everyone winds up dead."

"The High Lords will be arriving with a fleet of ships. And since the soldiers they bring with them won't be returning, I intend for them to load their vessels with as many civilians as can be fit aboard. Now perhaps you might reconsider your comment about me doing *nothing* for the people of Mudaire, Lord Calorian."

Killian was spared having to say anything as the doors to the balcony opened and Bercola leaned outside. "Grand Master Quindor to see you, Your Highness."

Malahi pointed a finger up at Killian, muttering, "This conversation isn't over," before gesturing for him to follow her back inside, tossing his coat over the back of a chair. "And please take some time out of your busy schedule to purchase some more fitting attire. You look like you were raised by wolves."

The Grand Master of Hegeria's temple was a man of middling years, tall and lean enough that his white robes adorned him about as well as they would a rake. His pale pinkish skin suggested he hailed from the central part of the kingdom, though Killian had no idea where the man had actually been born. A permanent frown marred the inked half circle marking him as a healer, and his overlarge green eyes immediately went to Killian. "Lord Calorian, did you not receive my note?"

"Just now," Killian said, extracting the crumpled paper from his pocket.

Quindor's jaw tightened. "A word in private, my lord."

Sighing, Killian joined the man in the corner of the room, bringing a drink and a tiny tea cake with him in the hope they would improve the conversation.

"You do realize that time is of the essence if we are to find her," Quindor said. "We've received conflicting descriptions of her appearance, which I hope you can clarify for us."

"She was old. Grey haired and hunchbacked. It was dark and the deimos bit half my shoulder off, so I wasn't focused on getting a good look at her"—Killian drained his glass— "Grand Master."

His attention shifted as the door opened. A servant girl carrying a tray entered the room, her head lowered as she began gathering empty glasses.

"Why a man in your situation would flaunt a royal decree is beyond my understanding," Quindor retorted. "You should be hunting her down, not loitering about drinking, gambling, and"—his gaze fixed on Killian's hand—"eating cake!"

"Hunting down rogue healers isn't my—" Killian broke off, his skin prickling even as he watched the color drain from Quindor's face, his attention all for the serving girl only paces away from Malahi.

"Corrupted!" the healer screamed, but Killian was already moving. He threw his heavy glass and it smashed against the girl's head, but the blow barely stunned her. Turning, she revealed eyes that were pooled black, irises rimmed with fire. "You weren't supposed to be here!"

Jerking out his sword, Killian lunged toward the assassin, but the women in the room screamed and scattered, colliding with him. One of them flung her arms around his neck. "Help me!"

"Move!" He lifted her out of the way even as Bercola swung her massive blade at the corrupted. The girl ducked under it with blinding speed, whirling to tackle Malahi, scattering coins and sending glassware crashing to the floor.

No.

Dodging courtiers, Killian reached for the corrupted to pull her off, but she skittered sideways, holding the Princess in the path of Killian's sword like a shield.

"Killian, help me!" Malahi's voice shook, but her face remained young and unchanged, meaning the corrupted had yet to use her mark. The assassin had come here to kill Malahi but had expected to flee unchallenged. His presence changed that. She needed a hostage.

The rest of the guards poured into the room, several of them carrying bows that they trained in the assassin's direction.

"Killing Her Highness will do you no good," he said to the assassin, keeping pace with the pair as they backed against a wall. "Let her go and I'll show you mercy."

"I don't think so." The corrupted girl was tiny, and Killian only caught glimpses of her livery around Malahi's gown. One naked hand was pressed against the Princess's throat. "Clear a path for me and I'll spare her."

Killian's mind raced through his options. If they attacked, she'd drain Malahi's life before he could kill her, but if they let her go with Malahi as her hostage, the result would be the same. And catching one of the corrupted in the teeming mass of humanity filling the city would be next to impossible.

"Tell them to clear the door!" The assassin's voice was shrill. Desperate. Young.

"Don't do it." The tears streaming down Malahi's face did nothing to detract from the resolve in her voice. "She came to kill me. There is no chance of her leaving me alive."

Killian's heart slowed, each beat loud in his ears. *Thump-thump.* His eyes went to the girls blocking the door, faces tight and weapons held at the ready. *Thump-thump.* To Quindor, half-hidden like a child behind a tapestry. *Thump-thump.* To the mirror in the opposite corner, its reflection revealing the assassin with her ear pressed against Malahi's shoulder. She was watching him. "Don't come any closer," she hissed. "I'll kill her; I swear it." *Thump-thump.*

The sword in his hand gleamed bright, the edge honed razor sharp. *Thump-thump.* It would slice through cleanly. Death would be quick.

"I'm sorry for this, Malahi," he said, and then he lunged.

The point of the sword slid through Malahi's shoulder like it was made from butter. Her eyes widened in shock, but before she could scream he jerked the blade out. "Quindor," he shouted, catching the Princess as she fell.

The assassin swayed, eyes staring blindly; then she dropped to the floor, blood running from one ear.

Killian shoved Malahi at the Grand Master. "Help her." Then he whirled back around, blade singing through the air as he brought it down hard, separating the corrupted's head from her neck.

Thump-thump.

She was only a child. Killian stared at the lifeless face, blood soaking into the carpet beneath her corpse. *Only a child.* Swallowing the rising contents of his stomach, he turned to Quindor, who was kneeling next to Malahi's prone form, his face withered and old. And angry. But the Princess's chest rose and fell evenly, so whatever the Grand Master had to say could wait.

"Felicity and Sara are dead." Bercola stepped between Killian and Quindor, jerking her chin toward the open door. Two dried-up skeletal forms lay in the hallway like bodies of aged hags long dead, a draft catching at their grey locks.

"How did she get past you?" he snarled at Gwen. "There's a list of approved people who are allowed past those main doors, and the Seventh knows, she"—he pointed at the dead girl—"wasn't on it."

Gwen whispered something that he didn't catch. "What?" he demanded.

She lifted her chin. "Asha *was* on the list. She's the daughter of the head chef—her family has served in the palace for generations."

"Shocking," Quindor muttered, going to one of the chairs on the far side of the room and sitting while he recovered.

Killian ignored the healer's comment and walked over to kneel next to the corrupted's corpse. He rolled the head faceup, peeling away the strands of bloody hair stuck to her skin. Recognition hit him like a punch to the gut. The darkness and flames had faded to reveal soft brown irises, the slack muscles no longer holding the wild hunger of those bearing the Corrupter's mark.

"I know you," he murmured, brushing her lids closed. Except the girl he'd interviewed months ago had been shy, sweet, and popular among the other servants. A faithful follower of the Six. He knew her mother, Esme, well, the cook integral to his attempts to keep Mudaire's orphans fed, and Killian's stomach hollowed at the thought of informing her that her daughter was dead. And that he'd been the one to kill her.

Malahi knelt next to him on unsteady legs, the bodice of

her gown soaked with blood. "She was only recently marked," she said, gently touching the girl's cheek with seemingly no regard for the fact that the child had come to kill her.

"A matter of days, I should think. Even if she was able to hide the changes in her eyes, the corrupted aren't known for their self-control. There'd be bodies." Killian sat back on his haunches, a sickening feeling filling him as he considered the deimos. The way they seemed to haunt *his* steps in particular. "The Seventh has his eyes on us," he said under his breath. "First the deimos and now the corrupted."

Malahi nodded slowly. "It makes sense for them to hunt you, but why me? No one—" She broke off, eyes shifting to Quindor uneasily, then in a barely audible whisper said, "No one knows about my mark."

"If you think the Seventh doesn't know, you're a fool. I think he knows precisely what you're up to, Highness."

The corpse twitched and both of them jumped, staring at the dead girl for a long moment. Malahi finally said, "He wouldn't bother trying to stop us if he didn't believe my plan would work."

"He wouldn't care if your plan worked or not if it didn't serve his purpose to keep your father in power."

Their eyes met, the gravity of Killian's statement not lost on either of them.

"My father treats the Marked like slaves and he's angered the Six. The Marked are meant to lead, not to be led. What greater confirmation of that truth do you need?"

Killian didn't disagree, but there were less risky ways to achieve the same ends. "Cancel the ball and meet the High Lords in Serlania. Mudaire is too dangerous by far."

"No. The people of Mudaire need to see that I haven't abandoned them like everyone else. Besides, I'll not be ruled by fear."

"Just idiocy."

Rising to her feet, she said loudly, "Remove the body. And consider allotting me more of your time, Lord Calorian. I would not like this to happen again."

Without a backward glance, she strode from the room.

"Go with her," Killian said to Bercola, and then to Quindor, "A word."

The Grand Master waited until the room had cleared before snarling, "You mad fool! The King will hear of this."

Killian toyed with a half-dozen choice remarks but settled on, "She's alive. I consider that a win."

"Luck." Quindor shook his head sharply. "That wound was mortal. A lesser healer would have succumbed, and then you'd have three corpses on your hands."

"Lesser healers don't become Grand Masters," Killian said, fighting the impulse to add, *Besides, it's about time you have a taste of what you expect of the healers you send to the battlefield.*

Quindor's face twisted, and he turned to leave.

"Wait." Killian stepped into his path. "You knew what she was, that she was corrupted. How?"

The Grand Master hesitated, head turning to the corpse on the floor. "She had too much life in her." Then he shook his head. "You'll have to excuse me; I have a rogue healer to find. I trust you won't mind me questioning your guardswomen. They might remember a detail you left out."

"By all means," Killian replied, knowing Quindor would search every residence Killian was associated with while he was at it. The same would go for all the ships leaving the harbor. No one would be able to board without putting a hand on whatever injured individual the temple had employed that day, and Hegeria's mark had a mind of its own. Unless it was on the back of a good horse riding at a near straight gallop to reach Abenharrow before dark, smuggling a healer out of the city would be next to impossible. "Best of luck."

The Grand Master shoved past Killian with surprising strength.

Killian let him go, his mind whirling as he carefully rolled the dead girl up in the ruined carpet, then lifted her in his arms. His own mark had warned him of the danger, but Quindor had known exactly what the threat was.

Hegeria's temple was keeping secrets.

Which wasn't surprising. Identifying corrupted was a skill that could be used, and the King already used them hard enough.

But was it also a skill *Killian* could use?

Ignoring the blood that had soaked through the carpet and was now seeping into the shoulder of his shirt, he considered the advantage of having a healer watching over Malahi. The trouble was, even if one could be spared, the tattoo on their foreheads made them easily identifiable and therefore useless for his purposes. He needed a healer whose mark was unknown, who hadn't been branded by the temple. One who could watch over Malahi undetected.

And he knew just the girl.

There were no coincidences in this world. Not when the gods were involved.

24

LYDIA

Lydia sat on the floor of the warehouse that the Crown had transformed into a shelter, her knees pulled up to her chest and her face buried in her skirts. Bodies pressed against her on all sides, strangers leaning on each other not for support, but because there was no room to move. They'd been packed into the stone building as tight as they could fit, children sitting on mothers' laps, and siblings wrapped around each other as comfort against the dark. Limbless soldiers sent back from the front lines wept in the darkness, haunted by nightmares that seemed to plague them sleeping or awake. The air felt thick and unbreathable from the smell of thousands of exhalations, and it was all Lydia could do to remain calm. To refrain from clawing her way over the sick and impoverished press of people to the doors and out into the wind and rain.

And the deimos.

Though the warehouse was stifling, Lydia shivered and wrapped her fingers in the wool of her dress. *It's safer in here,* she told herself. Yet it didn't feel safer. She felt like she was suffocating—like no matter how fast her breath came, not enough air reached her lungs. Her limbs were stiff from the forced immobility, but every time she shifted, it seemed her neighbors stole more of her space. There was no space allocated for a privy, and those who couldn't hold it were forced to urinate where they sat. The ground was damp with weeks' worth of filth, and she swore she could feel disease seeping into her skin. A few people had tallow candles lit, but rather than welcoming the faint bits of light, she worried what would happen if the filthy straw scattered across the floor caught fire.

Worse, in the darkness, she couldn't help but see the misty

flows seeping off those around her as time, illness, and starvation stole life from them. Many were dying; some would likely be dead by morning.

You could help them, her conscience whispered. *You could save them.*

But doing so would ensure she was caught. If that only cost her, it would be one thing, but too many lives depended on her returning to Celendor.

Guilt plagued her until exhaustion took over and she slipped into a sleep troubled with the vision of her skin crisping and blackening and the sounds of a thousand voices screaming, but none louder than her own.

Lydia jolted awake to the heat of a flame held in front of her face and fingers snatching at her dress, digging in her pockets. Blinded by the light, she lashed out at those around her, but her limbs felt numb and useless. "Let me go!" she shrieked, trying to move, trying to get away, but someone was standing on her skirts.

"It's her," a woman hissed. "I saw her in the market today. Check her pockets."

They were robbing her.

Panicked, Lydia fought harder. She *needed* that coin—if they stole it from her, not only would she lose her best chance at making it home to help Teriana, she might well starve. Her fists connected with flesh, and the woman swore and pulled back. In a second, three more were on Lydia. She lost count of how many women were attacking, holding her face down in the filth while they pummeled her with fists and feet.

"Help!" she screamed. "Someone help me."

No one would. The mass of refugees pressed away from the fight, a blur of faces in the dim light, watching.

"Here!" One of the hands digging in her pockets jerked out, and Lydia sobbed, knowing the fist contained all her silver coins. A boot stomped on her back, knocking the wind from her lungs, but they weren't paying attention to her now. They were attacking one another.

Silver coins rained down around her, and then it seemed every soul in the warehouse descended at once, the sight of the silver igniting their desperation. People screamed and shouted, fights breaking out all over the floor. Her handful of silver had set off a riot, but there was nowhere to move.

Blood pounding, Lydia fought her way out from under the mass of women, the blows landing on her body barely registering through her panic to get away. All around her, people were being trampled, little children screaming for their mothers.

The faint light of the handful of candles went out, and the riot ended as soon as it started. The mass of people swirled and jostled, each individual trying to carve out new space. Lydia collapsed against the wall of the building, the stone blissfully cool against her battered face. Adrenaline continued to course through her veins as she listened for any signs the women would come after her for more, but it seemed she had been forgotten. All around her, she could hear the moans of the injured, the ragged breaths of the survivors, and the silence of the dead.

Lydia clutched the wall like a lost sailor holding tight to a bit of driftwood in the storm, feeling the life all these people were shedding drifting over her. Clinging to her. Becoming part of her. And as it did, her injuries healed, the sensation prickling and unnatural and awful. Thunder shook the building, and she welcomed each boom because it drowned out the sounds around her. With no sense of time, the night seemed to drag on and on, and she forced herself to concentrate on each measured breath she took.

"I will survive this," she whispered. "I will find a way out of this city. I will find the Maarin, and I will make it home in time to help Teriana. In time to save my father. I will make Lucius Cassius pay for his crimes." She repeated her goals like a mantra, using the words to drive away her fear and refusing to acknowledge that she had no idea how to make them happen. Because it didn't matter.

"Whatever it takes," she said as thunder shook the walls of the shelter. "I'll do whatever it takes."

25

KILLIAN

Killian jerked awake, reaching for his sword and nearly falling off the side of the sofa.

Around the heavy velvet curtains, lightning flashed, thunder following straight on its heels, but in the room itself nothing stirred. Yet the anxiety racing through his chest didn't dissipate, his pulse rivaling the storm with the way it throbbed in his ears.

Unsheathing his sword, Killian crossed the room, his feet sinking into the thick carpets as he approached the bed. Easing aside the curtain, he listened to Malahi's steady breathing, a flash of lightning illuminating her face, blond hair spread out over her pillow. She stirred and Killian dropped the curtain so as not to disrupt her rest any further.

Rolling his shoulders, he retreated back to the sofa where he flopped down on his back, sword in easy reach. But no amount of twisting and turning made him comfortable enough to sleep, and with an annoyed sigh he dragged on his boots and made his way to the antechamber. Unbolting the door, he stepped out, nodding at the guards on duty. "Stay inside with her," he said to Sonia. "Keep the door locked until I return."

The Gamdeshian woman inclined her head. "Will you be long?"

"No."

Leaving behind the Princess's wing, he trotted down the servants' staircase, making his way into the bowels of the palace, feeling the heaviness of grief hanging over the halls despite nearly all being abed. The servants had taken the death of the girl—whose name was Asha—badly, many of them unwilling to accept that she'd been marked by the Seventh, most especially her mother. Esme had been inconsolable. It had required both Lena and Gwen to restrain her, the woman screaming that her child was chosen by the Six and then cursing Killian as a murderer. Even now, her voice rang loud in his ears, drowning out the sound of his boots as he approached the palace dungeon.

It was empty, but the cell where he'd locked Asha's corpse was surrounded by burning candles, melted wax pooling on the floor.

Resting his forehead against the bars, he stared at the shrouded corpse, guilt rising thick and sour in his gut. *She was only a child.*

Shoes scuffed against the floor, and turning, he found Esme standing by the entrance to the dungeon, her eyes swollen. Almost unrecognizable as the woman who snapped her dish towel at the heels of her assistants, coordinating night after night of elaborate feasts for Malahi and her court. He waited for the onslaught of words and accusations, but she only said, "Finn and his friends will be suffering a miserable night in this storm. The sewers will be raging."

"It's not the worst storm they've weathered."

"Still." Her throat convulsed as she swallowed, eyes fixed on the body. "It's no way to live."

Silence clung to the space between them without even the sound of thunder to dispel it.

"May I see her?"

Killian gave a slight shake of his head. "You don't want to. She's no longer . . . whole."

Esme flinched, a single tear running down her cheek. "Please. I wish to say good-bye to my girl before—" A sob tore from her throat and she pressed a hand to her mouth.

Before she was entombed in rock. It was what was done with the corrupted. Rather than burning them, the bodies were entombed in mortar or rock in a hole seven feet deep, binding the soul and denying the Corrupter his due. An eternity in limbo.

Knowing he might have cause to regret it, Killian reached into his pocket and extracted the key to the cell. The oiled lock made no sound, nor did the hinges of the barred door as he swung them open.

Her shoes made soft *pats* against the stone as she entered the cell, hands reaching down to the shrouded form, hesitating over the dark stains marring the white fabric. He heard her take a deep breath; then she untucked the folds to reveal the girl beneath.

Killian didn't want to see but forced himself to look anyway. To watch while the weeping woman kissed the cold grey skin of her daughter's forehead before carefully tucking the shroud back in place. Then she turned back to him. "Asha was a good girl. She wouldn't have chosen this. Couldn't have. She was already—" The cook broke off, shaking her head. "It's impossible."

Shifting his weight from foot to foot, Killian debated his words before coughing to clear his throat. "I killed one of the corrupted before the battle for the wall began." It was a story most everyone knew, but there were things that Killian had kept to himself. "Before she died, she seemed to have a moment of clarity. A moment . . . *free* from the Seventh's hold. And she told me that she hadn't been given a choice. That she didn't want to be a monster. I don't know if it's any comfort or not, but Asha may not have walked this path entirely of her own volition."

Far from easing his own mind, the notion that the Corrupter could force his mark upon anyone made his skin crawl. And yet if it were so easy, why were the corrupted so few in number? What held the Seventh in check?

"If Asha didn't choose it, why does she deserve an eternity of punishment?" Esme's eyes were full of a quiet plea. "Please don't put her in the ground."

It was law that he did so. To do otherwise bordered on blasphemy, and yet . . . A faint breeze blew through the dungeon, his skin tingling with the sense of being watched.

And of being measured.

"It's late," he said. "You should go."

Esme looked as though she was considering arguing, but then her shoulders slumped and she nodded once before departing.

Waiting for the sound of her footfalls to diminish, Killian stooped next to the cot on which Asha lay, gathering her up and lifting her slight form. But as he did, a piece of paper drifted from beneath her to land on the floor.

Skin crawling, he set the girl down and retrieved the paper, unfolding it to reveal a message.

The weak will always be tempted by the promise of strength. Especially when that which has been their strength has proven itself weak.

R

Rufina. Anger rose in Killian's chest, hot and wild, and he crunched the message into a ball before shoving it in one pocket. Lifting Asha, he carried her out of the cell and down the corridor to the room containing the trapdoor that led to the tunnels beneath the palace. With a torch in one hand, he balanced the girl on his shoulder, winding his way down until he could make out the sound of waves crashing against the cliffs.

The tunnel opened into a small chamber, at the far side of which was a barred opening leading to the sea. An escape route built by House Falorn when they'd constructed this palace generations ago. There were small boats resting against one of the walls, along with crates of supplies.

Placing the girl's body in one of the boats, he used the jars of lamp oil in the crate to soak her shroud. Then he unlocked the bars and pushed the boat down the carved stone steps onto the sea.

Clearing his throat, he shouted, "If you want her back, then take her!"

The roll of thunder from the storm grew quiet, the deluge of rain ceasing in the space of a heartbeat. The waves pushed against the boat and then fell still, the ocean smooth as glass.

Killian tossed the torch into the boat, watching as the flames took hold, then shoved the vessel hard. It drifted out into the ocean, a current taking hold of it and pulling it farther and farther from shore until all that Killian could see was the glow of flames.

"May the Six fight over the honor of holding your soul," he said, and without another word he retreated into the palace.

26

LYDIA

"Girl-with-no-name?"

Lydia opened her eyes, struggling to orient herself.

"Hello?" A hand waved in front of her face, and she blinked. "You alive?"

Lydia focused on the news crier sitting in front of her, knees pulled up to his chest. What had he said his name was? She wracked her brain, her wits foggy and slow. Finn, that was it. "I'm alive."

He squinted at her. "When was the last time you ate?"

"Dawn." Though calling it eating was a stretch—she'd scavenged the refuse piles along with the other homeless, forcing herself to chew and swallow the scraps of rotting vegetables and rancid meat. Keeping it down had been another matter entirely.

Frowning, the boy pulled a heel of bread from his pocket. "Here."

Lydia's mouth instantly watered. "I can't take that from you."

"Sure you can," he said. "Had my meal with a lord this morning—ate like the king I am, and there's no way I can fit another bite down my gullet. See?" He lifted his shirt and puffed out his skinny belly. "Full up."

No doubt he was telling another one of his fables, but the pinching pain in her stomach had no interest in selflessness. Taking the loaf, she tore into it, each mouthful utter bliss.

"Don't suppose you've any interest in a job?"

Lydia lifted her head, the bread souring in her mouth. There was only one job left in the city, and she'd be lying to say that she hadn't considered it. However, the current supply far outweighed the demand, and she wasn't quite hungry enough to give up so much for a day's worth of food. "I'm not a prostitute."

"Do I look like a cathouse madam to you?" He grinned. "Captain of Princess Malahi's bodyguard is looking for a new recruit."

"I'm hardly qualified," she muttered, remembering all too clearly the number of times in the past days when she hadn't even been able to protect herself.

He cocked one eyebrow. "Don't know how to fight?"

She opened her mouth, then thought better of what she'd intended to say. Admitting she was incapable of defending herself seemed like asking for trouble. "Not well enough to guard a princess."

"Well, if you want to get to Serlania, maybe you'll find a way to fake it."

"What are you talking about?"

"The Princess is heading to Serlania after her coming-of-age ball, and where she goes her bodyguard goes."

The idea of her as a bodyguard was absolutely ludicrous, yet if it meant making it to Serlania and finding a Maarin ship . . . "But I'm a girl."

"So's the rest of her guard," Finn replied. "And besides, I know the captain, and he owes me a favor or two. He'll owe me three if I deliver a girl he can use."

Lydia bit the insides of her cheeks, considering her options. If she refused Finn's offer, she'd almost certainly starve to death if she wasn't killed in the Crown shelters. Yet either death seemed merciful compared to being shipped off to a battlefield to age over and over again until she eventually succumbed. By taking a position among the nobility, she'd be hiding in plain sight. "When is the Princess supposed to sail?" she finally asked.

"The ball is a month from now."

A month? Could she fake it that long? Could she elude Killian Calorian and those he'd likely set after her? It was an enormous risk, but the reward was just as great, and already her mind was racing with strategies, with ways to change her appearance. She could do this. For Teriana's sake, she had to. "I'll do it," she said. "Take me to see this captain."

Finn's eyes went over her shoulder, and her stomach dropped as a familiar voice said, "I must say, that was much easier than I expected."

Whirling, Lydia found herself face-to-face with the very man she'd been desperate to elude.

"Hello again," Killian said.

The alleyway behind her was a dead end, and he was blocking most of the entrance. But she had to try. Launching herself forward, she was almost in the clear when a hand latched on her arm, jerking her back. She shrieked, fighting and kicking, but his grip was relentless as he dragged her farther into the alley. Desperate, Lydia twisted and bit down hard on his forearm. He yelped and she stumbled free, falling on something that squished, the sound of Finn laughing filling her ears.

"Gods-damn it!" Killian shook his arm, wincing. "Though I suppose I earned that."

"What do you want?" she demanded.

"Exactly what Finn told you," he said. "Just hear me out." Then his eyes flicked to the boy in question. "Finn, go sit your ass on the fountain in the square, and don't even *think* about eavesdropping."

The news crier grinned. "Wouldn't dream of it. Besides, I've had my entertainment for the day."

Killian waited until the boy was out of earshot; then he said, "Yesterday, Princess Malahi was attacked by one of the corrupted."

Lydia silently listened to the story, half her mind for what he was telling her and the other half trying to come up with a way to get past him.

"I need someone with Hegeria's mark who hasn't been branded by the temple to guard Malahi. Someone who will recognize the corrupted before they get close to her. I think that someone should be you."

The very idea of it was terrifying. Not only hiding in plain sight, but guarding against creatures that, if what he'd said was true, could drain the life from a person with a touch.

"You'll be fed the best food there is to be had in the city," he said. "Paid in silver. Malahi's entourage won't be subject to Quindor's scrutiny when they board the ship to Serlania, and once there you'll be free to track down a Maarin ship and head home." His head tilted to one side. "You also have my word that I'll keep your mark a secret."

"Unless I don't agree to your scheme, correct?" she snapped. "Which means it's no choice at all."

Rocking on his heels, he shook his head. "You have my word I'll keep your secret, regardless of what you choose to do." Then Killian turned on his heel and walked out of the alley, his voice trailing behind him. "You know where to find me."

A way to Serlania, where Lydia was certain she'd be able to find a Maarin ship. Which meant a way back to the Empire. But the Princess wasn't departing for more than a month. What were the chances of her father surviving Vibius's poison that long? What were the chances of Teriana and her crew surviving Lucius's inquisition that long? And there was the added risk of her mark being discovered. She'd be caught, her freedom gone and her life sure to follow.

But what were the chances of her making it back home any other way?

"Wait!" Lydia stumbled down the alley, rounding the corner to find Killian waiting, his dark eyes glinting with satisfaction. "I'll do it," she said.

"I know." He gestured for her to follow. "Let's go."

"Why are you helping me?" Lydia asked as she followed Killian through the city.

Reaching into his pocket, he extracted something metallic

and handed it over. Lydia's heart leapt at the sight of her spectacles, which she immediately placed on her face. The world came back into focus.

"I decided to confirm your story. Found those in the stream. And something else, too." He gave her an appraising look. "What in the depths of the underworld possessed you to touch a xenthier stem? Don't you know how dangerous they are? They're forbidden for a reason."

"That's nonsense. They aren't dangerous if you know where they go."

"Did you know?"

"Obviously not."

"Then my point stands."

"I would've died if I hadn't taken it." She blinked away the remembered fear of being underground. "I was trapped in a cave with no other way out."

"The old rock and a hard place dilemma." He stepped over a puddle. "Either way, I believe you. About everything. Your mark. That you're not from here."

"That still doesn't explain why you're helping me. You'll be punished if you're caught, so what's in it for you?"

He shrugged. "I'm oath sworn to protect the princess of the realm. To do that, I need someone who can recognize the corrupted for what they are. I'm not averse to stepping outside the boundaries of the law to make it happen."

"I've never seen one of them before. How will I—"

"Quindor said the corrupted have too much life in them; does that mean something to you?"

Life. With so many crammed into the city, it was everywhere, seeping off of the belabored people like a mystical fog. One glance at an individual told her whether they were long for this world, many of those sitting listlessly against the walls of buildings so faded as to be barely distinguishable from the stone. Killian, by contrast, was vibrant with it. Vital. Strong.

"Do I look well enough?" he asked, catching her staring.

Her cheeks warmed. "The theory makes sense to me, though I would have to see one of them to be certain."

"Let's hope it doesn't come to that."

An understatement. "On the assumption you don't intend to inform the Princess or the rest of her guards of the true nature of my role, I feel it necessary to point out that I'm lacking the skill set required to protect anyone, much less someone of her significance. How do you propose to convince them I'm an appropriate choice?"

One side of his mouth curled up with a hint of a smile. "By telling them so."

"And if they question you?"

"My gut tells me that won't be a problem."

"Most men use their minds to make decisions, but you follow the advice of your innards?"

"Daily." His half smile turned into a grin. "They follow a twisting path, but I find they always deliver. My brain is less reliable."

It took her a second, but then she snorted and shook her head, the jest reminding her briefly—painfully—of Teriana. "You'll be lying to them and, in doing so, putting them at risk."

"Telling them the truth makes them complicit, which puts them at equal risk." He exhaled a long breath. "Two of my guards were killed with their weapons still sheathed. They didn't see the threat, which meant they didn't have the chance to defend themselves or Malahi. You can give them that chance."

"How do you know I won't just run at the first sign of danger?"

"Because I've seen you in action. You're resourceful. You're not a coward. And you possess a certain quality that I consider integral to join Her Highness's guard."

"Which quality is that?"

"Selflessness." His eyes met hers. "It's the reason why I'm still alive."

Lydia tore her gaze away, unwilling to tell him that she'd no intention of risking her life for girls she didn't even know. Her father needed her. Teriana needed her. Which meant that until Lydia made it back to the Empire, the only life she intended to protect was her own.

Killian led her to the wall encasing Mudaire and up a narrow set of stairs onto the battlements. Fifty feet above the ground below, the view of the city and surrounding country was incredible.

Mudaire's footprint was tiny compared to that of Celendrial, which was to be expected given it was a fortress city. The wall was shaped as a five-pointed star and was thick enough that a pair of horses could've drawn a cart along the length of it. There were four gates: three were the end point of highways leading west, north, and south, and the fourth led to the harbor, which lay outside the confines of the wall. The harbor itself was smallish but was the only breach in the towering white cliffs. The palace sat on the edge of the cliffs with a wall of its own separating it from the city. And in the center rose the seven towers of the god circle, the faces carved into them seeming to watch her and Killian as they walked, making her shiver.

The land surrounding the city was brown and barren, broken up by copses of trees almost large enough to be called forests. In the far distance, mountains loomed, so tall as to be capped with white despite it being summer. Yet it was the veins of black running across the landscape that drew her attention, and she remembered stepping into one not long after she'd crawled out of the stream. How it had been slimy and smelled of rot. Even as the thought crossed her mind, the wind blasted her in the face, carrying that remembered stench with it. "That smell." She pressed a hand to her nose. "What is wrong with the land?"

"There's a blight spreading down from the mountains. It's rotting the earth, and with the tenders all working to feed the King's army, there's nothing to be done about it."

"What's causing it?"

"Depends on who you ask."

"I'm asking you."

Killian turned his head to regard the blight. "If you believe the King, it's a punishment for our lack of faith in the Six. But . . ." He gave a slight shake of his head. "I don't think it's that. The gods don't interfere directly like this; their work is done through those they mark."

Like her. And him.

"We've always known about the corrupted, and it's believed that their powers are the only mark the Seventh bestows. But maybe that's not the case."

Lydia frowned, recalling what she'd read in *Treatise of the Seven*. "You think the Seventh has different marks? Ones *no one* has seen before?" Pointing to the blight, she added, "You think a person did that?"

"It's a theory."

"If that's true, couldn't someone marked by Yara stop it? Couldn't they drive back the blight?" The goddess Yara had dominion over the earth and all the things that grew upon it, those she marked able to make plants grow and thrive even where they should not.

"It's possible." His gaze shifted to the palace. "But we'd need one willing to try."

"How many of them are there?"

"There used to be close to three hundred in Mudamora." This time his gaze flicked west to where the war was being fought in the shadow of the mountains. "But not anymore."

It wasn't long before they passed over the south gate, but instead of taking the stairs down into the city, Killian kept going, his eyes on the dozens of miniature palaces in the district below. Like most of the structures in Mudaire, they were built with a dark grey stone, their faces elegant but austere. Compared to the airy and open patrician homes of Celendrial, these structures seemed grim and claustrophobic, entirely closed off from the elements by glass and stone. All the properties were walled and gated, but no smoke rose from chimneys and all, as far as she could see, were devoid of life.

"Where are we going?" she asked.

"The Calorian manor. My brother is in Serlania, so the place is empty and therefore a good location for us to chat without unwanted listeners." He leaned over a parapet. "District was under guard until recently, which is why there are no squatters. But it's only a matter of time." Then he slung both legs over the edge and dropped out of sight.

Sucking in a sharp breath, Lydia leaned over the edge and saw Killian standing on a rooftop below, hands shoved into his pockets as he tapped one foot impatiently. "Madman," she muttered, then eased out onto the ledge, lowering herself until she dangled from her fingertips before letting go. She stumbled as she landed and would've fallen if he hadn't caught her by the elbows.

"You'd make a poor burglar."

"How tragic," she snapped, pushing her spectacles up her nose. "Is this it, then?"

"That one." He pointed across the distant street at a stately structure, galloping horses wrought into the gate barring the entrance. "Follow me."

He leapt off the roof onto a balcony and then onto the wall surrounding the home, walking along it as easily as a cat until he reached the end and dropped to the ground. With him pushing on her heels, Lydia managed to scale the wall, which he easily climbed; then they crossed through the neglected gardens toward the main doors.

Inside, the heavy drapes were drawn, but even in the dim light, it was obvious that whoever had decorated the home had excellent taste. The wooden floors were laid in a complex pattern and polished to a high shine, the walls were adorned with large pieces of art, and the furniture was carved from what looked like fruitwood. The air smelled faintly of varnish but also stale, as though it had not been stirred in some time. There was a large portrait hanging between a twin set of staircases, and Lydia gave a slight smile as she recognized a much younger version of Killian flanked by his older brothers, mother and father standing behind. He looked a great deal like his father, tall, with dark hair and eyes, skin a dusky olive hue. His mother, by contrast, was fair and rosy cheeked, with reddish-blond hair and a kind smile.

"The artist took license," Killian said, waving a hand at the painting. "She's the only person in the world whose temper I won't tempt."

"She's beautiful."

"You don't notice that when she's chasing you down the hall shouting threats."

He led Lydia through the corridors and into a large room, where he flung open one of the curtains to give them light. Her eyes immediately went to the chandelier hanging from the ceiling, taking in the layer after layer of crystal that must glitter like stars when it was lit. There was a table at the center, on which rested a large roll of paper. "Why are we here?" she asked.

"Because if we are to work together, I need the whole truth from you."

Reaching for the paper, he unrolled it, resting a pair of knives on the edges to hold it flat. It was a large map, the landmasses detailing those she'd only seen once—when she'd been spying on Marcus and Lucius. Like that map, judging from the symbol in the corner, it was of Maarin make. "We are here," he said, pointing to a dot labeled *Mudaire* on the western coast of the large Northern Continent. "Now where is Celendor?"

The Maarin had kept the East and West secret from each other for all of recorded history, and while it was obvious why they they'd kept the East ignorant, it was unclear to her why they'd kept the West equally so. Had it been to prevent these people from braving the Endless Seas, for if they successfully voyaged east, the Empire would surely learn of their origins? Or had there been a greater reason? Lydia didn't know, but right now truthfulness seemed in *her* best interest. "Do you have a pencil?"

He held one up. "I came prepared."

Eyeing the scale on the map of the West, Lydia flipped it over, and she began to draw. An artist she was not, but her father had provided her with an excellent education, which had included geography. The Empire grew beneath her hand, the vast central continent, then the islands. And as she drew, she spoke. "I was adopted at a young age by my foster father, who is head of the patrician family Valerius. His position gives him a seat in the Senate, which is the body that governs Celendor and its provinces. He is the equivalent of one of Mudamora's High Lords, though there are a little over three hundred senators."

"Good gods," Killian murmured. "And here I thought eleven plus a king was bad enough. The arguing must be endless."

"It is nearly all they do, though they prefer the term *debate*." She finished her outlines of the landmasses and began shading in the topography. "Only men may inherit in Celendor, and as my father has no son, the Valerius fortune and seat in the Senate must go to his nephew, Vibius, who despises me." The story poured from her lips and her pencil never stopped moving until she said, "So you see, it was either die in an underground chamber or risk the xenthier path."

Killian was leaning back in his chair, elbows resting on the padded arms. "Why in the names of all the gods would you want to go back?" He sat forward abruptly. "Don't get me wrong, I can understand not wanting to be *here*, but there are better places. Gamdesh, for instance."

It was time to tell the rest of the story. The part that haunted her night and day.

"Because I *have* to go back." Her hand shook, and Lydia labeled provinces in order to hide the tremor. "I made a mistake. I was careless, and it has cost people their lives. Will cost more people their lives if I don't get back to rectify it."

A single tear landed on the map, and she brushed it away with irritation. "As I'm sure you've surmised, the Maarin travel within the Empire—they have a treaty with the Senate that allows them autonomy, although they are beholden to the Empire's laws whenever they are within a port. As religion is outlawed they, by necessity, kept their worship of the Six a secret." Biting her lip, she said, "My best friend is Maarin. She confided in me her people's secrets, and when her mother refused to help me escape my betrothal to Lucius she gave me a book. *Treatise*—"

"—*of the Seven*," Killian finished. "I'm quite familiar with it. Why would she give you *that*?"

"I don't know. But I was careless and didn't hide it as well as I'd thought. Vibius found it, knew who'd given it to me, and he gave it to Lucius, who used it as grounds to search Maarin ships in port. What they found on the ships was . . . damning. The crews were detained, questioned about the maps detailing the Dark Shores, and tortured when they refused to reveal their route across the Endless Seas. Eventually they were executed.

"Once Lucius won the consulship, he used his power to send the navy after dozens of Maarin ships, including my friend's ship, the *Quincense*. It was towed into Celendrial's port the morning he tried to murder me, and I know he has Teriana and her crew and if I don't get back—"

"Wait." Killian held up his hand, interrupting her. "The *Quincense*? This Lucius Cassius is holding *Teriana* prisoner? And her mother? Triumvir Tesya?"

She blinked. "You know who they are?"

"That's akin to asking if I know who the gods-damned Sultan of Gamdesh is. Of course I know who they are. Never mind that they've sat at my family's dinner table more times than I can count." He was on his feet, pacing back and forth. "This is why you believe the Maarin will take you back?"

Lydia had known Teriana and her mother were important, but from the way Killian was talking, they sounded almost like . . . royalty? Shaking away the thought, she answered, "For the sake of so many of their people, I have to believe they'll bend their rules and take me as a passenger."

"They need to bloody well do more than that. They need to rise up. Fight to get them back."

A strangled laugh tore from Lydia's throat. "I think I've not conveyed the magnitude of the threat."

His eyes narrowed. "Convey it, then."

"This"—she darkened the border and then labeled the area—"is Celendor. It's the controlling nation of the Empire. The heart of it, if you will." It wasn't large. Smaller than Mudamora was, by contrast.

Killian stopped his pacing. "And what is the extent of this nation's control? Of the . . . Empire?"

She gestured at the map. "All of it."

His gaze lifted from the map. "The entire eastern half of Reath is controlled by *one* man?"

"One man with his eyes set on the West," she said. "One man with an army of over two hundred thousand strong. And if he can force the Maarin to bring the legions across, I assure you, the threat will be very real. Which is why I need to get back. Not only to save Teriana, who is like a sister to me, but because I can prove Lucius has broken the law. He will be stripped of the consulship and of power, and maybe it will be enough to stop the Empire's progress west before it even begins."

"And what will happen to you?"

Nothing good. "It doesn't matter. Don't you see? All of this began because of *me*. I have to stop it."

Killian's eyes were distant, as was his voice when he muttered, "There are no coincidences." Then his gaze focused on her. "A month feels too long for you to wait. We need to get you back sooner."

"If there is a xenthier stem—"

He gave a rapid shake of his head. "No. For one, there isn't a genesis stem within a day's ride of Mudaire. Two, if there were, it would be entombed, as are all the known genesis and terminus stems across nearly every nation of the West."

She stared at him in horror, and he nodded. "You might

have escaped that underground cave only to find yourself in a tomb with no chance of rescue."

"But . . . why?"

He shrugged. "No one likes another nation having easy access within one's borders. And to leave the genesis stems open would be negligent. A child could wander across one and no one would ever know what happened to her."

It made a certain amount of sense, but she still felt like pounding the table in frustration, because if there was a way here, there must be a way back.

Taking a deep breath to steady her anger, she said, "I sold my ring for enough to gain passage on a ship. I was going to try today, but—"

"I told you that Quindor has—"

"I know," Lydia interrupted. "And it doesn't matter anyway. I was mobbed in the shelter, and they took all of my coin. And now—" She broke off, the memory of all those hands holding her down sending a wash of panic through her.

"You stayed in one of the *shelters*?"

"I didn't want to waste my coins on an inn, though in hindsight . . ."

"I'm sorry. If I'd known, I'd—" Killian broke off. "The cost isn't an issue. If we can sneak you past Quindor's testers . . ." He dug into the pocket of his coat, then swore. "Gods-damn it, Finn. Of all the days for you to pick my pockets." More digging in his other pockets produced a handful of coins mixed in with random items: a pair of dice. A crumpled scrap of paper. A single cufflink shaped like a horse. Plucking out the coins, he pushed them into her hands, tossing the rest on the table.

She stared at the coins. "But you need me to guard the Princess until she's safe in Serlania."

"I do. But Teriana is my friend, and it seems there is much more at stake than Malahi's life. Besides, her safety is my responsibility, not yours."

Lydia stared at the glittering coins, all of them stamped with a scorpion except one dull piece of silver, which was stamped with a bird of prey. *A falcon.* She traced a finger over the tarnished silver, something about it familiar.

"Are you able to control your mark?" he asked. "I know it's possible—I've seen it done."

"I don't know. I've never tried." She'd been afraid to even make an attempt.

"Only one way to remedy that." Killian extracted a knife, the edge glittering. Pulling up his sleeve, he sliced it across the back of his forearm, blood immediately welling to the surface. It ran in little crimson droplets down the back of his hand, making soft splats against the floor. He held out his arm to her.

Lydia eyed the injury, remembering how it had felt to let go of her life to bolster his. How her heart had fluttered, how it had become hard to breathe. Though logically she knew this injury wouldn't cost her so much, her hand still shook as she reached out, because so much more than her own life hung in the balance.

Be brave, she silently commanded herself; then she wrapped her fingers around his muscled forearm, holding her breath.

She could feel it. Feel the injury. Feel the insistent tug at her core to right the damage.

No. She resisted, but it was like fighting the urge to breathe.

"You're shaking. They'll suspect if you act this way."

Focus.

Her chest hurt. Everything hurt.

"Breathe, Lydia."

If you don't get back, no one will ever learn the truth about what Lucius has done.

"Lydia?"

Do this, or Lucius wins.

"Breathe!"

Gasping, Lydia snapped open her eyes to find Killian staring down at her, his arms the only thing keeping her upright. "Are you all right?" he demanded, and only when she nodded did he let her go.

He held up his still-bleeding arm. "I'm not sure we can consider that a total success."

Eyes stinging, Lydia turned away. *Do not cry. You will not cry.* "I need to get home."

Killian was silent for a moment. "It's your choice. Delay a month and have the certainty of reaching Serlania or go now and risk a performance like this on the harbor docks."

Which was the better path?

Killian scooped the coins off the table, but instead of repocketing them, he took her hand and pressed them into it. "You don't need to decide right this moment. Think on it, but while you do, we'll carry on with our plan."

The sound of a door opening made them both jump.

"That will be Finn."

Sure enough, the boy sauntered into the room. "My lord," he said, bowing with finesse. "Mistress Lydia."

"Perfect timing, Finn," Killian said. "Take Lydia to the barracks and get her introduced. They're expecting her."

"Was my agreement such a sure thing?" Lydia asked.

Finn laughed and Killian shrugged. "Good instincts. They'll give you what you need. Finn"—he jerked his chin at the boy—"give her a story that won't invite questions."

"I only speak the unaltered truth, my lord."

Killian snorted in amusement, but there was affection in his gaze. The sort, Lydia thought, that one had for a younger brother. Protective.

"I need to be at the palace." He turned to go, but Lydia stumbled after him. "Killian!"

He turned, and she caught his bleeding forearm, holding it for a heartbeat. "Thank you." Then she trotted over to Finn and followed him out the door.

27

KILLIAN

Hours after he'd left Lydia in Finn's capable hands, Killian could still feel the sensation of her long fingers wrapped around his arm. Of the pain receding as his skin knit together, leaving not even the faintest of scars behind. The only proof the injury had been there at all was the blood staining the linen of his shirt.

"What do you think of this color?" Malahi asked, holding up a scrap of finely woven wool in front of his face. Killian frowned at it. "Seems a strange choice for a gown."

"For you, Killian. Not for me." She frowned. "Have you been listening to a word I've said?"

The honest answer was: no. The room was full of ladies, all of them agonizing over what they'd wear to the ball. Several dressmakers were in attendance, along with their assistants, and samples of fabric and lace and gods knew what else were floating around the room. With so many present, there wasn't a chance he'd leave Malahi's side, but remaining had meant offering his opinion on things far outside his area of expertise. "I . . ."

Malahi huffed out a breath of amusement. "This is why your mother still has to send you clothing."

Killian's cheeks warmed. "She does not—"

"This will do fine." Malahi handed the sample back to the waiting tailor. "Black embroidery, of course. Nothing else will suit."

"The jewelers have arrived, Your Highness," Lena announced from the doorway. "Are you ready to meet with them?"

"Yes," Malahi replied, and moments later two older women entered with two boys behind, a large chest suspended between them. Curtsying, the women showed Malahi tray after tray of jewels, only moving on to the other ladies after she'd made her selections.

"I've already acquired something new, thank you." Helene's voice dominated the room, demanding everyone's attention. "With a piece like this, I need nothing else."

"Lovely," one of the jewelers said. "Might I take a closer look, my lady?"

Helene pulled the ring she was wearing off her finger and handed it to the woman, who'd already extracted her magnifying glass. Holding the ring up to the sunlight, she examined the gemstone, turning it this way and that. "Exquisite work, my lady. And this color . . . I've never seen anything like it. Where did you say you acquired it?"

"A Maarin captain brought it back from across the seas."

Killian's ears perked, as did those of everyone in the room.

"Someone has been telling you tales, my lady," the jeweler responded with a nervous laugh. "The mark of a good salesman, yet—"

"Yet you've never seen anything like it." Helene's eyes were fixed on the gemstone. "And the Maarin do have their secrets." She smiled. "And all for a handful of silver."

"Let me see it, Helene," Malahi said, reaching out a hand.

The other girl dutifully plucked it out of the jeweler's hand and brought it to the Princess, who slipped it on her own finger. Killian stiffened as he recognized the ring as the one Lydia had worn. The one she'd sold in an effort to flee the city.

"It's beautiful." Malahi tilted her hand back and forth to admire the glitter.

"I couldn't say no to the poor girl," Helene said. "She was desperate to sell it. And I know Your Highness values charitable actions."

Killian ground his teeth, trying to keep his mouth shut. But it was a lost cause. "Charitable?" He gestured to the jeweler. "How much would you say this ring is worth?"

The woman accepted the gem back from Malahi before

conferring with her colleague. "Five hundred gold pieces, for certain, Lord Calorian." Then she rubbed her chin. "And if research proved it to be as unique as I believe it to be, upward of a thousand gold pieces."

"And all for a handful of silver." Leaning forward, Killian said, "That's not charity, Helene. That's extortion."

The girl's cheeks reddened, and she snatched her ring back from the jeweler, shoving it on her finger. "She offered it to me. If I hadn't bought it, no one would've."

"You swindled her. You should've given her the coin and let her keep her damned ring. You took advantage of her desperation to decorate your finger."

"I can't be giving away coin to every girl who begs it of me."

"Why not?"

"Enough!" Malahi climbed to her feet. "You two are like a pair of barn cats. I can't even have you in the same room together!"

Killian ignored her and said to Helene, "Sell it to me and give away the coin. Or keep the gold, if that's what your conscience tells you to do."

"I'll do no such thing."

"Five hundred."

"No."

"A thousand."

"You are intolerable, Lord Calorian," Helene replied, but Killian didn't miss the glint of greed in her eye.

"Fifteen hundred."

"Your wealth doesn't impress me."

"Two thousand." His brother Seldrid, who managed the family's finances, was going to kill him for this.

Everyone in the room was staring at them, courtiers, jewelers, and guardswomen alike. Helene's jaw worked back and forth, warring between her desire for the gold and her pride. Finally, she smirked. "For the opportunity of swindling you, Lord Calorian, how can I say no?"

Bending over the table, Killian took up a sheet of Malahi's

stationery, scribbled the details, and then signed it before pushing it over to Malahi to witness. Then he handed it to Helene. "The bankers in Serlania will make the transfer. Should help ease the sting of your father cutting your allowance."

She threw the ring at him and stormed out of the room. Killian shoved it in his pocket, not sure what sort of madness had possessed him, only that any amount of coin was worth getting it off that harridan's finger.

"I don't know what's gotten into you, but clearly you need to step away," Malahi muttered. "Come with me."

Abandoning the sitting room, he followed Malahi out into the corridor to find one of the guardswomen approaching. "A letter came for you with the supply caravan, my lady."

Taking it, Malahi motioned for Killian to follow her down the hall to her bedroom, where she latched the door behind them and opened the sealed letter. Her eyes scanned the contents; then she grimaced and handed it over.

Dearest Daughter,

It has come to our attention that the cursed creatures plaguing Mudaire's skies have taken to attacking ships within its harbors—a clear attempt to disrupt supplies intended for our armies. In response, I have ordered all vessels bearing goods destined for the front to make port in Abenharrow, where they will be met with an armed escort. As to your request that we seek aid from Gamdesh, I forbid you to do so. It makes us look weak at a time we can least afford it, and do not think for a moment that the Sultan won't take advantage while our backs are turned.

Keep your faith,
Father

Abenharrow was a fortress a day's sail south of Mudaire. If ship captains could sell their freight there for gold with no risk of deimos attack, they'd have no incentive to sail north to the capital. "Nothing will be coming into the city now," Killian muttered. "This is dire."

"We've been at peace with Gamdesh for over a century." Malahi took the letter back. "They are our allies. It's madness not to ask the Sultan for aid."

It was and it wasn't. Mudamora's navy had been decimated during the last war with the giants of Eoten Isle, along with subsequent civil war that had followed on the heels of the assassination of King Derrick Falorn. Only a handful of ships had been built in the intervening years, and the King had already conscripted their crews, leaving the vessels to languish in Serlania. Asking Gamdesh for aid would signal to rival kingdoms and privateers alike that Mudamora's shores were undefended and ripe for the picking. "There are always risks to admitting weakness."

"I'm going to do it anyway." Turning to her desk, she sat down and picked up a pen. "By the time my father realizes what I've done, it will be too late for him to punish me for it."

Killian snaked the pen from her hand. "I've a better idea. Let me write to Kaira."

Princess Kaira was the general of Gamdesh's armies and the Sultan's favored daughter. Killian knew her personally by virtue of them both being marked but also because his brother Seldrid was married to the Sultan's niece. Kaira could and would influence her father, but the fact remained that Gamdesh was on a totally different continent and any aid they sent might not arrive in time. Mudaire needed to find a way to fend for itself. To feed itself.

Frowning, Killian bent over the desk and scribbled a few paragraphs describing the woe, the need to evacuate, the lack of vessels to do so. Not a direct request, but Kaira would understand.

"It feels like the walls are tightening in on us," Malahi said, shivering. "Like Mudaire is a prison. And soon to be a tomb if something doesn't change."

A thought that had been niggling in the back of his head came to the fore—an idea he knew that Malahi wouldn't agree to easily. If at all.

"Then let's escape for a few hours," he said. "Trust me?"

Malahi cocked one eyebrow, then shrugged. "With my life."

Opening the door, he stepped out into the hallway. "Lena, come here for a minute."

The young guardswoman followed him back in, raising an eyebrow when he shut the door. "I need your clothes."

"Pardon?" Both Lena and Malahi said the word at the same time.

"You're the closest in size, so"—he waved his hands back and forth between them—"switch. Malahi needs a disguise so we can sneak out and you will stay in here as our decoy."

"Have you lost your mind, Killian?" Malahi was eyeing him suspiciously. "What exactly do you have planned?"

"A surprise. Now change clothes."

Both girls retreated behind a screen. A few moments later Malahi emerged dressed in uniform, Lena following in a silk wrap. She swiftly braided Malahi's hair, then perched on one of the chairs. "What do you want me to do?"

"Stay in here until we return." He gestured at the side table, which had a basket of fresh fruit. "Eat. Lounge. Pretend to be a princess. Just don't open the door. Malahi, put your hood up."

The stables were quiet, few horses remaining given the expense of feeding them. Two of them were Killian's: his black brute of a war-horse, Surly, and his dappled-grey mare, Seahawk.

Surly turned around to face the back of his stall at the sight of Killian, but Seahawk stuck her head over the door and whinnied loudly. "Hello, beautiful," he said, kissing her on the nose. "Care to go for a ride?"

"Half my court would sell their souls to hear those words from you and you say them to a horse?"

"My horse has no expectations beyond being fed."

"Unlike your conquests?"

His hand stilled on the animal's neck. It bothered him more than it should that Malahi believed the rumors about him. Not that he'd done anything to dissuade her from her belief in them.

"Denying a rumor only gives credence to it," his elder brother Hacken had told him years ago, back when Killian still asked for his advice on anything. "It's likely only some love-sick milk maid or dowdy courtier making up stories to impress her friends. It will blow over."

It hadn't blown over, but Hacken had been right about denying it being fruitless. Not even Killian's own father had believed that the rumors that his son spent his nights chasing skirts were anything less than the Six-sworn truth.

A groom appeared, sparing Killian from the conversation. "I'll saddle her myself," he said to the boy. "If you could ready Her Highness's mare for Lena, please."

It was a matter of minutes before both horses were ready and outside. "Remember, Lena is a terrible rider," he said into Malahi's ear before giving her a leg up into the saddle.

Malahi dutifully bounced like a sack of potatoes as they trotted through the city, but once they exited the west gate she pulled back her hood. "Race?"

"To Hammon's Rock?" he asked, naming the landmark.

The Princess only dug in her heels.

Their horses' hooves thundered against the road as they galloped west, neck and neck, though that wouldn't last. Hers was the faster mount and Malahi was less than half his weight.

But Killian had been riding before he'd learned to walk.

So he cut left, taking a shortcut. Behind, Malahi laughed as she followed, both of them leaping rickety fences and crumbling walls as they plunged through the farmland, scaring up birds as they went. The land should've been lush, crops rising high in the summer heat and livestock dotting green pastures, but instead it was brown. Empty. Nearly barren of life.

This is your fault. You let the Corrupter and his Marked in.

Shoving the thought out of his mind, Killian glanced backward. Malahi was gaining ground. Her braid had come loose, and her golden locks trailed out behind her. Her amber eyes locked with his and she grinned, her expression fierce and defiant and honest. A fighter. So different from the façade she put on for her court. The face of the queen this kingdom needed. "Try to keep up, Princess!" he shouted, and dug in his heels.

Seahawk surged forward, plunging between an abandoned farmhouse and a barn. Both had been looted, broken furniture and mud-soaked clothing littering the yard. The barn had been partially burned, scorched planks of wood reaching skyward like blackened fingers. The gate on the empty pigpen swung open and shut, and against one of the posts sat an abandoned doll, its eyes seeming to track Killian as he passed. *Where is its owner?* he wondered. *Is she safe with her parents somewhere in the South? Or is she trapped in Mudaire's walls like all the rest?*

Is she even alive?

Faster, he willed his horse. As if it were possible to outrun his own thoughts.

Malahi surged past him, racing toward a spot where the wall had crumbled. Killian kept straight on, Seahawk gathering herself beneath him and then vaulting the obstacle, her stride lengthening on the far side as they flew across the empty pasture.

One more fence stood between them and the road, and beyond loomed Hammon's Rock, the granite glittering in the sun. There was a ditch between the fence and the road, and he tugged on the reins to slow his horse's pace, not caring to risk her breaking a leg.

"I'm not going to let you win, Killian!" Malahi shouted, pulling alongside him. "And you're cooking me lunch as my reward!"

"Malahi, slow down!" he shouted. "There's a ditch!"

She either didn't hear him or didn't care.

His skin abruptly began to prickle, everything coming into sharp focus. "Malahi, stop!"

The wind stole his voice, carrying with it a fetid stench that made him gag. *Gods, no!*

"Malahi!" he screamed her name. "Don't jump!"

Her head whipped around, and she sat back, hauling on the reins.

It was too late.

Her horse leapt the low fence, Malahi losing her seat and toppling backward, barely missing the wall as she fell to the ground.

Killian flung himself off Seahawk's back as she slid to a halt, running to Malahi's side.

"I'm all right." She brushed away his hand as he tried to help her up. "My horse . . ."

A desperate, frantic whinny split the air. They both stumbled to the wall, leaning over the rough-hewn blocks of stone.

Filling the ditch between the wall and the embankment of the road was a river of black slime. And in the center of it struggled the horse, already up to her belly and sinking fast.

Malahi screamed.

Killian was already moving. He ran to Seahawk and extracted a length of rope from his saddlebags. Leaping over the wall, he slid down the bank to the edge of the blight, forming a loop, which he tossed over the mare's head and drew tight. He scrambled back up the bank and over the wall, fastening the other end to his saddle.

Malahi caught hold of Seahawk's reins, urging her to pull.

"Keep it taut." Sprinting back to the wall, which was nothing more than rocks that had been stacked on top of one another, Killian shoved his weight against it, sending the rocks rolling down the gentle slope. He slid after them and pushed the rocks into the murk, swearing as they sank into the spongy earth.

The mare's nostrils flared in desperation and exhaustion, her eyes rolling as she struggled.

"Easy, easy." Killian stacked more rocks to create enough of a bridge that he wouldn't sink himself, then picked his way out into the black flow. "I won't let it have you."

He stretched out his fingers toward the mare's nose, reaching for the reins. The rocks were sinking beneath him, the sludge rising up his boots. "Come on, lovely. Try. You need to try."

The horse stretched her nose toward his hand and Killian lunged, catching hold of the reins. "Pull!" he shouted, scrambling backward, lending his strength even as Malahi urged his horse on.

The mare squealed and struggled, and for a painful few moments Killian thought it was a lost cause. That whatever sickness the Corrupter's minions had put into the earth was too strong.

Then the horse began to shift, creeping forward inch by inch. When her neck and shoulders were free, Killian dropped the reins and reached for a stirrup, his boot heels digging deep into the ground as he hauled the horse free.

The mare collapsed on the bank, sides heaving even as the rest of her trembled.

"Malahi! Ease up!"

He was unbuckling the girth and pulling off the ruined saddle when Malahi slid down the bank. "Is she all right?"

"I don't know." Taking the saddle blanket, he used the side that had been pressed against the mare's back to clean off the sticky mess, feeling her legs for any sign of a break. "Just exhausted, I think."

In silence, they cleaned up the animal as best they could without water and, when she finally struggled to her feet, led her up the embankment and through the gap in the wall. Only then did Malahi say, "Did you know it was this bad?"

Killian shook his head. "I haven't ridden out this far in some time." And with the flow of refugees stopped, the only news came via the Royal Army's supply caravans. None of them had spoken of *this*.

"Do you think my father knows?"

Yes. "I don't know."

"Can it be stopped?"

His hands paused where they'd been rubbing the mare, trying to scrape the filth from her chestnut coat. "The tenders might be able to do it, but they're all with the army." His gaze shifted to Malahi.

"I can't." Her voice was wooden. "Even if I am capable of doing something to push the blight back, I can't do it in the space of an afternoon. I'd have to be out here daily, and everyone would know it was me. I'd have to leave to join the other tenders with the army, and that would be the end of my plans."

"I could sneak you out. No one has to know."

"*He'd* know."

"Maybe so, but your father can't do anything about it without risking everyone discovering that *he* has been lying to the entire kingdom, which we know he won't do."

"He can kill me. He *will* kill me."

"I won't let him."

Malahi shook her head. "I can't risk it. What was it that your father said? That even the Marked are fallible?"

That Killian was fallible. And yet thousands of people were starving. Were trapped with little chance of rescue. "If this blight reaches the walls, it might eat its way under them. They'll collapse." He eyed the slow-flowing ooze. "Perhaps that's its intended purpose."

"Maybe it is! But what are we supposed to do about it with my father in power?" Malahi's hands were balled into fists. "Until he's removed from the throne, anything we might do is just spitting into the wind. Only a month, Killian. Then I'll be queen and you'll be in command of the Royal Army and we can finally fight back against Rufina. We can win. And then we can make Mudamora strong again."

"And until then, we do nothing?"

"Yes." The muscles in her jaw stood out against the skin of her face. "Because to do *something* might get us caught. It's not worth the risk. And I know this is killing you. That you feel terrible enough about the suffering of our people—that you think it's your fault. That you're willing to do anything to try to help those who've been hurt most. But I need you to believe in me enough to understand this is the right path."

Clouds were rolling in overhead, promising rain, if not snow, the wind whistling through the dead grass. The sun descended in the west, illuminating the Liratoras with a red glow, as if the kingdom beyond—Derin—were the underworld itself. The shadows the mountains cast were long and black as the blight, reaching in their direction. They needed to get back to the relative safety of Mudaire. But not yet.

"Try." Killian jerked his chin at the blight. "Fix some of it. See if you can drive it back. Then at least we'll know whether it's even possible."

She stared at him, silence hanging between them. "That's why we're out here, isn't it? Not to escape for a few hours. Not to—" Malahi broke off, shaking her head, but before Killian could put much thought toward what she'd intended to say, the Princess picked her way back down the bank to the edge of the stinking stream of blackness. Leaving him to lead the two horses, she walked along it, following one of the branches, eyes fixed on the shifting murk as it slowly narrowed until it was little more than a grasping finger of rot. There she paused.

She pressed her hands against the earth, and Killian watched her eyes grow distant, the grass around her hands turning green and lush, growing taller and taller. But the blight did not recede.

"There's no life in it," she whispered. "There's nothing in it to grow."

Pulling her hands back, Malahi rose, and Killian's heart skipped at the first doubt he'd seen since she'd brought him into the fold of her plans. "Killian," she said. "I can't fix this."

28

LYDIA

Finn brought Lydia back to the same house where she and Killian had sought refuge the night of the deimos attack. They stopped up the street from it, and Lydia eyed the blue door apprehensively. "Does Killian own this property?"

Finn frowned at her. "Of course not. Don't you know the Marked can't own property? His brother owns it. Though you won't be finding *Lord Calorian*"—he put heavy emphasis on the title she'd failed to use—"here often. He stays with *Her Highness*. But this is where her bodyguard lives when they aren't on duty."

Lydia flushed at her social misstep, wondering if Killian had noticed. If he'd cared.

"Your story is this," Finn said. "You were the lover of a—"

"No," Lydia interrupted. "Pick something else."

"Fine. You are the *niece* of a ship captain who was supposed to be delivering you to family members in Serlania. You were on your way south from Axbridge when your uncle decided to make port in Mudaire. He gave away your place on the ship to a paying passenger, leaving you here with nothing but the clothes on your back."

Lydia started to argue that the story seemed improbable; then she thought of Vibius and said instead, "I've never been to . . . Axbridge. What if they ask questions I can't answer?"

"No northern girls in the guard, so it's not likely. And besides, none of them will pry." Giving her a sideways glance, Finn said, "The girls in the guard . . . They aren't High Lords' daughters, if you get my meaning. They understand not wanting to talk about your past. Besides, your story is the same as everyone else's. You're just trying to survive."

Finn opened the unlocked door without knocking, and Lydia followed him inside, an eerie sense of déjà vu coming over her. It was brighter now, the sun filtering through the panes of glass over the door. The wooden floor gleamed with polish, the drops of blood long since washed away.

Finn took a sharp left, leading her down a narrow hallway toward the sound of female voices.

"Good morning, ladies," he said to a trio sitting around a large dining table. "I'm delivering your newest recruit. This is Lydia."

The girls all lifted a hand in greeting, introducing themselves. One, a sturdy girl with pale freckled skin and sandy blond hair, stuck out her hand, which Lydia awkwardly shook, clenching her teeth as she felt a slight pull on her insides, her mark taking over.

But the other girl didn't seem to notice. "Gwendolyn. Gwen, to those who know me. I'm the day lieutenant for the guard, but I'm home today because something I ate played foul with my innards. Not much good to Her Highness if I'm constantly bolting off to the privy, right?"

I think I solved that problem for you, Lydia thought to herself, giving Gwen an amused smile as the other girls laughed.

Gesturing for Lydia to take a seat, the girl waved a hand at Finn. "Go flirt with the cook and get yourself fed."

Finn scampered off, leaving Lydia alone with the girls.

"Eat!" Gwen said. "It's a bit picked over, but you'll get your fill at dinner."

Perching on one of the benches, Lydia scraped what remained on the serving platters onto a clean plate. The meat was dry and salty, the unfamiliar vegetables bland, and the bread dotted with what she sadly expected were weevils, but the food tasted like the finest meal she'd ever had in her life. A young woman with russet skin, short brown hair, and large hazel eyes poured her a glass of water, which Lydia guzzled down.

"I'm Sonia," she said, her voice holding the same accent

as the Gamdeshian sailor Lydia had spoken to in the harbor. "You're from the North?"

Lydia's palms prickled with sweat. "Axbridge."

"High Lady Falorn's stronghold." Sonia nodded. "Mudaire is the farthest north I've ever been, but I should like to visit one day."

"Too cold for your summer blood, Sonia," Gwen said. "You'd freeze solid."

Sonia ignored the comment. "Even in Gamdesh, the High Lady is a legend. Have you met her?"

High Lady Dareena Falorn. Lydia remembered the woman from *Treatise of the Seven.* Not only was she marked by the same god as Killian; she was also the former King of Mudamora's younger sister. She governed over the north of the kingdom, and the book detailed an incident where she'd held back the enemy nation of Gendorn almost singlehandedly by holding a narrow pass until reinforcements arrived. Because it seemed a safe answer, Lydia said, "I've only seen her from a distance."

"Ahh." Sonia rubbed her chin thoughtfully, then shrugged. "Perhaps one day I'll have the good fortune. I hear she is as beautiful as she is fierce."

"Quit fantasizing about northern girls and go get some sleep," Gwen said, nudging Sonia with her elbow. "I'll show Lydia around."

Scooping the last scrap of food into her mouth, Lydia followed the other girl around the house, which was two levels and square, the middle boasting a large courtyard with a well at its center. There was a rack of dulled practice weapons and several straw dummies that someone had painted frowning faces on.

"Bit quiet today," Gwen said, drawing up a bucket of water from the well. "There were lots of comings and goings scheduled at the palace, so some of the night girls stayed on for that and they'll likely nap in the palace barracks rather than coming back here."

"If the palace has barracks, why do you live here?" Lydia asked, following her into a small chamber with a large copper tub and a smoking stove.

"I suppose a northern girl like you is used to female soldiers, especially given your High Lady is the most famous living warrior in the kingdom," Gwen answered. "It's not such a common thing here, and less so the farther south you go."

"Ah." Lydia frowned, her question not precisely answered. "Are you not allowed in the palace barracks, then?"

"We are. That's where we started, but we had some trouble with the men misunderstanding our presence, and the healers got tired of fixing their broken hands." Gwen laughed, the sound echoing through the room as she poured the water into a large kettle, which she set over the flames in the stove. "The Princess was of a mind to evict the men, but the captain had other plans."

"Oh?"

"Some sort of nonsense about us needing time away. That if we stayed at the palace, we'd always be on duty." Gwen shrugged. "I reckon it would be worth it given the inconvenience of traipsing back and forth across the damned city twice a day, but I suppose he knows of what he speaks."

"He stays there, then?"

"Mostly. And he's *her* sworn sword, so don't be getting any ideas about distracting him."

Lydia's cheeks burned hot. "I have no interest in—"

"Didn't say you did." Gwen gestured for Lydia to follow her back out into the courtyard, where she retrieved another bucket of water. "I'm only saying, don't find yourself discovering an interest. We have rules, and that's one of them. Start making eyes and you'll be dealing with Bercola, and she's got a heavy hand with the strap. Or so I've been told. Got no interest in men, myself."

"It won't be an issue."

"Excellent. Now why don't you set to filling up that tub while the water heats, and I'll get you some clothes. You aren't to be wearing your uniform when you're off duty, but it will do while you launder that dress."

Though Lydia had never done an ounce of labor in her life, there was something soothing about the methodical process of drawing up water and filling the tub. The water in the kettle boiled, and she used a folded towel to lift it off the fire, pouring it into the tub and then filling it up again. After stripping off her filthy dress, Lydia soaped it in a bucket, then rinsed it as best she could, though it would take further scrubbing to rid the fabric of the stains of her ordeal.

She poured the heated water into the tub, shivering as her spectacles went foggy with steam. Setting them aside, she picked up a bar of soap that smelled faintly of flowers, then stepped into the tub. The warm water reached up to her knees, and she settled into its depths. The chamber was dark and windowless, the only light the faint glow of the stove next to her. Steam rose from the water, filling the air, but rather than soothing her, it felt stifling. Suffocating.

"It's a just a tub, you idiot," she whispered. "Get clean. Get out."

Her hair was a tangled mess and needed to be washed, so she closed her eyes and slid down, dunking her head. But the moment the water closed over her, a snarling golden dragon appeared before her eyes, Lucius's laughter echoing in her ears.

I can't breathe!

Lunging up, Lydia gasped and spluttered, clinging to the edge of the tub. "It's not real. It's not real. It's not real."

The words did nothing to steady her racing heart.

Retrieving the soap, she washed her skin with shaking hands, digging grime out from under her nails. The wood in the stove snapped and popped as the fire consumed it, each sound causing Lydia to twitch like a skittish horse. Every time she blinked, she saw the baths in Celendrial. The sconces on the wall. That damned table with its decanter of Atlian wine.

Her breath came in ragged little gasps, her hands shaking

as she rubbed the soap in her hair, building a lather. *Get out,* instinct told her even as logic reasoned that she was being ridiculous.

"Lucius is on the far side of the world," she muttered. "And so is Marcus. They can't touch you. And when you do get back, it will be them who pay. You'll make them pay. You'll save your father and Teriana, and all of this will be over."

A bang sounded behind her, and Lydia screamed, spinning in the tub, certain she'd see Lucius. Certain she'd see the legatus, eyes full of resignation, reaching for her throat.

But it was only Gwen, her eyes wide, arms full of clothing. "I'm sorry," she said. "I knocked, but you didn't answer."

"It's fine." Lydia could barely get the words out, her breath coming in great heaving gasps.

Setting the clothing down on a stool and a pair of boots on the floor, the other girl walked to the door to the courtyard and opened it, the steam rushing out even as cold air rushed in. "Sorry, I know better than to startle a girl in her bath. It's my fault. But try to breathe."

Lydia couldn't find the air in her lungs to answer, her chest so tight it hurt, her body shivering despite being immersed in warm water.

Gwen crouched next to the tub, resting her hand overtop Lydia's. It was warm. Comforting. A choking sob tore from Lydia's chest, tears flooding down her face, and then the other girl had her arms around her. Holding her tight.

"It's all right," she said. "You're safe here, understand?"

"Nowhere is safe."

Gwen chuckled soundlessly, but Lydia felt it against her cheek. "Maybe not. But here you're as safe as you can be. You see, we don't just guard Malahi's back; we guard each other's. What you've joined here is a sisterhood who protect their own. You're not alone."

Fresh tears flowed down Lydia's face, but the aching pain in her chest eased. When her breathing steadied, Gwen reached down for a bucket of water, which she warmed with some from the kettle, saying nothing as she rinsed the soap from Lydia's hair, then picked up a comb and went to work on the tangles.

A sisterhood. Part of her yearned to belong to such a thing, to be surrounded by girls who were her friends in truth, not spies set to achieve the ends of men. There was a strange sort of autonomy in that, something she might never have appreciated if fate hadn't put her in this place.

This time you are the liar, she reminded herself. Nothing Gwen or the other girls thought about her was true. Not who she was, where she came from, or even the skills that she possessed.

Yet as she rose from the tub, Gwen handing her a piece of toweling, Lydia found her heart aching to be friends with these girls in truth.

29

KILLIAN

Killian hadn't believed the day could possibly get worse.

He'd been wrong.

Grand Master Quindor was waiting for Malahi when she and Killian had finally made it back through the palace gates, both of them sodden from washing the horse off in the warm waters of the spring and dusk heavy in the sky.

"Take him to the council chambers," Malahi told the servant who met them at the palace entrance, the woman giving her mistress a wide-eyed once-over of her ruined guardswoman ensemble. "Tell him that I'll be there in a few moments."

Now, freshly attired, she and Killian strode through the palace corridors, flanked by her bodyguards. "Do you know what this is about?" he asked under his breath.

Malahi only shook her head, waiting for Sonia to announce her before stepping into the council chambers.

"I hate to think," Quindor said, turning from his appraisal of the table, "what your father would say if he learned you were gallivanting about the countryside in these troubled times, Your Highness."

"I wished to see the spread of the blight, Grand Master." Malahi circled the large table, taking her father's seat, the scorpion of House Rowenes glittering above her head. "It was easier for me to do so in disguise."

"Surely others could've been sent to assess the problem." Quindor seemed to briefly consider sitting in one of the High Lord's chairs, then clearly thought better of it, choosing instead to hover near the table. Killian sat between them in his brother's chair, not caring whether it was his place to do so or not.

"My kingdom," Malahi said, resting her elbows on the arms of her chair. "My problem."

Quindor inclined his head. "I didn't realize that you'd taken such an interest in rule, my lady. Perhaps you might address the state of the crown shelters. They've become quite the source of illness."

"Better than a night with the deimos."

"It's just a slower way to die, my lady. We haven't the resources to treat them all."

Malahi's jaw flexed. "I'll address the issue. But I don't think that is the reason for this visit, so perhaps you might get to it. I've had a trying day."

"Of course, my lady. It's a matter of finances."

Malahi huffed out a breath. "Why am I not surprised? What do you need the gold for?"

"As you know, Highness, the Marked are typically brought to Mudaire for their training," Quindor said. "Due to the city's current predicament, we've chosen to keep them in Serlania until they are ready to join the King's army. But the cost of passage has become . . . prohibitive."

"What else? You know full well the Crown will bear that expense."

The Grand Master hesitated, and Killian knew that whatever subject he intended to broach would not be well received.

"Well?" There was an edge to Malahi's voice that suggested she was of the same mind-set.

"There is a matter of the cost of procurement."

Silence.

"The temple bears the cost of compensating families," Malahi said. "It's not a crown expense."

"Desperate times make the people less generous, Highness. The coffers grow thin."

"We're at war, Grand Master. Everyone's coffers are thin."

"Indeed." Quindor sighed. "However, what I'm referring to is the external sourcing of marked healers."

Malahi shook her head. "I don't know what you're speaking of."

"Your father asked me to make arrangements to procure Marked from other kingdoms, and agreed to fund the cost."

"What do you mean, *procure*?" The Princess's voice was acidic.

Quindor was silent, but Killian *knew*. And it took every ounce of control he possessed to keep his mouth shut.

"Explain yourself."

"We've had a long-standing agreement with King Urcon of Arinoquia," the healer said.

"Arinoquia has no king," Malahi interrupted. "Urcon is a clan lord, and a corrupt one at that."

"Even so"—Quindor's tone was delicate—"he's been facilitating arrangements in which Arinoquian families are compensated for allowing their marked children to come to Mudamora for training."

Spots of color appeared on Malahi's cheeks. "You mean Urcon's been selling marked children. And you've been purchasing them!"

"Highness, you twist my words."

"I don't think I do." Malahi was on her feet. "You're talking about buying children. About slavery. And if you think I'm going to provide the funds for such a venture, you are sorely mistaken."

"Highness, the King approved the transactions. You are in no position to flaunt his—"

"My father won't be king forever," she said. "And he isn't here. If I hear even a whisper that you've flaunted *my* orders in this, I'll have you kneeling before the headsman, and whatever punishment the Crown might visit upon me won't be enough to reattach your head."

Quindor blanched. "That's sacrilege."

"Maybe," spit Malahi. "But so is what you're doing."

She turned to walk out, and Quindor reached for her, quick as a viper.

Killian was faster. He knocked the slender man back. "Don't give me a reason, Quindor."

"Fools! Don't you see that there is no other choice? Without healers, Mudamora will lose this war. The Seventh will triumph."

"And you think he does not triumph when we engage in such behavior?" the Princess demanded.

"They've been marked for this fate—to withhold them from it would be blasphemy."

"I'm not listening to this." Malahi stormed out of the room.

Killian moved to follow, but Quindor caught his wrist, his grip painfully tight. "Hegeria marked them for a reason. It is the will of the gods that they use their gift to serve. To do otherwise would be courting the Seventh."

Killian met his gaze, horrified and fascinated by the fanaticism within them. The King believed that it was Mudamora's lack of faith that had brought this war upon them. And maybe he was right. But Killian couldn't help but wonder if it wasn't Quindor's sort of faith that would allow the Corrupter to win.

30

LYDIA

It was an evening unlike any Lydia had ever had.

The group of girls responsible for protecting Malahi during the daylight hours had returned just before dusk, all of them chattering about Killian sneaking the Princess out wearing a guard's uniform as disguise.

"They both came back as foul as thunderclouds on a sunny day," the girl whose uniform it had been, said. "So I expect things didn't go quite as intended. Also, they were both filthy and soaking wet. Hence my attire." She gestured at the servant's livery she wore in lieu of a uniform.

"Probably because he didn't give her that ring," one of the other girls said. "My gods. Two thousand gold coins for a trinket . . ."

Shrugging, the girl approached Lydia and Gwen. Lydia recognized her from the night of the deimos attack, although she hadn't appreciated then how pretty the other girl was with her copper-colored hair and rosy cheeks.

Rising on her toes, she kissed Gwen on the lips, long and deep enough that Lydia felt her face warm. "How are you feeling, my love?"

"As well as if Grand Master Quindor himself had made a house call."

It was a struggle for Lydia to keep from wincing. The first thing she needed to purchase with her wages was a good pair of gloves, or she'd be healing people inadvertently every which way she went.

"Good." Rocking back on her heels, the copper-haired girl smirked. "You would not believe the day I've had. I'm so stuffed full of fresh fruit, I'm not even going to eat dinner."

"Is that why you smell like you rolled out of the door of a cathouse?"

"It is." The girl linked arms with Gwen and then, to Lydia's surprise, with her, leading them both toward the dining room. "I understand you're our new recruit, Lydia. My name's Lena."

"As of this morning." Lydia bit the insides of her cheeks, waiting for the inevitable questions. "Finn—"

"—delivers the best girls," Lena finished for her. "Would you like to hear a story?"

She regaled the dozen girls with the tale of her four hours of *pretending to be a princess,* the whole group howling with laughter as she described trying on gowns and jewelry and perfume, all while eating every last thing there was to be found.

"She's going to notice you were digging about in her things," one of the other girls said. "You're going to be lucky if you aren't sacked."

Lena made a rude noise. "I was careful to put everything back as it was, and she's used to servants moving things about. Besides, I'm her favorite."

"Sonia's her favorite," Gwen said. "Everyone knows that."

Lena rolled her eyes. "Sonia's not nearly as fun as I am."

The loud shriek of a deimos shattered the conversation, and everyone went still, listening to the steady drum of wings as the creature circled overhead. A chill ran through Lydia, and she shivered.

"Sad as it is to say, there are easier pickings than us," Gwen murmured, patting her arm. "There's the dead littering the street, plus the sad souls who couldn't find shelter for the night."

"The nights are getting longer," one of the other girls said, jerking her chin toward the clock sitting on the sideboard. "Winter will be a fell thing."

The dining room filled with uneasy murmurs, and Lydia didn't blame them. She recalled the map of the West that Killian had shown her. Mudaire was far enough north that the winter nights would be long indeed.

"How fortunate that we shall all be in the lands of endless summer soon enough," Gwen said, silencing the chatter. "No cold. No deimos. And all the food you can eat."

"And southern boys!" shouted several of the girls.

"You lot are either gods-damned idiots or hard of hearing," Gwen replied, casting her eyes skyward with exaggerated annoyance. "We were talking about the positive aspects of our impending departure, not the burdens."

Everyone laughed, but Lydia leaned closer to Lena and asked, "What's the Princess like?"

"Better than most of her ilk," Lena replied. "She's fair and not prone to losing her head. But . . ."

"But . . . ," Lydia pressed, curious to know more about the girl she'd be watching over for the coming weeks.

"Have you ever met someone and felt like you might spend day and night with them and never know who they really are?"

Lydia had spent her life surrounded by politicians. There was nothing she knew better. "I know the sort."

"I'll let you form your own opinions, though." Lena smiled. "Tomorrow, you get to be my shadow."

With the sun barely above the distant horizon, Lydia walked with the other young women toward the palace, Lena filling her ears with instructions as they went, almost all of it related to manners and protocol. The sword she'd been provided hung from the sturdy belt holding up her snug trousers, the weight comforting despite the fact that she had no idea how to use it. Same for the knife sheathed on the opposite side of her waist.

"Technically, the captain is in command of us," Lena said. "But Bercola is the one who manages the day-to-day, including our training. She's a giant." Casting a sideways glance at Lydia, the other girl asked, "Have you ever met a giant?"

Lydia's guts swirled with trepidation, because she *had* met this particular giant. And she rather thought there was no chance at all that Bercola wouldn't recognize her. Silently, she cursed Killian for abandoning her without appropriate instruction. This was *his* insane plan, and yet she'd seen neither hide nor hair of him since the prior day. "I haven't," she lied.

"I hadn't, either, though I've heard there are more of them in the South. I'd always heard they were quick to temper, but Bercola isn't too bad."

"Just don't do anything stupid," Gwen chimed in. "Bercola doesn't have any time for foolishness."

They rounded a corner, and the palace came into view, partially hidden behind a stone wall that stood perhaps fifteen feet high. The two aged men standing inside the gates eased them open at the sight of the women. Beyond was a lane paved with grey stone that split and encircled a lawn that contained miniature versions of the towers of the god circle at the center of the city. The lawn was bordered with stone planters, but the crimson flowers within them were wilted and dying, though whether it was from neglect or the cold Lydia couldn't say.

The palace itself was a two-story affair made of the same solid grey blocks as the rest of the city, the vast structure curved in a half-moon shape. Wide steps led up to a twin set of solid wood doors, the planks reinforced with steel, but the guardswomen ignored them in favor of a narrow path leading them to a small side entrance.

Inside, the corridor was dark and narrow, lit by dripping candles set into sconces on the walls. It smelled like tallow, woodsmoke, and of something cooking, and Lydia could faintly hear the clatter of a kitchen preparing itself for the day.

They took a narrow staircase up to the second level, and it was as though Lydia were stepping into an entirely different building as they made their way out into the wide vaulted corridor. The floors were intricate parquet layered with elaborate woven carpets. The plastered walls were framed with polished wood that gleamed from the sun shining through windows set high on the walls, the building cunningly designed to allow natural light into the corridor despite it being enclosed by rooms on both sides.

Lydia's boots sank into the carpet as she followed Lena,

taking in the gilt-framed pieces of artwork hanging on the walls. Ahead of them, the corridor was closed off by a heavy door, which was flanked by two guardswomen, one of whom Lydia recognized as Sonia. The young woman's hazel eyes warmed at the sight of them.

"How was the night?" Gwen asked.

"Quiet." Sonia proceeded to give Gwen a detailed report of the evening, but as they were talking, Lena stepped to Lydia's side. "They tend to be a late-to-rise sort, so we'll likely be doing little more than standing right here for the next couple hours."

"Does the Princess often leave the palace?"

"Rarely. Her ladies are responsible for doing her good works in the city, but even they hardly venture out anymore." Lena's mouth curved up in a smile. "It can be very boring work."

"Then you, at least, will be pleased with Her Highness's plans for the day."

Lydia jumped and turned to find Bercola standing behind her, the giantess having come out while the other girls entered to relieve their counterparts.

"Good morning, Bercola." Lena smiled widely. "How is my largest and most favorite ray of sunshine on this fine day?"

The giantess exhaled a belabored breath. "I really need to figure out a way to get you fired, Lena. You're gods-damned irritating."

"It's why you love me," the guardswoman replied, but Bercola's eyes were fixed on Lydia. "So you're the new recruit."

Before Lydia could answer, someone said, "I was under the impression we had a sufficient number of guards in our employ, Lord Calorian."

Turning, Lydia found a young woman standing in the doorway, Killian behind her. She wore a high-necked gown, the amber velvet identical in color to her wide eyes. Her dark blonde hair was twisted back from her face, spilling down her back in thick ringlets that would've been the envy of any patrician girl in Celendor. Her skin was the color of sand, her cheeks rounded, and her small nose slightly upturned above bow-shaped lips. She was a good foot shorter than Lydia, her narrow waist and generous curves emphasized by the cut of her dress. She was lovely, but what struck Lydia was that she was *regal*. Undoubtedly, this was Princess Malahi.

In response to the Princess's query, Killian only shrugged. "I'm merely attempting to compensate for your recent decisions, Highness."

"Is that the reason?" Malahi's voice was light, but her eyes narrowed as she looked Lydia over. "What's your name, girl?"

"Lydia, Your Highness." She bowed, noting as she did that the other girl was wearing boots, suggesting this wasn't a jaunt down the corridor. Straightening, she added, "I'm pleased to be in your service."

Malahi inclined her head. "And I thank you for it. May the Six keep us both safe."

Without another word, she started down the corridor, Lena and Gwen hurrying to get ahead. Bercola and the rest of the guardswomen followed, but Killian caught hold of Lydia, his hand encircling her bare wrist.

"Against my better judgment, we're going into the city to tour the crown shelters," he said in a hushed voice, his eyes locked on hers. "You see anything, anything at all, that seems not right, you tell me."

She nodded, the warmth of his hand against her skin capturing her focus. This was the first time she'd seen him since they'd parted ways at the Calorian manor, and though she had accumulated a hundred questions to ask him, she felt reluctant to break the silence hanging over the corridor.

"You should be wearing gloves," he said. "Just in case."

"I'll buy a pair as soon as I get a chance."

Killian nodded. But he didn't let go of her, his other hand slipping into the pocket of his trousers as though to retrieve something. He swallowed and looked at his feet. "I—"

"Captain! Carriage is being brought around!" Lena's voice carried down the corridor, and Killian simultaneously let go of Lydia's arm and jerked his hand out of his pocket. Taking a long step back, he scrubbed a hand through his hair, looking anywhere but at her.

"I should go," Lydia murmured, his obvious agitation triggering her own.

Killian nodded, but as she started down the corridor he called, "Lydia."

She stopped and looked over her shoulder, seeing his throat move as he swallowed. But all he said was, "Be safe." Then he opened the door behind him and disappeared.

31

KILLIAN

There were more pressing matters, none the least convincing Malahi that to go into the city was an unnecessary risk, but Killian found himself backtracking into Malahi's rooms. Shutting the door and flipping the latch so a servant wouldn't catch him, he hurried to the massive closet containing her clothing, pulling out a drawer that had to have held at least three dozen pairs of gloves. He dug around, finally extracting a pair of black riding gloves, which he tucked into his belt.

As he rose to his feet, his eyes landed on one of the heavy chests containing some of Malahi's jewelry. Opening one, he lifted out trays of jewels, searching for something that would suit his purpose, finally catching sight of the glint of silver near the bottom. Malahi never wore silver, gold as much an emblem of the Rowenes house as the scorpion courtesy of the mines on their lands, so the absence of a silver chain wouldn't be noticed.

Unlike the ring burning a hole in his pocket.

32

LYDIA

It was raining.

A frigid wind drove the fat droplets against her face with such force that it felt like being struck by pebbles of ice. Her hair and clothes were drenched, and freezing water dribbled down her back, her skin prickled with goose bumps. Worst of all, the cold was making her nose run, and Lydia had nothing but her sleeve to wipe it with as she stood with the rest of Malahi's bodyguards, listening to Killian argue with the Princess.

"It's too risky!" he shouted into the open carriage door where Malahi sat with her arms crossed, eyes narrowed to slits. "There are tens of thousands of people in this city who resent you for no reason more than that you have food in your stomach."

"And you think me hiding in my palace will win their favor?"

"I think in the palace I have a fighting chance of keeping someone from sticking a knife in your back!"

"I believe you that it's dangerous, Killian. I believe you that there are threats out there. But I'm not a coward."

"No, you're a bloody idiot!"

Lena hissed through her teeth where she stood next to Lydia, and Gwen gave an answering wince. The argument had been circling around the same points for the past twenty minutes, escalating with each pass, but now they were both shouting.

"Gods-damn it," Lena muttered. "I don't know why he ever thinks he'll win against her."

"I think they both like to argue," Gwen replied.

"I think he wants to be able to say 'I told you so' when something goes wrong," another girl, Brin, chimed in before Bercola shot them all a look that said *shut your mouths.*

Lydia wiped the rain out of her eyes, only to be splattered with more as wind gusted against her, torrents running down the back of her neck to soak into her shirt. Though she didn't think the other girls were wrong, watching Killian's agitation made her wonder if there wasn't something *more* to his concerns. His eyes kept drifting from the argument toward the city as though he saw . . . no, *sensed* something to be wary of. As though his mark was warning him. Yet the rain, and an occasional piece of hail, pinged off the light armor he wore in lieu of his usual black coat, and she knew he wouldn't have worn it if he'd believed there was any chance of dissuading the Princess.

"I'm going to pretend you didn't say that." Malahi's amber eyes were narrow. "Perhaps if you could provide me with some more specificity about the threat?"

"You know that's not how it works." Killian's voice was low, his irritation drifting off him in waves. "It's not like Tremon is whispering instructions in my ears. All I know is that today the city has a bad feel to it."

"Will tomorrow be better?"

Killian didn't answer.

"The next day? The day after that?" She crossed her arms. "Maybe you ought to consider that me doing *something* might help the *feel* of the city."

Color rose on Killian's cheeks. "Have it your way," he snarled, then slammed the carriage door shut, coming over to Lydia and the others. "Lena, you ride inside with her."

Lena nodded but muttered, "Lucky me," under her breath.

"At least you get to stay dry," Gwen replied, slapping her lover on the shoulder as she walked toward the carriage.

While their backs were turned, Killian brushed against Lydia and she felt a tug on her sword belt, then he was stalking over this massive black horse, checking the saddle girth. Glancing down, she saw he'd tucked a pair of gloves into her belt, and while no one was looking she quickly pulled them on.

Killian swung into the saddle with practiced ease, then

turned to survey Malahi's bodyguard, plus the additional guardsmen he'd seconded from the palace walls. His dark hair was plastered against his forehead, skin glistening with rain that emphasized the hard lines of his cheekbones and jaw.

"Keep your heads up and eyes open. If things go sour, your priority is to get the Princess back to the palace or to one of the gatehouses," he said, then nodded at the coachman, who snapped the reins against the backs of the four-horse team.

Moving out at a walk, the women flanked the coach, the gates opening as they approached. Lydia adjusted her sword belt, despite knowing that it was for show. Her true purpose was to look for the corrupted. To warn the others. Though she was freezing, sweat pooled beneath her breasts and dripped down her back, and her hand went to the knife belted at her waist. Equally useless against the corrupted, if what she'd heard was true.

The carriage passed through the streets, moving slowly into the city. Mudaire was quieter than she'd ever seen it, all the bustle stalled as the people abandoned their business to watch their princess pass. There was no fanfare. Far from it. Women stood with crossed arms, eyes tracking the progress of the group. Children peered out of alleys, expressions feral and hungry. Lydia felt hunted, imagining corrupted hiding in every shadow, and she let her vision drift out of focus so that she could see the life emanating from the people watching them. Some were bright. Most were not.

"Gods-damn it," Killian muttered, his horse chomping angrily at the bit. He cast a glance at Lydia, and she shook her head. Nothing. *Yet.*

The carriage team's hooves clip-clopped in unison, the plump animals tossing their heads, the plumes of their trappings sagging in the rain. Lydia's skin crawled, and she fought the urge to step closer to Gwen. *Be brave,* she mouthed silently to herself. Then she looked over her shoulder.

The street was full of people, a silent procession following on their heels.

"Kil—" She caught herself. "Captain . . ."

"I know," he said. Reaching down, he pulled open the coach door and said something to Malahi that Lydia couldn't make out. But the angry twist of his jaw and the way he slammed the door shut told her all she needed to know. *Keep going*.

They wound through the streets, the crowd behind them growing. Then the carriage stopped. Lydia glanced once at the large warehouse, her stomach souring as she recognized the shelter. The smell of the place wafted over her, and she bit down against the panic rising in her chest. The feeling of being pressed in on all sides. Of being unable to breathe.

"Form up," Killian barked, snapping her back into the moment. Instinctively, she fell in next to Gwen, forming a protective barrier as Malahi stepped out of the carriage, a parasol balanced over her head to keep her golden ringlets out of the rain.

If the Princess saw the masses watching them, she said nothing, walking straight toward the shelter door. Killian and Bercola flanked her like twin towers. Several of the girls walked ahead and the rest of them fell in behind, leaving the old men to watch over the horses and carriage.

"What is that stink?" Malahi demanded the moment she was inside.

"Shit," Killian replied, then tilted his head sideways. "With hints of piss and vomit."

"I know that," she snapped. "*Why* does it smell like a latrine in here?"

"Because people must go where they sit." The words were out of Lydia's mouth before she could think. "They pack women and children and crippled soldiers in here as though they were cattle, no room to move. Barely air to breathe."

"Lydia, shut your trap," Bercola muttered under her breath, but Lydia barely heard the admonition as Killian's eyes tracked to her, the muscles in his jaw flexing. But he said nothing.

Malahi faced her, and for a moment Lydia was certain the other girl would reprimand her for speaking out of turn. But the Princess only said, "You stayed here?"

"For a night. It felt like a lifetime, so I can only imagine how those who've been staying here for weeks—for months—feel. But the alternative is facing the deimos."

The Princess's eyes panned over the other guards. "Have any of the rest of you stayed here prior to joining my guard?"

A few nodded.

"Is it as she says?"

More nods, and Lydia tried to curb her irritation at having her word questioned.

"Why didn't any of you say anything?" Malahi demanded.

The girls who had nodded looked at their feet and shrugged, and Lydia clenched her teeth against answering for them. Of course they hadn't said anything—to escape from that nightmare had been a dream, and *no one* was fool enough to jeopardize that by suggesting that the shelters the Crown had created were any less than adequate.

Killian cleared his throat. "Because they—"

"I gods-damned know why they kept quiet, Killian," Malahi snapped, then abruptly turned, picking her way through the filthy straw until she stood in the middle of the warehouse. "I want these shelters cleaned out every morning. Pay those staying in them to do it, if they are willing. And find more space for people. Another warehouse."

"There is no space, Malahi," Killian replied. "The city is full."

"Full of those without means," she replied. "I believe we'll find that those with means have fled south and that there are many properties vacant throughout the city."

"They'll be looted," he warned.

"I find myself not caring," Malahi said. "Break the locks. If need be, we'll break down the doors to the manors of the High Lords themselves."

A commotion at the entrance caught her attention, and Finn appeared, pushing his way between the guards. He scurried over to Killian, pulling frantically at his arm and whispering something that Lydia couldn't make out.

"We need to go," Killian ordered.

"I'm not finished—"

"Now."

For once Malahi didn't argue. Jerking her skirts up to her knees, exposing worn riding boots, the Princess ran across the warehouse, her guard forming up around her. Outside, the crowd was silent no longer, a swell of angry voices growing like a storm. There was a small half circle of space between the carriage and the crowd, which had nothing to do with the aging guardsman and everything to do with Killian's menacing war-horse. The animal stood where his rider had left him, but he pawed the ground restlessly, snapping his teeth at anyone who approached.

Killian had his sword in hand, keeping between Malahi and the crowd as he half-lifted her into the carriage. The other guardswomen had their blades out, too, and Lydia fumbled to get hers free, palms slick with sweat. They were all grabbing on to various handholds on the sides of the carriage, so she did the same, wishing her grip didn't feel so weak, her knees so wobbly.

"Go," Killian ordered the driver, and the woman snapped the whip. The carriage horses squealed and leapt forward, only to grind to a halt as the crowd refused to part.

"Make way for the Princess," Killian shouted, heeling his horse toward the crowd. For him, they scrambled back, moving out of reach of both his blade and his horse's teeth. The carriage surged again, and Lydia clung to her handhold, her eyes on the crowd that pressed in the moment Killian was out of reach. Their eyes were desperate. Hungry. And in an instant, Lydia realized what they wanted.

"They're after the horses," she shouted.

It was too late.

A stocky woman with a knife lunged, her blade slicing through a carriage horse's throat. It reared, slamming against the horse next to it, then dragged the whole team forward several paces before collapsing.

The crowd was upon it before the poor creature hit the

ground, those with knives or axes moving with speed to slaughter the remaining three horses. It was madness, women and children climbing over one another to cut loose handfuls of meat like wild animals, people fighting and being trampled.

"Gods," Gwen said. "Gods help us."

Because the crowd was surging against the carriage now, hands reaching up to claw at the gilt. *Not gilt*, Lydia realized. *Gold*.

Killian drove his war-horse through the masses, shouting at people to move; then he reached down and jerked the carriage door open. In a flash of skirts, Malahi was in the saddle in front of him.

"Retreat to the palace," he shouted at them. "Stay close."

Lydia flung herself after him, pushing and fighting through the crowd. Someone elbowed her in the face, and she tasted blood, panic roaring through her veins as she struggled in the black horse's wake. No one cared about her, only about the meat and the gold, but it was like trying to run upstream in a river. The other girls were punching and shoving their way through, some using their weapons out of desperation as they fought to protect their charge.

Then the mood of the crowd shifted once again, more and more eyes shifting to Malahi.

"She's wearing gold and jewels!" a woman shouted. She screamed the words over and over, trying to rally those around her.

"The Seventh take you," Gwen swore at the woman, then shouted at Lydia, "Watch my back!" before striding toward the woman and slugging her in the face. But the damage was already done. The incensed crowd pressed closer, and Lydia saw a blade flash. Lunging, she tried to get her sword in between, but it was knocked from her grip, another blow sending her stumbling. A second later, she heard a scream of pain.

Barely managing to keep her feet, Lydia searched for Gwen's red and gold coat, but all she saw was a blur of angry faces. Lydia threw herself into the crowd, shoving her way to where

Gwen had fallen, the desperate and starving people buffeting her from side to side.

"Move!" she screamed, but her voice was one of hundreds, and no one listened. People were pushing back against the flow, splattered with blood and carrying chunks of horsemeat or pieces of the carriage with them. A nightmare.

Then she caught sight of a red-clad figure on the ground, people stepping on and over the individual with as little regard as they did the cobbles. "Gwen," she shouted, but the figure didn't move, and with the press of humanity even Lydia's mark wasn't enough to tell her if the other girl was alive.

Weight slammed against Lydia's back, and then she was on the ground, crawling, trying to keep the pace even as boots and bare feet alike stepped on her legs and hands. She shrieked as one of her fingers broke beneath a heel but kept going, falling across Gwen's still form.

"Get up!" She dragged on Gwen's arm, but the other girl barely stirred.

Lydia tried to rise to her feet but was knocked down time and again. Gasps that were half sobs tore from her throat, exhaustion deadening her limbs as she protected Gwen's body with her own. Unless they got clear of the crowd, they were both dead.

Gritting her teeth against the pain, Lydia forced herself onto her hands and knees, lifting her head to search for the other guardswomen. For anyone who might help them. Then through the masses of civilians, her eyes latched on a hooded figure that stood amidst the chaos. It seemed to burn with life, the mists seething around it bright as the sun. But instead of being transfixed by the beauty, Lydia's guts heaved, her throat burning with bile as dark eyes rimmed with fire looked over the crowd. Not human.

Corrupted.

33

KILLIAN

People flung themselves out of the way of his horse and Killian urged the animal to greater speed, its hooves ringing against the cobbles as they flew up the street. Killian held tight to Malahi with one arm, the Princess sitting sideways across his lap, her cheek pressed against his chest.

"My guard," she shouted over the noise. "Are they with us?"

"They can take care of themselves," Bercola bellowed from where she ran next to them, the only one capable of keeping his pace. "And it's you the crowd is after, not them."

Killian cast a backward glance over his shoulder, counting red coats even as he searched for black hair and a pale face.

There.

Lydia was pushing through the masses, her expression unreadable from this distance but her head moving from side to side as though searching. She staggered as a woman carrying a handful of horsemeat slammed into her, colliding with another woman. Then the crowd surged again and Lydia disappeared from sight.

Without thinking, Killian dragged on Surly's reins, the stallion sliding to a stop even as Killian pushed Malahi into Bercola's arms. Then digging in his heels, he galloped back toward the crowd.

"Stay with the Princess," he shouted at the guards he passed, digging into his pocket and pulling out a handful of coins, which he tossed ahead of the pursuing crowd. The civilians dropped to their knees, fighting over the silver and gold, then turning on one another.

His horse shrieked, reaching out to snap at any who came close, and Killian rose in his stirrups, searching for Lydia's familiar red coat. But there was crimson everywhere, the people splattered with blood from the carriage horses and the blood of one another, dozens lying still, their bodies tripping up those trying to flee.

A flicker of motion caught his eye, a pale face splattered with mud and blood, and he dug in his heels. "Move!" he roared at those in his way, a path clearing ahead of him, revealing Lydia sprawled over Gwen's still form.

Leaping off Surly's back, he left the stallion to fend off the crowd. "Lydia!"

She looked up, green eyes full of panic but very much alive. Relief flooded his veins as he caught her under the arms, lifting her upright, then pulling her against him as she swayed. "Are you all right?"

"Yes," she gasped, wiping blood from her eyes. "Gwen's not."

"Shit!" He let go of her, bending to pick up Gwen's limp form. Blood soaked the girl's coat, but he felt a whisper of breath against his cheek. "Get on the horse. You'll need to hold her."

"Killian!" There was urgency in her voice. "There's one of the corrupted in the crowd. I saw her."

His stomach flipped. "Where?"

"I don't know. I only caught a glimpse."

He searched the diminishing crowd, ignoring those who jostled against him, but he saw nothing. Except that didn't mean Lydia was wrong about what she'd seen, and he'd left Malahi alone with only a handful of guards.

"Lydia, get on the horse!"

She scrambled onto the stallion's back, and he eased Gwen across the saddle in front of her, unleashing a stream of profanity at the horse as he shuffled sideways and tried to bite. Grabbing the reins, Killian broke into a run, trusting Lydia had the wherewithal to hold on.

He sprinted through the streets, knowing the route Bercola would take, and it didn't take long until he caught sight of the group, Malahi surrounded by her guards.

They whirled at the sound of hooves, and ignoring Bercola's admonition that she keep running, Lena sprinted toward him. "Gwen!"

"She's alive," Killian replied. "We'll send for a healer as soon as we reach the palace, though the temple will be strapped dealing with that mess."

"Take her straight there," Malahi said. "Bercola and the others will remain with me."

"My priority is getting you back to safety," he snapped. "Your decision put us in this mess, Malahi, so for once, maybe you could refrain from arguing."

Color leached from the Princess's skin; then her eyes flicked to Lydia. "You take her, then. You look in need of a healer yourself."

Killian clenched his teeth. The last place he wanted Lydia going was Hegeria's temple, but he had no argument to stand upon for it being someone else. And as it was, he could see Lydia's wounds were slowly beginning to heal, the slice across her temple no longer bleeding. Without the excuse of a healer having seen to her, someone was bound to ask questions. He had to trust that Lydia was clever enough to see this through.

"Take Gwen to the temple," he said. He flipped the reins over his horse's head, holding the stallion steady until she had him in hand. "Tell the healers Her Highness sent you. When you're through, head back to the barracks. One of the other girls can bring the horse back to the palace."

Lydia nodded, and he gave Surly a slap on the haunches, watching as the stallion cantered up the street, taking her out of his reach to protect.

And praying he wouldn't have cause to regret not going with her.

34

LYDIA

Foul-tempered as the stallion was, he was well trained, and despite being only a middling rider, Lydia managed to guide him to the temple while keeping Gwen balanced in front of her.

The other girl was hurt badly, and in the few moments she gained consciousness she sobbed in pain, the sound tearing at Lydia's heart.

You could help her, a voice whispered inside her head. *You could take away her pain.*

But at what cost?

It was that question that stilled her hand, that caused her to take care that she did not touch Gwen's exposed skin. That caused her to dig in her heels, urging the stallion to greater speed.

There were already dozens of wounded making their way into the god circle, and those helping them eyed Killian's horse warily. But it was not their eyes that Lydia felt most keenly. Turning her head skyward, she regarded the seven stone towers looming above, all of them carved with reliefs to resemble the gods, with the exception of the tower of black stone, which possessed only the suggestion of eyes.

Her skin crawled as she passed into the circle, her heart catching as the towers seemed to bend forward, faces coming closer to peer at her intently, the wind whispering between them as though they spoke to one another. Then she blinked, and they were once more inanimate structures. Stone carved by the hands of mortals.

Hegeria's temple was no taller than the rest, but its base was broader than the others, the size necessary given the number of individuals the goddess marked. Riding right up to the open doors, Lydia called out, "I'm here by order of Her Royal Highness, Princess Malahi."

Only then did she see the dozens of injured laid out in rows, individuals in white robes moving among them carrying cases of bandages and other supplies. She watched with fascination as a girl, who could not have been more than thirteen, reached inside a man's opened guts, deep wrinkles forming around her eyes, her hair turning to grey. But the concentration on her face never faltered as she drew the skin of his belly together, sealing it but stopping before the wound was fully healed. Then she picked up a length of catgut and a needle and without pause began to stitch the deep slice in his leg

"Sent by Malahi, you say?"

Lydia jerked her attention away from the surgery to find a thin old man with his hand resting on the horse's neck, his white robes stained with blood. "Yes, Gwen was hurt in the riot."

The old man's mouth tightened, but then he nodded. "Let's get her down."

Showing surprising strength, he caught Gwen in his arms as Lydia slid the other girl off the saddle. Dismounting, Lydia helped him carry Gwen inside, laying her on one of the many cots that had been set out. Straightening Gwen's legs, she looked up to discover the healer was no longer an old man, the age having receded from his face. It was both strange and magical, made more so in knowing that the same thing happened to her when she used her mark.

He looked up and caught her staring, and Lydia recovered by asking, "Will she be all right?"

"Yes, yes. We'll send her back to the Princess when she's rested. Now get that animal out of my temple."

Heat rose on her cheeks, and she hurried to the door to retrieve Surly's reins, leading the horse back outside. But instead of mounting, she stood next to the animal's shoulder, watching as the healer gestured for two boys in white robes to attend him. With bloody hands, he gestured as he worked, obviously instructing them, though Lydia was too far away to hear.

But she was desperate to know what he was saying, to learn how her mark worked, even if she was never to use it. Dropping the horse's reins and muttering at him to stay put, she crept back inside, leaning against the doorframe.

". . . broken ribs . . . perforated . . . must repair them manually prior to . . ."

She caught only snippets of what he said, but as he slid a scalpel down Gwen's abdomen and then reached inside to right her broken rib cage, Lydia found she could see where he was directing the misty flows of life. That she could see his essence, as well as that of the two boys, diminishing, while Gwen's gained in strength.

Then the healer lifted his face and caught her staring, his brow furrowing as he studied her. Lydia's skin turned to ice, certain that she'd been discovered, but he only said, "Get back to your mistress, girl."

35

KILLIAN

They reached the palace without further incident, though the city simmered with tension and fear.

"Keep the gates shut," Killian ordered the old men standing guard. "I'll arrange for reinforcements."

He turned back to Malahi, wanting her inside the palace and behind locked doors, but she was striding across the lawn toward the stables. "Update the men on guard," he said to Bercola, and then started after the Princess.

"Malahi!" he called, but she ignored him and kept walking.

Breaking into a run, he caught up to her, catching her elbow, but she jerked it out of his grip.

"What are you doing?"

"What I should've done a long time ago. What I would've done, if I'd known just how desperate they were."

Pushing open the door to the stables, she walked down the rows of stalls, stopping in front of one holding a chestnut carriage horse. Clipping a line to its halter, she went to the stall and retrieved its teammate, leading both animals down the aisle.

He stepped in her path. "I'll get someone else to take them."

"No." She lifted her chin, wet hair clinging to her cheeks. "You were right that the city is dangerous, Killian. But you are wrong to think that means I should hide from my people. They need to know that I will stand by them. That I'll fight for them."

There was one of the corrupted prowling the city—Lydia had seen it. But he couldn't very well admit it without compromising her secret. "You could've been killed in that riot. And if that means nothing to you, remember that Gwen nearly *was* killed."

"Then I'll go alone."

"Malahi—"

"I'm going, Killian. Whether you follow is your own choice."

"The Six grant me patience," he growled, but he stepped out of her path, following as she led the animals to the palace gate.

Malahi walked down the street, Killian and the rest of her guard following at her heels. The civilians who caught sight of them followed, but the feel of it was different than it was before, the animosity gone. The Princess reached one of the city squares, leading the animals to the fountain at the center, where she stepped up on the edge.

Without saying a word, she gestured to a tall woman standing nearby to approach and handed her the lead to one of the horses. "Share with those in need." The woman nodded, leading the animal away. Malahi did the same with the other horse, the crowd calmly accepting the animal—a far cry from the frenzied mass they'd been less than an hour before.

But she wasn't through.

As Killian watched on, Malahi took off her heavy cloak and gloves, handing them off. Then her jewelry: gold bracelets, earrings, hairpins, and a necklace that alone could purchase a city block. She handed them to the people, saying always the same thing: "Share with those in need."

Her boots followed; then she turned to him. "Unbutton my dress."

He silently obeyed, unfastening the tiny gold buttons that ran down her back, helping her step out of the heavy velvet gown, which she gave to a woman with three children clinging to her legs.

Malahi stood before her people dressed only in a silk slip, the falling rain soaking her loose hair. Then with hundreds of her people watching, she caught hold of the hem and lifted it over her head so that she stood before them in nothing at all.

"You are my people," she shouted, handing over the garment to a woman. "And all that I have to give is yours."

And without another word, she stepped down from the fountain, the parting crowd dropping into bows and curtsies as their princess walked back through the streets. Naked. But very much a queen.

36

LYDIA

The house was quiet as Lydia lay on her back in her narrow bed, listening to Lena's steady breathing and Gwen's much louder snores. Exhaustion pressed her against the mattress like lead weights, but for hours sleep had eluded her. The balance of the day had been uneventful, but she'd been unable to shake the frantic tension of the morning's events, visions of the knife flashing, of Gwen falling bloodied beneath the crowd, of her own gods-damned uselessness dancing across her thoughts.

Rolling over in bed for the hundredth time, she tried to calm the escalating beat of her heart, the panic that made her feel as though she would vomit. When the clock downstairs chimed the midnight hour, Lydia climbed out of bed and roamed down the hallway to Killian's study, having seen a glimpse of bookshelves in passing. With the exception of a dog sleeping on a chair, the room was empty.

Trailing a finger along the spines, she examined the titles, which showed topics from history to philosophy to law to poetry. None of which she could imagine Killian reading and none of which were what she was looking for. Dropping to her knees, she examined the bottom row, smiling when she lighted upon *The Art of Swordsmanship*. Plucking out the book, she sat on the floor rather than shooing away the dog.

The book was light on words and heavy on diagrams, and she swiftly read through the contents, then set it aside to retrieve another volume on a similar topic. She read until her eyes burned, and it wasn't until she felt a hand shaking her shoulder that she realized she'd fallen asleep.

Alarmed at being caught, she jerked upright, her forehead collided with something hard.

"Gods-damn it, woman." Killian crouched next to her, rubbing his chin. "What are you doing in here?"

"Sorry," she muttered, acutely aware that she was sitting on the floor of *his* study wearing nothing more than a cotton nightdress. "I was . . . Why do you smell so awful?"

"Because I was in the sewers. It's the only way to traverse the city after dark, but unfortunately, the stink clings." Pulling off his coat, he tossed it across the room. Then he picked up one of the volumes, frowning at the title before tossing it aside with equal carelessness. "This is useless. You can't learn how to fight from a book."

"I beg to differ." She carefully shelved the rest of the books before he could damage them as well. "You can learn anything from the right book. And for someone with such a large collection, one would think you'd hold them in more esteem."

Killian eyed the shelves while he pushed up the sleeves of his shirt. The knuckles of his hands were scraped and bleeding, and she wondered what he'd been doing. "I've always considered them more decorative than useful, frankly."

Lydia crossed her arms, trying to focus on his view of literature rather than the way the candlelight illuminated the muscles of his bare forearms. Or on how his dark hair fell over eyes bright with humor. She wished a clever retort would come to mind, but her brain seemed intent on failing her.

Killian was quiet for a long moment; then he ran a finger down the spines of the books. "Why would a scholar like you be interested in books full of pictures of men waving sticks?"

"Why do you think I'm a scholar?"

The corner of his mouth turned up. "You shelved my books in alphabetical order, which I doubt was the state in which you found them."

There was nothing to be gained or lost in denying it, so she nodded. "Incompetence irritates me, particularly my own. I hoped the books would help rectify my limitations."

"I believe you," he said. "Only that's not the reason you're sitting here in a nightdress when you should be asleep." His attention didn't stir from her face, but she flushed nonetheless.

"I didn't want to wake Gwen or Lena," she said, then sighed, the excuse weak even in her own ears. "It concerns me that the other girls might depend on me to fight again and that I'll fail them." Like she'd failed Gwen today. Like she'd failed Teriana. Like she'd failed herself.

"Today wasn't your fault. It was mine. I had a bad feeling about Malahi going into the city, but . . ." Shaking his head, he sat on the floor and rested his elbows on his knees.

"Gwen could've died because I didn't know what I was doing." She stared at the floorboards between them. Her hair fell forward to pool in her lap as she thought of how very different things would be if she'd been able to fight off Spurius when he'd chased her down, stopping her from warning Teriana. Or if she'd been able to hold off Marcus long enough for help to arrive. Or if she'd been as good with her fists as the women who'd attacked her in the shelter and stolen her coin. "I'm tired of being helpless."

Of being a victim.

She clenched her hands into fists, her nails digging into the palms of her hands. Her body was so tense it hurt, each breath a struggle, though there was no reason for it. Her pulse roared in her ears, and all she wanted was to escape, to find some form of release from the fear that had hung over her from the moment Lucius had captured Teriana's ship. A violent shiver took hold of her, though she wasn't cold, and she clenched her teeth to keep them from chattering.

Then Killian's fingers, warm and rough with callus, cupped her cheek, and she exhaled in a loud whoosh, leaning against his hand though she knew she should not.

"Breathe," he instructed, and she drew in a ragged mouthful of air. "You aren't helpless. You saved my life from the deimos, and I'm fairly capable with a sword."

"Luck."

"No, it wasn't." His thumb traced over her cheekbone. "You aren't helpless. Your presence gives the other girls a fighting chance if one of the corrupted comes for Malahi, because without you, there is no warning. And without a warning, they don't have a chance. You're risking *your* life for them. There's a word for *that,* but it isn't *luck.*"

She squeezed her eyes shut and shook her head until his fingers caught in her hair, his other hand rising to hold her face steady. "Lydia, look at me."

"I'm tired of being afraid," she whispered, refusing his request. "Do you even know what fear feels like? What helplessness feels like?"

He hesitated, then said, "Yes. Every day. Every minute."

Something about his tone—the truthfulness of it—steadied her heart, and she opened her eyes. His were dark, all humor gone. Then he looked away, shaking his head. "Everyone knows. Everyone in the gods-damned kingdom knows, but not you. Not the girl from the far side of the world."

"What do you mean?"

"This war is my fault," he said. "My mistakes were what allowed Rufina and her army to invade Mudamora."

Lydia listened in rapt silence as he explained what had happened at the wall. The death of the corrupted woman. The subsequent attack from the rear that he saw coming a heartbeat too late.

His last conversation with his father.

"I've never told anyone that part," he said, then shifted his weight to extract the sword belted at his waist. "This was his."

It was an infinitely finer blade than the one Lydia had been given—and had subsequently lost—the steel engraved with a cursive script she couldn't make out. The grip was well worn, but a large sapphire was set into the pommel and it glittered in the candlelight. "I think it's the only thing I own that I couldn't bear to lose."

"It's beautiful."

"It was a gift from King Derrick Falorn. They were friends,

and my father was his sworn sword. I was—" He broke off, shaking his head. "It doesn't matter."

Neither of them spoke, but there was something comforting in the silence. As if what was conveyed unspoken was more powerful than words.

Finally, he said, "I know Teriana gave you a copy of *Treatise*, so you know that the strength of the Six depends on the belief of the people. It's not so much belief in their existence, but the belief that the Six will protect their faithful followers. And that protection most visibly comes through those the gods mark, which means that our actions impact the strength of belief."

Our. Because she was marked, too.

He rubbed his chin, eyes distant. "If the Marked aren't where they are needed, it damages faith. If they don't do their duty to the people, it damages faith. If they fail to protect the people, it damages faith. And *that* is what gives the Corrupter his power."

It was an incredible burden to bear—more than she'd even realized.

"The only way I can redeem myself is by winning this war. Driving Rufina back. But Serrick forbids me to fight, because he believes Tremon and the rest of the Six have turned their back on me." He sighed. "I am terrified of what is to come. And I feel helpless to stop it."

She understood that weight of guilt. To have made a mistake that cost those one loved so very much. That it hadn't been intentional didn't matter—the fault was still there. And to be denied the chance at atonement . . . That she understood equally as well. Reaching out, she took his hand, her heart skipping as her mark took hold. "Hegeria marked me to save your life because Tremon asked her to, Killian. But maybe it wasn't just to save your life—maybe it was also to bolster your faith."

"My faith's just fine."

She tightened her fingers. "I'm not talking about your faith in them. I'm talking about your faith in the Marked." *In your-self.*

A draft gusted through the room, and the candle flickered, sending shadows dancing across the wall. The sensation of being observed made Lydia shiver.

The corner of his mouth turned up and she knew he felt it, too. "They're always watching. I'd like to tell you that you'll get used to it, but I never have." Then he gave a slight shake of his head. "I almost forgot the reason I came here tonight."

Reaching into his pocket, he extracted a silver chain with something dangling from it. Lydia's eyes widened at the sight of her ring. "How did you . . . ?"

"Never mind that." He lifted the chain over her head, the ring falling to hang between her breasts, still warm. "Remember who you're fighting for."

Her father. Teriana. All of the Maarin who'd been captured. "I'm afraid I'll fail them."

"What would ease that fear?"

Always she'd tried to fight her battles with words, but some people refused to hear her voice. "I want to learn to fight."

He nodded slowly, then said, "I can't turn you into a warrior in a few weeks. That's something that takes months, years, even."

Her heart skipped. "But you'll teach me?"

"I will. Every night I can get away until Malahi sets sail. Meet me at the Calorian manor after your day is done tomorrow. Tell the others there's a girl you fancy and that you're meeting up with her in the city. They'll understand—half of them are supporting lovers and family with this job."

He stood in one smooth motion before reaching down to extract one of the volumes from the shelves. "This one isn't too bad."

And without another word, he disappeared into the darkness of the hallway.

37

KILLIAN

Light was already growing in the sky by the time Killian made it back to the palace.

He jumped down from the top of the wall and rolled, coming to his feet in time to see the door to the stables open. One of the boys who cared for the horses led out an agitated pair and turned them loose to graze the grounds, fattening them up for their eventual slaughter, which had been the fate of most of their fellows. Both galloped to the far side of the palace grounds. The boy disappeared inside; then a moment later a shout of dismay cut through the air.

Skin prickling, Killian ran toward the large building. The light was dim inside, but he could hear Surly and Seahawk rustling uneasily about their stalls. And over the smell of horse and manure, his nose picked up the scent of blight.

The stableboy stood with his back against the wall, his face drained of color, eyes fixed on what lay beyond in the stall opposite. The one belonging to Malahi's mare.

Swearing under his breath, Killian strode down the aisle and looked inside, barely keeping the contents of his stomach in check at what he saw.

"She was fine last night, my lord," the boy blurted out. "I swear it."

"This isn't your fault." Taking the boy by the shoulders, Killian examined his face. He and Malahi had cleaned the mare up in a spring prior to bringing her back in the city, but this boy was with these horses constantly. If he'd been infected . . . "Do you feel sick? Any symptoms at all?"

The boy shook his head rapidly. "No, my lord."

Thank the Six. "Good. That changes, you come to me directly.

Now I need you to run to Hegeria's temple. Tell them I sent you and ask to speak with the Grand Master. Explain to him that we have a horse infected with blight. Tell him to come immediately."

The boy sprinted out of the stables.

The other horses were turning circles in their stalls, ears pinned and eyes rolling, so Killian swiftly turned them out, all of them galloping to the opposite side of the grounds before turning to stare back in his direction. *They knew.*

Then, taking a deep breath, Killian went back to the mare's stall. She lay on her side in the straw, flanks rising and falling rapidly, nostrils fluttering as she struggled. Her eyes were glazed with pain, but as he knelt in the straw to stroke her cheek they focused on him. She'd been with him since she was a yearling. He'd trained her, taken her with him nearly everywhere he'd been for the last three years. She'd been one of the few horses to survive the battle at the wall, having carried one of his men in their wild dash to safety despite having been injured herself. She was one of the best mounts he'd ever owned, and it had only been because Malahi had fallen in love with the mare that he'd gifted her to the Princess.

And now she was dying.

Steeling himself, Killian forced his eyes away from the mare's face to her forelegs. Her hair had fallen out, the skin beneath a strange grey. Pulsing black veins rose up her shoulders, the same way the blight crawled across the landscape, but a thousand times more sickening, because there were places where the skin had ruptured, black sludge dripping into the straw. And the smell . . . never in all his life had he experienced anything like it.

Heels clicked against the stone of the stable aisle, the measure deeply familiar. Scrambling to his feet, Killian stepped outside the stall, pulling the door shut behind him and stepping in Malahi's path. She'd clearly dressed in a hurry, her hair still tangled from sleep. "It's bad, Malahi. You don't want to see this. I'll take care of it."

"She's my horse."

"All the more reason for you not to see."

Malahi's face was blanched, but she shook her head. "Let me pass."

Wishing he could force her to see reason but knowing it wasn't right to do so, Killian opened the stall door.

Malahi's shoulders rose and fell as she took a deep breath; then she rounded the corner and stepped inside. A soft gasp of horror tore from her lips and she swayed. Killian reached forward to steady her, but she only brushed his hands away, going to kneel next to the mare's head.

The night guard had followed Malahi in, and even Sonia's russet skin seemed waxy and pale. "All of you out," he ordered. "You too, Bercola. I've sent the stableboy for Quindor. If he isn't here in the next half hour, you fetch him yourself. No need to prolong this." Then he went inside the stall.

Malahi was stroking the mare's cheek, murmuring soothing words.

"She needs to be put down." He knelt next to her. "I've sent for Quindor. If the blight can do this to a horse, it can do it to a person as well. The healers need to be prepared. But—"

"I know," Malahi interrupted. "I know he won't expend the energy to heal a horse."

"I'm sorry."

A tear dribbled down her face. "It's my fault. If I'd been paying attention . . ."

"I brought you out there." And he was the one who was supposed to have been protecting her.

Soft footfalls echoed through the stables, and a heartbeat later Quindor appeared in the entrance to the stall. His brow furrowed at the sight of the horse, and he gave the faintest shake of his head. "How did this happen?"

Killian cleared his throat. "We had the horses out for a run. She leapt a fence and landed in a ditch filled with blight. We got her out, but she was covered in it."

The Grand Master knelt next to the horse, his hand resting

on her neck, eyes unfocused and yet somehow intent. Then he pointed at her forelegs. "She was injured?"

Killian nodded. "Scraped up her forelegs getting out." Then he looked at his own hands, which had been nicked and scraped in the same ordeal. "I'm fine."

"You're marked, Lord Calorian," the Grand Master replied. "I think you are not a good test case." Then his gaze shifted to Malahi. "What of you, my lady? You were there as well, yes?"

Killian's chest tightened, but Malahi had a lifetime of experience hiding her mark. "I was wearing gloves. Everything I was wearing was burned. And I've no open wounds."

"That might well be all that saved you from this fate."

Killian's stomach churned with nausea. Lydia had stepped in the blight on her way from the xenthier stem to the city, and her bare feet had been scraped bloody. But she'd also been marked less than two hours later. His palms turned to ice at the thought of what would've happened if she had not.

Quindor was still frowning at Malahi, assessing her in that strange way all healers did their patients. "I think it best if you refrain from leaving the palace grounds, my lady. For your own safety."

"Never mind me." Malahi's voice was fierce. Angry. "What of my horse? The blight closes in on Mudaire with every passing day. We need to know how it infects and whether the effects can be counteracted by a healer."

The Grand Master exhaled a long breath. "She's near death. Even if I can reverse the damage, I'll not save her. Not when there are lines of civilians in front of Hegeria's temple in need of my strength."

Pragmatic prick, Killian thought, despite having known Quindor would say as much.

Quindor moved his hands from the horse's neck to her chest, pausing there. "Strange," he muttered before shifting so his hands hovered over one of the pulsing veins of black running up the animal's shoulder. "Dead."

Malahi turned her head to meet Killian's eyes. She'd said almost exactly the same thing when she'd tried and failed to drive the blight back.

"Utterly devoid of life." The Grand Master's hands flexed, still hovering above the blight. "I've never seen anything like it. Not from poison or infection. Not from frostbite or burns. This . . . this never lived."

"Obviously that's not the case," Malahi pressed. "Can she be healed?"

Quindor didn't answer, but his reluctance was palpable. Sweat broke out on Killian's back, all of his instincts screaming a warning, but they had to know if the blight could be fought.

Taking a deep breath, the Grand Master of Hegeria's temple pressed one hand against the flow of black.

Time seemed to freeze even as panic rose on the man's face. Killian lunged, catching hold of the healer's shoulders and jerking him away from the horse, the force of the motion sending them both sprawling.

Clambering upright, Quindor clutched his hand to his chest. "This is an abomination sent by the Seventh!"

"She's just a sick horse!" Malahi said, resisting Killian's attempts to move her a safe distance away.

"Not anymore." The Grand Master eyed the dying animal like she was a venomous snake. "Kill it. Burn the body. The last thing we need is some fool thinking the meat can be salvaged."

Killian extracted a knife, pushing Malahi out the door to the stall. "She's my horse," the Princess snapped. "It was my mistake that caused this, so I'll put her down myself."

"Admirable sentiment, my lady," Quindor said. "But better that Lord Calorian do it. We don't know for certain yet how the blight infects and we dare not risk your life. Not with a knife, Lord Calorian. It is in the horse's blood, and the last thing we need is the entire stables contaminated."

Killian waited until Quindor had led Malahi from the stall;

then he moved to the horse's head. The veins of blight had already risen up her neck, reaching like grasping fingers toward her head. The mare's breath was coming in great ragged gasps, her brown eyes fixed on him.

He'd had to put animals down before when they were injured beyond hope of recovery, but it had never gotten easier for him. Just as he'd never gotten used to the way they watched him as he did it. The way they always seemed to *know*.

"I'm sorry," he murmured, taking hold of her chin and drawing her head back, bracing one foot against the base of her skull. "You deserved better."

Then a shadow passed over the mare's eyes, and what was looking back at him was no longer a horse. She started to move, lips pulling back to reveal her teeth. Killian's instincts kicked in even as his mind recoiled, and a loud crack filled his ears as he broke the creature's neck.

38

LYDIA

Lydia had spent one of the duller days of her life outside the door to Malahi's suite, the Princess having remained closeted in her rooms, apparently distressed over the death of her horse. Lydia heard from the other girls some of what had happened, that the animal had been infected with blight and had been put down. As she'd been exposed to the black sludge herself, the story had made Lydia shiver, knowing in her heart that if she hadn't been marked she might well have suffered the same fate.

Her back and feet ached from standing, but worse than that, the idleness had given her far too much time to think about her lesson with Killian. Instead of sleeping, she'd crouched over the book for the better part of the night, drinking in the diagrams and explanations of style and form until her candle flickered out. Throughout the day, she'd been practicing the forms every time she visited the privy, and her daydreams evolved with each passing hour until she was certain Killian would be stunned by her natural skill with a blade.

Now she stood outside the gates to High Lord Calorian's manor watching the dying sun, wondering if all her daydreams were better classified as wishful thinking. Killian had not spoken a single word to her all day, standing outside the Princess's bedchamber with crossed arms and a face like a thundercloud. Given the events that had transpired, Lydia was not so self-involved as to believe his fell temper had anything to do with her, but she was beginning to wonder if he'd found another activity to relieve his mood.

Just as it was growing dark enough that she'd need to sprint back to the barracks to beat the arrival of the deimos, a tall shadow materialized up the street. Saying nothing, Killian boosted Lydia up so she could reach the top of the wall, pushing on her feet until she was able to scramble over.

"We've only got a few hours," he said, dropping next to her on the far side. "There are other matters requiring my attention."

Curbing what was an unjust sense of disappointment, she followed him into the manor.

He led her once more to the ballroom, and after helping him light a handful of lamps she carefully extracted her sword and assumed the stance the book diagrams had detailed.

Killian looked her up and down, then said, "Well, I suppose that explains the length of your breaks today. Lena was quite certain last night's stew had not agreed with you."

She gaped at him, her face burning hot.

"The first thing we need to work on is that draw of yours. It will signal to any attacker you come across that you haven't the first idea of how to use that weapon. Which isn't ideal."

Her whole body felt like it was being consumed by the flames of embarrassment.

Pulling off his coat and gloves, Killian tossed them to one side of the room before returning to the center. "This," he said, "is how you draw a sword." He proceeded to extract his blade with both speed and flourish.

Lydia eyed him dubiously, wondering if traveling this path was more likely to get her killed by accident than see her to Serlania. "What good is knowing how to pull it out if I haven't any idea how to use it?"

He started to grin and she scowled at him. "Keep your jokes to yourself and answer the question."

"It's a bluff," he replied, the corners of his mouth twitching with unspent laughter. "Like when you play cards."

"I don't gamble." She instantly regretted the admission as he lifted one eyebrow in horrified disbelief.

"How can you be friends with Teriana if you don't gamble? The girl could fleece one of the Six in a game of cards."

Teriana had taught her a few games, but unlike her friend, Lydia took no pleasure from risking her coin. Besides, Teriana always won. "We do other things."

"Fair enough. But you *do* understand the premise of a bluff?" She nodded.

"Good. Your draw, then, is your bluff. If you do it with enough skill, you can trick your opponent into believing you have the hand to back it up." He waited for her to nod again before continuing. "If your opponent has a bad hand and believes your bluff, they fold and you win."

"And if they have a good hand?" she asked, sticking with his stupid analogy. "What if they call my bluff? What do you propose I do then?"

"We'll get to that part. Now why don't you give it a go."

Lydia took hold of the sword and heaved. Instead of the cruel snick of metal Killian's blade made when he drew it, hers made a grinding noise, then stuck, the bottom of her scabbard flipping up. "Blast it," she muttered, her belt riding high. She adjusted it, trying to regain her composure and hoping he'd mistake the flush on her cheeks for exertion. When she finally looked up, all the humor was gone from his expression, and for the first time she saw a hint of doubt in his eyes.

He shook his head once, then nudged her into the center of the room. "Try it again."

She managed to get the blade out this time, but the sound of the metal grinding against the scabbard set her already-frazzled nerves on edge.

"Again."

The results were the same. "I think the scabbard is too snug—" Before she could finish, he reached over and tugged her sword out with the same ease as his own. He lifted one eyebrow, then shoved the blade back in. "Again."

"Perhaps rather than mocking me, you might provide some semblance of instruction," Lydia said between clenched teeth.

"Widen your stance. Bend your knees. Hold it like this." He held out his own sword to demonstrate but shook his head when Lydia tried to replicate the position. "That's not right. And quit squeezing so hard; your knuckles are whiter than a corpse's. It will give you away to anyone who knows their business."

Frustrated, Lydia snapped, "Just fix my hand for me then."

"Fine." Gripping her by the shoulders, he spun her in a circle so that her back was to him. Prying her clenched fingers off the hilt of the sword, he adjusted her grip, his breath warm on the nape of her neck. "Relax."

As if such a thing were possible.

"May I adjust the rest of you?"

Lydia nodded, her heart a thundering drum in her chest.

His hands moved over her body, gently but firmly, adjusting her posture, the toe of his boot knocking at her ankles until she widened her stance. "Like so," he said. Then he closed his hand over hers, warm fingers concealing hers entirely. "Breathe."

She sucked in a breath.

"Once more."

She inhaled and he moved, guiding her arm and the blade with a speed and grace she hadn't believed her body possessed. The steel glinted in the lamplight, and as she stared down the empty room she felt like she could fight anyone or anything that came at her. She was powerful. Capable. Fearless.

Then Killian let go of her hand and the tip of her blade wavered, the feeling vanishing. He came around in front of her, for once his expression unreadable. "Now do it again."

She shook her head. "What was that?"

He looked away, jaw working back and forth. "It's the reason I'm not a very good teacher."

"Because you're marked." She eyed him, wondering what it would be like to walk through life with such a sense of invincibility. It certainly explained his penchant for risk taking. And his ego. She'd read a great deal on god marks in *Treatise of the Seven*, but the god of war's mark was an elusive thing, much of it impossible to distinguish from natural talent.

Those marked were stronger, faster, able to sense what their enemy or opponent intended. They easily mastered all forms of fighting, had a mind for strategy, a gift for leadership. Above all, they were brave.

"Do you ever wonder how much of it is the mark and how much of it is you?" she asked.

The way his shoulders stiffened told her that he had. "The mark gives me aptitude," he said. "But I still had to study and learn and train every day for years to master these skills. And I decide what to do with them."

"Still—"

"Never mind my mark," he interrupted. "I'm not going to spend my days holding your hand to lend you competence, so best you start practicing. Now do it again."

He had her repeat her draw over and over until she was drenched with sweat, her muscles screaming from the un-accustomed exertion. "Set aside your spectacles for the next part," he said. "I'm not sure there's a lens maker left in Mudaire, so we shouldn't risk them unnecessarily."

It only went downhill from there. He chased her around the room, barking orders and battering at her sword, hands, wrists, and arms, until she was too flustered to remember anything she'd read, all of it exacerbated by the deimos circling and screaming above, which he barely seemed to notice.

"Move your feet," he snapped, and she shuffled sideways, trying to parry while not tripping over her own boots. "Not like that. Pick them up!" He scrubbed a hand through his hair, clearly as frustrated as she was.

She looked at her feet, trying to will them into behaving, and his padded sword caught her across the forearm. "By the Six, how are you planning to block a blow staring at the floor?"

"How am I supposed to do anything with you yelling at me?" she retorted. "I'm only trying to do what your stupid books said to do."

"I told you you couldn't learn how to fight from a book. And you're doing a fine job proving it."

She blinked furiously. She did not cry. Not ever. And she refused to debase herself by doing so in front of him. Instead, she let her anger take hold, and with one violent motion she flung the blade end-over-end across the room, where it thudded against the wall.

Killian eyed the shadows where it had landed. "Out of curiosity, will you be allowed to carry a sword when you return to Celendor?"

A vision of her gliding into a dinner party in a silk dress and high heels with a sword belted around her waist floated up in her imagination, and an involuntary laugh tore from her lips. "No."

"Knives?"

"It would be frowned upon."

"Never mind frowns. If Malahi can hide two blades up her skirts, then so can you."

Lydia bit the insides of her cheeks, wondering how he knew that particular piece of information.

"I think it best we move on to the weapons you'll always have with you."

Without further explanation, he dropped his blade and swung at her with his fist.

Lydia dodged, feeling his fist brush against one of her braids.

Killian laughed. "I knew those instincts were in there."

"You just tried to hit me!" She stared at him in indignation.

"Your point?"

There was a gleam in his eye that suggested he knew exactly what her point was but fully intended on making her say it. "A gentleman should *not* hit a woman."

"Which liar told you I was a gentleman?"

She gave him a flat stare.

"Fine, fine," he said, circling her. "What about in such instances where the woman has requested said gentleman teach her how to fight?"

"Surely you can teach the mechanics without trying to blacken my eyes."

"That's about as good as you trying to learn from a diagram in a book."

Lydia bit the insides of her cheeks, annoyed, though she wasn't sure whether she was annoyed with him or with herself. "I don't want it to hurt."

"Fighting hurts. Part of learning to fight means learning to deal with just how much it can hurt." He rocked on his heels, brown eyes fixed on hers. "So what will it be, Lydia? Do you want to be a *lady* who needs someone like me to watch her back, or do you want to be a *lady* who can take care of herself?"

She glared at him. "You know the answer."

Killian gave a slow nod suggesting that he *had* known but had also hoped she might change her mind. "If it's what you want."

"It is."

"So be it. Now get your hands up in front of you to protect yourself and try to hit me."

A slight thrum of fear filled her stomach, because she'd been struck before. By Vibius. By Lucius. By the women who'd attacked her in the shelter. Lydia was not keen to experience that sort of pain again. But as much as she was afraid of the pain, she was more terrified of the helplessness she'd felt in those moments. And because she never wanted to feel that way again, Lydia took a deep breath and swung wildly with her fist.

Killian blocked the blow, then caught her with his own just below the ribs. Lydia stumbled, gasping for air, because it *hurt*. But her blood was racing, and she found the pain didn't make her want to cower. It made her want to *fight*. So she attacked again.

They fought in earnest and in near silence. It was a lesson, but it was taught with actions, not words. With the reward of a blow landed. The pain of a missed block. He was stronger. Infinitely more skilled. But more than she'd realized, her mark had put power behind her fists. Made her faster. And the bruises he inflicted faded in an instant, the pain fleeting and inconsequential. It made her feel invincible.

You won't have these advantages when you go back. You'll just be yourself. Weak.

The thought stole her focus, and Killian took advantage, hooking her leg out from under her so that she fell, the impact rattling her teeth. She didn't struggle as he pinned her wrists, the fight gone out of her.

"You all right?" A drop of blood from a cut on his brow dripped onto her face, and she twitched.

"Sorry." He let go of her wrist, wiping the blood away with his finger. Then he paused. "See if you can stop yourself from healing me."

"Am I *that* terrible a fighter?" Lydia tried to keep her voice light, but her stomach clenched at the thought Killian might be reconsidering their arrangement.

His face remained serious. "We both know that the sooner you can get away from Mudaire, the better. Might as well use what chances you have to practice controlling your mark."

He was right. Yet her arm still trembled as she reached up to cup his cheek, the tips of her fingers touching the injury. Immediately she could feel the pull, the insistent tug against her core, but she bit down on the insides of her cheeks and resisted.

Except her attention wavered from the injury to Killian's eyes, which regarded her steadily. The lamplight flickered off them, illuminating the shades of umber and walnut and bronze, like polished tiger's-eye stone, but warmer. Lydia was quite certain she'd never seen eyes like his, although perhaps it was only that she'd never been this close to someone. Never been so captivated—

Her mark jerked free of her control, life flowing from her into him, and the cut sealed into a faint white line, the swelling around his other eye fading into nothingness.

"Perhaps you're not the best test subject," she mumbled, embarrassed about losing her concentration.

"Why is that?"

"Because . . ." She trailed off, keenly aware of the warmth

of his body over hers. The roughness of his cheek against her palm. The raggedness of her breath, and the way his shirt strained against the muscles of his shoulders.

He didn't let her go.

She didn't want him to.

The hand still holding her other wrist loosened, turning to catch hers, their fingers interlocking. Heat flushed through her, and she didn't know what to do with it. She'd never been kissed. Never been touched. Had never met anyone she wanted to touch her. Until now.

He's sworn to the Princess for life. He belongs to Malahi. The thought slapped her in the face, and she squirmed out from under him. "It's late." Late and she needed to sleep and the last thing she should be thinking about was a young nobleman who was far too attractive for his own good. Her mind needed to be focused on getting back to Celendor. On Teriana. On her father. On making Lucius pay for what he'd done. Not on kissing.

Killian was on his feet with enough speed that she strongly suspected he'd allowed every punch she'd landed. Reaching down, he pulled her up before dropping her hand as though it had burned him. While she donned her spectacles, he circled the room retrieving his coat, gloves, and several of the buttons that had torn from his shirt while they were fighting. "Let's go. I'll show you the route back to the barracks."

The sun had set hours ago, but even though the shrieks of the deimos echoed through the night sky, Killian showed no concern. Keeping close to the wall of the property, he trotted along, stopping when they reached the corner. "This is the fun part," he said. "Up and over, then down into the sewer on the other side of the street. Grate's open."

He eyed the starry sky, absently linking his fingers. "Go."

Heart hammering, Lydia placed a boot into his hands, and then he was lifting her. Her fingers found the edge of the wall, and she slung her legs over right as the deimos screamed. Fear ricocheted through her body, and she dropped down the other side with no concern for the distance, twisting as her boots hit and then sprinting across the street. The dull metal of the grate beckoned her, and she fell to her bottom, grasping hold of the edge and lowering herself into the darkness.

She was suspended by her elbows when she heard the thud of Killian landing on the ground, followed immediately by the clatter of hooves. Swiveling her head, she saw the deimos galloping up the street toward them.

"Move!"

She leapt into the sewer, stumbling out of the way as something heavy slid across the paving stones. Then Killian dropped into view, landing with both feet on the other side of the sludge running down the middle of the sewer.

He was laughing.

The deimos pawed the ground overtop of them, teeth snapping at the opening. "Try again on the other end," he shouted at the creature, then caught Lydia's hand, leading her out of the pool of moonlight and into the blackness.

"The system runs through the entire city and empties into the sea," he said, stooping to pick up a lamp that inexplicably waited for them. "I can get almost anywhere I wish to go as long as I plan ahead and make sure the grates aren't rusted shut. It's a bit on the filthy side of things, but at least the rats are no longer a problem."

Her stomach turned at the reason for *that,* but of more interest was the feel of his hand gripping hers. *You're an idiot,* she told herself. *He's only helping you because he thinks you can't take care of yourself.* Yet for all her admonitions, it was still a struggle to pull her fingers from his grasp.

It didn't take them long to reach the sewer grate closest to the barracks, Killian pushing it open, then peering at the sky before scrambling out. Sword in hand, he reached down to pull her up, keeping to the shadows of the buildings as he led her to the familiar blue door.

"Are you going back to the palace?" she asked.

"Eventually." He pushed open the door. "Good night, Lydia." Then without another word, he retreated the way they'd come.

Eventually? Where could he possibly be going?

She stood in the front entrance for several long moments, knowing she should go up to bed. Knowing it wasn't any business of hers what he spent his evenings doing. Knowing it was utter lunacy to tempt the dangers of the night just to satisfy her curiosity.

And yet she found herself easing open the door just in time to see him dropping into the sewers.

Where is he going?

Knowing if she thought about it she'd talk herself out of it, Lydia scampered down the street and eased herself into the hole, dangling from her elbows for a moment before letting herself drop. Her feet landed on either side of a stream of filth, but though she looked both ways, there was no sign of Killian. She allowed her eyes go out of focus so that she could see the drifting streams of life that she usually ignored.

It seeped off every living creature, and even without light she was able to follow the trail he left in his wake. She meandered through the sewers with no sense of direction, no idea what lay above her or how she'd find her way back. Before long, the sound of voices reached her, bouncing off the slimy walls and beckoning her closer.

"What's this?" The voice was familiar, and after a moment she placed it as Finn's.

"Pineapple." Killian's voice. "No, don't eat the skin."

Curious, Lydia edged around the bend until she saw them. They stood next to a hand-drawn cart full of foods of all sorts. Finn had a piece of yellow fruit in his hand, the juices dribbling down his chin. "That's good."

"Don't get too attached. I'm not sure another shipment is forthcoming."

"Trouble with supply?"

"That's my problem, not yours. Let's go."

Lydia trailed after them, and it wasn't long until more voices filled the tunnels. Children's voices. Then all of a sudden they were coming from every direction. She ducked into a small side tunnel before dozens of ragged and filthy children passed, some leading younger siblings by the hand. They converged on the cart, and Killian and Finn doled out the food. Fruits and vegetables. Salted meat. Sacks of oats. Sweets. And from Killian's pockets she heard the clink of coins, bits of copper pressed into grubby hands that tucked it away in pockets and waistbands.

Then they all disappeared as swiftly as they'd arrived, leaving the two alone with an empty cart. "Can you make the delivery yourself tomorrow?" Killian asked.

Finn scuffed his worn boots against the stone. "It gets out of hand when you aren't here. The strongest children take from the weakest without you watching over the process, if you get my meaning."

"The Seventh at our doorstep and I'm playing gods-damned nursemaid." Killian scrubbed a hand through his hair. "Fine. Same time tomorrow, then. I need to get back to the palace."

Lydia retreated into the tunnels before he could catch sight of her, so focused on finding her route that she didn't see the children until she was upon them.

They'd created a nest of ratty blankets and sacking, their eyes gleaming in the light of the single candle burning in their midst. They scampered away at the sight of her, her age making her a threat in this strange world ruled by orphans.

"I won't hurt you," she called after them, but none stopped.

Sighing, she started to move on when the sound of coughing caught her attention. Buried in the mess of rotten fabric, she found a little boy, the glow of life about him so faint that she wouldn't have noticed him but for his cough.

He was dying.

Her body moved almost of its own accord. There was no doubt in her mind of what she needed to do. Dropping to her knees, she touched a hand to the boy's clammy forehead and dragged life out of herself, forcing it into him. Her heart fluttered as she watched the skin on her hand wrinkle and mottle, but the child's breathing steadied and his cheeks flushed with health.

A shoe scraped on the stone behind her, and a child's voice said, "You're a healer."

Lydia stumbled to her feet, jerking her hood forward to obscure her face. "No, I'm . . ." The children who had fled stood before her, their faces pale, many with crusted eyes and injuries bound with dirty rags. But their expressions were full of hope.

This was precisely what she'd been hiding from—being forced to heal others over and over, her life stripped away to save the casualties of war. Helping them could kill her. Would kill her if she kept it up. Except if she didn't, how many would die? And how could she live with the knowledge that she could've saved some but had chosen not to? She imagined explaining her choice to Teriana. Imagined her friend's expression when she heard Lydia had left children to die so as not to jeopardize her own fate. Already she could see the condemnation.

Taking a deep breath, she said, "I can't help everyone tonight. But I'll help those who need it most."

39

KILLIAN

He pushed the cart through the darkened sewers, moving between the circles of moonlight shining through the regularly spaced sewer grates. The recent rains had washed away much of the filth, but it had come at a cost. The damp made the place a breeding ground for disease, and he hadn't missed the endless coughing of the children waiting for their rations.

Yet another problem in a sea of problems.

He and Quindor had agreed that the progress of the blight needed to be tracked, for if it reached the city, hunger would rapidly become the least of Mudaire's concerns. Quindor would undertake the task of warning the people of the dangers of the blight, while Killian would assign some of the few remaining men in the city guard to monitor the spread. What they could do to stop it was another problem. Trenches. Dams. All things that required manpower, which would mean employing civilians to do the labor. And the last thing Killian wanted was them near the foul substance.

Ideally, he'd track down the source, but even if he wasn't under strict orders by the King to remain in close proximity to the city, leaving Malahi alone for that length of time wasn't a risk he was willing to take. It was something the King should've had the tenders addressing, but he claimed they were too strapped with the task of growing food to feed the army. Though perhaps he might change his mind on that count once he received Quindor's and Malahi's letters on the subject of the horse.

Reaching the open grate near the palace wall, Killian pushed the cart into a dark side chamber for later use and then went to stand in the pool of moonlight, digging into his coat pocket to retrieve the delicate roll of paper he'd received just prior to departing the palace to meet Lydia.

Lydia. He stared up at the moon overhead, barely seeing it. Time and again, he'd lost his train of thought when those up-turned green eyes fixed upon him, and whenever she spoke the low, lilting tone of her voice drowned out the shrieks of the deimos. Even sweating and red-faced, she was pretty. More than pretty, if he was being honest with himself—

"You are an idiot, Killian," he told himself, shoving away *those* particular thoughts. "A gods-damned idiot. What are you even doing?"

Because *preparing her* wasn't the whole truth. Yes, she needed to be able to protect herself while watching over Malahi. And yes, she needed to be able to hold her own against those who'd wish her harm once she'd returned to Celendor. Not only did Teriana and the rest of the Maarin depend on it; his gut told him the stakes were even higher than that. But he could've asked Bercola to teach her—she was a better, more patient instructor than him. Yet the thought hadn't even crossed his mind, not when teaching Lydia to fight would give him the opportunity to spend more time with her himself.

"Idiot," he repeated, but the admonition did nothing to temper the sudden wave of bitterness that passed over him. He'd never taken up with a girl—it had never felt like the right thing to do, not when he had so little control over his own future. He'd been deployed throughout the kingdom, never knowing where or when he'd be moved next. His life was spent in army camps or fortresses or sleeping in the dirt, never with any respite. And now . . . Now he was sworn to Malahi for *life*. His whole reason for being was to keep her safe, and what girl in her right mind would be content with always playing second fiddle to the Princess?

"Lydia's leaving anyway," he muttered. "So get your head on straight and focus on your damned duties."

Lifting the paper he still held in his hand, Killian scanned the note, which was from his mother.

Killian,

Seldrid has conveyed to me your deep distress over the plight of the orphans of Mudaire. While your brothers and their fellows seem of the belief that the navy ships sitting in our docks cannot be adequately crewed, Adra and I suffer from no such limited thinking. Three naval vessels will depart for Mudaire, albeit a day after Hacken leaves for Her Highness's ball. One of them will be under strict instruction to take aboard all of your young charges, and I will personally take control of ensuring their welfare once they arrive.

Mother

The image of his mother in one of her fancy gowns waving at Hacken as he sailed north only to turn around, commandeer three royal ships, and crew them with women filled his mind, and Killian smiled. Then he squinted at the note, picking out the hidden message. He'd struggled with learning codes when he was young, and it had been his mother who'd instructed him for hours until he'd grown fluent in their use.

Watch your rear.

His first reaction was to flinch at the reference to his defeat at the wall, but that passed as he considered the warning. An attack that she didn't believe he'd anticipate. Trickery. But too bloody vague for him to do anything about.

Bad news all around, for though he now had a way to get Finn's orphans out of Mudaire, he wasn't certain they'd last that long. Food he might be able to scrounge up, but if plague struck there was nothing he'd be able to do to save them. The ships his mother was sending would sail back next to empty.

The sound of footfalls echoed through the tunnel, snatching him away from his thoughts. Someone was running this way.

"Lord Calorian! Lord Calorian! Wait!"

Finn's voice.

The boy careened around the corner, nearly colliding with Killian. "What's wrong?"

"It's the girl!" Finn's eyes were wide with panic. "Your new girl. I think she's dead!"

40

LYDIA

"You insane, idiot, fool of a girl." Killian's voice sounded distant, but fabric pressed against her cheek, her nose full of the familiar scent of soap and steel. She felt strong arms holding her close.

"Can't breathe," she whispered, her chest aching as her heart skipped and faltered.

"Hold on." His breath came in fast little pants. *He is running,* she realized. *Carrying me and running.*

And she couldn't hold on. She was fading, the few remaining wisps of life drifting away no matter how hard she clung to them.

"Almost there, almost there." There was desperation in his voice. "Hold on."

Everything went black.

And then she could feel it. Could feel life flowing into her, coating her skin, filling her lungs. Her eyes fluttered open, revealing mist flooding down from above, the air thick with it.

Her heart steadied, and in the moonlight filtering through the grate she watched a loose lock of her hair change slowly from white to black.

Killian's breathing was ragged. He was on his knees, one arm under her legs and the other around her shoulders, his grip hard enough to bruise. Slowly turning, she looked up at him. "Where are we?"

"As close as I could get to one of the shelters." His face was concealed by shadows. "There are hundreds of people above us."

"I know," she whispered. "I can feel them."

"On the battlefield," he said, "when a healer does too much, we drag them out among the healthy and uninjured men and it usually brings them back from the edge."

From the edge of death. Lydia pulled her ring out from beneath her shirt, gripping it tight and trying not to think of how close she'd come to losing her everything.

"Are you feeling stronger?"

She nodded, then wished she hadn't when he eased her onto the dry side of the tunnel, the comfort she'd felt in his arms falling away, leaving her cold.

"What were you doing in the sewers?"

She swallowed, her throat dry. "I followed you, and after . . . When I was finding my way out, I came across a sick boy and his friends. I . . . I couldn't leave them like that."

Killian shifted his weight, the moonlight falling across his jaw and cheek, and Lydia felt the urge to reach up and touch him, to feel his skin beneath her fingers. To—

"You put both of us at risk," he said, interrupting her thoughts. "By now, all the hundreds of children down here will know there was a healer here tonight." The muscles in his jaw clenched. "You aren't trained, Lydia. You don't know how much healing a particular injury will take out of you, and if Finn hadn't recognized you and run to find me, you might have—"

"And you aren't taking a risk every time you bring food to them?" She sat up straight. "Those deimos are watching for *you.* They're hunting *you.*"

He shrugged. "The children don't have anyone looking out for them. What does it matter if I'm risking my life if it will save hundreds? It's what I'm for."

She frowned. "You're marked to fight. For war."

"No, I'm marked to *protect.* The rest is just a consequence."

"To protect Malahi."

"It's not that simple." He scrubbed his hand through his hair. "At least, it isn't for me. It's like a compulsion. . . . I can't *not* do it."

A deep understand of *exactly* what he meant filled her. The desire to help those suffering around her had been growing and growing, the sick children finally overwhelming her fear of using her mark. The fear of the *consequences* of using her mark.

"If you get caught," Killian said, "you won't get back to Celendor to set things right. Your father, Teriana, the rest of the Maarin? Is risking them worth saving a handful of lives?"

It felt like she was being torn in two. Like there was no choice that wouldn't cost her. "My father . . . my father is likely already dead." Saying the words made her chest tight, like she could scarcely breathe. "And Teriana will never forgive me if she learns that I could've saved the lives of children but didn't for fear of risking her."

"If it was just her life, I'd agree. But the stakes are much larger than that. You need to get back."

He was right. She knew he was right. But she didn't think she could live with herself if she stood by and did nothing. Nearly all her life she'd hidden alone in the library while the world passed by, doing nothing to right the wrongs she saw but chose to ignore. She refused to go back to being that girl. She refused to go down without a fight. "Why can't I do both? Why can't I help those who need it right up until the moment I board the ship to Serlania? It would give them a fighting chance of surviving."

"Because you risk being caught. You risk *dying* if you make a mistake."

"I'm not worried about being caught. Or of dying." She grinned, feeling the rightness of the moment. "Because I'll have you to watch my back."

41

KILLIAN

"You can't wear what you're wearing," Killian muttered, rooting through the wardrobe. "The last thing we need is anyone figuring out who you are."

Lydia stood a pace behind him, holding up the lamp. "Whose clothes are these?"

"Adra's, I think." He pulled out a bright pink gown trimmed with gold. "Definitely hers. She's married to my middle brother, Seldrid, but she's Gamdeshian—niece to the Sultan. Which is why her closet looks like a gods-damned rainbow."

Slamming the wardrobe shut, he motioned for Lydia to follow him out of the room, trying not to notice the faint smell of scented soap that hung in the air around her. As he'd been trying to ignore it all evening. How she managed to smell so clean after an entire day of work plus two hours of training was a mystery to him.

"You didn't spend much time here growing up, did you?"

There was something about Lydia's voice that he liked. A purposefulness that suggested she only spoke when she had something to say. Or, more often, there was something she wanted to know.

"Why do you say that?"

"You don't treat it like home."

"I don't really have a home. I've never spent more than six months in the same place since I was a child." Stopping outside a pair of doors, he rested his hands on the knobs, reluctant to open them. "Though I suppose if I had to name a place, it would be Teradale."

"Where is that?"

"On the southern coast, about a dozen leagues north of Serlania." He scowled at the doors, annoyed at his own reluctance to go inside. "It's my family's estate and where our horse-breeding farm is located. My mother lives there, and it's where I lived until I was seven."

Turning the knobs, Killian shoved open the doors and stepped inside.

The drapes in his parents' rooms were drawn, Lydia's lamp casting shadows over the heavy furniture and thick carpets, the air stale after months of being left undisturbed. He'd expected to feel echoes of his father's presence. But the room only felt empty. Lifeless.

Going into the adjoining chamber, Killian opened up the long series of doors to reveal his mother's garments. "After this, I'm hoping that squatters take over this house," he said, "because otherwise she'll *know* I was in her things." He shook his head. "She'll know I was in here even if I don't touch a damn thing."

Lydia stepped forward, her elbow brushing against his sleeve as she ran her finger along the hanging dresses. "I don't remember my mother." Her hand paused on a velvet gown, rubbing the fabric between her fingers before moving on. "She was murdered. My father found her dead outside the gates to his home with me in her arms."

"I'm sorry."

She gave the slightest shake of her head. "I was two, so I have no memory of the event. And who my real father was is of equal mystery."

Her fingers paused on a white wool cloak that Killian had never known his mother to wear, she being fond of darker colors. Reaching up, he unhooked it from the hanger, draping it over Lydia's shoulders. It had a deep hood trimmed with ermine, the buttons running up the chest polished silver disks. It sparked a memory, and he pulled open drawers of accessories until he found what he was looking for.

Extracting the mask, he held it up. "You won't be able to

wear your spectacles, but this should solve the problem of anyone recognizing you."

Lydia's brow furrowed; then she nodded. "Everything I need to see will be up close, so I should be fine. Will you put it on for me?"

Pulling off her spectacles, she tucked them in the pocket of the cloak and turned her back to him. With her holding the mask in place, Killian looped the laces behind her head, her hair like silk beneath his fingers. This close, the scent of her was strong in his nose, making him fumble tying the knot. "Please don't tell me you're spending coin on special soap."

Why in the name of all the gods did you just say that?

"I haven't." Turning her head, she looked up at him, and even with the top half of her face concealed by white satin and sparkling crystals, she was more beautiful than he felt comfortable admitting about a subordinate. "I use the same soap as the other girls."

"Oh." His face felt like it was on fire. "You smell different, is all."

She bit her bottom lip and looked down at his boots. "Well, I haven't had the opportunity to bathe since before dawn."

"No, it's nice. You smell nice."

Nice?

Grinding his teeth, Killian mentally berated himself for saying anything at all. "Most soldiers aren't particularly fastidious about bathing, is all. Can get hard on the nose. Now let's go. We've wasted enough time raiding my mother's closet."

Outside, the deimos were circling overhead, waiting for them to exit, but he'd brought his bow with him this time, and as he walked out of the shadows the creatures took one look at him and flapped their wings, soaring out of easy range. Arrow nocked, he shadowed Lydia as they walked over to the grate, waiting until she was in the tunnel before jumping down himself.

"I told Finn to have those who need to see a healer organized beneath one of the shelters," he said, leading her through the tunnels. "But you need to be cautious. We don't need to repeat what happened last night."

She nodded, the crystals on her mask glittering as they passed beneath a grate. "I wish there was a book I could read on the subject."

"You and your books." He held out his hand, helping her over a pile of debris. "The temple here in Mudaire has a library, so there are undoubtedly books on the subject given it's where Mudamora's healers are trained."

"I know it's not possible, but I would love to see it." Her voice was wistful. "It's what I miss most about home."

Killian was not inclined toward books, primarily because he was not inclined toward sitting still. "How did you meet Teriana if you spent all your time in a library? I can't say I've ever known her to lose herself in the stacks."

"You'd be surprised. A good many of my favorite linguistic texts came courtesy of her. She speaks every language on Reath, and her grammar is impeccable." Lydia hopped over a puddle of filth. "But as to your question, we met when her mother was negotiating the latest iteration of the agreement between the Maarin and the Empire. One of the senators involved overestimated his proficiency with Trader's Tongue— that's what Mudamorian is called back east—and Teriana and I bonded over the humor of it all."

"You lost me at *favorite linguistic texts.*"

She laughed, the sound filling his head and drowning out everything else. *You are her senior officer,* he reminded himself. *You are helping her out of obligation. Your loyalty is to Malahi.* But the logic spun away as she stepped into another pool of moonlight, looking for all the world like some mystical princess of the icy north.

"Sparkly!"

Killian jumped, sword half-drawn as he whirled around to find Finn standing behind him, hands held up in mock defense.

"I don't believe I've ever gotten the jump on you before, Lord Calorian."

"Don't get used to it," Killian growled, shoving his sword back into its sheath. Finn's eyes were gleaming with amusement in the light of the candle he held. *What?*

"Nothing," the boy said, laughing. "I didn't say a thing." Dodging around Killian, he made his way to Lydia, pulling up her hood so that it shadowed her face. "No more use of names, all right? I've started a few rumors about who is coming to do the healing tonight, and I'd hate for my hard work to be for nothing."

Even with her face concealed, Killian could sense Lydia's frown as she asked, "Who do they believe is coming?"

"Hegeria herself."

Before Lydia could respond, Finn trotted off. "This way."

They followed the boy, Lydia's unease palpable. "I don't even know what I'm doing," she murmured. "They'll know I'm not her."

"That doesn't matter." Killian understood the pressure she was feeling. The pressure to be infallible. To be perfect. "All that matters is that they don't know it's you."

He could feel that his words had done nothing to ease her concern, so he kept talking. "There will be many of them. More than you can possibly help in one night. How do you want to prioritize them?"

"I'll be able to tell who is the worst off," she answered. "We'll prioritize those."

"There still may be more than you can help in one night. Pulling someone back from death's door is no small thing. Even for you."

Her hooded head turned toward him. "What do you mean, *even for me?*"

You're stronger than most. Exhaling, he considered his words. "I've been near death several times in my life. Because I'm marked, it has usually taken two, sometimes three healers to set me to rights. You did it yourself, and I don't even have a scar to show for it."

Ahead, Finn turned his head sideways, clearly listening, but there was no helping it. Not in the tunnels. And as it was, there wasn't a person in Mudaire other than Bercola whom Killian trusted more than the boy.

"I've seen healers working in army camps more times than I care to count," Killian continued. "They don't heal every last scrape and bruise; their efforts are more . . . targeted." Frowning, he considered his own experiences. "I couldn't tell you how they do it, but they can focus their marks on the worst of the injuries. Sometimes they'll only take the edge off. Stop the bleeding and then stitch and bandage or do whatever needs to be done. It allows them to save more lives."

Except he also knew Serrick wasn't allowing the healers discretion in this. He was forcing them to heal the soldiers enough that they could fight. Healers were burning out and dying in unprecedented numbers, and it wasn't sustainable.

"Do they study how to do all this?" she asked. "At the temple?"

"Yes. It's a school of sorts, I suppose. There's a similar institution in Revat, though the healers in Gamdesh have choice in whether or not they wish to attend."

Killian didn't have a chance to say more on the subject. The quiet chatter of children's voices reached his ears, growing until he and Lydia rounded a bend and encountered the group waiting for them. It was the same spot he'd brought her the prior night, almost beneath one of the shelters, and he didn't miss the way Lydia cast her gaze upward before focusing on the children.

Many rested on the sewer floor, coughing or still, brought by their friends and siblings in the hope they might be saved. And there were so many. Dozens and dozens, and it made him feel sick, because he knew their faces. Remembered when they'd been strong and healthy. When they'd had hope.

She is their hope.

Lydia stepped away from him, moving among the children, many of them reaching up to touch the hem of her cloak, whispering Hegeria's name. The handful of candles made the crystals on her mask sparkle, her skin nearly the same shade as the satin, full lips a pale pink. She bent from time to time, touching foreheads and whispering words, every eye fixed upon her. With every moment, Finn's story that it was Hegeria visiting the tunnels seemed more like the truth.

Finally, she turned, gesturing to Killian. "This girl first," she said. "Then this boy."

Picking his way through the children, he bent to pick up the girl, his chest tightening at the sight of her familiar face. She was the one he'd given his cuff link to. The one he'd promised to protect.

One of many people he'd failed.

Resting her on the floor a short distance from the group, Killian moved back to give Lydia space to work. The girl stirred, her breathing labored, face colorless, and Lydia pulled down the collar of her ratty dress, pressing her palm against the child's chest.

Though Killian had seen healers at work hundreds of times, it was as astonishing now as it had been the first time. The girl's breathing steadied, losing the wet rasp, and her skin lost the waxy tone of near death. Her eyelids fluttered and opened, and she jerked in alarm.

Killian dropped to his knees next to her, holding the candle up to illuminate his face. "Easy, little lady," he said. "You're with friends and you are well now."

Her eyes widened with recognition, and then her arms were around his shoulders. The girl clung to him for a minute, then reached into her pocket and extracted his cuff link. The damned thing was made of gold and jet and she could've traded it for something to eat. A clean place to stay. "It keeps me safe," she whispered, and the words carved out his heart.

Lydia spoke. "Finn, get her something to drink. Something to eat. She's still weak. And then bring me the boy."

She healed the boy, then two more before Killian asked her to stop, sensing she was at her limit. A limit she'd push right through if left to her own devices. "We have time," he said. "All night, if need be."

"What about the Princess?"

Her voice was changed, raspy with age, and it was a struggle not to push back her hood and take off her mask to see how far gone she was. All he could see were her hands, which bore little resemblance to those of the girl he knew. An old woman's hands. "Malahi doesn't need me. Bercola and Sonia, plus eight other guards, are watching over her."

"Wouldn't she prefer it be you?"

There was curiosity in her voice, the question a larger one than he cared to answer. "Malahi knows I'm in the sewers with the orphans. They're her people—she understands."

Except she *didn't* understand. Didn't understand why Killian needed to be down here himself, why he didn't delegate the responsibility to the girls in her bodyguard, who were just as capable of doing what he did. Didn't understand that half of his motivation for being down in these sewers was selfish—he needed tangible proof that he was doing *something*. That he needed to atone for bringing this suffering down upon them.

What about your time spent with Lydia? How do you justify that?

"I've heard them call you her sworn sword. What exactly does that mean?"

That was the last thing Killian wanted to talk about with her, but if it meant her taking a few more minutes to recover, then talk he would. "It means I'm sworn to stay by her side and protect her for the rest of my life."

"Whether you want to or not?"

"Why wouldn't I want to?" he retorted, then instantly regretted his tone. "I'm sorry. I—"

"It's fine. I shouldn't have pried." She rose to her feet, bracing her hand against the wall. "Bring me the next child."

She swayed and Killian caught her arm. It felt fragile beneath his grip, his fingers encircling her bicep, but she tugged away with surprising strength. "I'm not stopping until everyone I believe might not make it until tomorrow night has been treated."

Phrased like that, it was impossible for him to argue.

It was the darkest hour of the night before Lydia decided they were finished, the children who remained instructed to return to the same place tomorrow night. They slowly filtered away to the narrow side tunnels with their nests of blankets and rags, leaving Killian alone with Lydia and Finn.

"I'll stay with her until she's recovered enough to go back to the barracks," Finn said, gesturing to Lydia, who'd fallen asleep, her head and shoulder resting against the wall of the sewer. Finn himself looked dead on his feet, the shadows beneath his eyes not entirely from the dying flame of the singular candle.

Going back to the palace meant a hot bath. Clean clothes. Something to eat and something expensive to drink. It meant the sofa in Malahi's bedroom, which would be warm and dry and quiet, and he could sleep until late morning. It was where he was supposed to be. Where he was duty bound to be. "It's fine. I'll stay until she's ready. You get some sleep."

Sitting on the cold stone next to Lydia, Killian pulled off his coat and stuffed it behind his head, eyes on the shadows moving beyond the sewer grate. The deimos were prowling, their wings a steady drumbeat, their shrieks like shattering glass. But he hardly noticed them as Lydia shifted, her head falling against his shoulder. The hood of her cloak concealed her face, the fur trim tickling his neck. But the slender hand resting against his hip was changing, like the slow bloom of a flower, becoming young again.

Finn flopped down on the floor next to him, and Killian gave him a little shove. "Don't even think of trying to use me as a pillow."

The boy shifted a little farther away, but Killian couldn't

help but notice how skinny his arms were, brown wrists bare beneath a threadbare coat that was already too small for him. There was a hole in the toe of his boot, and his curly brown hair was tangled and matted. Finn curled up in a ball, but as the candle flickered out, Killian saw that he was shivering.

Sighing, Killian pulled his coat out from behind his head and tossed it at his young friend. "You pick my pockets again, I'm going to hold you upside down by your ankles and shake you until I get all my coin back."

"I've never picked a pocket in my life," came the muffled reply, but it was only moments until his breathing took on the rhythm of sleep.

An hour, Killian told himself. *You can stay for another hour; then you need to go back.* But the minutes ticked by. Then the hours. And he didn't stir from where he sat until the glow of dawn filtered into the tunnels.

42

KILLIAN

"Killian, would you please *not* do that."

"Do what?" he asked, leaning farther over the balcony, attempting to determine precisely where the cave opening below was. The damned thing flooded at high tide, but he was relatively certain the Rainbow Ballroom was right above it.

"Lean over the edge like that," Malahi said. "You're going to fall and get yourself killed."

He made a face at the ocean below. "I'm not going to fall. And even if I did, it's not *that* far."

"Far enough!"

"Let's find out." Hopping up onto the balustrade, Killian balanced easily, walking back and forth along it.

"You wouldn't." Malahi sat perched on a delicate metal chair, the hand holding her teacup frozen midair as she watched.

"Don't tempt him," Bercola grumbled. "Teriana, one of the Maarin Triumvir's heirs, indoctrinated him into the joys of cliff diving when he was twelve. He'll jump if for no other reason than to prove he can."

At the mention of Teriana, Killian's attention shifted to Lydia to see if she'd heard the reference to her friend, but she was inside the ballroom itself, helping Lena set up for archery practice. As if sensing his scrutiny, she turned, a faint smile rising to her lips.

A gust of breeze came from nowhere, buffeting him. Killian swayed, nearly losing his balance before jumping onto the balcony to conceal his loss of concentration.

Bercola was glowering at him and Malahi's face was blanched, the cup in her hand trembling. "You worry too much," he said, picking up the pot of tea and filling her cup before flopping down on the chair across from her.

Taking a sip, Malahi said, "You're in awfully fine spirits."

Killian *was* in good spirits.

True to her word, Malahi had slowly given up the horses to be slaughtered, the only two remaining in the stables Killian's own, which she'd reluctantly spared because he'd need them in the weeks to come. She'd stripped the palace of blankets and excess clothing and had it distributed to those in need, and on top of improving the existing Crown shelters, she'd commandeered a number of empty residences, opening the doors to those who had nowhere to sleep. Circumstances were no less dire, but she was deeply in favor with the people.

Though if he was being honest with himself, Malahi's popularity had little to do with his mood.

For nearly three weeks, he'd been meeting Lydia each night for a training session before they moved into the sewers, he and Finn handing out rations while Lydia, her face always carefully concealed, healed the children who required it. Finn's kingdom of orphans wasn't exactly thriving, but they were surviving. Not one had died since Lydia began her rounds, and if things continued this way the ship his mother was sending would be full to the brim with children when it departed for the safety of Serlania.

Sensing that Malahi was waiting for an answer, he shrugged. "It's a beautiful day." And because he knew it would annoy her, he added, "And I've just had breakfast with a beautiful girl." Never mind that his stomach still growled, less than satisfied with his rations.

Malahi rolled her eyes, but he was spared the sharp side of her tongue when Lena called, "We're ready, Captain."

Offering Malahi his arm, Killian led her inside the ballroom, where she ensconced herself at a table filled with her writing materials, content to address her correspondence while he saw to the training of her bodyguard.

He'd had neither the time nor the resources to ensure the

young women he'd hired were trained prior to beginning their duties, which had necessitated much of it happening on the job. Every one of them except Lydia was adept in a fistfight and handy with a knife, but for most, that was where their martial skill sets ended. Bercola handled much of their training, her ability to explain technique infinitely superior to his own, but he also relied a great deal on their ability to teach one another. Sonia, in particular, had a great deal of knowledge to share. She was currently leading the lesson.

"Surprised your northern girl isn't better with a bow," Malahi remarked, watching as Sonia showed Lydia how to hold her weapon. The young Gamdeshian woman's brow creased as Lydia peppered her with endless questions, and Killian struggled not to smile. "She's a brawler. And she'll bite if pressed, so I wouldn't advise it."

"Doesn't look like a brawler. She has all of her teeth."

"So do I." He grinned at her, hoping to deflect her interest from Lydia. Because Malahi wasn't wrong: nothing about Lydia suggested a street fighter from Axbridge. Her posture was as perfect as any courtier's, her teeth were intact, her nose was too straight to have ever been broken, and her skin was devoid of the inevitable scars that came from combat. And those damnable spectacles didn't help. "She's good in a fight; trust me."

Lydia chose that moment to send an arrow sailing sideways into one of the curtains. Malahi arched one eyebrow, then shook her head and went back to her writing.

Leaving the guardswomen to Sonia's instruction, Killian prowled around the ballroom, his mind on other things. In a matter of days, this room would be full to the brim with nobility and Malahi would be at risk for every second of it. For the next hour, he scoured the room until he knew every inch, coming up with plans for fortification and escape routes, one of which he was going to have to build himself. He was assessing the glass doors to the balcony when an exclamation of surprise caught his attention, something clattering to the floor near his feet.

Lydia's spectacles. Reaching down, he plucked them up and turned. Lydia was staring at him with dismay. "Are they cracked? The string caught the frame, and—" She broke off, color rising to her cheeks.

Polishing a fingerprint off one of the lenses with his sleeve, Killian said, "No damage." He handed them back to her, feeling the smooth brush of her fingers against his as she took them, her hand warm from exertion.

"Thank you."

They stood staring at each other; then Sonia appeared at his arm, causing him to jump. "It's your elbow, Lydia," she said, then to Killian, "She needs to see. She learns by watching. You, Captain. You show her. Your form is satisfactory."

"Satisfactory?" He looked at Sonia, thinking it was a joke, but there was no humor in her hazel eyes.

"Exemplary aim, of course. But form"—she shook her head—"satisfactory."

From across the room, he could hear Bercola howling with laughter. Feeling more than a little self-conscious, Killian took the bow and arrow from Lydia. Drawing it, he aimed at the target, which was laughably close.

"Hold there please, Captain."

Killian dutifully stood still while Sonia's small hands poked him in various places as she explained form and stance, Lydia asking the occasional question. But when Sonia adjusted his elbow, Killian gave her a dark glare. "I don't think so."

"Even you can stand to improve, Captain."

He allowed the string to slip from his fingers, and a heartbeat later there was a loud thunk as the arrow hit the target. He knew without looking it would be at the center of the bull's-eye.

Several of the girls whistled with appreciation, but Sonia only lifted one eyebrow and tucked a lock of her short hair behind her ear. Taking the bow from him, she retrieved an arrow and in a blur of motion let it loose, splitting his arrow shaft in two.

"I fought for General Kaira," she said, naming the marked Princess of Gamdesh. "In comparison to her, you are just a boy playing with toys. Now if you'll excuse us, Captain, you're interrupting my lesson."

Shaking his head, Killian started toward Malahi, who was watching him, her expression unreadable. Before he could reach her, Gwen stepped inside the doors to the ballroom and cleared her throat. "High Lord Hacken Calorian is here to see you, Your Highness."

Then the doors swung the rest of the way open, and Killian's older brother stepped inside.

43

LYDIA

Everyone stopped what they were doing as a man of perhaps twenty-five years of age came into the room. Even without having seen his likeness on several paintings in the Calorian home, Lydia would have known the man was Killian's eldest brother. They had the same dark hair and eyes, sculpted features, and darker skin, both of them possessing slightly fuller bottom lips that would make anyone with eyes look twice.

It was there the similarities ended.

Where Killian was broad shouldered and muscled, High Lord Calorian seemed almost slight in comparison. Lydia put him at around her height at six feet, but that still made him half a head shorter than his younger brother. And where Killian was covered with tiny scars from a lifetime of combat, his nose crooked from being broken, Hacken was . . . flawless. Beautiful.

But there was something in his eyes that made Lydia want to step back. To look away. To avoid his attention landing on her at all.

Bercola bowed deeply as the High Lord approached, Malahi rising from her chair and dropping into a curtsy. "High Lord Calorian. We were not expecting you so soon."

He took Malahi's hand, raising her up before kissing her knuckles. "I found after your last letter that I could no longer sit idle, Your Highness. You painted a heartbreaking picture of the plight of our capital, though I must say, the reality is far worse."

"It is dire." Malahi didn't pull her hand from his grip. "But the people know that without your continued generosity, it would be far worse."

Hacken inclined his head, then led her back to her seat.

Setting the small box he carried on the table, he said, "A little thing to brighten your day."

All of the women in the guard collectively leaned forward as Malahi opened the box, a small smile growing on her face. Extracting what looked like some sort of sweet, she popped it in her mouth, sighing deeply as she chewed. "Thank you."

Hacken Calorian lifted his shoulder in a graceful shrug. "I know you're fond of them and they took up little space on the ship."

Malahi straightened. "You brought supplies?"

Hacken sat in the chair Bercola had brought over. "A full ship. My soldiers are already in the process of distributing it throughout the city to those who need it most."

"Thank you." Malahi seemed to almost breathe the word, her eyes fixed on the High Lord. "You and your continued generosity are all that's stood between Mudaire's people and starvation. But I can hardly bear to think of the cost—"

"What is wealth compared to lives? We have plenty. It is the *least* I could do." Then his eyes shifted Killian's direction. "Brother."

Having heard there was little love lost between the two, Lydia fully expected a snide comment, but the younger Calorian only bowed. "Your Grace."

"I set aside some provisions for the orphans you've taken such an interest in. I understand many of them are too fearful to venture out of the sewers?"

"They've reason to be afraid."

"Even with *you* watching over them?" Hacken's voice was light, but there was a hint of mockery in his eyes that set Lydia's teeth on edge. He reminded her of the senators who ruled the Empire. And though they looked nothing alike, there was a cunning in his gaze that reminded her of Lucius.

"I do what I can for them, but my duty is to Malahi."

"Of course. Even in Serlania, we hear that you never leave her side. As always, Killian, your dedication to your duties is admirable."

There was nothing but sincerity in Hacken's tone, but next to him Malahi's brow furrowed.

"As it is," Hacken continued, "I've brought enough that they should be well fed for a few days."

Killian inclined his head. "Thank you for thinking of them."

Hacken waved a hand as though it were nothing; then his gaze moved past his brother to Lydia and the other guards. "So these are the women you entrust your life to, Malahi?"

"Some of them," she answered, but Hacken was already crossing the room. He stopped in front of Brin, whose cheeks colored as she executed a strange combination of bow and curtsy, everything she'd learned in her months of service apparently forgotten.

"What's your name?"

"It's Brin, Your Grace. Brin Hammel."

"And where are you from, Brin?"

"Blackbriar, Your Grace. Though me and my mum have been in Mudaire since—" Her gaze flicked to Killian, then back to High Lord Calorian. "My pa was with the Blackbriar garrison. Was him who taught me about fighting with a sword and such."

"My condolences on your loss."

Blackbriar, Lydia had heard, was one of the town garrisons that had been decimated on the wall.

"Thank you, Your Grace."

"And how did you come to be part of Her Highness's guard?"

"The captain—he knew my pa. We got to talking when he came to see after my mum and saw me swinging a stick in the yard. Offered me a job."

"From swinging a stick in the yard to protecting a princess," Hacken murmured. "What a story."

Then he moved on to the next girl and then the next, asking their names and where they were from. Lena flirted outrageously with him. Gwen gave him one-word answers. Sonia spoke to him in Gamdeshian, in which he proved to be fluent. Lydia he approached last, her skin turning clammy as she dipped her head.

"Last, but not least," he said. "And what is your name?"

"It's Lydia, Your Grace. From Axbridge."

"Lydia from Axbridge." He rubbed his chin thoughtfully. "Has anyone ever told you that you look like a younger version of High Lady Falorn?"

She shook her head.

"It's striking." Reaching up, he removed her spectacles, then used them to lift her chin so they were staring into each other's eyes. "More so without these concealing those beautiful eyes of yours."

"What you consider concealing I find quite revealing, Your Grace." Lydia extracted her spectacles from his grip, feeling his index finger slide along her palm, his skin as free from callus as her own. It was a struggle not to cringe, and she hid her discomfort by polishing the lenses on her uniform before replacing them on her face.

Hacken chuckled softly. "And how long have you been in service to Her Highness?"

A variation upon the question he'd asked everyone else. "Three weeks."

"Not long at all." He gestured to the bow. "Why don't you give a demonstration."

"Oh." She looked wildly to Sonia, searching for reprieve, but the young woman only shrugged, leaving Lydia to mutter, "I'm afraid I'm not much of an archer."

Hacken leaned forward and whispered conspiratorially, "Neither am I."

Lifting the bow, Lydia shrugged her shoulders to release some tension. Her hair had fallen over her right shoulder and her skin crawled as Killian's brother ran his hand along the nape of her neck to draw her braid back to center, his fingers brushing the chain holding her ring between her breasts. "That's better," he said.

"His Grace makes an excellent point," Sonia said loudly. "Those of you with long hair should not leave it hanging. It catching in your bow is the least of your worries. Here, Lydia, let me help you." The shorter woman edged between Lydia and Hacken, reaching up to twist her braid into a knot at the nape of her neck. "Now try."

Lydia aimed, feeling the eyes of everyone in the room upon her as she released the string. The arrow sailed past the target to clatter against the stone wall. Cheeks burning, she turned, expecting to see dismay in High Lord Calorian's eyes, but they were shining with delight.

"Keep practicing." As he walked past a glowering Killian, he added, "I look forward to seeing more of you, Lydia of Axbridge."

"I'm quite certain I've never seen a prettier man in the whole of my life," Lena declared, putting her bare feet up on the arm of the sofa.

"So you've mentioned," Gwen replied, shoving Lena's feet away from her face. "*Three* times. A point you already made clear with the outrageous way you flirted with him."

"I *wasn't* flirting." Lena moved to sit in front of Lydia, which was a silent cue for her to braid the other girl's hair. "I was being polite. He's a gods-damned High Lord—to be otherwise would border on stupidity." She gave Gwen a pointed look.

Most of the girls of Malahi's day guard were sprawled across the furniture of the parlor, a fire roaring beneath the thick stone of the mantle. It was rare for Lydia to be here at this time of night. She nearly always met Killian for training after she'd eaten dinner with the other girls—and he with Malahi—after which they'd meet up with Finn to see to the well-being of the orphans in the sewers. It was always close to the second or third hour of the morning before she'd creep back inside the barracks, silently falling into the bed in the room she shared with Gwen and Lena for a few hours of sleep.

But tonight Killian had some other matter that required his

attention, and he'd been insistent she not meet with the orphans alone. "They'll be fine for one night," he'd said, having caught her alone in the servants' stairwell. "And I don't want us to have gotten this far only to have you caught or killed days before setting sail for Serlania."

Part of her had wanted to go anyway out of fear that there might be a child waiting for her, that someone might die while she lounged around drinking cheap wine with the other girls, but in the end she'd conceded that Killian was right. She was too close to jeopardize her chance at reaching Serlania.

Though by all rights, she could have been on her way already.

Guilt filled Lydia's chest at the thought, but despite her best attempts, she couldn't push it away. For some time now, she'd been able to control her mark. Been able to assess the sick and injured children without Hegeria's power taking control, and once she did decide to use her mark she could direct it to heal only that which required urgent attention. If she could do that, there was no reason she couldn't control it well enough to bypass Quindor's testers on the docks, and the coins Killian had given her, along with the wages she'd earned, were more than enough to pay for passage.

Yet here she remained.

She told herself that it was because it was too risky. That it was better to get back to Celendor late than never. That her control over her mark wasn't certain, something proven by Killian testing her with whatever injuries he garnered during their training, which she inevitably healed despite her best efforts.

Have they been your best efforts?

She bit down on the insides of her cheeks, uncertain about the answer. Uncertain whether her failure was more purposeful than she cared to admit.

Tying off one of Lena's braids with a bit of twine, Lydia paused in the task to press a hand against the ring hanging between her breasts, the feel of it comforting. The ring her father had given her. The ring she'd sold to try to get back to Teriana. The ring Killian had paid a fortune to give back to her because he'd known how much it meant . . .

You are a terrible friend, she silently accused herself. *And a worse daughter.*

"What do you think, Lydia?"

The sound of her name pulled Lydia from her self-flagellation of her character, and she looked up to find the other girls staring at her. "Pardon?"

"I thought he was awfully liberal with his hands," Gwen said.

"Who?"

"High Lord Calorian." Gwen frowned at her. "Haven't you been listening?"

"Sorry, I was lost in thought." Frowning, Lydia divided the hair on the other side of Lena's head into sections, considering Killian's brother. As uncomfortable as the attention had made her, Lydia had spent enough time around political men of Hacken Calorian's sort to know that it had nothing to do with attraction and everything to do with demonstrating power. And she suspected it had nothing to do with her and everything to do with either Killian or Malahi, perhaps both.

"I thought he was kind to show interest in us," Brin muttered. "We spend all day watching over Malahi and her ladies, and not one has ever so much as asked me my name."

Lena laughed and Lydia tugged on her hair to keep her still. "Gods, Brin. You don't want women like *Helene Torrington* knowing your name. And even a farm girl like you should know by now that if a man pays you a squirt of attention, it means he wants something. High Lord Calorian was likely just buttering us up to please Her Highness."

"Quit gossiping about your betters, you damned foolish girls."

Every head in the room turned to watch Bercola enter, an oversized cup in one hand and a teapot in the other.

"They aren't better." Gwen scrunched up her face. "They're just rich enough to make everyone think so."

"Philosophical enlightenment from Gwen—my day is made and I shall rest easily." The giantess shooed one of the girls out of her chair. "How about this: Quit gossiping about those powerful enough to make your life difficult should they not like what you say."

"You know the Calorians best," Lena said, ignoring Bercola's warning. "What's Hacken like?"

"He's ambitious and nothing like Killian, so don't presume to know one because you know the other."

"Nothing wrong with ambition," Brin said. "Won't get far in life without it."

"Drop the subject."

"So you're saying he wants to be king?" Lena persisted.

Bercola glared malevolently at the pretty girl. "If I tell you a bedtime story about the Calorians, do you promise to go to sleep and leave me in peace?"

Lena grinned and nodded. "Tell us about how you came to be in their service."

"Fine. Fine." Bercola leaned back in her chair. "I was part of a landing party during the last war between Eoten Isle and Mudamora. We'd rowed up into the swamps with the intent of coming at Serlania from the rear, but we were set upon by High Lord Calorian's forces. The *former* High Lord, not the one Brin's mooning after."

Brin's cheeks turned bright red and she crossed her arms but said nothing.

"Anyway, the bastards rained arrows down upon our boats and there was little to be done, sitting ducks that we were. So we jumped in the water, trying to escape by swimming upstream beneath the murk. Unfortunately, the waters down there are rife with crocs. Damned creatures finished what the Mudamorians started."

"But what about you?" Lena demanded.

"Shut your gob, girl; I'm getting to that." Bercola took a sip from her steaming cup. "I was swimming hard toward the bank when one of the crocs caught me by the leg. A big bastard it was, and every time I got out of the water it dragged me back. Jaws like a damned vise."

Her jaw tightened, and Lydia thought she must be remembering the pain.

"Figured I was done for, then *twang!*" She half-shouted the word and all the girls jumped. "Arrow straight into the beast's eye. And I looked up to find the High Lord himself, bow in hand. Without saying a damned word, he came down and pried the beast's jaws open and then dragged me up the bank, all his soldiers watching on. I was certain that they'd do their best to extract what information they needed and then string me up—but he just walked away."

"That's it?" Lena demanded. "But how—"

"Quiet!" all the girls shouted, including Lydia, and Bercola lifted her teacup in salute.

"I watched him walk away while I bled into the mud and I shouted after him, 'Finish the job, you Mudamorian coward!'"

All the girls leaned forward. "What did he say?" Lydia finally asked, curiosity getting the better of her.

"He said," Bercola replied, taking a long pause, "that anyone who fought that hard to live deserved the chance to do so."

That sounds like something Killian would say, Lydia thought. *Like something Killian would do.*

"At any rate, the gods in their infinite mercy decided not to take my soul that day or in the days after, leaving me with the predicament of owing a life debt to a Mudamorian. So once I recovered, I had to track him down and explain as much. He told me the only thing he had need for was a bodyguard for his youngest son, and I, in my infinite foolishness, didn't question why he'd struggled to find someone willing to take the job. In hindsight, I should've let the crocodile eat me."

All the girls laughed, but Lydia was still curious. "Why do the giants go to war so frequently?" She'd heard that it was because they had vile, aggressive tempers, but Bercola had anything but.

"Because it's good fun chopping off Mudamorian heads."

Lydia eyed the giantess for a long moment and then shook her head. "What's the true reason, if you don't mind me asking?"

Allowing Lena to fill her teacup, Bercola stared at the contents for a long moment, then shrugged. "We do it to celebrate the marking of a new summoner."

All the girls were paying attention now. Gespurn only marked giants, much as Madoria only marked the Maarin, and from what Lydia could determine, the nature of those marks was not well understood by those outside the two peoples.

"There are never more than twenty-four summoners alive at any given time," Bercola continued. "When one passes on to the gods, a year must always pass until another is marked by Gespurn. In that year, we are mandated to be vigilant, lest the winds over the Endless Seas rise while our summoners are weakened. Only when the twenty-fourth is marked are we allowed to turn our spears to sport."

Lydia shivered at the mention of the winds over the Endless Seas. Or the lack thereof. In Celendor, they called the stretches running north to south the doldrums. They were what prevented the Empire from exploring the limits of the Endless Seas—likely all that had kept them from discovering the existence of the Dark Shores. The Colleges believed them naturally occurring, albeit inexplicable, phenomena, but hearing Bercola's words made Lydia suspect it was the work of Gespurn and his Marked.

Shaking her head to clear away the thought, Lydia asked, "Is twenty-four a significant number?"

Bercola shrugged. "On Eoten Isle, it is said that there must be balance between the gods, and thus there must be balance between the Marked." She set aside her cup. "Hegeria's mark is strong but is tempered by the great toll it takes, so she is generous with her gift. Yara and Lern grant untempered power to their Marked, and thus are more moderate in their gifting. Madoria gifts her chosen with the ability to breathe under the sea, but also to manipulate it, which has far-reaching effects. But to command the elements? To be able to turn the skies into a weapon? That is a vast power for one individual to hold."

Lydia frowned. "It makes a certain sense, but what of Tremon's mark?" All eyes shifted to her, so she added quickly, "Not that Kil—err, the captain isn't impressive in his skill, but no matter how good he is with a sword, surely that doesn't rival the power to control a storm?"

Bercola's colorless eyes regarded the steam rising from her cup for a long time. Then she said, "You are correct that a sword is nothing compared to a storm, but you are incorrect to presume that weapons and martial prowess are the limits of Tremon's Marked Ones."

Outside, the deimos screamed, the steady thump of their wings audible even through the walls, but Lydia paid them no mind, her attention all for the giantess.

"We look to the Six for protection," Bercola continued, "and in this there are none we look to more than Tremon's Marked. Theirs are both the most miraculous of achievements and the most catastrophic of failures, for there is no power on Reath that rivals that of a leader of men."

44

KILLIAN

Hammer and chisel in hand, Killian chipped away at the mortar surrounding the block of stone, channeling his irritation into his construction project.

The corridors of the palace were heavy with the cloying scent of the countless tropical flowers Hacken had brought with him, Malahi's rooms filled with candies and chocolates and expensive wine, much to the delight of her ladies, whom he flirted with outrageously. But Hacken was no fool. True to his word, he'd brought a small fortune's worth of food and supplies, all of which had been carefully distributed throughout the city by the soldiers Hacken had brought—all of it touted as *gifts from Princess Malahi Rowenes.*

Not that the people in the city didn't know *exactly* where—and whom—all the goods had come from. The Calorian banner hung above the palace, its white horse galloping next to the Rowenes scorpion, and the lone ship in the harbor flew the same.

It drove Killian mad that Malahi and Hacken were playing at politics, courting the favor of starving people in order to further themselves. But that wasn't what had his temper in a fire. It was the way Hacken had put his hands on Lydia that morning. It had nothing to do with her being pretty and everything to do with Hacken abusing his power. He'd done it because he could. Because he was a High Lord and above consequences.

Killian slammed his hammer against the chisel and was rewarded with a satisfying crunch as the block came loose. Bracing his heel against it, he shoved the block into the next room, eyeing the wall for a few moments to make sure it wouldn't all come toppling down on him.

To top off his day, three wagons' worth of injured soldiers had returned to Mudaire from the front lines. Men who'd lost limbs or been incapacitated in a way that couldn't be mended by a healer's touch and thus were of no use to Serrick on the battlefield. They'd been bandaged and loaded into wagons, and when Killian had met the caravan at the city gates half of them were near death from infection. Some of them *were* dead, the flies of war swarming thick as the wagons had trundled through the city streets toward Hegeria's temple, civilians stopping in their tracks to watch them pass.

They should have been easy pickings for the deimos and other fell beasts that roamed the night, but the wounded soldiers had made the entire journey to Mudaire unmolested, and if it all hadn't made Killian sick to his stomach he might have applauded Rufina's strategy. She'd break the hearts and minds of every person in Mudaire, so when she finally reached the city walls there'd be no fight left within them.

He was about to start loosening another block when his skin prickled with the sense he was being watched. Dropping the chisel, Killian retrieved his sword and scanned the empty ballroom. The exits were all secured, the drapes pulled shut across the expansive windows and doors leading to the balcony. Lifting the blade, he walked toward one of the curtains and was about to draw it back when a knock sounded on the door.

"It's Hacken."

Scowling, Killian dropped the curtain and started toward the entrance. He lifted up the beam he'd recently installed and cracked the door open. "What?"

His brother stood in the hallway, a bottle of whiskey and two glasses in hand. "It's three in the morning, Killian, and it sounds like you're trying to pull the palace down on our heads. Since sleeping through it wasn't an option, I decided to keep you company."

"You could always go stay at your house." Not that Killian wanted *that*. It would mean losing his place for training Lydia. He'd had to miss seeing her tonight in favor of this particular task, and he didn't want to lose his last chances to spend time alone with her. She was both his respite from the world and his ally in saving this corner of it, and the fact that their days together were numbered troubled him more than it should.

"Both the deimos and the threat of squatters make staying at the house rather inconvenient. Now let me in."

It was tempting to slam the door in his face. But Killian was smart enough to know that Hacken wasn't here because he couldn't sleep.

Opening the door enough that his brother could pass, Killian shut and barred it, crossing back over to his abandoned tools.

"What in the underworld . . . Are you making a *hole* in the wall of the Rainbow Ballroom?"

Killian grunted an affirmative. "Escape route. Didn't like the available options, so I decided to make my own."

Hacken eyed the wall warily. "How do you know the whole wall won't collapse?"

"I don't." Killian hefted his hammer. "But sometimes you need to roll the dice."

With one block removed, the work was easier, and within the hour Killian had a pile of stone sitting next to him and a hole in the wall leading into the adjoining chamber. Motioning for Hacken to follow, Killian ducked under and, when Hacken was through, pulled up the heavy Gamdeshian carpet to reveal a trapdoor. "This was already here," he said. "Leads into a storage room in the lower level. Two doors down is the access to the underground tunnels. Tide will be low while the party is underway, so the cave opening will be clear."

Hacken nodded approvingly. "Boats?"

"Two. Both already supplied. If things sour the night of the ball, stay with Malahi. Bercola knows the plan."

His brother was silent for a long moment as Killian replaced the carpet. Then he said, "I'm surprised you're including me in your escape plans."

It would be tempting to leave Hacken to fend for himself for once, but their mother would never forgive Killian if he let his older brother get killed. "I'll have plans for all the High Lords. Our lot won't be improved if all of you are dead."

"I'm touched by your sentiment."

Killian snorted, then motioned for Hacken to go back through the hole. Pushing the backless cabinet in front of the opening, Killian climbed through, shutting the doors behind him. He carefully tacked the panel of silk back to the wooden casement, then straightened and turned to the pile of stone. "You going to help or just stand there and watch?"

"That seems like a *you* job." Hacken eyed the mess on the floor. "I'll sweep."

Sighing, Killian pulled off his already-sweaty shirt and set to carrying the heavy blocks of stone out onto the balcony, where he tossed them over the edge. The cool night air was blissful against his overheated skin, and the wind coming off the sea drove away the stink of the blight. When he went back in, Hacken had finished sweeping up the dust and crumbled mortar and was holding Killian's sword, the blade glinting in the lamplight. It was a struggle not to snatch it out of his hands.

"His armor and ashes came back to Serlania, but not this."

Killian shrugged. "He left instructions. I got the sword. Sel got the Serlania house. You got everything else."

"Father never cared much about everything else." Hacken's voice was light, but Killian heard the bitterness. The resentment.

"That's not true." Killian bent to pick up his shirt, fiddling with one of the buttons as he added, "He was the sworn sword of Derrick Falorn—it was his duty to be at his side. And when Serrick took the throne, Father swearing to lead the Royal Army was what ended the civil war between the Twelve. What he *wanted* wasn't a factor."

"Except he got exactly what he wanted. His horse and his sword and a tent. An army. *You*." Hacken made a noise of irritation, then handed over the sword. "I don't know why I still care. He's ash on the wind."

"Then let it go. We've bigger problems."

"That we'll *all* soon be ash on the wind?"

"If you're going to keep on with such morose topics, I'm going to need you to pour me a drink."

His older brother laughed, retrieving the bottle and pouring generous measures into both glasses before handing one to Killian. "To Father."

"To Father." They clinked glasses and Killian drained the contents of his, setting it on the floor in favor of putting on his shirt.

"Speaking of estates, Seldrid was in a frenzy over your recent purchase. That was quite a large sum of coin, Killian. And all to piss off Helene Torrington."

Killian ground his teeth, waiting for the inevitable reprimand.

"I told Sel to let it slide—it isn't as though this is a habit of yours. But"—Hacken paused, bending over to refill Killian's glass—"I'd ask that you ease off on baiting Helene. I realize she's a loathsome girl, but she's also Torrington's heir, and I'd rather not have to deal with a feud between our houses because you couldn't keep your mouth shut."

"Noted."

"Good. Now where is it?"

Shit.

Finished with his buttons, Killian picked up his glass and took a sip. "Where's what?"

"Gods, but you're bloody annoying. The ring."

"In one of my pockets, probably." A lie, because he knew exactly where it was—on a chain hanging around Lydia's neck. Where it would remain.

"You haven't done something stupid like giving it away?"

"Now to whom would I have given something like that?"

Knowing Hacken was after more than just a bauble, Killian made his way onto the balcony, hoping the shrieks of the deimos over the city would throw his older brother off his game. Sitting on the balustrade, he watched with amusement as Hacken paused in the doorway, eyes shifting skyward.

"Can they land here?"

"Easily. And they have it in for me, so they might well try." Killian eyed the sky. "They're no fan of fire, so we'll have a few dozen torches burning to ward them off the night of the party. Keep them from trying to eat Malahi's guests."

Hacken muttered a few choice curses, then strode onto the balcony. "I'll recompense you for the ring; just give it to me."

"What do you want it for?"

Silence.

"Let me be blunt," Hacken said, his eyes still on the sky as he spoke. "I want that ring as part of my proposal to Malahi."

Killian choked on his mouthful of whiskey. "What?"

"Don't act the fool. You know that this is ultimately about marriage." Hacken topped up his glass. "You know why all the High Lords are risking coming to Mudaire. Serrick will be Mudamora's downfall, but trust me when I say that there is *no* consensus on which house should take the crown. And to start a civil war over the throne when we're in the midst of one would be as damning as leaving the crown on Serrick's head. So we'll make Malahi our puppet queen and then orchestrate the shift of power to one of the other houses after you win this war for us."

"After I win it." As if beating back the Derin army were going to be the easiest of all the obstacles facing them.

"Yes. That *is* Malahi's plan, isn't it? Dareena at the head of the Royal Army would be the safer bet—she's got a decade of experience on you and an intact reputation—but having the High Lady of House Falorn save our necks does not send quite the right message for a Rowenes girl with her eye on the crown. Whereas her sworn sword defeating Rufina and her Seventh-cursed army makes *Malahi* look good."

"She doesn't care about such things."

Hacken gave him a pitying look. "Malahi cares, and that's not a bad thing. Shows foresight, which is an important quality in a queen."

"Especially one *you* are of a mind to marry."

Hacken spread his arms. "You have to know that the choice of who Malahi will wed is purely political. Queens don't wed for sentiment."

That wasn't what bothered Killian. It was that Malahi deserved a hundred times better than a reptile like his brother.

"You look upset."

There was a faint gleam in Hacken's eye, one Killian had learned a long time ago meant that his brother was taking pleasure from his distress.

Laughing, Killian drained his cup. "You mistake the source of my suffering, Hacken. I know Malahi's plans, and I know what part I play in them. What troubles me is that you want to propose using a ring that Malahi watched *me* purchase." Sliding off the balustrade, he slapped Hacken on the shoulder. "This, Brother, is why despite all your wealth and all your power and all your good looks, you never get the girl. And that makes me feel badly for you."

"Give me the ring, Killian. It's not a request."

Walking backward to the doors leading inside, Killian held up his hands. "If you can find it, you're welcome to it. But you'll have to excuse me, Your Grace, because I've better things to do tonight than search my rooms for a shiny bit of rock."

Hacken glared at him, saying nothing, but as Killian made his way through the ballroom he had the sickening sense that this conversation wasn't over. And when it resumed, it would be his brother who'd have the final word.

45

LYDIA

Lydia's skull thudded into the floor for what seemed like the hundredth time. Her eyes glazed, but only for an instant; then she blinked and twisted. She flipped Killian on his back, her knees on either side of him, one hand locked around his wrist and the other holding a silver butter knife to his throat.

"Did you let me do that?" she demanded, leaning so that her face was only inches from his.

Killian shook his head, but she only had a heartbeat to enjoy her victory before he had her shoulders once again pressed against the floor, butter knife spinning off into a corner. "Never let your guard down."

"You're rather cheap with your praise, you know." She met his gaze steadily.

Letting go of her wrists, he eased up. "I'll praise you when—"

Lydia caught hold of the back of his head and pulled down and to her left, her back arching as she twisted. Killian cursed as his shoulders hit the floor. With her free arm, she swung, stopping her knuckles just shy of his nose. "Never let your guard down."

He grinned at her. "Well done."

He'd been training her almost every night since she'd joined the guard, and she could count on one hand the number of times he'd said those words. Every single time had felt like a triumph. Not against him, but against those who'd harmed her in the past. Those who'd try to harm her in the future. She grinned back, but it was all teeth.

"Victory suits you," he said, and something in his expression made her cheeks burn. Flustered, Lydia rose to her feet and crossed the ballroom to the table where a jug of water and two glasses sat. Filling one, she took a long drink. "One victory in a hundred fights isn't very good," she said, keeping her back to him. "Still means me dead or worse ninety-nine times."

"Ninety-nine times out of a hundred you won't be fighting someone as good as me," he replied. "And that one time that you are, your opponent is going to underestimate you just as I did now. You look weak, but you're not. And a blow that would knock another woman senseless barely slows you down. You can take advantage of that and have a knife in the man's ribs before he has even a hint of how dangerous you are."

"Most of that is my mark," she muttered, her elation already dissipated. "I won't have that back in Celendor."

"Are you certain about that?"

Lydia wasn't certain. Just as she wasn't certain anymore whether the loss of her mark would be a blessing or a curse, only that it was imminent. Tomorrow night was Malahi's ball, and the next day the Princess and her retinue would sail for Serlania.

But not Killian.

He hadn't said anything that would lead her to believe he wouldn't be going south with the Princess, but she knew him well enough to know that he wouldn't abandon Mudaire and its people without a fight, which made his silence telling

Regardless, tonight would be her last night alone with him, and that truth sat heavily in her stomach. *Say something!* a voice screamed inside of her head. But all the things she wanted to say to him were things that needed to remain unsaid, so Lydia stayed silent.

"We should go," he said. "We'll both need our wits about us tomorrow night, and that's not going to happen with no sleep."

"Do you believe something will happen?" she asked. "Do you believe the corrupted will attack?"

"I do." Picking up his sword, he belted it on. "And I want you to stay as clear of it as you can. Give the warning, but don't engage. You need to get out of here alive."

She gave the slightest of nods, and Killian lifted his head and frowned. "I'm serious, Lydia. Remember, the whole point of you taking this job was that it was a way to get back to Teriana."

"I thought the point of me taking this job was to protect Malahi."

He looked away. "Things change."

Gods, but didn't she know that. *Remember who you are,* Lydia silently berated herself. *Remember what your goals are. Rescue Teriana. Avenge your father. Force justice upon Lucius.* "I'll stay out of the way."

"Good." He didn't sound convinced. "Let's go."

Lydia followed him out into the darkness of night. It was cloudless, as it had been for days, rain a distant memory for the belabored city. Stars twinkled above them, the moon only a sliver of light. Perfect for deimos on the hunt, though none circled above.

"Where are they?" she asked as he unlocked the gate, easing it open for her to exit before locking it again behind him.

"Good question."

They walked across the road and dropped down into the sewer, but the second Lydia's feet hit the tunnel floor the rank scent of rot slammed her in the face. "Gods," she whispered. "That smells like—"

"Blight." Killian swore under his breath, then said, "We need to find where it's coming from."

Together they made their way through the tunnels, Killian navigating without hesitation with his uncanny sense of direction. They passed several groups of children, and he asked them to try to find Finn before carrying on.

"Where are we going?" she asked.

"Toward the western part of the wall."

The smell grew stronger, bad enough that Lydia covered her mouth with her sleeve, breathing shallowly. They turned a corner and a faint glow appeared ahead, illuminating a slender figure. Beyond, the sewer was a dead end, but that wasn't what stole Lydia's attention: it was the blackness seeping through the cracks in the bricked-up wall.

The figure holding the candle reached out with one hand as though to touch the blight and Killian shouted, "Finn, no!"

The boy jumped, the candle nearly slipping from his hands as he whirled about. "Lord Calorian?"

"Did you touch it? Did you get any of it on you?" Killian's voice was frantic as he grabbed hold of the boy's hands, searching them for blight.

"Of course I didn't." Finn's voice was indignant. "What sort of fool do you think I am? I was only having a closer look."

"I don't want you going anywhere near it."

While the pair argued, Lydia took Finn's candle and approached the wall. The blight wasn't coming from above but from behind, seeming to be eating away at the mortar between the bricks.

Lifting one foot, she nudged a brick with the toe of her boot. It gave easily, sliding backward into the wall. Then, with Lydia watching in horror, it slid forward again and kept going until it landed with a crack on the tunnel floor. "Shit," she whispered right as Killian said, "What in the underworld was *that*?"

Blight flowed through the hole the brick had left in the wall, a thick and viscous slime flooding down the walls and onto the tunnel floor.

Lydia backed up rapidly, colliding with Killian, the three of them retreating as the blight followed them up the tunnel.

"Finn, round up all the children you can and take them to the eastern half of the city," Killian said. "As close as they can get to the harbor. Now run!"

As the sounds of Finn's boots echoed off into the distance, two more bricks pushed loose. Then another and another. The blight flooded out in great gouts, flowing down the tunnel like sewage.

"We thought it had stopped its progress," Killian said, shaking his head. "But it had only gone underground. It's beneath the wall, destroying the foundation."

"How do we stop it?" Lydia demanded, backing away.

"Get supplies down here. Shore it up."

"It's the middle of the night!"

"Do you think I don't bloody well know that?"

They retreated, step by step. Blight had poisoned Malahi's horse, and Lydia had heard the warnings to avoid contact with the foul substance at all costs. And if they were to avoid contact . . . "Killian, is the only source of water in the city wells?"

He stopped in his tracks. "Without rain, yes."

"What if it's contaminated the water?"

Grabbing her hand, he led her at a run until they reached an open sewer grate. "I'll cover you against the deimos," he said. "You check the well water."

Her skin crawling with the sense she was being watched, Lydia kept to the shadows of the building until she caught sight of one of the public fountains. With Killian's bow nocked and his eyes on the sky, she knelt next to the basin. In the darkness, the water appeared black, but she knew that was an illusion.

The stench of rot filling her nose, however, was undeniably reality.

46

KILLIAN

Dawn saw the arrival of two things: utter panic among Mudaire's civilians and the fleet of ships carrying Malahi's esteemed party guests.

All through the balance of the night and through the day, Killian had been out in the streets directing the migration of people away from the western quarter of the city where all the wells were, or soon would be, contaminated by blight. Malahi had ordered the doors to the houses of the High Lords be opened, and hundreds of terrified civilians were escorted into those polished manors. Finn's army of children had been relocated to the Calorian manor, which Hacken had already arranged to have emptied of anything irreplaceable.

But the blight spread swiftly, and with every passing hour the city lost another source of water as the rot crept toward the ocean. And with the skies devoid of clouds, the loss of the city's well water would soon prove to be catastrophic.

The ships carrying the High Lords and Ladies had been packed to the brims with soldiers and supplies. But it wasn't enough. Not nearly enough when there were close to a hundred thousand civilians crammed within Mudaire's walls.

Not enough food.

Not enough water.

And only enough room for two thousand souls aboard the High Lords' ships when they sailed south. Two thousand, out of a hundred thousand. As for the rest—

"Thank you all for coming." Malahi's voice pulled Killian back into the moment, his eyes focusing on the men seated around the table, who were all watching the Princess with interest.

Calorian. Torrington. Hernhold. Trian. Cavinbern. Pitolt. Nivin. The seven High Lords Malahi had set her eyes on as supporters, both Falorn and Serchel having declined the invitation, Damashere and Keshmorn out of her reach given they rode at her father's side.

"Congratulations on your coming-of-age, Your Highness," High Lord Pitolt said, the old man's ruddy jowls shaking. "Seems just yesterday you were a wee bit of a thing. Still are, really. Short stock, the Rowenes clan. Could use a bit of height added to the bloodline, if I do say so myself. My son Rodern—"

"Thank you for your well-wishes, Your Grace," Malahi said, inclining her head. "But I think given the gravity of the situation, we should move straight to the purpose of us gathering together, which is not for a party. As you all—"

"With respect, Highness . . ." Hacken rose, gesturing at Malahi to take a seat. "It pains me to remind you, but your presence here is a courtesy. A nod, if you will, to the important role you have played, and will continue to play, in the coming days and months. As is my brother's."

His eyes flicked to Killian, and it was all Killian could do to not lift his hand in a universally insulting gesture. But getting himself kicked out of this meeting would be a mistake.

"Of course." Malahi's voice was frigid, but she sat in her father's chair, smoothing the silk of her skirts.

"Thank you, Highness." Resting his hands on the table, Hacken looked around the chamber, meeting the gaze of each of his fellows in turn. "Gentlemen. We all know why we're here. Our Royal Army is being pushed back step by step, and with Serrick in command it won't be long until Mudaire is lost. Until Mudamora is lost."

The High Lords all nodded and made noises of agreement.

"And yet he refuses to see reason!" Hacken pounded a fist against the table. "This is no simple war between men. This is a war between the gods, and while the Seventh sends his champions to fight, ours languish. Dareena wasted in the North fighting bushmen and Killian reduced to teaching little girls to swing sticks! It's no wonder our Royal Army falters—the Six must look at us as fools deserving of our fate!"

Killian glowered at the slight against Malahi's guard, but there was no sense interrupting. Not when Hacken's goals ultimately aligned with his own.

"But Serrick is the King." Hacken paused, surveying the group. "And we have not the power to overturn his decisions. We have not the power to send my brother or the High Lady Falorn to take command. And in fairness, it should be said that the High Lady's absence today demonstrates that she's washed her hands of responsibility."

Next to him, Malahi shifted in her chair, but when Killian glanced down, her face was smooth. Serene. Seemingly as entranced in his brother's performance as the others.

"The only power we have, gentlemen, is to decide whether to keep Mudamora's crown on Serrick Rowenes's head or whether we tear it from his brow! And yet . . . ,"—Hacken lowered his voice, scanning the table with widened eyes—"we do nothing. Mudamora falls beneath the hand of the Seventh, and yet we do nothing. Why?"

All the High Lords shifted in their seats, Torrington drinking deeply from his wineglass, though the rest left theirs untouched. And even he glared at the contents, then set his glass aside.

"Why?" Hacken pushed his chair back and circled the table. "You know the reason as well as I—it's because even in these desperate times, we cannot put aside the enmities between our houses long enough to choose a king from among ourselves. Despite Mudamora being united for centuries, we still behave as though we're twelve separate kingdoms squabbling over a garden plot of land! And since we cannot fight together, it seems we are all destined to die together!"

Killian had known his brother was the consummate politician, but it was another thing to see him in action. And even knowing Hacken as well as he did, Killian found himself caught up in the rise and fall of his brother's voice. Felt his blood boil with the need to take action.

"Thank the gods there is one among us who had the wisdom to see a better path." Hacken had circled around to Malahi's chair. Reaching down, he took her hand, helping her stand. Though this was the moment she'd fought for these long months, the moment of reckoning, Killian had to curb the urge to shove his brother away from the Princess.

"A girl of only just eighteen," Hacken said. "Yet it was she, not any of us, who found a way to spare my brother from Serrick's blasphemy. It was she who remained in Mudaire, despite the dangers, in order to care for its civilians. It was she who saw how Mudamora might be spared despite all of our pettiness and infighting. And I say we make her our figurehead in our fight against the Seventh and his sorceress. I say we make Malahi Rowenes our queen!"

The High Lords roared their approval, and as one they stood, bowing low to Malahi.

Hacken turned on Killian. "What say you, Marked One?"

It was a struggle not to grimace at that blasted title, though Killian had known coming into this meeting what role he was to play. "In the names of the Six, I swear that this vote has been conducted lawfully, and that all have acted of their own accord and without compulsion."

"Then it is done." Hacken reached into his coat, extracting a sparkling tiara, which he placed on Malahi's head. "May the Six guide and protect Her Royal Majesty, Queen Malahi Rowenes!"

Everyone in the room bowed low; then Hacken took Malahi by the elbow. "Let's go make the announcement to your guests, shall we?"

The group rose, the other High Lords going first. Outside the council chambers, a young boy stood with the guards. He pushed through toward Hacken, handing him a note, a slow smile rising to Hacken's face as he read the contents.

Casting a backward glance at Killian, he said, "Looks like we won't be needing Mother's ships after all."

Killian's heart skipped.

Watch your rear.

47

LYDIA

Lydia rested her shoulders against the wall outside the council chambers, wishing she could shut her eyes for a moment without fear of a reprimand from Bercola. Last night had been sleepless with its mad dash to attempt to warn the civilians of the tainted water with the deimos flying overhead, and then much of the day spent assisting with the evacuation. The well at the barracks was foul, so all of Malahi's guards had moved to the palace.

Not that it mattered much given that every one of them was on duty tonight.

And given that Malahi intended to set sail at dawn.

They'd be undertaking the journey on High Lord Calorian's ship. The Princess had limited her ladies to two chests of belongings each, and other than Helene, none of them had argued. They'd wanted to be gone weeks ago, and Lydia was certain that if they'd been told they could bring nothing more than the clothes on their back, none of them would've cared. With the city losing wells to the blight by the hour, even the most privileged were starting to feel the walls closing in.

Tonight would be her last night in Mudaire. And the beginning of the end of her time in the West.

This is what you've been working toward, she reminded herself. *Going home to help Teriana. To, hope against hope, save your father.*

And even if the worst happened and she failed in both of these things, to have her revenge on Lucius.

What she should be feeling was anticipation. Eagerness. Even a bit of fear.

Yet all she felt was hollow as she surveyed the young women

she'd befriended over the past month, her mind going to all that she'd be leaving behind the moment she boarded a Maarin ship. The life that she'd made for herself. That she'd chosen for herself.

How can I go back to life in Celendor?

At the thought, she viciously bit at the insides of her cheeks until she tasted blood. *How selfish can you be,* she silently screamed at herself. *All of what has happened to the Maarin is the result of your carelessness. Even if you can free them, things will never be the same. You'll need to spend the rest of your life atoning.*

"What is that noise?"

She jumped at Gwen's voice, but now that she was pulled from her thoughts, she heard exactly what the other girl was speaking about. A growing roar. The sound of hundreds, possibly thousands, of angry voices.

Bercola jerked her chin at Lydia and Gwen. "Go see what that is."

Elbow to elbow, they hurried down the hallway together toward the main door of the palace. The large foyer had a scattering of party guests, women in elaborate gowns and men dressed in embroidered coats, boots polished to a high shine. All were turned toward the open doors of the palace, silently watching what lay beyond.

Following Gwen, Lydia stepped closer to the door and looked outside, her eyes immediately going to the crowds of civilians beyond the palace gates.

"The Six help us," Gwen whispered, and Lydia felt her stomach drop.

There were thousands of them, the square and the streets beyond full of faces marked with anger and desperation and fear.

And hunger.

The walls were lined with the soldiers the High Lords had brought with them. Hundreds of trained and hardened men. But they seemed a pittance compared to the crowd, who, despite the sun being only a faint glow in the west, showed no signs of dissipating.

A soldier in a dark uniform with the Calorian horse embroidered on the chest appeared in front of them. "Where is Lord Calorian?"

"In council with the High Lords and the Princess," Lydia answered.

"Inform him his presence is required," the soldier said. "We need his order to use force against the mob."

Which wasn't an order Killian would ever give. "They'll go home once the sun sets for fear of the deimos."

As if on command, there was the flap of wings overhead and a shriek pierced the night. There were shouts of fear from the crowd, people casting their eyes skyward, but instead of being driven to safety they only pressed against the gates, the metal groaning.

The soldier's jaw tightened. "Fetch Lord Calorian, girl. Now."

Gwen hauled on her arm, and they hurried through the anxious guests in the direction of the council chambers.

"What in the name of the Six are they talking about in there that's more important than *this*?" Gwen asked.

The door to the council chambers opened and the High Lords exited, looking pleased as cats with cream. Behind them, Hacken appeared, Malahi on his arm. And Lydia's eyes went straight to the tiara on her brow.

The one that hadn't been there when she'd entered the room.

"They made her queen," she murmured, but Gwen didn't hear, too busy weaving her way toward Killian, who was watching his brother with a furrowed brow. But his attention snapped immediately to Gwen when she spoke, listening carefully, then shaking his head.

High Lord Calorian and Malahi set off down the hallway, Killian shadowing their steps as they made their way toward the main staircase.

With Sonia and three other guards in the lead, they started

down the wide hallway leading to the ballroom. Glowing lamps hung from the paneled walls, illuminating their progress, the soft laughter and conversation coming through the twin doors at the end in sharp contrast to the sounds coming from outside.

Then High Lord Calorian ground to a halt. "Before we go in, Your Majesty, might I have a word?" His eyes shifted to his younger brother. "Alone."

"Not a chance," Killian growled. "We are going to make this announcement, and then this party is over."

"It won't take but a moment."

"No."

Hacken grimaced. "Do not presume to order your betters about, little brother. The Queen chooses where she goes and with whom, not you."

Out of the corner of her eye, Lydia saw Malahi stiffen.

"What is it that you want, Hacken?" Malahi asked. "Killian is correct that our time is short."

"I would speak of it in private, only, my lady."

"Why?" Killian demanded, and Lydia's eyes flicked to his gloved hand, which kept twitching toward the hilt of his sword. "What is it that you wish to say that you don't want me to hear?"

"Nothing!" Hacken practically spit the words, but Lydia had spent her life surrounded by politicians—his anger was false. "It's only that I wish for *her* to be the one to respond to my words, not you. And with you present, Killian, that seems an impossibility."

"We've a mob of starving civilians outside the palace gates." Killian's hand was on his sword now. "There's not a chance that I'm letting her out of my sight. Say what you need to say, and be done with it."

"For the love of the Six!" Malahi flung open the door to a side chamber. "Killian, you wait here while I talk to the High Lord. I'll be in plain sight the entire time."

Hacken inclined his head and started into the room, but

Killian caught the Queen's arm as she went to follow. "Malahi, no."

Malahi hesitated.

"You are Queen of Mudamora, my lady." Hacken's voice held a bite that it had not before. "Yet why should the realm follow a woman who allows herself to be bullied about by her own watchdog?"

Malahi's face hardened. "Stay here, Killian."

"I don't want you alone with—"

"She need not be alone, you imbecile. You." Hacken snapped his fingers at Lydia. "You seem like a girl who knows her place. Get in here and watch over your mistress."

Lydia froze. Why had he chosen her? Out of all the guards-women standing in the corridor, why did it have to be her? From the tightening of Killian's jaw, he was thinking the same thing.

"Surely a woman you handpicked to guard Her Majesty will be more than capable of forestalling any untoward behavior on my part, Brother." The corner of Hacken's mouth turned up in a sneer. "The gods may have gifted our family a great deal of brawn, but as everyone knows, every last bit of it went to you."

"Get in here, Lydia," Malahi hissed. "And be quick about it."

Lydia's feet felt like lead blocks as she walked past Killian, his expression full of warning. As if she didn't know she was walking into the lion's den.

Malahi slammed the door behind them. "I know you're up to something, Hacken, so why don't you spit it out."

"That's a bit of the pot calling the kettle black, *Malahi*," High Lord Calorian answered, taking a seat on one of the so-fas. "After all, it is *your* plotting that has brought us all together this fine night."

"You're in the middle of a starving city, so I fail to see how the night is fine."

"Fine in that tonight will be the beginning of the end of Mudaire's plight. And fine in that you'll be choosing yourself a husband."

Lydia trailed after them, stopping a few paces back from the chair on which Malahi sat. There was only one entrance to the room and no windows. No closets in which attackers could be hidden, no shadows of feet behind the heavy drapery. Hacken Calorian was the only potential threat to the Queen, and it wouldn't be a physical attack—it would be with words.

"Yes, Hacken. After the war is won."

Hacken exhaled a long breath. "No, Malahi. You will announce your betrothal tonight or I will withdraw my support. And without it, you will cease to be queen and all of this will have been for naught."

"And am I to assume that the betrothal I'm announcing is to you?" Malahi's voice dripped with venom. "Let me remind you that if the other High Lords were interested in you as king they would've skipped my little scheme and bent the knee to House Calorian."

"And yet you've shown my house such favoritism." Hacken rubbed his chin. "Why do so if you didn't intend to choose me when all was said and done?"

The Queen went still, not even seeming to breathe.

"You never intended it to be me you wed nor, I think, any of the other High Lords you enticed to your party." He cocked his head. "It was a fine little ruse. You quite nearly had me convinced you were true to your word with the obvious measures you were taking to bolster my name with the people, making it seem as though I were singlehandedly holding the kingdom together with my wealth and resources and connections. With my . . . *charitable* nature. I confess, I've never felt quite so popular."

"How sad for you." Malahi's voice was stiff.

Instead of acknowledging her retort, Hacken's eyes flicked to Lydia. "Lydia, is it? A strange name for a northern girl, but what does a name matter with a face like yours?"

She didn't answer, his scrutiny drawing a cold sweat to her skin.

He gestured for her to approach. "Sit, dear. I don't want you to miss anything when you report back to your captain, who I'm sure is about ready to break that door down."

The last thing Lydia wanted to do was go any closer. "I'm accustomed to standing, my lord."

"And I'm accustomed to being obeyed."

"Do it, Lydia." Malahi's amber eyes went to hers. "Just sit down so we can get this over with."

Rounding the table, Lydia perched gingerly on the sofa next to Killian's brother, cringing as he played with hairs that had come loose from the knot at the base of her neck. "Do you suppose he chooses pretty ones on purpose?"

"They aren't all pretty." Malahi's voice was frigid. "Get on with it."

Hacken continued playing with Lydia's hair. "As I toyed with what your end game might be, Majesty, the question arose in my thoughts: Why go through all that effort to bolster *my* name if you had no intention to wed me? And it dawned on me that perhaps it was not *my* name you were bolstering, but my *family's* name. A name which I am not the only man to hold."

Killian.

"A vision of your intentions rose in my mind: We would replace your father, whom everyone despises, with *you*. You'd then dispatch my dear younger brother to win this war against Derin, which would of course make him a hero to the people, for there is nothing anyone likes better than a tale of redemption. Just as there is nothing the people would love better than for you to take the handsome, marked, hero of the realm and put a crown on his head. More perfect still, for Killian has no taste for rule, and therefore would be quite content to be relegated to the role of consort, leaving Rowenes as the ruling house and you an autonomous woman. There's just one problem."

"And what is that, Hacken? That you'll no longer support my rule if it means your younger brother having power over you?"

"Oh, I've no fear of that, Malahi." He chuckled. "You thought it would be easy, didn't you? Winning Killian over? Except, as I'm sure you've come to discover, my brother's reputation as a womanizer is . . . *grossly* overstated. If you'd come to me, I might have told you the truth: Killian would fall on his own sword before bedding a girl he isn't in love with. And he's not in love with you."

Malahi didn't react. Didn't seem to even breathe. "What makes you so sure about that?"

Hacken's fingers twisted into the collar of Lydia's coat, and with a sharp jerk he snapped the chain. Examining her ring, he then dropped it on the table before Malahi with a loud clatter. "Seldrid nearly fell off his chair when he learned our little brother had spent two thousand gold coins on a trinket, but what I found most interesting is that Killian didn't give it to *you.*"

Malahi's eyes were fixed on the ring, her face filled with naked hurt.

"I can explain," Lydia blurted out. "It was mine. I sold it to Lady Helene because I was desperate, and Lord Calorian only bought it back because he knew how much it meant to me."

Yet even in her own ears, the words sounded hollow. Most everyone in the city had lost everything they valued. Most of the girls in Malahi's guard had lost everything. That Killian had done this for her was damning enough, but the sheer amount of the expense . . .

"Makes you wonder where he goes every night, doesn't it?" Hacken leaned back on the sofa, resting one polished boot on his knee.

"The children in the sewers." Malahi's voice was shaking. "He feeds them. Cares for them."

"All night?" His eyes slid to Lydia. "And this one, from what I hear from Brin, is also notably absent in the midnight hours." He reached into his pocket and withdrew a handful of buttons, along with a cuff link shaped like a black horse. "I went to my own residence today to ensure anything of material value was removed to my ship, and it was clear it had seen some visitors."

"It's not what you think. He's . . . we're . . ." Lydia trailed off. Telling them Killian was teaching her to fight would only invite more questions, none of which she could answer. Yet as a single tear ran down the Queen's cheek, Lydia wanted desperately to tell her the truth, because she knew what it was like to be subjected to a speech like Hacken's.

"Don't weep, Majesty," Hacken said, reaching over to wipe the tear from Malahi's face. "You've come too far to debase yourself like that."

"What do you want?"

"For you to reign as queen, of course." And when Malahi lifted her head in surprise, he added, "Yet like all things, it will come with a price."

48

KILLIAN

Killian paced back and forth in front of the closed door, his heart thundering in his chest.

Watch your rear.

His mother's coded warning repeated through his head, her meaning all too clear. Hacken had been the one reading her correspondence. He was up to something, and whatever it was would be motivated by self-interest, not the good of the realm. Not that Killian could do a damn thing about it out in the hallway.

"You don't think he'll try any funny business, do you?" Gwen's voice cut through his thoughts. "Because if he does, brother or no brother, I'm going to crack his skull."

Killian gave a sharp shake of his head. "He won't touch Malahi."

No, it wasn't her physical safety that worried him. It was what Hacken was saying to Malahi right now. It was that he was comfortable saying whatever it was in front of Lydia, which meant whatever it was, he didn't care about Killian finding out after the fact. It was that it had been *Lydia,* of all the girls standing in the corridor, whom Hacken had chosen to bring in with them.

The door abruptly swung open and his brother exited, Malahi on his arm. Pointedly looking anywhere but at Killian, she said, "My guests will be wondering where I've wandered off to. Shall we?"

Killian cast a backward glance into the room. Lydia stood frozen in place, that damnable ring dangling from the broken silver chain in her hand.

Twisting on his heel, he broke into a run in the direction Malahi had gone.

"Killian, wait!" Lydia's voice called from behind, and part of him wanted to turn back. But Mudamora depended on Malahi and her plan and Killian getting back in front of an army, and if his brother intended to disrupt it then Killian needed to stop him.

Ahead, he heard Malahi's and Hacken's titles announced as they entered the Rainbow Ballroom, the nobility clapping and calling well-wishes for Malahi's coming-of-age.

"Killian!"

He slowed to a walk as he entered the ballroom, but Malahi and Hacken were already deep in the crowd, moving toward the steps leading up to the balcony. Easing his way between the wide skirts of the noblewomen, he pressed after them.

Malahi had reached the top of the steps, Hacken at her elbow. As he turned, he held up a hand for silence. "Without preamble, allow me to announce that I, as well as the other High Lords with us tonight, have cast our votes for a new ruler for Mudamora."

The room went silent.

"Allow me to present Her Royal Majesty, Queen Malahi Rowenes."

No one seemed to breathe.

"Thank you, all." Malahi's voice streamed out over the crowd. "For the well-wishes and for the risk you took in coming to be with me tonight."

"Move," Killian muttered to a nobleman in his way, forcibly shoving the man aside when the word was ignored.

"We stand here"—Malahi's voice took on a serious tone—"under the guise of celebration. Yet I fear we have little to celebrate. War is on our doorstep. Our countrymen starve. Our very skies turn against us the moment night falls."

A hand closed on Killian's wrist, jerking him back. He turned his head to see Lydia behind him, her face devoid of color. "He's tricked her into believing I'm your mistress."

"I gathered." He pulled her along with him through the crowd, his eyes fixed on Malahi. "But he's after more than just spreading gossip about me."

"Yet there is hope!" Malahi's voice rose, clear as a bell. "Thanks to my sworn sword, Killian Calorian."

What?

"In a moment, I'll have you all join me on the balcony to watch as the fleet sent by our ally and friend Sultan Kalin of Gamdesh arrives in our harbor. A fleet sent at Killian's behest."

Lydia said something into his ear, but whatever it was, the cheers that filled the ballroom drowned it out, all eyes going to the sea, which sparkled with countless lights. Ships. Dozens of them. Except Killian knew it hadn't been his letter that had brought them here, because this would've taken weeks to organize on top of the time to sail the distance. This was Hacken's doing—he not a pawn in Malahi's plot, but rather she in his.

"The fleet brings supplies and soldiers," Malahi shouted. "But of equal importance, the ships will assist with the evacuation of the people of Mudaire, allowing us to turn our full attention to driving our enemy back across the wall."

The room shook with shouts of delight.

"He's not spreading gossip," Lydia hissed, trying to pull him back. "Will you listen to me!"

"In these dark times," Malahi cried, "unity is what will save us. Faith in the Six and those they've marked is what will save us. And to that end, High Lord Hacken Calorian and I are so pleased to announce my betrothal—"

"You gods-damned bastard," Killian snarled, dropping Lydia's hand, knowing he needed to stop this. Because the last thing Mudamora needed was his brother as its king. "Malahi!"

Her eyes lighted upon him, and the hurt in them, the defeat, made his feet freeze in place. "Yes, Killian. You should be up here."

The crowd quieted, stirring to create a path for him. Lydia's hand dropped from his wrist. Warily, Killian walked toward the steps, ascending them to Malahi's side. With his back still to the crowd, he glanced first at the arriving fleet and then turned his eyes on his queen. "You don't need to do this, Malahi. You don't need him."

Hacken made a noise of amusement, a false smile on his face as he panned the crowd.

"Except that I do need him." Her face was smooth and serene, but her eyes glittered with tears, gaze fixed on his chest. "I'm sorry. I know this isn't what you want, but please know that I'm doing it for the sake of Mudamora."

Catching her hand, he squeezed it, knowing that he had one moment to convince her. One moment to stop this. "The only ruler Mudamora needs is *you*."

Her face tilted upward, their eyes locking. Then Hacken's voice broke the stillness. "It seems Her Majesty finds herself overwhelmed with emotion. Allow me to announce for her, then, that at her behest, I have agreed to her betrothal—"

He broke off, smiling at the crowd, before adding, "To my younger brother, Lord Killian Calorian. May the Six bless their union."

49

LYDIA

Killian looked like he'd been slapped across the face.

And though Lydia had known it was coming, she still felt gutted. For failing to warn him. For being the tool his brother had used to manipulate Malahi. For falling in . . .

Lydia forced the last thought from her mind, there being far larger problems facing her now. She'd gotten herself wrapped up in a political web as complex as what she'd left behind in Celendrial and, in doing so, had jeopardized her chance to get free of this place. And Teriana and the Maarin would pay the price. Her father likely already had.

High Lord Calorian said something to Killian, who rigidly leaned down to kiss Malahi's cheek before taking her arm and facing a crowd who appeared as stunned as Killian, the High Lords glowering with obvious displeasure.

Lydia took one step back. Then two. She needed to be gone from this place. As much as Hacken's accusations about her and Killian were a lie, it wasn't a lie she could put to bed, because the truth was far worse. She needed to slip out and collect her things. With luck, it might be possible to sneak aboard one of the Gamdeshian vessels in the madness of the evacuation.

Then Killian's face turned in Lydia's direction, and she found that she could barely breathe, much less move. He swayed, almost imperceptibly, as if he might drop the Queen's arm and come down the steps, but Lydia gave a violent shake of her head. *No.*

She took another step back; then motion behind them, beyond the glass and on the balcony, caught her attention. The large torches lining the balcony to repel the deimos were extinguishing, one by one. There were guards out there, and indeed, she could see figures moving. But there was something . . . *wrong* about them. The life surrounding them shone with the brilliance of stars that had stolen the light from all else in the universe. Not beautiful, but . . . *terrifying*.

"Corrupted." The word came out strangled, unnoticed in the commotion of those around her, but Killian stiffened. Of its own volition, Lydia's hand went to the sword at her waist, drawing it out. The weight gave her strength. "Behind you!"

She ran forward, but Killian was already moving, hauling Malahi down the steps, shouting orders. The doors to the balcony exploded inward behind him, and a woman dressed in riding leathers and a hooded cloak strode through, the top half of her face concealed by a black mask. The aura around her was ghastly bright, but even without, Lydia would've known what she was, for her eyes were infinite pools of blackness rimmed with flame.

"Such a lovely party, Your Highness. Oh, excuse me. It's *Your Majesty* now, isn't it?" The woman paused at the top of the steps, taking stock of the chaos below her. "I can only assume my invitation was somehow lost. It is so difficult to get a courier through in these *troubled* times."

"Rufina, I take it." Malahi's voice was steady.

"Not just a pretty face, are you," the Queen of Derin purred. "Though you've already proven your intelligence in abundance."

Lydia pushed her way next to the other guardswomen, who were being buffeted by the fleeing nobility, soldiers herding lords and ladies out the side exits, under instruction to take them to rooms upstairs where they'd be barricaded in until the fighting was over. Only Killian stood steady, sword out, Malahi slightly behind him with Bercola at her side.

"And you, Lord Calorian. This is the second time I've come from behind you—it's starting to become a pattern."

He didn't answer.

Rufina's gaze shifted beyond them, and she chuckled. "Look

at them run. They won't get far, I'm afraid. I opened the palace gates on my way in. Stood there before that horde of your starving people and I said, 'Inside is enough food to feed you all. Take it, with my blessing.'" She exhaled a deep breath, then smiled. "Fatten them up healthy before we come for them."

Rufina's voice took on a soft lilt as she said the words, her eyes drifting over those who remained as though they were delicacies meant to be consumed. It was sickening. Perverse.

"Barricade the main doors," Killian ordered, and the soldiers who hadn't gone with the High Lords rushed to comply. Seconds later, there was a roar of noise outside, then fists hammering against the heavy wood.

"What are you waiting for, Killian?" High Lord Calorian hissed. "Kill her!"

Killian tilted his head, eyeing the Queen. "You didn't come here tonight *just* to allow Mudaire's citizens to ransack the palace, did you, Rufina?"

The corrupted smiled, and it was all teeth.

"Who cares?" Hacken was shaking, his gaze ripping back and forth between Rufina and the shuddering doors. "She's alone and this is what you're bloody meant for. Kill her!"

"She's not alone." The words tore from Lydia's throat. "I saw two more of them on the balcony before. And something . . . something else is out there."

The corrupted's gaze shifted to Lydia and one eyebrow rose. "Clever clever, Lord Calorian, to hide a lookout in your midst. It seems you do learn from past mistakes."

Lydia flinched, knowing that she'd revealed herself as marked to the creature, but Rufina didn't seem to care. "My followers had other business to attend to. As to the something else . . ." She lifted one shoulder in a shrug, then whistled.

The deimos walked in from the balcony, the clip-clop of its hooves echoing through the room. The creature had its eyes half-shut against the bright lights of the ballroom, but that wasn't what stole Lydia's attention. It was the saddle on its back.

"Bercola, get Malahi to safety!" Killian moved, a knife flying from his hand. Rufina laughed as she knocked it aside, but then her eyes widened when she realized he was already halfway up the stairs, sword in hand. "Go!" he shouted.

Rufina jerked out her own blade and steel sang against steel. Lydia stared, mesmerized by the speed and intensity of the fight; then a hand hauled on her arm.

It was Lena. "We need to go," she hissed. "Our duty is to protect the Princess. He can take care of himself!"

But she couldn't go. Couldn't leave him to fight that . . . *creature*.

"Lydia, come on!" Lena screamed the words in her ear. And she knew. Knew that if she didn't go now, she'd be trapped in here with the corrupted. With the deimos. And, soon enough, with the starving civilians of Mudaire.

Killian sidestepped a swipe of Rufina's sword, his fist catching her in the face and driving her back. But instead of attacking, he turned, his eyes locking on Lydia's. "Run!" he screamed.

Lydia ran.

50

KILLIAN

Steel met steel with enough force to produce sparks, Killian driving Rufina toward the balcony.

But he couldn't focus on the fight. Not with Lydia still in the room. Not with every move he made intended to keep himself between her and the demon that stood before him.

"Run!" The word tore from his throat. And out of the corner of his eye, he saw Lena dragging Lydia through the hole in the wall. *Safe.* And then the world around him fell away, leaving behind only the fight.

Their swords slammed together, hilts locking, and his eyes met Rufina's between the crossed blades. She hissed, "I'm going to enjoy taking your life, Lord Calorian."

"You can try." He swept out a leg, sending the corrupted stumbling back even as he flipped his sword around and lunged.

Rufina deflected the blow, but Killian got past her guard and slammed her into the wall of glass, both of them falling together as razor shards rained down upon them, pain blossoming across his body.

They rolled, losing their blades as they grappled, Killian coming up on top.

He slammed his fist into her face, hearing the crunch of bone; then motion flickered in his periphery as the deimos attacked.

Diving sideways, he felt the heat of the creature's mouth as he passed under it, coming to his feet in time to see Rufina kick his sword out of reach. Behind them, the main doors to the ballroom burst open, civilians pouring inside, not even the sight of the deimos stopping them from running toward the tables full of food.

"Go play with the rabble," Rufina told the deimos. "He's mine."

The deimos snorted and trotted inside, and a heartbeat later screams echoed from the ballroom.

Her gaze locked on Killian, Rufina tossed her own weapon aside. "Your life is too good to waste on steel." Then she lunged, as swift and deadly as any snake.

Killian darted back, dodging each swipe of her deadly hands. Hands that reached for his throat. For his face. For any inch of bare skin that might allow her to drain the life from him. Back, step by step, until he reached the balustrade.

And overhead, he could see the flicker of flames carried by riders on the backs of at least a dozen deimos, all of them soaring in the direction of the harbor. And the fleet.

No.

Killian struck with his knife, and the corrupted side-stepped him, only to reach out, her fingers grazing the skin of his throat.

He spun away, but he still felt a *tug*. Minutes of his life stolen. Maybe hours. Though if this creature got the better of him, he wouldn't live long enough to care.

She was too damn fast. And unlike most of her kind, Rufina knew how to fight.

But so did he.

Killian feinted, then slashed at her right side.

Rufina danced out of his reach, leaping onto the balustrade, then using the height to launch herself at him with blinding speed.

His shoulders hit the floor with enough force to rattle his teeth, but he somersaulted backward, slamming his knife into her side even as he flipped her over his head.

On his feet, he pulled another knife and threw it, but Rufina batted it aside. Walking backward into the ballroom, she pulled the knife he'd embedded in her ribs out, inch by inch, coughing up blood.

Attack her now, instinct ordered him, but the deimos was

terrorizing the civilians; half a dozen bodies lay still on the ballroom floor. Those inside were trying to flee, but they were met with a sea of starving people unaware of the danger inside. The deimos was slaughtering them, but just as many were dying beneath the feet of their friends, the air loud with screams. So instead of lunging at Rufina, Killian grabbed hold of a lamp and threw it at the curtains.

Glass exploded, spraying oil in all directions, igniting the fabric.

Shouts of "Fire! Fire!" filled the air. The tide of civilians caught sight of the flames rising to the stone ceiling and turned, trying to flee. The deimos shrieked in fear, galloping to the balcony, but Killian didn't have a chance to see where it went before Rufina slammed into him. His head cracked against a column, agony racing through his skull, but he saw her reaching fingers—

Killian ducked, ignoring the pain as he rolled, retreating until the stars faded from his vision.

Then he attacked, knocking aside her hand and punching her in the face. She reached for a fallen knife, but he kneed her in the gut, then slammed her against the floor, punching her in the still-healing wound in her side, again and again, feeling her ribs break, her blood coating his fingers.

But it wouldn't be enough to kill her.

Killian threw himself at the knife, snatching it up and throwing before he'd even regained his feet. It sank deep into her shoulder, but she only pulled it out, her teeth bared.

Behind her, the drapery was an inferno, the air thick with choking smoke. Killian coughed, his head still spinning and now his lungs burning, but he had to kill her. Had to finish this.

Picking up the blade of a dead soldier, he stalked toward the corrupted queen, driving her onto the balcony.

"Nowhere to go, Rufina," he said, backing her against the balustrade, trying to regain his senses. To regain his breath in the choking haze. "You made a mistake coming here tonight."

Her smile chilled him to the core. "Mistakes were made; that much is certain, Lord Calorian," she said. "But not by me."

Lifting her fingers to her lips, she whistled.

Swearing, Killian lunged, sword tip out, but the Queen of Derin twisted and dived off the balcony. And seconds later reappeared, clinging to the saddled back of a deimos. Righting herself, she called over her shoulder, "You should've taken more care with your charge, Killian. This will be the second princess I'll have killed under your watch."

The wind hurled itself at the balcony, driving away the smoke, and as he blinked back stinging tears, Killian's heart plummeted at the scene on the ocean before him.

Lifting his sword, he ran back into the inferno.

51

LYDIA

With Lena clutching her arm, Lydia sprinted to where Gwen stood wild-eyed and holding back a curtain covering a hole that had been knocked in the wall. "Hurry!"

Lydia pushed both girls through the hole first, allowing the curtain to fall behind her as she scrambled through the cabinet hiding the opening on the opposite side. The antechamber contained Malahi, her guardswomen, and one man: High Lord Calorian.

"My brother?" he demanded.

"Buying us time." She could barely get the words out.

Bercola pulled up the trapdoor in the floor that had been concealed by a heavy carpet while Sonia and Brin worked to barricade the door to the hall. Beyond, screams pierced the air as the civilians sacking the palace encountered fleeing nobility and soldiers, the latter clearly cutting down those who got in their way with no regard for the fact they were countrymen.

Angry tears streamed down Malahi's face. "This isn't how it was supposed to go."

"Things very rarely go as planned," Bercola snapped. "Which is why Killian built you an escape route. Use it. Fight another day."

"I can't leave my people."

"You can't help them if you're dead." The giantess loomed over the Queen. "Now climb down that hatch or I will toss you down."

Scrubbing tears from her face, Malahi complied, fighting with her voluminous skirts to get through the opening. The group dropped one at a time into the chamber below, Bercola coming last and pulling the trapdoor closed with her.

They were in the sublevel of the palace, below ground, the air cold and stagnant, for the space was used for little more than storing supplies. Cracking open the door, Bercola peered out into the corridor and then pulled it shut, swearing under her breath. "They've made it down here already."

"How many?" Sonia whispered.

"Ten, that I saw. Hopefully the sight of swords will send them running. The room we need is the one two doors down and on the left. Go."

The door swung open and the giantess charged out, weapon in hand, Sonia and five others on her heels.

"Go," Lena said to Malahi, gently pushing her and the High Lord out into the corridor. She and Gwen flanked them, Lydia and the rest bringing up the rear.

Lydia's heart hammered in her chest, the palm of her hand slick with sweat as she gripped her sword, casting backward glances as they moved up the hallway, but it was empty. And ahead, Bercola had chased off the looters and was unlocking the door.

"In, in, in!" she hissed, piling everyone into the room before shutting the heavy door and latching it. A lone lamp burned in the empty chamber, at the center of which a steel trapdoor was set into the floor. Pulling it up, Bercola took a torch from a stack sitting against the wall, lighting it and handing it to Gwen. "You and Lena go first. Follow the route marked with white chalk. Don't deviate."

"Gods, Bercola." Lena's face blanched as she eyed the black opening. "A daylight practice run would've been nice. What the hell is this place?"

"A secret way out, which is why we didn't tell any of you loose-lipped jabber-mouths. Now go!"

The tunnels beneath the palace were narrow, the shadows from the torches dancing on the walls. The heavy breathing of the women was loud, the only other noise the scrape of boots against the stone floor. No one spoke, and Lydia wondered if they were thinking the same thoughts as her. That there was no way to know what was happening in the ballroom. Who was alive. Or who wasn't.

Down and down they went, following the white chalk on the walls. Several tunnels branched off from the main path, though where they led, Lydia could not have said. Then the silence was chased away by the roar of waves smashing against the cliff. Fresh air hit Lydia in the face, her boots splashing in puddles as she entered a chamber that opened to the sea.

Two black-painted boats sat on the ground above the waterline, both containing oars, black tarps, and a crate of what Lydia suspected were supplies. Ready and waiting in case the unthinkable happened. Which it had.

The opening to the sea was secured by a gate of steel bars draped in seaweed, but Bercola was already unlocking the heavy padlock and swinging it open. Waves splashed against a set of stairs that had been cut into the rock, leading down to where the boats could be launched.

"We get out," the giantess ordered. "Make our way to one of the ships and set sail immediately."

While the others worked to move the boats, Lydia picked her way down the steep steps to where she could see the ocean beyond. What she saw stole the breath from her chest.

The sea was illuminated, bright as day, by countless floating infernos.

"No. Gods, no."

Lydia turned to discover Malahi at her shoulder, eyes reflecting the flames consuming the Gamdeshian fleet.

"Shit!" Bercola slammed her fist against the bars. Then she shook her head. "Doesn't matter. We row down the coast until we reach Abenharrow. Now get those boats down here!"

"Wait." Lydia pointed out across the water. It was too dark to determine what sort of vessel it was, but she could see the life of the people aboard. "Someone's coming this way."

"Probably sailors who escaped the ships. Now quit standing there, Lydia, and help!"

"In a moment," Lydia muttered, something catching her eye.

The vessel came closer, and a figure that burned unnaturally bright stepped out from behind the others. "They aren't Gamdeshians," she shouted. "There's one of the corrupted with them. Look!"

Even as the words exited her lips, an arrow sliced past her face, embedding in the boat behind her. Lydia grabbed hold of Malahi and shoved the Queen farther back into the chamber, everyone ducking for cover behind the boats.

"We can't go out there!" High Lord Calorian was crouched behind the same boat as Lydia and Malahi. "They'll pick whoever is manning the oars off and we'll be slammed against the cliffs. It would be suicide."

"I'm aware," Bercola snapped. "We need to get that gate shut."

"I'll do it!" Lena darted out from behind the boat, dodging arrows as she slammed the gate shut.

"Lena!" Bercola bolted after her, shoving the girl out of the way right as a flurry of arrows shot into the cavern.

Lena rolled across the ground, the padlock in her hand slipping from her fingers to tumble into the water even as Bercola recoiled, an arrow embedded in her shoulder.

"Bercola!" Lena screamed, but the giantess only growled at her to stay down.

"We'll wedge the gate shut with the boats," Lydia shouted. "Push them closer. Push! Push!"

Together, they slid the heavy vessels against the gate, wedging it shut while arrows flew through the bars.

"There's more of them coming." The words came out from between Bercola's teeth, her face lined with pain. "We need to backtrack. Find somewhere to hide in the palace. Sonia, hold them off for as long as you can, then retreat."

The Gamdeshian guardswoman's gaze was fixed on the inferno consuming the fleet of her countrymen, but at Bercola's order she nodded. "Go."

Her bow twanged over and over, providing the rest of them cover as they ran through the chamber and back into the tunnel.

"The trapdoor leading back into the palace is solid steel set into rock," Bercola said. "They won't be able to get through it. We can hide in the storage rooms until the rioters get what they came for. Most of them are unarmed civilians—they won't trouble us. We'll wait for help to come."

"And if it doesn't?" Hacken demanded.

"Then we'll see what daylight brings and go from there."

"That's not much of a plan."

Bercola gave the High Lord a dark glare, the torch flames casting shadows on her face. "You come up with a better one, by all means let me know."

They were nearly back to the entrance to the palace, all of them breathing hard from the climb, when a shout echoed up from behind. Sonia's voice.

"They're almost through!"

"Get that trapdoor open!" Bercola bellowed.

Brin climbed the ladder and shoved a key in the lock, the mechanism releasing with a clunk. Her arms shuddering, she pushed, but the door didn't budge.

"There's something on top," she muttered. "I can't lift it."

"The gods spare me from you little weaklings," Bercola growled. "Let me do it."

But as Bercola reached for the ladder, the trap snapped open and two arms wearing rags reached down and jerked Brin upward. A piercing shriek filled the air, and blood splattered down on the guardswomen below.

"Brin!" Bercola started to climb, but more rag-clad arms reached down, faces appearing in the opening as they fought against one another to get through the trapdoor.

Their faces were an ashen grey, black veins running up the sides of their necks. But it wasn't until one of them twisted to look at the group with eyes devoid of humanity that Lydia knew what was wrong with them. "They're infected with blight!"

"Pull back!" Bercola shouted, and then they were all running.

Lydia looked over her shoulder as they rounded a bend, terror racing through her veins at the sight of infected civilians with blight toppling down into the tunnel, one after another, only to rise and give chase. "Run!"

With Bercola in the lead, the group careened downwards, everyone tripping and stumbling. Lydia's elbow slammed against the wall of the tunnel, but the pain was inconsequential compared to her fear. Sonia appeared ahead, panting and wide-eyed. "They'll be through by now. We have to go!"

"Way back to the palace is blocked by the enemy." Blood streamed down Bercola's arm from the arrow wound. "We're trapped."

"We go down the other tunnels." Malahi's voice cut through the heavy, panicked breathing of the group.

"I have no idea where they go," Bercola said. "They could be dead ends."

"We have no choice." The Queen's face was streaked with dirt, but it did nothing to diminish the authority in her voice. "This way. Now."

Torches in hand, Lena and Gwen led the way down a dark branch of tunnel. It bent and wove, narrowing in places only to open up wide, everyone fighting to keep their footing on the slimy rock. Lydia's pulse raced, her breath coming in fast little pants as the ceiling lowered, forcing them all to duck, Bercola nearly bent double.

The giantess was struggling, the confined space and her injury slowing her to a crawl. Falling back, Lydia whispered, "Let me help you."

But Bercola shook her head. "You get caught, he gets caught. I've had worse. Keeping going."

Yet even over her roaring pulse and rapid breath, Lydia could hear the sounds of feet racing up behind them. Not the boots of soldiers, but the bare feet of Mudaire's poor. Women. Children.

She and Bercola reached a spot where the tunnel widened enough for them to stand straight, and there the giantess stopped, setting her torch against the wall. "I'll hold them off here. They'll only be able to come through one or two at a time. Go."

Lydia didn't move, watching the light from the rest of their party diminish. "I can't leave you alone."

"There isn't room for both of us to fight. You'll only be in my way. Go! You'll have your chance to die soon enough."

Bercola was right, and Lydia knew it. But at least she could give the giantess a fighting chance. Reaching up, she pushed the arrow the rest of the way through the woman's enormous shoulder, and before Bercola could react Lydia directed her mark at the wound until the bleeding stopped.

"You're an idiot," Bercola muttered, then shoved Lydia up the tunnel.

Despite the darkness, Lydia moved swiftly, keeping one hand in front of her and the other against the tunnel wall, following the trails of life the group had left behind them. It wasn't long until she caught sight of their torchlight.

The skin on the back of her neck crawled as Lydia approached, meeting Sonia, who was guarding the rear, first.

"Where is Bercola?" The other young woman's eyes were wide with alarm.

"Holding them off. She told me that we should keep going."

Several of the other guards turned, their expressions grim.

"Is it a dead end?" It was a struggle to get the words past her lips, fear strangling her.

"Not exactly," Lena replied, stepping aside. "Look for yourself."

Stepping into a small chamber, Lydia's eyes locked on the stem of xenthier glittering at its center.

And from behind them, Bercola roared a battle cry.

52

KILLIAN

Sprinting across the ruined ballroom littered with bodies, Killian exited the main door. Only to find himself met with a tide of civilians, all coughing and choking even as they ransacked the palace, running with loaded arms out the front entrance and into the night.

The main staircase bristled with soldiers, their duty to protect the High Lords hidden in the upper level, not to protect the palace. Killian prayed the fire he'd set would remain contained to the ballroom, or the strategy would see half the power of Mudamora dead in one night.

But he didn't care about that now.

He'd seen the smaller vessels bristling with men heading toward the cavern entrance, and his gut told him they weren't full of Gamdeshians. Malahi was trapped.

And Lydia was with her.

Shoving his way clear to the soldiers, he shouted, "Fifteen of you with me. The Queen's escape has been compromised. We need to get her upstairs."

The soldiers the High Lords had brought with them were well trained, following him without argument as they pushed their way down the hall to the narrow stairs leading to the sublevel.

Screams erupted in front of them, and suddenly people were running and pushing. "Get out, get out!" someone shouted. "They're inside! They're in the palace!"

"Corrupted?" muttered one of the soldiers, but Killian pressed onward, lifting his sword as the hallway cleared.

There were bodies on the floor, some moaning, some still. But while most had been crushed, several of them were clawed up and scratched, their hands and arms covered with . . . bite marks?

Edging down the stairs, Killian picked up the sound of shuffling feet. Of many mouths breathing. And in his nose, the awful stench of blight.

Steeling himself, he stepped out of the stairwell.

And found himself behind a horde of civilians, all of them fighting one another in an attempt to get into the room containing the trapdoor leading to the tunnels.

None of them spoke, only pushed and strained against one another, bare feet crushing those who fell. And those who fell uttered not a sound of pain, only attempted to crawl through the legs of their companions toward the trapdoor.

"The Six protect us," one of the soldiers whispered. "Some of them are children."

And as one, the horde turned, revealing grey faces lined with blight, eyes reflecting the underworld that had stolen them.

Killian lifted his sword.

53

LYDIA

Everyone in the group jumped at Bercola's battle cry, Malahi and Hacken turning from their wary inspection of the xenthier stem.

"Bercola's holding them off," Lydia repeated. "She doesn't know it's a dead end."

The Queen closed her eyes, grief passing over her face. Then she turned to Hacken. "We don't know where it goes. It could take us to the bottom of the sea. Or to a chamber a league beneath the ground. Or to a terminus that's been entombed in rock."

Or somewhere far away from here.

"Gods-damned Falorns," Hacken muttered, running his hand through his hair in a gesture reminiscent of his brother. "They built this castle. It's full of their secrets."

Malahi turned away from the xenthier. "Sonia, how long can we hold them off?"

The small woman exhaled a long breath, then shook her head. "Against those things . . . Hours, I should think. They were unarmed, but if they keep coming . . ." She trailed off, leaving much unsaid because everyone was thinking it. The guards would fall one by one to the onslaught, and if no help came they might all die before Malahi and Hacken were driven to risk the xenthier. "But," Sonia added, breaking the silence, "that's only if one of the corrupted doesn't arrive. I'm out of arrows, and no one here is fast or strong enough to defeat one of them, especially not in close quarters."

There'd been one of the corrupted in the boat. And Lydia was sure everyone was thinking the same thing: that it was only a matter of time until it hunted them down.

Faint grunts of effort echoed up the tunnel. Thumps and thuds and the loud clang of a sword hitting rock. Bercola fighting off those poor souls who'd been inflected by the blight. But notably absent were screams. As though those she cut down felt no pain at all. *Because they aren't alive*, Lydia thought. *Merely hosts for the blight to control.*

"For now, we hold our position. Help may well be on its way." Malahi stepped away from the xenthier. "But if one of the corrupted comes, we use the xenthier. All of us."

Hacken huffed out an aggrieved breath. "It might follow. Better for some of your soldiers to try to hold it off. That will give the rest of us a chance to run."

Malahi's eyes flared with disgust. "No. We live together or we die together. That's an order."

"Do not presume to give me orders, girl," he snarled. "Without me, you're nothing."

All the guardswomen shifted angrily, but Malahi waved a calming hand at them. "Oh, I don't presume to order you to do anything, *High Lord* Calorian. By all means, if you wish to stand here, sword in hand, giving us all a fighting chance of survival, I will ensure you are honored for your heroism."

Hacken's gaze was vitriolic, but Malahi only frowned, assessing the group. "You," she said, pointing at Lydia. "Go inform Bercola of our plan, then stay there. If one of the corrupted comes, you'll be the only warning we have."

Not a random choice. Lydia met Malahi's cool amber gaze, then nodded.

"She shouldn't go alone," Gwen protested. "Just in case."

"It only takes one person to shout a warning."

Never mind that the person doing the shouting wasn't likely to make it back to the xenthier before the corrupted caught up to her. To refuse to go and necessitate someone else doing it would be cowardice, and if it weren't for the fact that so many other lives depended on her, Lydia wouldn't have hesitated. But Teriana needed her. Her father needed her. The Maarin needed her.

Her mark made her stronger and faster, and it allowed her to endure and survive what others couldn't. Of anyone standing in this room, *she* was the one most likely to make it back to the xenthier alive. "I'll go."

Before her courage could abandon her entirely, Lydia started up the tunnel, moving by feel as the light behind her faded. It was only when she was in the darkness entirely that Lydia realized the faint sounds of Bercola fighting weren't growing louder, they'd vanished entirely.

What if Bercola had been overwhelmed?

What if the horde of poisoned civilians was silently coming in her direction?

What if their grey hands were reaching toward her?

Every step was a force of will, Lydia peering into the blackness even as she listened for the sound of breathing. For the shuffle of bare feet. Then ahead, she made out the flickering glow of a torch. And faintly, almost so imperceptible that she wasn't certain what she was hearing, came the sound of weeping.

Sword pointed ahead of her, Lydia crept down the tunnel. As she rounded the last bend, the stink of blood and blight hit her in the face, her eyes landing on Bercola's broad shadow, and beyond . . .

The small chamber was painted with gore, bodies and body parts layered upon the floor. Not soldiers, but Mudamorian refugees. Women and children, all barefoot and clad in ragged clothing, their bodies emaciated from hunger.

Lydia gagged, turning to press her forehead against the cool wall until she regained control. When she turned, Bercola was scrubbing tears from her cheeks.

"They wouldn't stop coming." The giantess's voice was hoarse, pleading. "I tried just knocking them back. Knocking them down. But they kept coming."

It was then Lydia saw the rips in Bercola's clothing. The stains of blood. The scratches and bite marks on her enormous hands.

"I tried." Bercola's shoulders bowed, the tip of her sword resting against the ground. "They aren't the enemy. They are . . . were, our people."

This had broken her. Not physically, for Lydia knew the giantess's wounds weren't mortal. But her mind would never be the same. There was no coming back from this.

Which was exactly what the Corrupter wanted.

Chaos. Anger. Fear. That was what the god desired. What fueled his power. He'd trapped all these thousands of people in the city they'd once called home. Taught them to fear the dark. Their empty stomachs. And now one another.

"They weren't themselves." She offered the words as sympathy, knowing they'd make little difference. "It was the blight within them, and it knows only one master."

The slow clap of hands made Lydia jump and Bercola whirl around, blade rising in defense.

On the far side of the chamber stood a man dressed in black riding leathers. He was young, his skin the same dusky hue as Killian's, hair a dark brown, but the eyes regarding them were black voids rimmed with flame. "Poetics in such a dark hour," he said, nudging one of the corpses with his foot. "Not that this rabble deserves it."

"Lydia," Bercola hissed. "Run!"

But the corrupted was across the chamber in a blur of speed. He knocked aside Bercola's sword in its downward stroke, sparks flashing as the blade hit the metal of his wrist guard, then tackled her against the floor with a bone-shattering crunch.

Lydia opened her mouth to scream a warning; then she heard shouts coming from the tunnel the corrupted had come from. They were calling Malahi's name. Hacken's name. Help was here, if only she and Bercola could hold off the corrupted long enough.

The giantess grappled with the corrupted, but the creature's strength was more than enough to counter Bercola's skill. They rolled, slamming into Lydia's legs as she tried to stab at the thing. He twisted, reaching up to yank the sword from her hands and toss it across the chamber.

Bercola took the opportunity to punch the corrupted in the face, his jaw cracking, head snapping back. But he only hissed in irritation, catching her arm and slamming it against a ridge in the stone floor, breaking the bone with an audible snap. Bercola screamed and Lydia stabbed with her knife, but the blade only skidded along the corrupted's ribs.

Snarling, he rose and, before Lydia could dart backward, backhanded her, shattering her spectacles and snapping her head backward.

Agony fired across her face and she fell onto her bottom, her neck screaming in pain; blood dripped down her cheeks. Sobbing, she tried to regain her footing, but her vision was doubled, the world spinning.

Get up. Get up.

Bercola screamed, and as Lydia's vision finally cleared, she saw the creature had a naked hand around the giantess's throat, his teeth bared in a smile.

Instinct took over.

Lydia flung herself at the corrupted, grabbing him by the waist. They rolled, slamming into the wall, tiny pieces of rock raining down on them. She smashed her elbow against his nose, blood splattering her face even as his fist took her in the ribs.

Agony split her torso, every gasping breath sending sharp stabs of pain through her body.

You'll heal! Lydia silently screamed the words at herself. *Just hold him here until help arrives!*

The corrupted's fists hammered her body, her wrist snapping as she deflected a blow aimed for her face. It hurt. It hurt with an intensity she'd never experienced. Never dreamed of.

Hang on.

Boots pounded down the tunnel, coming closer. The corrupted turned his head, listening, then tried to shove Lydia aside. "I've more important targets than you."

She lunged, grabbing the corner of his coat and pulling, but he only smacked her arm away with a force that made her cry out. "Bercola, help!"

But the giantess was on her knees on the floor, too injured to move.

The corrupted sprinted in the direction of Malahi and the others.

Go!

Lydia tore after him, running faster than she'd believe herself capable of as she pursued him down the twisting tunnels, following the foul brilliance that illuminated him. Ahead, light bloomed, and with all the strength she possessed she threw herself forward. The corrupted went down but twisted as he fell, and Lydia landed on her back with him on top of her.

"Fine," he hissed. "If you must have it this way."

His hand slapped against her cheek.

It felt like her insides were being torn out, her skin burning, her heart hammering, a frantic and primal need to fight rising in her chest.

"No!" Lydia screamed the word in the corrupted's face. Ripping free one of her gloves, she grabbed the creature's bare throat and dug her fingers into his flesh. And she *pulled*.

Life surged back into her, what he'd taken from her and more, her injuries melting away as she pulled and pulled even as her mind recoiled from the strange pleasure that came with it. The corrupted's eyes widened in shock and he reared backward, her fingers slipping loose from his throat a heartbeat before a sword blade sliced his head from his neck.

Blood gushed from the stump as his body toppled onto her and Lydia screamed as it splattered her face.

Then hands were under her arms, pulling her free.

"Are you all right?"

Killian's voice. Wiping blood from her eyes revealed his face. His left eye was swollen shut, a deep cut on his temple dripping blood down his cheek. His clothes were torn and covered with gore, but he was here and he was alive.

"I'm fine." Her voice rasped, her throat dry as sand.

"As are the rest of us, thanks to you, Lord Calorian."

Twisting, Lydia looked over her shoulder to see the group standing next to the xenthier, all eyes on her. Including Malahi's.

Killian let go of her shoulders, stepping past to Malahi's side, both the Queen and the High Lord immediately demanding answers as to what had happened.

Had they seen what she'd done?

Only Lena was watching her now. "Is Bercola . . . ?"

Injured. And badly. "I'll go to her now."

Lydia took Lena's torch and ran back into the chamber, hating how *alive* she felt. How *good* she felt in the face of what she'd done.

The giantess lay on the floor, groaning but not fully conscious. Easing the woman onto her side, Lydia grimaced at the sight of the jagged split in her scalp and the fractured bone beneath. *A mortal wound.*

Six more soldiers ran into the chamber. "That way." Lydia gestured down the tunnel. She waited until they were gone, then pressed her hand to Bercola's head injury, pushing life into it. Bone solidified and the bleeding of the brain ceased, the giantess's skin knitting beneath Lydia's hand. She gave Bercola all that she had taken from the corrupted. Only when she felt once again herself did she remove her hand and slump against the wall. There were bodies everywhere. All around her.

Bercola lifted her head from the floor, eyes searching. "Where is it? The corrupted?"

"Dead."

And Lydia was covered in his blood, her skin coated with it.

"Malahi?"

"Killian's with them."

There was blood in her mouth. She could taste it.

A soldier came back in their direction, his eyes landing on Bercola before moving to Lydia. "The Queen is safe. We'll secure the passage and get you all out of here." Then he nodded once. "Well done."

It didn't feel well done.

A rhythmic rattle caught Lydia's attention. Her scabbard, tapping the stone floor. Only then did she realize she was shaking. Crying. Her breath came in escalating pants, not enough air reaching her lungs.

"It's all right." Bercola eased upward, wrapping her unbroken arm around Lydia's shoulders and pulling her close. "It's over. Deep breaths."

It didn't feel over. Instead, waves of fear and remembered pain washed over Lydia, smothering her. Yet it was nothing compared to the panic that rose up like bile when she thought of what she'd done. The way it had felt. How some part of her, deep, deep down, wanted to feel that way again.

Sonia appeared from around the corner, quickening her step at the sight of them. Gwen and Lena arrived on her heels. "How badly are you hurt?"

"I'm fine," Lydia said. "Bercola needs to see a healer."

Despite Lydia's protests, Lena hauled her up; both Gwen and Sonia helped Bercola to stand. Two more of the guardswomen appeared, then Killian and Malahi. The Queen's jaw tightened as she surveyed the dead civilians littering the chamber; then she inclined her head to Bercola. "You saved our lives. Thank you."

Without another word, she carried on.

Hacken raised one eyebrow as he passed, murmuring, "I believe she's disappointed you survived."

There was no answer to that, so Lydia kept silent, watching as the rest of the guardswomen and soldiers made their way through the gory chamber until only she and Lena remained.

"Come on." Her friend tugged on her arm. "We'll get you cleaned up."

"You go. I need a minute."

Lena opened her mouth as though to protest and then nodded. "I'll make sure they don't lock you down here, but don't take too long, all right?"

"I won't."

Picking up the flickering torch, which burned low, Lydia waited for the sound of footsteps to fade, and then she went in the opposite direction.

The tunnel was a mess of bloody footprints from all who'd passed, the corpse of the corrupted shoved to one side. Lydia avoided looking at the dead man's face as she skirted around his decapitated head, her boots sticking in the pooled blood.

The xenthier stem was as thick as her wrist, jutting three feet out of the rocky floor, her face reflecting in its multitude of facets. "Where do you go?" she asked. Picking up a small stone, she tossed it at the stem. It disappeared, already somewhere far away.

She knew the risks. Knew that reaching out to grasp the xenthier might result in her dying in an instant. In an hour. In a day.

But it might also deliver her from the horrible trap that was this city. To stay meant death one way or another, and there was no chance Malahi would allow her on any ship she boarded—High Lord Calorian had ensured that.

Teriana needs me.

My father needs me.

And if it came to pass that Lydia was too late to save them, then Lucius Cassius needed to be brought to justice for his crimes.

There is nothing for you here.

Her eyes burning, Lydia tightened her grip on her sword. Then she reached out her fingers toward the xenthier stem.

54

KILLIAN

Lunging, Killian caught Lydia's wrist and hauled her backward with enough force that she crashed into him, the torch in her hand falling to the floor.

She struggled, then realized it was him, her eyes widening. "What are you doing here?"

It was more of an accusation than a question. "I've got good instincts. Which is fortunate for you."

She jerked her wrist out of his grasp, bowing her head even as she balled her hands into fists. "I need to get home, Killian. And that means getting free of this cursed city however I have to."

"With this?" He jabbed a finger toward the xenthier, wishing there was a way to smash it. To break it. To eliminate any chance she'd ever go near it. "You have no idea where it goes."

"Anywhere is better than here."

"You bloody well know that's not true."

"Teriana needs me!" Lydia screamed the words, her whole body shaking. "Everything that happened to her, to her people—it is my fault! There is no risk too great if it means I might have the chance to save her life." Then she dropped to her knees, sobbing. "It's been a month. She's been a prisoner for a month, and all I can imagine is the things that Lucius has done to her. And my father . . . I've nearly lost hope that he's still alive." Lifting her face, she stared up at him, black lashes glistening with tears. "Every choice I've made has pulled me farther away from them."

He knew she didn't mean distance.

Dropping to his knees, Killian gripped her hands, wishing

he had a way to stop her shaking. "Every choice you've made since I've known you has saved lives."

Her hands tightened on his, her pale skin sticky with drying blood. Yet despite it, she was the most beautiful girl he'd ever met. Lydia was no fighter, but she was a warrior in her own right. In her own way. Clever. Fierce. Selfless. "Hegeria chose well when she chose you."

She gave the faintest shake of her head, fresh tears cutting tracks through the blood on her face.

"The sun will be up soon," he said. "We'll know better then the state of the Gamdeshian fleet. With the vessels that survived, we'll begin immediate evacuations. The city is lost. Everyone has to leave, one way or another, and there isn't time for Quindor's little tests. I'll get you out of here."

"And if the fleet is lost entirely?"

Killian sucked in a breath, unwilling to consider the magnitude of such a loss. "Then I'll make sure you're equipped and supplied, and you can take your chance with the xenthier."

"You won't try to stop me?"

Every part of him would want to. Not just because of the risk of the xenthier, but the danger he knew Lydia would face once she made it home. Killian knew the sort of man this Lucius Cassius was—not the sort that would take kindly to his power being contested, especially by a young woman. And in trying to save Teriana's life, Lydia might well lose her own. But keeping her here was no safer. He could not protect her, and even if he could, Killian knew she didn't want that from him. "It's your choice, not mine."

Though by the gods, he wished it could be different. Except he was sworn to Malahi, was *betrothed* to Malahi, and he would not dishonor her, never mind that none of this had been his choice. No matter that he could feel Lydia's breath against his cheek, her full lips so temptingly close. No matter that all he wanted to do was peel away clothes stained with the horror of the night and lose himself in her. Not for a night, but for as long as she'd have him.

Yet what Killian wanted had never mattered. And it did not now.

Rising to his feet, he helped her upright. And that's when he heard the sound of running feet. Lena burst into the chamber, dropping her torch to rest her hands on her knees, panting. "Thank the Six. I was starting to worry that you two star-crossed lovers had chosen to abandon us to wherever that *thing* goes."

"Lena." Killian glared at her. "You really need to learn to keep some thoughts inside your head."

"Right. Well, since you're still here." She handed him a tiny scrap of paper, the sight making his skin crawl with trepidation. "This came in by pigeon from the Royal Army."

Killian read the few sentences, his heart sinking in his chest as he eyed the date.

"What is it?" Lydia asked.

"The rest of Rufina's host flanked the Royal Army two nights ago." Shoving the paper in his pocket, he started up the tunnel. "More than twenty thousand enemy soldiers are marching on Mudaire and there is nothing in their way capable of stopping them."

55

LYDIA

Killian led them at a run through the tunnels, both Lydia and Lena struggling to keep his pace.

Just as it was a struggle not to look at the faces of the bodies they passed. More blight-infected civilians, most of whom Killian had killed from behind as he had raced to rescue Malahi, and Lydia couldn't help but think about Bercola. How the giantess had seemed . . . *broken* in a way no healer could fix.

How much worse was it for him?

No one knew better than her how dedicated Killian was to protecting the people of Mudaire, and to have been forced to slaughter them? She could only imagine the toll it must be taking on him, though he wasn't showing it.

"Captain," Lena called, but Killian didn't slow. Didn't show any sign that he heard at all, even when Lena repeated his title. Finally, the other girl shouted, "Killian, will you listen to me?"

He slid to a stop and Lydia nearly slammed into his back, catching herself against the wall.

"What?" he demanded.

"You might want to go ahead of us," Lena said. "Her Majesty is waiting where you left her and she's . . ." Lena's eyes went to Lydia. "Might be better if we followed along after, if you get my meaning."

Killian was silent for a long moment; then he said, "The reason I came back was that I'm not leaving *any* of you down here alone. That hasn't changed." Then he twisted on his heel, heading in the direction of the torch light ahead.

"Don't say I didn't warn you," Lena muttered. Catching Lydia's arm, she said, "Listen, I know the heart wants what it wants, but this is going to cause you a world of trouble." Her grip tightened. "Just keep your head down, all right?"

There was little to do but nod, though apprehension bubbled in Lydia's chest as they followed Killian.

Malahi and the rest of the group stood waiting at the base of the ladder leading up to the palace. Someone had dragged the bodies to the side, but there were still smears of blood and blight across the stone floor, the hem of the Queen's gown smearing it as she paced back and forth. She stopped in her tracks as Killian approached, shadows from the torches dancing across her face.

"Oh, how wonderful," she snapped. "It appears our dear Lydia is alive and well."

Killian didn't answer, only moved to go around her. But Malahi shifted into his path.

"We are about to have an enemy army knocking on the gates to Mudaire, Your Majesty. Perhaps we might prioritize *that*."

"How nice to see that there is *something* you care about more than her welfare."

"I'm not having this conversation right now."

"Yes, you are." Malahi's hands balled into fists. "This is twice now that you've abandoned me in favor of protecting her. Explain yourself."

"Abandoned you?" Killian braced his hands on either side of the tunnel. "I've never left you without at least a dozen armed guards standing in my place."

"Which begs the question of why you don't send them instead of going yourself."

Lydia held her breath, because this wasn't just a question of those two moments. It was all the times he'd left Malahi in the palace to see to the well-being of those other than her.

"Because I don't like to put others unnecessarily at risk."

"You swore an oath to me, Killian Calorian." Malahi's voice was a mix of anger and hurt. "And yet most days it feels like you are my bodyguard in name only."

Silence.

"In name only." There was a faint shake to Killian's voice that made Lydia want to step forward. To stop this. But Lena's hand closed over her wrist, pulling her back.

"Do you have any concept of what I had to do to save your life tonight?" He shouted the words, his voice reverberating off the walls. "Do you have any concept of the number of people I killed so that you could live?" Reaching down into the shadows, he jerked up one of the corpses, the small and lifeless body hanging in his hands as he shoved it in Malahi's face. "I killed her. I remember slicing through her spine while I fought to get to *you*. And I have to live with it."

Malahi recoiled from the corpse and it was then that Hacken stepped out of the shadows. "Enough, Killian."

In a flash of motion, Killian dropped the corpse, slamming his brother against the wall, once. Twice. Three times. All with a cold fury that rendered him nearly unrecognizable to Lydia. Always she'd known that he was dangerous, but never had he made her feel afraid. This wasn't him.

Something wasn't right.

Lydia tried to intervene, but Lena and some of the other girls held her back.

"Do you think I don't know you're the one behind all this?" Killian shouted. "Do you think I don't know that you're the one to blame?"

"Blame for what?" Hacken shouted back, struggling ineffectually. "Putting you in the position you needed to be to win this war? You're a pair of children more concerned with your feelings than with doing whatever it takes to defeat our enemies, so I took matters into my own hands."

Sonia chose that moment to shove between the pair of them, her face intent, but Lydia could already feel the rage fading from Killian, his grip on Hacken slackening.

"We are going to go upstairs and gather the High Lords," Hacken said. "And then you're going to war against the Derin army. And you're going to win."

"Why?"

Killian whispered the word, but Lydia heard it. Knew the real question he was asking.

"Because," Hacken said. "This is a war between the gods, and thus a war between the Marked. It's not enough for you to just fight, Killian. You must lead us to our salvation."

Every instinct in Lydia screamed that the High Lord's words were a lie buried in the truth. That despite war being at his doorstep, his ambitions for himself were what had motivated him to force this union between Killian and Malahi.

And yet Killian allowed Sonia to push him back. Saying nothing, he went to the ladder, climbing upward and disappearing from sight.

"After you, my lady." Hacken gestured for Malahi to climb, but the Queen instead turned to Lydia.

"You are a liability," she said. "Get out of my palace."

Then she climbed in a swish of skirts and disappeared. The guardswomen followed at her heels, their faces full of apology as they left Lydia alone with High Lord Calorian.

"I'm sorry," he said to her, wincing as he rubbed what was likely a badly bruised shoulder. "I don't use people lightly. But surely you see it was for the greater good?"

"All I care about is getting to Serlania," she lied, her skin prickling. "That's all this was ever about."

He smiled. "Smart girl."

Lydia followed him up the ladder, her stomach twisting as the carnage filled her gaze. Bodies thick upon the floor, but the first face her gaze lighted upon was Brin's, the dead guardswoman's eyes glassy and unseeing.

Which was why Lydia didn't miss it when Hacken Calorian stepped square on the girl's back as he strode from the room.

56

KILLIAN

Don't think about it. You've more pressing problems, Killian told himself, but repeating the order over and over in his head had little effect. Because it was impossible to forget the rage that had fallen over him in the tunnels. Impossible to forget how close he'd come to killing his own brother.

The group climbed the stairs to the main level of the palace, stepping over bodies and avoiding pools of blood as they went. Spotting one of the men he'd put in charge of securing the High Lords' safety, Killian waved him over. "We have control of the palace?"

"Yes, sir," the man replied. "We've swept all the rooms. Anyone who shouldn't be here is dead."

Dead Mudamorians. People you were supposed to protect. "Start clearing the bodies out front and then burn the lot. Use oil and make sure those doing the work wear gloves. Then burn the gloves."

"Yes, sir."

But he hadn't protected them. Instead, he'd killed dozens of civilians who'd been infected by blight. Not that he'd had much of a choice. The blight turned them feral and vicious, attacking anyone they crossed paths with who wasn't likewise afflicted. They didn't speak. Didn't seem to feel pain or any emotion beyond rage. But they'd still been his people, and every time he blinked he saw another one fall beneath his sword.

It hurt to breathe.

"We need to convene the High Lords." Hacken had come up from behind and was eyeing Killian warily. "We don't have time to waste."

As if Killian didn't know that. "Have the High Lords assembled in the council chambers," he said to the soldier. "Full escorts."

"May I change my clothes first?" Malahi's face was drawn and pale, and she hugged herself as though cold.

"Do what you want," Killian replied, not caring when she flinched. And then immediately feeling guilty for it. *What's wrong with you? This is the girl you're going to marry.*

The reminder was jarring, the knowledge that he was betrothed still feeling like a bad dream from which he needed to wake.

"I'll meet you in the council chambers," Hacken said, then headed in that direction, stepping over bodies like they were nothing more than fallen branches on the ground.

Anger bubbled up in Killian's chest, but he tamped it back down. "Sonia, keep an eye on him. The rest of you with me and the Queen."

They started up the main staircase, and his gaze went to Lydia, who trailed uncertainly at the rear. She was covered in blood and missing her spectacles, which he knew made her uneasy. *You can't keep her here. You can't push Malahi any further than you already have.*

But that didn't stop his stomach from souring at the thought of Lydia being out of his sight. What if she ran afoul of some of the infected? Or worse, one of the corrupted? What if she tried to go back to the xenthier?

Your duty is to Malahi. That you're pissed off at her doesn't change that. Nothing changes that.

So he fell back. "Wait until the sun's up, then go into the city," he said under his breath. "I'll find you when I know more. Stay safe."

Nodding, Lydia stopped on the bottom step, and it took every ounce of willpower Killian had to walk away from her, following Malahi up the stairs.

The upper level was broadly untouched, the soldiers who'd defended it having done their duty, but the carpets were marred with dirt and bloody footprints, several plants knocked over and pictures askew. Reaching out, Killian straightened one of them, then bent to right a plant, not knowing why he felt compelled to do so.

What is wrong with me?

They reached the doors to her suite, which were flanked by the soldiers guarding the ladies within. Inside, Malahi went directly to her bedroom, and Killian mechanically swept the chamber to ensure it was empty.

"I need a minute," she said. "One minute alone."

"Fine." Shutting the door behind him, Killian leaned against the wood, barely seeing the comings and goings around him. The stench of blood rose from his clothing, filling his nostrils and making him want to gag. Tearing off his coat, he flung it across the hallway, but it did no good. The blood had soaked into his shirt, coated his hands, crusted under his fingernails.

All of it Mudamorian blood.

"Are you all right?"

Gwen's voice tore his attention from his hands, and he looked up to see the guardswomen watching him uneasily.

They're looking to you for strength, he berated himself. *You cannot falter. Not now.* "I'm fine."

"What's going to happen?"

"Sunrise will allow us to determine the state of the Gamdeshian fleet." It was a concentrated effort to keep his voice steady. "We'll begin evacuating Mudaire immediately."

"But the whole sea seemed like it was on fire." Gwen dabbed at a cut on her cheek, then stared at her sleeve as though she wasn't sure where the blood had come from. "What if they all burned?"

"That's unlikely." *But possible.* "There is no point speculating now when another hour will give us facts."

Which was true, but he still needed to come up with plans for every scenario, and his mind was giving him nothing. Nothing but visions of bodies and limbs and—

"Incoming," one of the girls muttered.

A soldier strode down the hallway, and Killian's skin prickled with unease. "Message for Her Majesty, sir." He handed over the tiny roll of paper that had obviously come by pigeon. "And unfortunate news. High Lord Torrington is infected with blight."

Killian swore, handing off the message to Gwen, who disappeared inside Malahi's chambers to deliver it. "How?"

"It appears he consumed something tainted. He was on his way to the council chambers when he suddenly—" The soldier broke off, giving a violent shake of his head. "He changed, sir. Turned feral. We were able to restrain him and return him to his rooms. Grand Master Quindor is with him now."

Killian moved so Gwen could step back into the corridor. "He's the only one?"

"Yes, sir. The rest of them are convening in the council chambers. They've been instructed not to eat or drink anything."

A vision of Torrington sipping wine during the vote slapped Killian in the face. "It's the decanter in the council chambers that's been poisoned. Go! Ensure it's disposed of."

Eyes wide, the man bolted in the direction of the council chambers. But the damage was done. High Lord Torrington was a dead man; it was only a matter of time.

Grinding his teeth, Killian debated asking one of the guardswomen to inform Helene about her father before deciding better of it. "Keep Malahi inside until I'm back."

Striding down the hall, he entered the sitting rooms where Malahi's ladies were holding on to one another, faces streaked with tears. "The palace is secure," he said, and all of them sighed with relief. "But I have unfortunate news. High Lord Torrington has been infected with blight."

Helene clapped a hand against her mouth. "Is he . . . ?"

"Quindor's with him." Killian gave a slow shake of his head. "But you need to prepare yourself for the worst. I'm sorry."

A ragged sob tore from her lips and she doubled over, the other girls trying to comfort her, but she only brushed them away. Climbing to her feet, she demanded, "Where is he? Where is my father?"

"In the other wing, but you don't want to see him like this, Helene. Trust me on that."

"I trust you with nothing," she hissed, then shoved past him into the corridor. Clenching his teeth, Killian motioned to a soldier to follow her. Then his eyes lighted on Malahi's open door. To the Queen standing in the opening.

"I'm afraid circumstances are even worse than we realized," she said, holding up the roll of paper. "The Royal Army is abandoning Mudaire. We are on our own."

Within an hour of receiving Serrick's message, everyone had gathered in the council chambers.

Which meant they were all present when Helene entered the room, her eyes red and swollen as she silently circled the table and took the Torrington seat, now High Lady of her house.

"I'm so sorry, Helene," Malahi said. "May the Six keep and comfort his soul."

Helene gave a curt nod; then the doors opened once more to admit Quindor. The Grand Master's face was aged and drawn from using his mark and his white robes were stained with blood and blight.

"I'll not mince words," he said, holding on to the edge of the table for balance. "Those infected by blight cannot be saved."

Murmurs of distress filled the council room, but Killian asked, "Why is the infection taking hold so swiftly? It took days for Malahi's horse to succumb and she was coated in blight."

"Most likely because the infected individuals consumed tainted water, allowing the poison to reach the brain more swiftly," Quindor answered. "Or else the blight has grown more potent; there is no way to say for certain. I can say that once it takes hold, the individual entirely loses their mind, a strange madness taking hold. They feel no pain. Seem to feel nothing at all but the desire to attack those not similarly afflicted."

A strangled noise exited Helene's throat, and Killian knew she'd been there in those final moments. That she'd seen. It would take a long time for the haunted expression in her gaze to fade.

If it ever faded at all.

"The city must be evacuated," Quindor said. "But I expect you already realize that. Now if you'll excuse me, there are more patients requiring my attention."

Without a word, he left the room, leaving everyone in muted silence.

"So," Hacken said. "Which will do the job first: Rufina or the blight?"

"Rufina," Killian answered. "We're stockpiling clean water, and more can be retrieved north and south of the city during the daylight hours. Whereas the Derin army will be here"—he looked at the map, considering the math—"in three, possibly four, days."

"And Serrick's abandoned us," High Lord Cavinbern shouted, slamming his fist down on the table. "The Seventh take him, doesn't he realize half the ruling houses of Mudamora are stuck in this cursed city?"

"He's not stupid," Hacken interjected. "He knows *we'll* get out before the siege begins."

All eyes went to the hastily scrawled message in Serrick's own hand, the ink smeared from where the paper had been rolled before it had dried. Then all eyes went to Killian.

This is what you do, he reminded himself. *Not politics and lies and manipulation, but war.* He cleared his throat. "High Lord Rowenes likely doesn't believe the Royal Army will be able to catch the Derin army before it reaches Alder's Ford, and in that he's probably correct. What Rufina will do once she passes the river Tarn is split her army into three. Part to hold the ford, part to sack Mudaire, and part to go south to the coast to take Abenharrow. So what High Lord Rowenes is going to do instead is march the Royal Army hard south and east, cross the Tarn here"—he pointed at the map—"and intercept the Derin army before they can reach Abenharrow, where the Royal Army will make its stand."

The whole room erupted in outrage, and from behind Malahi, Killian heard Sonia snarl something in Gamdeshian that he was fairly certain translated as *Craven yellow-haired worm*. In truth, Serrick's decision was strategically sound. Mudaire itself was lost. The wells were poisoned and there was no reliable source of food. What were a hundred thousand lives compared to the millions living in the southern part of the kingdom who'd be at risk if the Royal Army wasn't able to intercept the enemy?

But just because something was strategically valid didn't mean it was right.

"What is our strategy, then?" Malahi asked.

"I'll take all the soldiers at our disposal and try to cut Rufina's army off. Buy some time."

The door opened then. A Gamdeshian soldier in a lieutenant's uniform entered, the man bowing low. His clothing was both singed and salt stained, a still-bleeding cut marring one of his russet-brown cheeks. "Your Majesty. Your Graces."

Malahi rose. "You have a count, then? How many ships are sailable?"

"Yes, my lady. Four ships."

She blanched and Killian felt his own stomach flip. He'd known it was bad, but . . .

"Four ships?" Malahi repeated. "Out of one hundred?"

"Yes, my lady. Four sailable ships." The Gamdeshian lieutenant's face was grim, the muscles beneath his skin flexing periodically as though he was struggling to maintain his composure.

"And your number of soldiers?"

"Five hundred, give or take."

"Of?"

"Two thousand, my—" The man's voice cracked, his head bowing.

"Gods." Malahi pressed a hand to her mouth. "I am so sorry. May the Six take and comfort their souls."

The lieutenant took a deep breath and squared his shoulders. "This is not a war against Mudamora, Your Majesty. It is a war against humanity. Against the Six themselves. If there was any doubt in the minds of my soldiers as to why we are here, last night vanquished it."

"Good." Killian straightened. "Then they'll be ready to march by midmorning. I assume you will be in command of the Gamdeshian force?"

The man's gaze shifted past Killian to the guardswomen standing behind Malahi. Killian lifted one eyebrow. "Or am I to presume that Sonia will resume her role as captain, then?"

The guardswoman snorted. "You can't do that."

"Why not?" Killian asked. "I trust you. They trust you. Seems a splendid idea. What say you, Lieutenant?"

Ignoring Killian, the man saluted Sonia. "I'll ready our soldiers to march on your order, Captain."

"This is madness, Killian." Hacken threw up his hands. "You can't really mean to strip Mudaire of every soldier it has?"

"I mean to strip the city of every person in it who is willing to fight," Killian answered, forcing himself to meet his brother's gaze. "The city isn't defendable. We have less than a thousand trained soldiers, and it would take three times that number to defend a wall of this size against a force as large as Rufina's. And that's if the wall was whole and strong, but we know the blight has undermined the foundation. It won't be long until sections in the western quarter begin to collapse."

"But—"

"There are no buts, Hacken. Rufina's army will be here in three days. You have only four ships to evacuate a hundred thousand people to Abenharrow where they can caravan south to safety. At best you can expect two round trips per day, which means you'll have evacuated fewer than five thousand people by the time the battle begins."

No one in the room spoke.

"Our only option is to try to stop them from reaching the city in order to buy you more time." Smoothing the map, he pressed a finger down on a spot west of Mudaire. "The only place suitable for an army to cross the river Tarn is here at Alder's Ford. It's narrow and steep, and we'll have the high ground. We should be able to hold them back for a couple of days before we're over-run. Which should give you five days, at least, to evacuate."

Not nearly enough time, and everyone knew it.

"I've drafted a document detailing that we've voted to put Malahi on the throne." Hacken's voice cut through the noise. "We'll sign it and have it dispatched immediately to the Royal Army." Picking up a pen, he signed his name, passing the document on to Cavinbern, who signed it as well. The document circled the table, finally landing in front of Helene Torrington, who sat silent and red-eyed at the far end of the table. The vote they needed for a majority. The vote Malahi needed to remain queen.

Slowly, she lifted her face. "You want me to support the *girl* who caused all of this? Whose meddling and scheming got my father killed? Resulted in the sacking of the royal palace and the burning of an entire fleet?" She laughed, the sound piercing and shrill. "And for *what*? To save those Mudamora is better off without at the risk of the good and hardworking souls of the South who depend on our army to keep them safe?"

Killian shook his head, having known this was coming. But he still twitched as Helene rose in a flurry of motion, her eyes full of fury. "You want me vote for the girl who intends to marry *him*?"

"Helene, enough," Malahi said. "You've made your point."

"Shut up, Malahi. You no longer have the privilege of telling me what to do." Helene leaned her hands on the table. "And neither do the rest of you. So if you'll excuse me, I'm going to go retrieve my things, and then I'm going to go board one of those ships." Without another word, she stormed out of the room.

Hacken turned a dark glare on Killian, tempting him to point out that his conflict with Helene wouldn't matter if Hacken and Malahi hadn't forced this bloody betrothal down his throat without asking. Not that it was looking likely that he'd live long enough to attend his pending nuptials.

"We need to get word to Serrick!" One of the High Lords banged his fist on the table. "Advise him that we have forces on the way to hold the ford."

"I've sent word to Abenharrow already," Killian answered. "They'll send riders to meet the Royal Army, but by the time they reach them it's likely going to be too late. And anyone we send will have to find their way through the Derin army and its scouts. We must plan for the reality that we are on our—"

"Where are my boys?"

At the sound of the familiar female voice, Killian broke off, his head whipping to the doors right as they swung open and his mother strode in, a grey-haired giant at her heels.

Everyone, including Malahi, rose at the sight of Lady Calorian, who surveyed them all with a glower. "Well, haven't you all managed to botch things right up."

No one answered. No one, Killian was quite certain, dared.

His mother circled the table until she stood in front of him. Reaching up, she took hold of his chin and pulled him down to her level, brow furrowing as she inspected his swollen eye. "This the worst of it?"

"I'm fine, Mother."

She huffed out an exasperated breath. "You could be run through and bleeding everywhere and you'd still say the same thing."

Not waiting for an answer, she continued in her progress around the table until she reached Hacken. "Well?"

He blinked at her.

"Move, Hacken. I've just walked all the way up from the harbor and my feet hurt."

Color rising to his cheeks, Hacken rose from the Calorian seat and pushed it under their mother while she smoothed her black skirts. "I've brought five vessels with me, all full of horses, weapons, and supplies, which my crews are in the process of unloading. I will, of course, be taking full control of the evacuation. It's a matter that requires organization, which makes me best suited."

"Mother—" Hacken said even as Malahi blurted out, "Lady Calorian, surely—"

"I believe you have other matters requiring your attention,

Your Highness," Lady Calorian interrupted. "And Hacken, you couldn't organize a closet without somehow making it political."

Killian cleared his throat. "Mother, it would be safer for you to leave with the first round of evacuees."

Silence. Then her eyebrow slowly arched. "Safer?"

"The palace is destroyed. There are bodies everywhere and the Six know what will happen once the sun goes down again."

His mother leaned back in her chair. "Killian, I stayed with your father through the sack of Serlania during the Giant Wars. Do you honestly believe I'm going to turn tail when faced with hungry civilians?"

"It's worse than that."

She made a noise that told him to shut up while he was still ahead. "How many days do we have?"

"If we can beat them to the ford, five."

"And nine ships in total." Pulling a sheet of paper in front of her, she picked up a pen, gesturing to the giant. "Ivan here is a summoner. He'll turn the winds in the favor of our ships. Draw in some rain so those who wait have something to drink that isn't full of poison."

The giant spoke. "Eoten Isle stands against the Seventh. So today, that means we stand with Mudamora." He lifted a huge shoulder in a shrug, his face splitting with a grin. "You are our favorite to cross swords with, and we would not care to see you fall to another foe when we have long wished for you to fall to us."

"It's good to have aspirations," Killian said, and the giant filled the room with his thundering laugh.

Lady Calorian finished her calculations, lifting her head and tapping the pen against her chin.

"Well?" Killian asked her. "Can you find enough seats at the table?"

His mother set down the pen, giving him a look that would've sent him running if he were still a child. "If you can give me six days, I can do it."

57

LYDIA

Lydia sat on her bed in the barracks, staring blankly at the worn wooden floor while she picked blood and grime out from under her fingernails.

The house was silent. Empty. Little more than a day had passed since it had been abandoned, the well contaminated by blight, but already it felt lifeless. As soon the whole city would be.

Coming back here had been a mistake. Or at the very least, lingering had been.

Too many memories.

Too many reminders of what, briefly, she'd had. And what she had lost.

Exhaling a ragged breath, she stood and undressed, her uniform stiff with dried blood and sweat. She left the ruined garments on the floor and retrieved her one dress, the wool smelling like soap, though it wouldn't for long given how filthy she was. But a bath was out of the question; the bucket of water she'd drawn up from the well was grey and smelled of rot. Her mark might keep her from being poisoned, but she'd rather not tempt fate.

Pulling her hair up into a messy twist, she buckled her sword belt over her dress, put her meager belongings into her satchel, and started downstairs, intent on walking to the harbor and washing up in the ocean. Reaching for the handle, she pulled the door open.

To find a startled Killian standing on the doorstep.

"What are you doing here?" she blurted out even as she took in the pieces of armor and chain mail he wore. His black war-horse stood on the empty street, his saddlebags bulging. "You're leaving?"

He nodded. "I'll lead our forces and try to hold back Rufina's army long enough to evacuate the city."

"What about the Royal Army?"

"Moving south to protect the rest of the kingdom."

"Oh," she said, the realization of what that meant hitting her like a battering ram to the stomach. "I see."

It wasn't a march to victory. It was a march to die so that the people of Mudaire might have a chance to live.

A tremor shook her hands, hundreds of words rising to her lips. A thousand words. All of them designed to keep him from going. To keep him alive, no matter the cost.

She said none of them.

He cleared his throat, eyes shifting up the street before moving back to her. "My mother, of all people, is organizing the evacuation. There's no reason you shouldn't be able to get on one of those ships, but if anyone gives you trouble, you find her and give her this." He handed her a letter. "They are going to be unloading the ships at Abenharrow, and from there people will travel to Serlania on foot. But you should be able to hire passage from another vessel in one of the port towns and get there sooner."

She nodded, her eyes burning.

"Once you're in Serlania, you need to get in touch with my brother Seldrid. Use my name, if you need to. Then give him this." He handed her another letter. "Tell him about Teriana, her crew, the Empire. All of it. He'll get you in contact with Maarin crews and make certain you have everything else you need. He's a good man—you can trust him."

Her jaw was trembling. Speech was impossible, so she only nodded again.

"You get back home, all right?" His hands caught her elbows, holding her steady. "You unseat that bastard Cassius. You get

Teriana and the rest of the Maarin free. And if Hegeria is still with you, use your mark to heal your father."

"I will." A hot tear rolled down her cheek.

"And you go with Teriana." His voice was hoarse. "Stay with the Maarin or sail with them until you find somewhere you love. Then make a good life for yourself. Don't let those Cel bastards keep you."

His grip on her arms was tight, and Lydia stepped forward, only inches separating them. "I could come back."

Wind whistled down the street, an empty straw basket tumbling along with it. The war-horse pawed the ground, pinning his ears before trying to kick the basket. But Killian didn't answer.

Then his hand slid down her arm to grip her hand. "In another life, I'd get down on my knees and beg you to come back. Might beg you not to go in the first place."

Her heart was beating so very quickly, a promise sitting on her tongue, waiting to be spoken.

Only to be silenced as Killian shook his head. "Don't come back to Mudamora, Lydia. There is nothing here for you but pain." He lifted her hand to his lips, kissing her knuckles. "Good luck. May the Six guide and protect your steps back to Teriana's side."

Turning, he strode toward the enormous horse and swung into the saddle, heeling the animal into a swift canter up the street.

He didn't look back.

Lydia didn't know how long she stood there unmoving. A minute. A lifetime.

There is nothing here for you. Not in Mudaire. Not on a Maarin ship. Not in Celendor. Was there something for her anywhere? Was there anywhere that she belonged?

Silencing the thoughts, she shoved the letters into her satchel and closed the door, heading up the street in the opposite direction toward the harbor.

A scuffle of sound caught her attention, and she peered into the blurry shadows. Wary of those who might attack her to take the few possessions she had, Lydia extracted her knife, moving to the center of the street and stopping in her tracks as Gwen stepped out from an alley.

"Been looking for you," the other girl said. "You disappeared."

"I was fired, remember?"

"Still could've said good-bye."

Gwen was right. She should've. These girls had been her friends for the past month. Had held her hand when she'd cried. Guarded her back. Made her laugh when she believed laughter impossible. Good-bye was the least of what she owed them. "I'm sorry."

Gwen started toward her, hands in the pockets of her coat. "Come back to the palace with me. Do things right before you hightail it south."

The skin on the back of Lydia's neck prickled, and she turned to see two of the other guardswomen walking up the street behind her, Lena following reluctantly in their wake. *What was going on?*

"Seems like I can say my good-byes right here." The palm of her hand holding the knife was slick with sweat.

"Better if you come with us."

They were approaching her on all sides. None of them had weapons in hand, but neither did they need them. All of them knew how to use their fists. "What's going on?"

Gwen's face was grim, and she gave a weary shake of her head. "I told you not to get involved with him. Told you it would be the worst sort of trouble. But you didn't listen."

"It's not like that." Lydia's free hand balled into a fist of frustration. If only she could tell them the truth: About her being a healer. About Killian hiring her because she could see the corrupted. About how he was helping her get back home. That he'd been teaching her to fight so she could protect herself.

But was that the whole truth? Or was the person she was lying to herself?

"We followed him here," Gwen said. "And from our vantage, it looked exactly *like that.*"

Run.

Lydia bolted, trying to get past Gwen, but the other girl dived, hitting her in the legs. They tumbled across the cobbled street, Lydia's knife flying from her hand.

Elbowing Gwen in the face, Lydia rolled the other girl off and scrambled up. But before she could regain her feet, someone else hit her in the back, sending her sprawling.

The other girls dog-piled onto her, pinning her legs and arms.

"Don't hurt her!" Lena shouted. "Malahi said she wasn't to be harmed."

Probably so that she can do it herself, Lydia thought bitterly. It was the last thought she had before Gwen clamped a foul-smelling rag over her mouth and everything went dark.

Lydia blinked, the world blurry and unfocused, but not, for once, because of her missing spectacles.

The room was well-appointed with heavy crimson curtains, furniture of polished wood, and several paintings hanging on the walls, though she couldn't tell what they were of. The window was cracked open, and from it came a breeze carrying the salty tang of the sea.

She was in the palace.

Lydia's head ached abominably, but as she tried to lift a hand to rub her temple, rope dug into her wrist. Both her arms were bound to the chair she was sitting on. Legs too.

Biting her teeth against the pain, she pulled against the ropes, but they were too strong. Too tight for her to do more than abrade her flesh. Her wrists grew slick with blood, and with a muttered curse she gave up.

The door to the room opened, and Malahi walked in, pulling it shut behind her before turning the bolt. "I told them that if they followed Killian they'd find you. Turns out I was right."

Anger chased away Lydia's fear. "Your kingdom is crumbling and your people are dying. But instead of focusing on that, you used your resources to have me dragged here. And for what? To have a jealous spat over a boy?" For the first time in her life, Lydia spit on the floor, immediately understanding why Teriana found it so satisfying. "You're pathetic."

Other than raising one eyebrow as she circled Lydia's glob of spit, Malahi showed no reaction as she approached, pulling a chair opposite Lydia and taking a seat. "We are here because of your relationship with Killian, Lydia. But let me assure you, jealousy has naught to do with it."

"I find that hard to believe given the way Hacken Calorian played you like a love-sick girl."

Malahi cast her eyes skyward. "Please. Sometimes it's best to allow the player to believe you're being played, because then they won't expect your attack from the rear."

Perhaps some of that was the truth, but Lydia had seen Malahi's reaction. Even if the Queen knew that there was nothing between Lydia and Killian, having his lack of sentiment for her shoved in her face had hurt. Badly.

"Hacken's soldiers guarding the palace ensure I can't sneak much past him," Malahi continued. "He believes I'm in here having my revenge on you, but the truth is a much different beast. You're going to do something for me."

"Give me one reason why I shouldn't just start screaming."

"No one will come."

"Bercola—"

"Is still in the infirmary waiting for a healer to tend to her injuries." Rising from her chair, Malahi went to the sideboard and poured herself a glass of precious water, drinking deeply before she added, "You only healed her enough to keep her from dying, didn't you?"

The blood fled from Lydia's skin, leaving ice in its wake. "I don't know what you're talking about."

Malahi sighed, then came back across the room. "Don't bother denying it, Lydia. It's easy enough for me to prove." Reaching down, she took hold of Lydia's wrists, her fingers uncharacteristically stained with ink. Then she pulled back the rope, revealing the healing abrasions. Moments passed, red fading to pink and then to white before disappearing.

Undeniable proof of her mark.

"You're the healer who saved Killian's life from the deimos. The healer no one has been able to track down in the month since. The healer he's doggedly refused to describe, despite the danger aiding you puts him in." Malahi removed her fingers from the rope. "The healer he hid in plain sight as one of my bodyguards, knowing it was the one sure way to get you past Quindor's testers when I sailed south for Serlania."

And to help keep you alive until you were safely there, Lydia wanted to add, but did not.

"I suspected some time ago who you really were." Malahi pulled on the bit of string looped around Lydia's neck, extracting the ring. "When he didn't give—" She broke off, giving a sharp shake of her head. "When I asked Helene to describe the girl she'd purchased this from, she said you were filthy, built like a boy, and ghastly tall. Probably northern. And lo and behold, the clean version of such a girl arrives in my employ not two days later. One my sworn sword abandons me in the middle of a riot in order to go back and save."

Malahi's voice was steady, her face serene but for the throbbing vein in her forehead that gave away her anger. Her hurt. "Then the rumors began that Hegeria herself was walking the sewers at night to care for Mudaire's orphans with a marked swordsman guarding her back."

"Someone needed to care for them." And it should've been the Crown. Most were the children of men fighting in the King's army, and even if they weren't, they deserved better than sewers and scraps.

"Peas in a pod." Malahi gave a slight shake of her head. "Both of you seeing only the suffering in front of your faces with no mind for what good you could have done for those fighting to defend those children."

"Then why didn't you stop us? If you knew who I was, why didn't you turn me in?"

"Because," Malahi said, "what you two were doing in those sewers did more to bolster the people's faith in him than anything I ever did. Your identity might have been a secret, but the whole city knew that the swordsman was Killian."

Neither of them spoke, the only sound the faint crash of the waves below.

"So now that I've done my part in rebuilding your future husband's credibility, am I to assume you intend to turn me over to Quindor?" Lydia stared Malahi down, clenching the arms of the chair to hide the tremor in her hands. Once she was in the hands of the temple, there'd be no escape.

Malahi gave a slight shake of her head, but instead of relief, Lydia felt trepidation as the other girl said, "I've different plans for you."

Sitting back in the chair, Malahi smoothed her skirts. "Let me articulate our circumstances so that you understand my predicament. Rufina's army marches on Mudaire. They will be here in three days' time unless Killian and those under his command are able to beat them to Alder's Ford, which is the only reasonably defensible position. If, by some act of the Six, they make it in time, it will be Killian's two thousand men and women, only half of whom are trained soldiers, against an enemy that numbers in the tens of thousands. There is no chance of them prevailing—they are sacrificing their lives to give us a chance at evacuating the city. And even then . . . There is a chance it won't be enough. That Rufina's army will arrive while Mudaire is still full of innocent undefended people. And that she'll slaughter every last one of them."

All her life, Lydia had heard talk of military strategy. Her father and his peers sitting on couches, wineglasses in hand, while they discussed which legion would be moved where. The gains and losses. Who'd be saved and who'd be sacrificed. It had always seemed so distant to her—not real lives, but game pieces on a board. To be in the midst of it, with lives that she knew, lives that she had touched, at risk, was another thing altogether.

"You're queen now—take control of your army."

Malahi's jaw tightened. "Unfortunately, High Lord Torrington was killed last night. His heir is Helene, and she finds herself . . . disinclined toward supporting my reign, particularly if it means a Calorian on the throne beside me. I've sent word of our situation to High Lady Falorn, but there is no love lost between our families, so I have little confidence that she'll vote for me no matter how dire the circumstances. As it is, I don't see how she could make it here in time."

It was sickening. Sickening that people were dying and these men and women were scrambling for power rather than scrambling to save every soul they could. Yet the question remained. "What does any of this have to do with me?"

Malahi didn't answer, and the tension that hung between them was thick enough to cut with a knife. A thousand scenarios ran through Lydia's mind, but none of them—none at all—ended with her boarding a ship south to Serlania.

"There's another way for me to remain queen."

Lydia's blood chilled, because *gods* she knew what was coming.

"Both Hacken and Lady Calorian brought horses with them. Fast horses. And Killian didn't take them all."

Lydia's breath was coming in fast little pants, her ribs aching from the violence of her beating heart.

"The Royal Army will be expecting messengers from us. It will be easy to give you one, which will allow you access to my father. Then you'll kill him."

The light seemed too bright. Too intense. And because the alternative was to cry, Lydia laughed, the sound wild and manic in her own ears. "You want to use *me* as an assassin? I can barely unsheathe a sword without risking my own foot, whereas your father is surrounded by trained soldiers."

"I don't want you to kill him with a blade." Malahi's face was steady, though the throbbing vein in her forehead remained. "I want you to kill him and make it look like the enemy is responsible."

Bile rose in Lydia's throat, and she swallowed it down. "How could I possibly do that?"

Silence.

"I didn't send you to stand watch with Bercola in that tunnel because I wanted you dead," Malahi finally said. "I sent you because I knew your mark would make you more likely to survive anything that came at you. I didn't realize how right I was."

It hurt to breathe.

"I *saw* what you did to that corrupted." Malahi leaned forward, her face intent. "Everyone else was too busy trying to protect me to notice, but I saw. I saw when he took life from you. And when you took it back."

"I don't know what you're talking about."

"You can do what *they* do."

Lydia shook her head wildly. "I'm not corrupted."

The curtains sailed inward on a gust of wind, and both of them jumped. Rising, Malahi went to the window and pulled it shut, the curtains settling back into place, making the room still. Silent.

"No. But you could be." Malahi remained staring out the window. "The same power, but turned to a different purpose. Two sides of the same coin." She turned back around. "Do you think, if Killian hadn't arrived and removed his head, that you'd have killed that man?"

Yes. Lydia kept the thought to herself, straining against the ropes binding her wrists, feeling blood trickle down her skin, the arms of the heavy wooden chair groaning. Her body screamed with the strain, sweat breaking out on her brow, but whoever had tied the ropes had known her business.

"You're my only hope. Mudamora's only hope."

I am Teriana's only hope. My father's only hope. The only person who knows the truth about what Lucius has done. "I can't help you."

"Can't? Or won't?"

"Both."

The other girl was across the room in an instant, Lydia's head cracking sideways as Malahi slapped her with surprising strength. "You selfish bitch! People are going to die, and you don't even care."

The accusation couldn't be further from the truth, because the Six knew, she cared *too* much. The plight of this city, of its people—it was her plight. She'd felt the same hunger. The same exhaustion. The same fear. And she'd risked everyone she loved in order to help them. Night after night after night she'd braved the darkness and the filth, giving up her life to those who needed it most, aging and nearly dying over and over and over. Yet never had she felt more alive. Never had Lydia felt more like she was in the place she needed to be. And to abandon them now cut her to the core. But not only was the cost of staying more than she wished to pay, what Malahi was asking her to do . . . "I'm not a murderer."

"He's not a good man." Malahi hissed the words. "And even if he was, what's one life compared to the lives of thousands?"

Nothing. And everything. "There are other people who need me, too. Who are depending on me. Even if I was willing to steal life like one of the corrupted, doing so would mean abandoning those I care about."

"What about Killian? Don't you care about *him*? He's going to die if we don't enable the Royal Army to march to his aid; don't you understand that?"

Lydia's eyes burned, and she looked away, unable to meet Malahi's gaze. She knew. Knew the guilt he felt about not fighting to the death to hold the wall. That he blamed himself for every life that had been lost since. That he'd fight back the approaching enemy until they cut him down.

You could save him, a voice whispered inside her head.

I'd be sacrificing Teriana for him.

Teriana might already be dead, the voice countered. *Your father, too. You know Killian's alive.*

He wouldn't want me to kill anyone to save him.

True, the voice conceded. *But what about to save his people?*

"I'll give you some time to consider," Malahi said, tearing Lydia back into the moment. "But know this: You getting on one of those ships isn't going to happen. You ride west and assassinate my father or I hand you over to Quindor. And lest you think me a total fool, you take that horse and try to run, I'll use every resource at my disposal to hunt you down."

There was no way out. No escape.

Lifting the hem of her skirts, the other girl extracted a knife, slicing through the bindings on Lydia's wrists and ankles. "And if you don't like those options," she said, gesturing to the window, "you can always jump."

Waiting until the door had slammed shut behind Malahi, an exterior bolt turning, Lydia tore around the room, searching for tools she might use. A weapon. Something to pry the door open. Anything.

But there was nothing.

Even if there were, she strongly suspected there were guards outside her door. The girls she'd called friends, but their loyalty was to Malahi, never mind that they all believed the worst of her.

Panic rose, hot and fierce, her heart threatening to tear out of her chest.

Think!

Sitting back on the chair, Lydia forced herself to consider her options. She could lie to Malahi and agree to the mission, then try to ride south until she reached a port. The risk was that both pigeons and ships would beat her there, and there was no chance that Malahi wouldn't send word ahead with her description and a reward for catching a rogue healer. Same if she rode north—the Princess was too clever to be fooled by that.

Be smarter than her.

She needed to give Malahi a reason not to spend resources trying to hunt her down, and the only way that would happen was if she believed Lydia were dead.

You can always jump.

Her eyes flicked to the window. Walking over, Lydia flipped open the latch and swung in the pane of glass, the wind immediately sending the curtains billowing. Below, the ocean crashed against the cliffs, and in the distance she could vaguely make out the longboats ferrying evacuees to the ships anchored farther out.

Even if she survived the fall and managed to swim to one of them, only children and their mothers were being evacuated today. They'd send her right back to shore.

She could try to make it to the harbor, hide in the city for a few days, then try to board one of the ships. Except Malahi might not be so quick to believe the fall killed her and would have her description passed around. Would give it to Quindor, who was known for his talent in tracking down rogue healers.

She needed another path.

The xenthier.

The trapdoor to the tunnel had been locked and secured, but Lena had dropped the lock to the gate barring the ocean. It was possible that the lock had been replaced in the intervening hours, but in the chaos . . . it was just as possible the gate remained unlocked. If she could get inside, it would be easy to retrace her steps to the xenthier stem.

You have no supplies.

You have no weapons.

"It might be my only chance," she answered the voice, climbing up onto the windowsill. "Teriana's only chance."

What about Killian?

What about the people of Mudaire?

Jump, and you condemn them all.

Lydia stared at the water, so very far below. "I can't save them both."

You know you can save Killian. You have no such certainty about Teriana.

Closing her eyes, Lydia allowed her doubts and fears and hopes and desires to twist through her thoughts. To fight with one another as the wind buffeted her unfeeling body. It was Killian or Teriana. One or the other. A hot tear ran down her cheek.

Choose.

Lydia jumped.

58

KILLIAN

Dread slammed into him like a battering ram, and Killian whirled his horse, staring back at the distant shadow of the city.

Go back.

His marching army parted to go around him, but he might as well have been alone on the plain.

She's in danger.

"What's wrong?" Sonia had circled Seahawk around next to him. "Is it Malahi?"

Lydia.

"Do you need to go back?"

Yes. Even as Killian thought the word, he turned his head back west, marching men and women flowing up the road. The only hope for saving an entire city.

He felt torn in two separate directions, between the desire to protect two different things that mattered to him so very much.

Choose.

"No," he finally answered. And nudging his horse into a canter, Killian rode toward war.

59

~~~

LYDIA

The wind whistled past Lydia's ears, her arms flailing as she fell, the sea rushing up to meet her with impossible speed.

But she still had time to regret her choice.

The toes of her boots slammed into the water, and then she was plunging down and down. Bubbles rushed past her face, pressure building in her ears, and when she looked up, the surface seemed terribly far away.

Kick, you fool!

Her legs churned, and she rose. Only not fast enough. Her chest burned, the desperate need to breathe sending flashes of panic through her veins. Then her head broke the surface.

She had the chance to suck in one breath before the waves slammed her against the cliff wall. Her wrist snapped, her forehead slicing open against the rocks; then the water was dragging her backward. Frantically, she searched the cliff walls for the opening. But there was nothing.

How was that possible?

High tide.

Her error slapped her in the face as the waves surged again, her feet slamming against the uneven rocks. Her ankle cracked, and she choked and floundered, trying to swim with two broken bones. Her mark was healing her, but not quickly enough.

Swim!

Body burning with pain and exertion, she dived, kicking as hard as she could in an attempt to get farther out to sea. The ocean flung her backward, the cliff rushing toward her. She was going to hit it again.

Swim, gods-damn you!

Pain exploded across her body as she hit the rocks, her body breaking. The sea pulled her back again, though she barely had the strength to stay afloat.

She'd made a mistake.

She was going to drown.

She'd failed Teriana.

She'd sacrificed Killian for nothing.

Water closed over her head, and she couldn't move. Couldn't swim.

Madoria help me.

But blackness only filled her eyes as her consciousness slipped away.

Then sunlight burned into them.

Lydia choked and coughed, rolling on her side to throw up before resting her face against the gritty damp sand. Her whole body was in agonizing pain, but she was healing.

"I was of a mind to let you drown, but Magnius thought otherwise."

The familiar voice filled her ears and, still coughing and spluttering, she rolled onto her back and looked up. "Bait?"

"Hello, traitor," he said, resting a dagger against her throat. "Fancy meeting you on this side of Reath."

Her rattled brain struggled with his words, and then she understood the accusation. "I didn't tell Lucius anything. I swear it on the names of the gods."

"Invoking the names of the Six, you godless Cel wretch!"

Her throat stung, and Lydia felt hot droplets of blood dribble down her skin as she gasped, "I didn't betray you." It was hard to get the words out, her lungs feeling like they'd never have enough air again.

"Prove it." His eyes were black and stormy, and then water surged over her legs and Magnius was in her mind. The demigod delved into her memories, and she relived the moment of learning the *Quincense* was in danger, of running through the gardens toward the gates, desperate to warn her friends. Worst of all, that painful moment when she learned the *Quincense* had been taken. Only then did Magnius release her mind, her vision clearing to reveal Bait's stunned expression. And she knew he'd seen it all.

"Gods, Lydia," he breathed, pulling the knife from her throat and shoving it into the sand. "I'm sorry . . . We assumed . . ."

"It's fine." She caught hold of his arms. "Please tell me Teriana's with you."

Bait slumped and exhaled a long breath.

Lydia's body turned icy cold, her heart beating like a drum. "Is she . . . ?"

He shook his head. "She's alive. The Cel have landed on the Southern Continent, in Arinoquia, and they have her with them. Tesya is a hostage in Celendrial."

Teriana wasn't in Celendor. And the Cel were here.

Easing up, she sat in the wet sand, her head resting on her knees. Finding a way home to help her friend had been her goal, what had kept her focused through everything that had happened, and now . . .

"She's alive," he repeated. "Magnius, at least, would know if she wasn't. But Lydia, how is it that you're here?"

"Xenthier. There's a stem in the outtake tunnels of the baths in Celendrial."

Bait whistled between his teeth. "And you took it, not knowing where it went?"

"I didn't have a choice. Lucius tried to have me murdered."

Bait's jaw dropped and stayed that way as she told him the story. "Lucius is blackmailing the Thirty-Seventh Legion's legatus, and he ordered him to shove me into the drain so my body wouldn't be found and it would look like I'd made good on my attempt to escape."

"Legatus *Marcus* of the Thirty-Seventh?"

She nodded and Bait spit into the sand. "You know him?" she asked.

"Aye. I know him."

Lydia's skin felt like ants were marching across it, her mouth turning sour as she listened to Bait tell her everything that happened in her absence, though there was one detail that captured all of her attention. "Marcus has Teriana?"

Bait's eyes were inky waves as he nodded. "Keeps her with him at all times. In his own gods-damned tent. And Lydia . . . He's as clever as they say."

She knew. But gods, all she could think of was that Teriana was the prisoner of a young man entirely under the control of Lucius. "Has he hurt her?"

Bait shook his head. "I saw her a few nights ago, and she was fine. But then again, she hasn't given him reason to harm her. Yet."

For several painful moments, neither of them spoke, Lydia coming to terms with the fact that Teriana was imprisoned by a man who had a secret he was willing to murder to protect. A secret that Lucius knew and had no compunctions against exploiting.

Lifting her head, she said, "Whatever Lucius is blackmailing Marcus with has something to do with his family—his real family, not the legion. He said he *knew* me, which—"

"Makes sense," Bait interrupted, "because he's a Domitius."

Domitius? Lydia stared at Bait in shock. The head of that family was not only her neighbor; he was the wealthiest man in the Empire. She'd grown up with Cordelia and Gaius and . . . "Gods, Bait. Senator Domitius had a second son named Marcus that went to the legions. It's *him*."

He was the one she'd played with in her father's library when they were small children. Except something about that truth jarred with her memory. Lydia rubbed her temples, trying to figure it out, but it had been so long ago. . . .

Bait's eyes had shifted into the brilliant blue waves of excitement. "Do you know what Cassius has against him? We could use it. Force Marcus to give her back to us."

"He didn't say. It could be anything. The Domitius family has their fingers in politics and business across the entire Empire."

They sat in silence; then Lydia finally said, "We have to rescue Teriana. We can't leave her with him."

Bait rested his forehead against his knees, then in one sudden move slammed his fist against the sand. "She doesn't want to be rescued."

"But . . ."

"If she escapes, Tesya and the other Maarin prisoners will suffer the consequences," he said. "She thinks she can sabotage them. That's why I'm here. I heard the Gamdeshian fleet was on its way to assist Mudamora, so Magnius and I took a xenthier stem north in hopes of sending them back. But . . ." He lifted a hand, gesturing at the harbor full of burned-out wrecks.

It was no coincidence that the Cel had set their eyes on the West right as the army of the Seventh had marched to war. Everyone believed the Gamdeshian fleet had been burned to prevent Mudaire from being evacuated, but with this news from Bait . . . Lydia wondered if the Corrupter had much more far-reaching plans. From the look on Bait's face, he was thinking the same.

"Lydia, if the legions can find land routes to and from the Empire, the West is going to be pinioned between two armies."

And the legions would find the xenthier paths; it was only a matter of time. The Senate would pay desperate men and women by the hundreds to travel through unmapped stems in the East in the hope one of them would get lucky. And the legions in Arinoquia would have the gold needed to do the same.

"What do we do?" she asked, more to herself than to her friend, because the idea of doing nothing made her sick.

Bait exhaled slowly. "Do you think I haven't been asking that very question since the moment the *Quincense* was captured?"

Perhaps her going back to Celendor and implicating Lucius would be enough to prevent the horror that was to come. "Can you get me back to Celendrial?"

Both his eyebrows rose. "Do you think you can stop Cassius?"

"He broke the law," she said. "And trying to have me murdered is the least of it. The truth might see him removed from his position as consul."

But would that be enough to stop the invasion? Never mind that the Senate had no ability to contact the legions on the Southern Continent, there were many others like-minded to Lucius in their desire for conquest. Others who might pick up his torch and carry it onward, especially if they discovered Marcus had been successful in his venture. The more she thought about it, the more she realized that the only sure thing going back would accomplish was seeing Lucius dangling from a noose.

Was vengeance worth sacrificing Killian's life? The lives of all those in his army? All those who couldn't be evacuated in time? Never mind that Lydia possessed information the West might use against the Cel.

"Lydia?"

Bait's voice tore her from her thoughts. He was staring at her broken wrist, the swelling and bruising fading as the fracture knit. He gaped at her. "Did Hegeria mark you?"

Denying it seemed like a waste of time. "Almost as soon as I arrived."

"Teriana always believed you were from the West. That you were from Mudamora." A faint smile rose to his lips. "Looks like she was right."

His words sank into her soul, the truth of them ringing like a bell. This was where she was from. This was where she belonged. This was where she needed to stand her ground and fight, no matter what she had to do. No matter what it cost her.

"I can't leave," she said. "I can do more good by remaining than by going back."

"That's insane, Lydia. You don't want to be in this city during a siege, and you certainly don't want to be here when it falls." He caught hold of her wrist and pulled. "I can get you out of here."

She shook her head. "You need to go. Convince the Sultan

of Gamdesh that the Cel are as great a threat as the Seventh's army. Convince him that maybe . . ."

"There's a link between the two."

Lydia nodded. "And you need to get back to Teriana. If she can find out what the Domitius family has done that would allow Lucius to blackmail Marcus, maybe we can use it."

"It will take me some time to get to Gamdesh. There's no underwater xenthier paths on this coast that run south, so Magnius and I will have to swim."

Swim? Then she understood. "You're marked by Madoria." Which meant he could breathe underwater. And turn the tides.

He winked and grinned, his teeth white against his ebony skin. "A pirate of the seafloor, Domina. You didn't think the *Quincense* got so rich selling to cheap Cel scum, now did you?"

An idea rolled into her thoughts, something she'd barely been willing to consider. "Bait, does your mark work when you're in the East?"

He nodded. "I don't play much with the currents and the tides while we're there, though. Too much chance of being caught."

Clenching her teeth, Lydia dug deep for the courage to ask her next question, dreading the answer but needing to know. "Was my father still alive when you left Celendor?"

Bait blinked. "Yes. Why?"

"Thank the gods." The words rushed from her mouth, relief filling her core. "His nephew, Vibius, is in league with Lucius. He's been poisoning my father with the aim of taking control of the Valerius seat in the Senate."

"And you're wondering if your mark will work if you go back."

Lydia gave a tight nod.

"If it did, they'd know about us," Bait said slowly. "And that's a secret Teriana's fighting to keep. She's got the odds stacked against her enough without the Cel discovering the truth about god marks."

"He'd keep it a secret. I know he would."

Exhaling slowly, Bait said, "I believe you. But the truth is, I'm not sure it would work. Hegeria's not going to help someone who doesn't believe."

And her father was Cel to the core. There was no chance of that.

"I'm sorry. But if it's any consolation, your father is the one keeping Captain Tesya. Teriana was none too happy about that, but given what you've told me, I think he's protecting her from Cassius. Which means he *knows* Cassius is up to no good."

If Teriana was upset about Lydia's father keeping Tesya, then . . . "Does Teriana believe that I betrayed her?"

Bait nodded, and Lydia's chest tightened. If her friend believed that, then she believed all that had happened, and all that would happen, was her fault. "If you can get to her, make sure she knows the truth—that I love her, and that I'd never betray her."

Her hand drifted to the scabbard at her waist, the blade in Malahi's possession. Even so, it reminded her that she was no longer quite the helpless girl she'd once been. "And make sure she knows the truth about the man she's bargained with."

60

KILLIAN

Icy water dripped down the back of Killian's neck, and he winced as a blast of sleet-filled wind hit him in the face. He spared a longing thought for his fur-lined cloak, but the aging soldier he'd lent it to needed it far more than he did. If only he had two hundred more to give.

The weather had turned foul overnight, a blizzard of wind and sleet that was bound to turn to snow by nightfall, likely thanks to the summoner's meddling with the winds on the coast. What was already a hard march delayed by the need to build bridges over streams of blight was made worse by a road now turned to muck, and his hopes of reaching the ford by nightfall were diminishing by the second.

His war-horse's teeth snapped in his direction, but Killian only pushed the stallion's nose away before glancing up at the two exhausted greybeards perched on the black brute's back. The pair probably weighed less than Killian in armor, but the other horses were showing the strain of carrying two riders, heads hung low, the mules pulling the small catapults no better. There was no helping it. There was no time to stop. No time to rest.

Two thousand men and women marched at his heels. Five hundred Gamdeshians. Three hundred old men who'd made up the city guard. Six hundred soldiers the High Lords had brought with them. And the rest were women who'd volunteered to fight. Some of them were warriors, but most were civilians here to give the families they'd left behind in Mudaire a chance to flee. A chance to live. There were some who'd call this army weak, but Killian knew better. These men and women had something to defend, and while they might die fighting, they wouldn't break.

"Scout," Sonia muttered from where she strode next to Killian, seemingly unaffected by the abysmal conditions despite having been born and raised in the balmy heat of Gamdesh. Likewise, the soldiers she led pressed onward without complaint, the loss of their comrades when the fleet was razed fresh in their minds. They wanted revenge.

Killian knew the feeling well.

Peering through the sleet, he watched the scout gallop toward them, the pace alone telling him all he needed to know.

The woman slid to a stop. "The advance force is only a few hours' march from the ford, my lord," she gasped, dismounting next to them and leading the tired horse.

"Shit," Killian said under his breath, exchanging a quick glance with Sonia. The Gamdeshian captain knew as well as he did that if Rufina's men made it to the ford ahead of them the battle was lost and Mudaire would be at the mercy of their enemies.

"Off," he ordered the men on his horse, then swung into the saddle. "Archers on horses! The rest of you, double time."

Sonia was already on Seahawk's back, organizing the archers with the ease of someone used to command, and within moments the force was rallied around them. "We have less than an hour to make the ford and get that bridge down," he bellowed. "Now ride."

Digging in his heels, he gave the stallion his head, mud splattering high as he tore down the road. It wasn't long until only Sonia kept pace, but that didn't matter. The two of them alone could bring down the bridge.

If only that was all it would take to stop Rufina's army.

The rolling farmland turned to forest, the branches giving some respite from the wind, if not the mud. The stallion leapt over a stream of blight that crossed the road, then slid, struggling to keep his footing. Then they were out in the open, the great ravine containing the Tarn cutting across the landscape. Killian stopped on the lip of the steep incline leading down to the narrow bridge spanning the river. The embankment on the far side was lower and not as steep, but as on this side, the road disappeared into the trees, hiding whatever marched upon it. Not that it mattered—his gut told him they were close.

Sonia behind him, he eased his horse down the slurry of mud and rock, dismounting next to the bridge.

"You call this a ford?" Sonia muttered, eyeing the churning rapids of the Tarn as Killian extracted the canisters of naphtha from the sack attached to his saddle.

"It's doable," he replied. "Bridge gets washed away in floods every few years. It's only waist deep, but it's cold enough to freeze your balls off."

"How fortunate I was not cursed with such vulnerable body parts," she replied, and despite the gravity of the situation, Killian laughed.

They walked onto the bridge, pouring the liquid onto the planks and dousing the thick pillars holding it out of the rapids. Wind blasted against them with such strength that it seemed to suck the air from Killian's lungs, whipping away the stink of the liquid. Which gave him an idea.

Back on their side of the Tarn, Sonia pulled a flint stone from her pocket, but Killian shook his head. "I've a better idea."

Retreating up the slope, he explained his plan to the young woman.

"You're worse than Kaira," Sonia said when he was finished, but she took the reins of both horses and led them back down the road to meet the rest of the archers.

Crouching behind a boulder, Killian extracted a tinderbox and started a small blaze that would attract no notice. Then he settled down to wait.

The setting sun was barely visible behind the haze of cloud when Sonia arrived with the archers, all of them creeping up to hide behind cover. Their arrival wasn't a moment too soon.

Out of the trees came a line of riders moving at speed. Their mounts were scruffy ponies, the legs of the men atop them hanging almost to their knees. The soldiers themselves were dressed in furs, but Killian could make out the glint of metal. They were well armed, which was unsurprising. Rufina knew she needed this ford—she'd have sent her best.

They picked their way down the slope, weapons out and eyes searching for any sign of danger. There were fifty of them, and Killian easily marked their commander, a small man with a sharp nose that protruded from his hood. From this distance, there was nothing about the man that set him apart, but Killian noted the way his men gave him wide berth. The nervous way his pony shifted from side to side, ears pinned, as though a mountain lion sat in the saddle rather than a man. *Corrupted.*

"You and you," the commander shouted, pointing at two of his men. "Scout ahead and see how much time we have until they arrive."

The two soldiers heeled their horses up the slope, and Killian let them pass unmolested. Sonia met his eyes. There were archers waiting down the road ready to take out the enemy scouts.

The bulk of the men began crossing the bridge, two abreast, but ten remained on the far side. Killian grimaced. Those would be hard shots in this wind, but he had no intention of allowing any of the enemy to escape to warn the main force. "I'll deal with those on the west bank," he whispered to Sonia. "You handle those on this side."

Out of the corner of his eye, he saw her nod, her weapons already in hand.

"We need to hold the high ground," the commander ordered from below. "Start building fortifications at the top of that slope." He dismounted and handed his reins to one of the men. Then he went still, head cocked as though smelling the air.

"Ambush!" he shouted, and Killian laughed, his bowstring twanging. The burning tip of his arrow sank into the man's left eye, and the corrupted toppled back onto the bridge, where the flames ignited the naphtha. Killian sent two more arrows through the air, and within seconds the bridge was an inferno. He turned his attention to the fleeing soldiers on the far side of the river, leaving Sonia and the Gamdeshians to handle the enemy charging up the embankment toward them.

He hit three men in the back in quick succession, missed one, swore, then caught him on the next shot. All it would take was one of them making it back to Rufina to turn this into a failed gambit.

Bows twanged to either side of him as Killian took down two more fleeing men. Only there were too many attackers on this side of the river to kill with arrows alone, and it would only be seconds until they were upon Killian and the archers. "Cover me," he said to Sonia. "I've four left to kill."

"Hurry!"

Killian aimed, judging the wind and the distance as he shot arrow after arrow. Two more men toppled from their horses—alive, though neither would make it far. But the front-runners were up the slope and galloping toward the trees.

"The Seventh take you!" Killian leapt onto the rock for better vantage and let an arrow fly. It sank into the back of one man's skull. The next missed. "Come on," Killian snarled, aware that the enemy was upon him.

His bowstring snapped forward, and the arrow caught the galloping horse, which went down hard. But the man was up and running. Killian nocked an arrow, aware of the enemy soldiers riding at him, hearing their battle cries. Knowing that this risk would have been for nothing if he missed.

He tracked the fleeing man's progress, then let the arrow fly.

Killian didn't have time to see whether he hit his mark. A blade swung at him, but he dived under it, slamming into the side of the man's horse and knocking it from its feet. They fell in a tangle of limbs, the animal sliding down the slope as it struggled to right itself, the man screaming until his head cracked open against a rock.

Dodging the flailing hooves, Killian leapt to his feet, sword in hand. He carved into the enemy even as Sonia's archers dropped their bows and drew their blades, screaming their own cries as they leapt into the fray.

It was over almost as soon as it had begun.

Slitting the throat of a dying man, Killian straightened and wiped the blood from his face. "How many did we lose?"

"Two." Sonia wiped her sword on a dead man's cloak. "Six wounded."

Nodding, Killian turned to the distant bank, hoping the loss of those two men had been worth it. His eyes landed on the dead horse in the distance, then skipped ahead to where its rider should be.

There was only empty ground.

Killian's heart sank, and he let loose a blistering string of oaths before a flicker of motion caught his attention. Just before the tree line, the enemy soldier was crawling away, an arrow protruding from his back.

"Won't make it far enough to matter," Sonia said. "Not worth crossing the river to kill him."

"I don't need to cross the river." Picking up the bow he'd dropped, Killian nocked an arrow.

All the world fell away as he aimed, the voices a muffled blur of noise. The string slipped from his fingers, his eyes tracking the fletching as the arrow carved through wind and sleet. The soldier twitched once. Then went still.

When Killian turned, Sonia was staring at him, jaw slightly parted. Then she shrugged. "I never said your aim was poor. Just your form."

"I believe the word was *satisfactory*," he replied, then turned to the archers standing behind him. "Leave the dead," he ordered in Gamdeshian. "Start felling trees. We have a wall to build, and we've only got a few hours before Rufina's army is upon us."

61

KILLIAN

Killian peered through a narrow opening in the hastily constructed fortifications, trying to count the campfires spreading back from the western bank before swearing and giving up. His time would be as well used trying to count stars in the sky.

They had at least ten times his numbers, and when they decided to come no amount of strategic advantage would stop them.

"I've got a rotating shift of archers watching our rear," Sonia said, coming up next to him. She took a long swallow from a waterskin before continuing. "We've got the tree line pushed back a hundred yards, but it's dark. Anyone with stealth could get close with no one the wiser. Setting some torches burning in the open space would rectify that problem."

"No," Killian replied, watching the flickers of light and motion on the riverbanks below, his archers taking shots at them when the mark was good. "The deimos are overhead, and while they might be able to see in the dark, their riders can't. As it stands, they don't know just how undermanned we are, and I'd like to keep it that way."

Not that he could keep it from them forever, but that wasn't the point. He was buying time for Malahi and his mother to evacuate Mudaire as best they could. *Time*—that was what he was fighting for. Nothing else.

Yet reminding himself of that fact didn't stop Lydia's face from swimming into his thoughts. She should be on a ship headed south by now, and then it was only a matter of time until she'd track down a Maarin vessel and make her way back to Celendor to help Teriana. He had no doubt that she'd succeed. And that her success would come at great personal cost.

Sonia grunted, pulling Killian back into the moment. "It's only another hour until dawn, anyway. They'll attack at that point, and it won't take them long to figure out where we stand."

"They aren't going to wait until dawn."

"They have to—it would be suicide to try and cross that river in the dark. They'll lose countless men in the effort."

"I don't think Rufina cares." Killian held a finger to his lips. "Listen."

They'd been treated to the sound of deimos wings overhead through the night, but the pair above them had a labored and unsteady beat. There was a whistle of something falling through the air, then a massive crack as it hit the ground on one of the banks.

"What in the name of all the gods was that!" Sonia exclaimed, peering through the opening.

Another set of labored wingbeats filled the night; then another enormous crack split the air. "That's wood," Killian muttered. "They're dropping building supplies for a bridge."

"Do you want us to set it aflame, sir?" one of the archers standing near them asked.

"No."

Even in the darkness, Killian could tell everyone within earshot was staring at him.

"But sir," the man said, "they'll get across the river."

"That they will." Killian turned to Sonia. "Move your soldiers to the rear. The deimos have been ferrying men across all night, and they'll attack us shortly to provide a distraction for their comrades trying to cross the Tarn."

The Gamdeshian woman moved down the line, barking orders, men and women moving into position. Killian stood listening to the sounds of the enemy working down by the river below. Then he moved down his line, explaining the plan to his soldiers, clapping his hand on shoulders and offering words of encouragement where needed.

Until he heard a familiar high-pitched voice.

"How many of them do you think there are?"

Striding toward the figure, Killian jerked the helmet off the boy's head. "Gods-damn it, Finn! What are you doing here? You're supposed to be on a ship to Serlania with the rest of the children."

Finn stared at him, then squared his shoulders. "I'm not a child. No chance of me fleeing or hiding behind walls like some sort of coward."

"You *are* a child. You're supposed to hide behind walls. That's what they're for." Killian wasn't sure if he was furious, terrified, or both. He'd been making decisions based on the need to buy time, not with the mind to get his soldiers through this alive. But now . . .

He didn't get a chance to finish the thought before battle cries split the air behind them. Turning, he peered into the rising dawn, watching as the enemy ran toward the line of archers standing at the ready. "Loose!" Sonia shouted, sending volley after volley into the ranks, and when those who remained standing were almost upon them she pulled her blade and charged into their midst with the rest of the swordsmen.

"Lord Calorian, they're across!"

Killian jerked his attention back to the river, pulling Finn with him as he moved to a position where he could see. "You stay with me, Finn—do you understand? Do not leave my side unless I say otherwise."

If the boy answered, Killian didn't hear, his attention all for the enemy's activities by the river. In the faint dawn light, he could make out men wading across the river with ropes, which they secured on the eastern bank. Then they hauled the thick tree trunks across the water, which they lashed together to form a rough bridge. They kept casting backward glances at the fortification, and Killian knew they were wondering why there'd been no attack. Knew that rather than filling them with confidence, it made them more afraid of what was to come.

"Hold," Killian said, sensing a tremor of unease run through his force as the enemy poured down the western bank. To those manning the small catapults, he said, "Mark your distances. There's no room for error on this." Then he picked up his bow.

As the enemy swarmed across the makeshift bridge, the catapults began to loose small, carefully weighted stones. Small or not, they killed those they struck, and bodies floated down the rapids or tangled up the limbs of their comrades. Still, they were crossing by the dozens, barely pausing to get their bearings before clambering up the steep slope toward Killian and his soldiers. The fortifications they'd built began to feel flimsy and insubstantial.

"Hold," he shouted, counting those crossing by the tens, then the hundreds, knowing he was dancing the fine line of making this gambit count and losing the battle. "Hold!"

The men charging up the slope were close enough that he could see the sweat on their bearded faces, their eyes wild as they screamed.

"Now!"

The catapults snapped forward, launching the thin bladders of liquid toward the bridge. On his next breath, he shouted, "Rocks," and soldiers sliced the ropes holding the traps, sending an avalanche of boulders cascading down the slope. One of the soldiers standing next to him handed him an arrow, flames flickering around its tip.

Killian's ears filled with screams as stone smashed bone and tore into flesh, but his attention was for the bridge and the panicked expressions of the men who'd realized the nature of the liquid they'd been drenched with. The catapults snapped forward again, splattering the horde on the opposite bank, and Killian fired. The arrow sank into the bridge, and within seconds it was engulfed.

Men were on fire, diving into the waters and fleeing toward both banks. They crashed into the masses of their comrades who'd been waiting to cross, igniting them and sending flames chasing up the western slope.

"Archers, loose," Killian shouted, firing shot after shot of his own, keeping to targets on this side of the Tarn in the hope the arrows could be retrieved later.

He sensed the Gamdeshians he'd deployed to the rear returning to bolster his ranks, the archers picking off those who remained alive below until there were no more screams.

Only the stink of scorched meat.

It was done.

Gesturing to the women who'd released the rocks, he said, "Ten of you go retrieve weapons—you have until the count of five hundred; then I want you back on this side of the wall. Prioritize arrows that can be reused."

One of the soldiers shouted the count while the women dropped over the walls, knives clamped between their teeth. Anyone they found alive would not stay so for long.

Killian tracked down Sonia, who was watching the men pilfer the dead for weapons. The stink of burning meat followed him, and he voiced a silent prayer to Gespurn to turn the wind in the other direction.

"We lost twenty to their archers, and another ten aren't likely to last until nightfall," she said. "You?"

"None," Killian said, casting his gaze over the Derin dead, noting that there were many different races among them. Faces that looked as though they hailed from Mudamora and Gendorn and Anukastre and even Gamdesh, though he wasn't certain how that could be. Bending down to look more closely at one of them, Killian frowned. The dead man was filthy and scrawny, with lice crawling in his hair and beard. "They all like this?"

Sonia nodded. "The Derin army is as hungry as those we left behind in Mudaire."

And both of them knew that only made the enemy more dangerous.

"Guesses as to the number of casualties they took?" Sonia asked.

"Five hundred." He tried breathing through his mouth, but

that only made it worse. "Probably be six hundred by nightfall unless they have healers in their midst. Which I doubt."

Sonia whistled approvingly, but Killian only frowned, something about how the battle had gone troubling him. "I don't think Rufina is with them. They gave up too easily."

"I'm not sure *easily* is the correct word. You burned them alive."

His stomach flipped and he swallowed hard. "Maybe. But you didn't see the way they fought at the wall—like what stood behind them was more terrifying than anything we could throw at them. This was different."

Not waiting for Sonia to answer, Killian started walking. His guts felt sour, and he needed to get away from the smell. He pushed through the lines of horses, inhaling their familiar scent, but it was no good. Dropping to his knees, he retched until his stomach had forgotten that it had ever known food.

Something bumped against his arm and, turning his head, he saw Finn standing behind him holding out a waterskin. His dirty face was streaked with the tracks made by tears, and he was shivering. "You told me to stay close."

"I know." Accepting the water, he rinsed his mouth, then spit into the dirt before taking a long swallow.

Finn crouched next to him, hugging his arms around his skinny knees, eyes haunted in a way they hadn't been before. A dull ache filled Killian's chest—a useless wish that there was a way to wipe the memory from the boy's mind.

"They won't stop, will they?"

Killian shook his head. The enemy would attack again, and swiftly. And the same ruse wouldn't work again. Maybe they could hold them a second time, and third, but each time they'd lose more soldiers, and the outcome would be inevitable.

You are buying time.

"I'm afraid," Finn whispered.

Killian eyed the smoke still rising in the air, grey and stinking. "So am I."

62

LYDIA

Lydia peered through falling sleet at the sprawling mass of men and horses trudging across the countryside and tried to muster the courage she needed to approach the Royal Army and complete the task she'd came for.

That she'd made it this far at all was nothing short of a miracle. At first, she'd tracked Killian's army, wishing to the depths of her soul that she could ride up and find him. But she knew he'd stop her from completing the task Malahi had set her, and Lydia couldn't allow that to happen. So instead, she'd bypassed them in the night, leading her horse so as to not accidentally fall afoul of a stream of blight.

Once past them, she'd galloped hard, crossing the bridge where Killian would make his stand and then riding around the terrifying horde of the Derin army. It seemed impossible that he'd have a chance against a host that large.

Which was why she couldn't fail.

Letting her reins go slack, Lydia allowed her tired horse to nibble at the browning grass, tucking her frozen fingers under the armpits of her coat as she considered the plan Malahi had given her.

Lydia had returned to the palace soaking wet from her plunge, the guards at the palace gates allowing her back inside only by virtue of them believing her still Malahi's bodyguard. Not caring about protocol, she'd entered through the main entrance, trudging upstairs and down the hallway until she found the door Gwen and Lena were guarding. They'd both gaped at the sight of her. "You did not," Lena said. "That's not even possible—"

"Find Malahi," Lydia had interrupted, unlatching the door

and reentering. "Tell her I said I'll deliver her message. But before you go, I want both of you to hear the truth from me."

A cough caught Lydia's attention, and she twisted in her saddle to find two men on horseback with arrows leveled at her head.

She stared at them.

They stared at her.

And because there was nothing else *to* say, she said, "I have a message from Her Highness, Princess Malahi, for His Majesty." Slowly, because it seemed prudent, she extracted the letter and held it up. One of the scouts lowered his bow and rode closer, eyeing the seal before nodding. "We'll take you to him."

Flanked by the pair, she rode down the slope and into the horde, which seemed to be setting down to camp for the night. Though why they were stopping when time was of the essence, she didn't know. The soldiers all walked slowly, listlessly, as if they didn't care, all of them dirty and malnourished. They looked like what they were: An army that was losing a war. An army without hope.

Lydia and her escort approached an enormous white tent resplendent with banners of crimson and gold. The guards standing outside leaned heavily on their spears.

"I'll take your horse to the picket lines," one scout said, and Lydia struggled to hide her dismay as her escape route, along with her sword, was led away.

One of the guards checked her for weapons, and then a livery-clad servant escorted her inside the tent, through a series of antechambers, and into a high-ceilinged room lavish with plush carpets, overstuffed furniture, and a heavy map-inlaid table that must have required four men to lift.

"A messenger from Mudaire, Your Majesty," the servant said, bowing low. Lydia followed suit, then lifted her head to regard the man she'd been sent to murder.

King Serrick Rowenes was a small, delicate man, with the same light brown skin as Malahi, his long blond hair braided in a single plait down his back. He wore heavy red robes, the collar embroidered with golden scorpions. His watery amber eyes burned with an intensity that made Lydia want to run from the tent and never look back. He nodded at her. "You bring word from my daughter?"

"Yes, Your Majesty." Lydia's gaze skipped to the tall healer standing behind the King. Like Lydia, she had northern features, but the healer's were marked by age, the wrinkles around her slanted eyes deep, her long braid laced with grey. She regarded Lydia with obvious interest but said nothing. There was one other man present. He was older but dressed in armor, and there were sheaves of golden wheat gilded on his dented breastplate. *High Lord Damashere.*

"Give it here then, girl."

Lydia jumped, then realized the King was asking for the letter. Hurrying forward, she handed it to him, averting her eyes from his searing gaze.

Serrick broke the seal and scanned the contents. Lydia knew what it said—there'd been no chance of her delivering a message without reading the contents, so she'd lifted the seal with a hot knife on the journey. Within it, Malahi outlined the direness of the situation in Mudaire, begging her father to ride in all haste to the aid of the city. Though she obviously believed they were wasted words, or Lydia wouldn't be here at all.

His brow furrowed, the King set down the page and retrieved a sheet of paper from a lockbox sitting on the table. Referring to the page, he silently circled certain letters in Malahi's message, and Lydia's stomach dropped as she realized what he was doing. There was a code hidden in the message.

She leaned forward, trying to read the coded message as the King transcribed it, but without her spectacles everything was blurry.

The King held up the scrap of paper so that the healer could read it, and the woman's eyes widened in surprise before furrowing into a frown. Then, to Lydia's dismay, the King held the transcription over a candle until it caught fire, tossing it into a silver basin, Malahi's original letter following suit.

"Give the order to break camp in two hours," the King said to High Lord Damashere. "We march to Abenharrow with all due haste."

"But the scouts tell us that the forces from Mudaire are successfully holding the ford," the High Lord protested. "If we come up behind them, we can crush them and end this war today."

"And risk the ford falling while we are on the way to their aid," the King snapped. "Once across, the Derin army will split their forces to hold us to this side of the ford, and we will have lost any chance of beating them to Abenharrow."

"But Mudaire—"

"Mudaire is lost," Serrick interrupted. "I'll not risk the rest of Mudamora for the sake of the handful who willingly gave up their lives to hold that ford. The Six will take their souls and reward them for their sacrifice."

Killian was one of those souls. And not just him. The Gamdeshians who'd sailed north to assist Mudamora and had already suffered so much. The civilians who'd volunteered to fight to give their loved ones a chance to flee. Even the Mudamorian soldiers whose duty it was to defend that ford deserved more from their king. Lydia's heart hardened as she stared at Serrick Rowenes. It was him who didn't deserve to live.

And it was clear High Lord Damashere agreed. "Your Majesty, with respect—"

"Damashere, you overstep yourself. You've spent your lifetime counting shipments of grain. Who are you to contest my strategies?"

"But—"

The healer spoke, her voice raspy. And strangely familiar. "His Majesty was chosen by the gods for this task, Your Grace. When you question him, you question the Six."

The High Lord paled. "My apologies, Majesty. I let my sentiment overwhelm my good sense."

Serrick gave the man a withering glare. "As you so often do. Go give the order; we have no time to waste." Then he turned his head back to Lydia. "You may go."

She was dismissed. Stomach hollowing, Lydia grasped about for a reason to remain. For time to do what she came for. For a plan that would see this monstrosity dead without costing her own life. But her mind came up blank.

Backing away, she retreated into an antechamber and, not knowing what possessed her to do so, she ducked behind one of the dangling tapestries.

Idiot! she silently screamed. *What sort of plan is this? Do you think no one will notice that you never left?*

Only before she could duck back out, the air filled with voices and the smell of food, servants coming and going. To appear from behind a tapestry would invite more questions, so she stood her ground, knees trembling, knowing the longer she remained the more contested her exit would be, but not knowing what to do about it.

Time passed. People came and went. Lydia did not move.

She was ravenous and desperately had to relieve her bladder, but peeking under the edge of the tent canvas revealed a perimeter of guards, the ground illuminated by dozens of torches. There was no sneaking out.

Darkness fell completely, the weather worsening, the wind shaking the tent. Lydia was almost glad of it, because it hid her uncontrollable shivers. *Do not faint,* she told herself. *Don't you dare.*

Consumed by her own discomfort, it took her longer than it should have to notice that silence had fallen over the tent.

Peering around the tapestry to ensure no one was there, Lydia sank to her knees, fighting to regain her bearings after standing still for so long. Blood roared in her ears, but gradually the nausea faded and she picked up the faint sound of snoring.

This was her chance. He was alone. No one knew she was here.

But with the opportunity came a thousand doubts she hadn't had before about whether she was capable of murder.

Calculated and cold-blooded. And the means by which she was supposed to do it . . . She remembered the feel of the corrupted's life flooding into her in those dark tunnels beneath the palace. The pleasure of it. Like a drug. What would it do to her to take a life in its entirety? Would it make her corrupted herself?

Easing aside the drape, Lydia peered inside. The King rested on his side beneath a heavy blanket, barely visible in the dim light. Unarmed. Unconscious. Helpless.

It's one life, she told herself. *One life, and in exchange you will save so many. You'll save Killian.*

She hesitated, swaying on her feet, palms damp with sweat. He was a terrible man and a terrible ruler; that much was true. He needed to be replaced, and while Lydia had no fondness for Malahi, surely she'd be a better choice. Especially with Killian at her side.

The thought of it made her cringe, and Lydia took a step back, bumping against the desk, setting the lamp to rattling.

Clenching her teeth, Lydia reached out to steady it, her eyes latching on the piece of paper illuminated by the flame.

It was the cipher.

You don't have time for this, she silently told herself. *You need to get this done and then figure a way out of this tent.*

Yet the page tempted her. What had Malahi written to her father that she hadn't wanted anyone else to know?

That she hadn't wanted *Lydia* to know.

Picking up a pen, she dipped it in a pot of ink and then drew a blank page in front of her. She needed to remember what Malahi had written exactly or this wouldn't work. Even the smallest error would render the task fruitless. Closing her eyes, she envisioned Malahi's letter, falling back into the moment when she'd crouched next to a tiny fire, reading and rereading the message before resealing it. The page came swimming into focus behind her eyelids, and she read the contents once more before opening her eyes and starting to write.

The letter flowed swiftly onto the page in the Princess's overly

{ 437 }

flowerily prose, a plea for her father to help the innocents, to not abandon his people. And when she'd finished, Lydia drew the cipher next to it, carefully circling the letters until she'd reached the end. Then she sat back, reading and rereading the message.

Citizens evacuated to Abenharrow. March to them with all haste. Mudaire is lost.

It was a lie. Mudaire was not evacuated, and with the Gamdeshian fleet burned and sunk, there had been little chance of it being so before the arrival of the Derin army. A lie that seemed to have no other purpose but to ensure that the Royal Army bypassed the ford, abandoning the soldiers there as well as the city they protected.

But why? What could Malahi possibly gain from doing this when it risked so many lives?

Think, Lydia, she screamed at herself. *This girl is a politician. You know politicians. What is her end game?*

If Malahi saved Mudaire and its civilians after they'd been abandoned by the Royal Army, the people would support her rule. And if Killian defeated Rufina alone, it would certainly bolster the people's faith in him. If they pulled it off, no one would question their reign, not when it would seem to be mandated by the gods themselves.

Yet if that was her plan, why bother sending a message to her father lying about the evacuation of Mudaire? Why risk it when her father was already doing *everything* Malahi wanted him to?

Lydia's hands abruptly turned to ice as she understood.

Malahi hadn't just lied to her father; she'd lied to everyone.

The King never intended to abandon Mudaire. At least, not until now. Malahi was gambling with the lives of everyone, and all to ensure her own rise to power was seen as mandated by the gods.

Heart in her throat, Lydia entered the King's sleeping quarters, approaching the divan. And though she was loath to do so, she put one hand on his bare wrist.

It was warm, his life swirling around her fingertips.

Take it.

The urge to do so hit her with an indescribable intensity, as though she'd been deprived of water for days and a cold cup of the liquid sat before her. One sip wouldn't be enough.

One life wouldn't be enough.

Lydia recoiled from the compulsion, landing hard on her bottom and then scrambling backward.

This was not who she was. Not *what* she was.

All her life she had questioned her purpose. Her role. But in the weeks since she'd been marked, Lydia had discovered the answer to that question. She was a healer, and that meant preserving life at the risk of her own.

Not taking it to save her own skin.

Reaching out, she took hold of the King's arm once more, but before she could do anything, hands latched on her shoulders and jerked her violently backward.

She slammed against the carpet, gasping for breath as she looked up into the eyes of the King's healer, inexplicable terror filling her chest.

"What is the meaning of this?" The King had jerked upright from the commotion. "Why are you in here?"

"Please, hear me out!" Lydia gasped, struggling against the healer's strength. "You need to know. Malahi didn't send me here to deliver a message—she sent me here to murder you."

63

KILLIAN

"You stay up here," Killian instructed, balancing Finn on the saddle in front of him until the boy had clambered into the tree. "Climb up high so that no one can see you, then tie yourself to a branch in case you fall asleep. Keep that blanket wrapped around you so you don't freeze."

"I'm not going to fall asleep." Finn's voice was sour, the boy not at all pleased that Killian was keeping him out of the fight.

"Just do it." Killian waited until his friend had complied. "And you stay put until this is over, all right? You wait a good long time after the Derin army has passed and then you follow the Tarn down to the coast. Don't drink anything but rainwater, do you understand? Don't eat anything but the supplies I've given you. And once you reach the coast, you use the coin in your pocket to book passage to Serlania, not to buy sweets."

"You've told me all this. Three times."

It was impossible to see in the dark, but Killian was quite certain Finn was glaring at him.

"And none of it matters anyway, because you're going to win."

Killian wasn't going to bother arguing with him. "Take care of yourself, Finn." Then he heeled his horse back toward the wall, knowing that time was short.

The night was quiet with no wind, the snow falling steadily around them. His soldiers stomped their feet and kept their hands shoved deep in their pockets, a nervous edge to the air keeping all of them silent, necessary words spoken at a whisper. They'd long since ceased glancing skyward at the sound of the deimos passing back and forth, delivering soldiers behind the lines to attack when the moment was right.

And there were sure to be corrupted among them this time.

Killian rode the lines, his armor clicking with the motion of his horse. Waiting. Waiting. Then there was a shift in the air, and he knew it was time.

Clearing his throat, he waited until all eyes were on him, then shouted, "Were I commanding a force of spineless cowards, I would stand before you and boldly sell you lies of our certain triumph. But the men and women I see are not weak, so instead I give you the truth.

"Tonight we fight not for glory, for victory, or even for our own lives. We fight for those we've left at home. We bleed in the hope our families will be spared such a fate, that the gods will take our sacrifice and spare the lives of those we love most. Our dying cries will be but the first trumpets of a day that we will never see, but will be the first of *many* your children see without the dark shadow of war biting at their heels. Let us fight for that dawn, and all the dawns to come. Let us pay the price on behalf of those we leave behind and march toward the gods' eternal embrace."

The roar of approval was almost enough to drown the sounds of men on the move, flowing down the western bank, faint splashes and muttered oaths echoing up as they waded through the Tarn.

"Hold them on the other side as long as possible," Killian said to Sonia. "Then kill as many as you can when they get through."

The woman nodded, seemingly unconcerned. "It's been a privilege fighting for you, Lord Calorian."

"Likewise." Reaching down, he clasped her arm. "May the gods fight long and hard over who gets the privilege of hosting your soul."

"Not too long, I hope," Sonia replied. "I'm looking forward to some rest."

Laughing, Killian trotted to the rear line, eyeing the raised and fortified platforms holding half of his archers. Extracting his bow from the wrappings keeping it dry, he nocked an arrow, holding it at the ready.

"The corrupted won't come first," he said, walking his horse behind the men and women, all of them tilting their heads to listen. "They'll let us exhaust our supply of arrows on the unmarked soldiers; then they'll move. Which is why half the archers will hold back. It's up to the rest of you to keep the enemy off them. Once we've put the lot of them down, you'll turn to reinforce the front. Then we'll make those bastards pay for this ford in blood."

"Dark Horse, Dark Horse," the men and women chanted, and it was picked up by the soldiers at the wall until the air shook with their voices, the stomp of their feet, the hammering of blades against shields. And Killian wondered, as he listened, when the moniker for his shame had turned into a symbol of his redemption.

Holding up one hand, he silenced the line. "They're coming."

The enemy came as they had the prior night, a roaring wall of men charging out of the blackness of the trees.

"Shoot at will," he ordered those who'd been instructed to engage. "Make them count."

The air filled with the twang of bowstrings and the whistle of arrows. Then the screams of men. Killian picked off target after target until his quiver was exhausted. Then he pulled his sword and bellowed, "Charge!"

The soldiers on horseback dug in their heels; then they were flying forward.

And there was nothing like it.

The rush, the roar of blood in his ears, the echoing impact of two armies colliding.

His war-horse slammed into the running men, crushing three beneath his hooves, teeth snapping at anyone in reach, as much a weapon as the blade in Killian's hand. He took the head off a man with the momentum of the charge, then an arm off another, who fell screaming. Then it was a blur, a bloody dance, as he carved through the ranks. Some landed blows on him, but his armor and adrenaline did their duty, and he barely noticed.

Then he saw them.

A blur of black sprinting out of the trees. Two of them cut toward him, and he dug in his spurs, horse leaping over the fallen as he plunged toward the corrupted.

One of them leapt into the air, and Killian lifted his shield. She slammed into it, the impact numbing his arm, but she flipped over his head to land heavily.

The other dived at the horse. The huge animal squealed and staggered, but before he fell Killian flung himself free, dropping his shield and rolling to his feet, another blade in his free hand.

The corrupted circled him warily, weapons out, though he knew they'd prefer to use their mark.

"Rufina has offered a thousand gold pieces to whoever brings her your head," the man said.

"I'll give you two thousand if you leave it where it is," Killian replied, slicing at the woman as she approached. "I've been told I have a very nice neck."

She danced back, grinning. "I've heard the life of the god-marked tastes twice as sweet, Lord Calorian. I'll enjoy drinking yours."

"Hopefully I age gracefully, or your reward might be in jeopardy."

She frowned, and he threw the knife at her face. When she reached for it, he struck, opening her from stem to stern, then twisted, slicing through her spine. The other corrupted shrieked and attacked. Killian turned, his sword taking the man in the chest. The corrupted kept coming, his naked hands reaching.

They went over backward, Killian grabbing the man's wrists and forcing him away. But the corrupted was impossibly strong. Wedged against the corpse of the dead woman and a tree stump, Killian couldn't move, and the man's hands dropped lower and lower. Then Killian lost his grip, and the man had him by the throat.

The corrupted's eyes filled with delight, and Killian felt the pull. He'd been healed more times than he cared to count, and while that felt like warmth and life, this was cold. This was death.

Fight.

The instinct that had been marked into his soul surged, and he smashed the bridge of his helmet against the man's face.

The corrupted hissed and pulled back, and Killian reached between them, finding the hilt of his sword. He pulled, carving the blade through the man's guts until he let go of Killian's throat. He punched the man in the face, knocking him back enough that Killian was able to get out from under him.

He clambered on hands and heels, trying to regain his feet when a massive shadow charged. His horse appeared out of the darkness, bleeding and angry, and his hooves slammed against the corrupted's back and neck until one steel-shod hoof crushed the man's skull.

"Easy." Killian caught hold of the reins. The horse was too injured to ride, so he added, "Stay out of trouble." Then he broke into a run across the field.

His soldiers had held their own better than he'd expected, but they were still being pressed hard. One of the corrupted knelt over a dying Mudamorian woman, his expression filled with ecstasy as he drained her life. Killian took off his head, then threw himself into the battle.

The enemy was flowing over the top of the wall. The Mudamorians and Gamdeshians struggled together to push them back, but there were too many. And he knew on the far side there were hundreds clambering their way up the slope, standing on one another's shoulders or pulling themselves up with rope or ladder. And beyond, thousands more ready to follow.

"Retreat to the wall," he shouted, and those who could ran in the direction of the fortification.

Killian cut down two more men, then followed at a sprint. But it was done. The wall was breached, his soldiers fighting on the ground rather than trying to hold them back to the far side. They were falling, dying, and the walls were shaking and swaying with the press of too many men. He fought alongside them, exhaustion slowing his arm, the blood of a dozen injuries slicking his skin as he tried to hold the line even as it fell back, step by step, the battle moving past the wall and into the field.

Just kill as many as you can, he ordered himself. *Every minute you slow them down counts.*

But it was over. He knew it was over. Victory had never been in the cards.

Then a low rumble filled the air, the ground trembling.

"What is that?" someone screamed, but then a horn sounded over the field. Not the deep bellow of the Derin army, but a high, clear call that made Killian's heart skip.

"Split the line," he roared. "Move to the flanks!"

Sonia echoed the order and their soldiers scrambled to comply, the enemy flooding through the gap they'd formed even as the rumble turned to thunder.

Then cavalry burst from the tree line, hundreds of soldiers on horses caparisoned with Falorn black and green. They spread across the field, a wall of horseflesh and lances and steel, and at their head galloped a woman in shining armor.

Dareena's eyes latched on Killian and she lifted one hand in salute. Then she slapped her visor into place and lowered her lance. "For Mudamora!" she shouted over the noise. "In the name of the Six, let's drive these bastards back!"

Mudamorians and Gamdeshians alike echoed her call, rallying as the Falorn cavalry hurtled toward the enemy.

The Derin soldiers wavered, then broke, racing back toward the sagging wall.

But it was too late.

The collision was deafening, lances breaking, the screams of men and horses filling the air as the Derin soldiers tried to retreat through the gap, clambering overtop only to be picked off by Falorn archers. When they tried running down the length of the wall to escape into the trees, Killian lifted his blade. "Show them no mercy!" he roared; then he led the charge back into the fray.

64

KILLIAN

"Wake up, you idiot!"

Killian felt the impact of a palm against his cheek, and he jerked upright, nearly colliding with the sturdy old woman leaning over him. Blinking, he stared at her before recognition set in. "Glenda?"

"That's Councilor Glenda, to you, Lord Calorian," she snapped, straightening her white robes.

Pushing up onto one elbow, he took in the interior of the unfamiliar tent. "What's happened? Did we lose the ford?"

"What's happened is that you were found half-buried under corpses, your skull split open and a dozen other wounds besides. You're lucky to be alive." She said the last bit rather pointedly and then strode off without another word.

Killian slumped against the pillow. Lifting the blankets, he examined his naked skin, noting several stitched wounds and countless livid bruises. Trust Glenda not to waste her energy on something that wasn't life threatening.

His armor and mail lay scattered about the tent, obviously having been removed from him in great haste and left where it had fallen. The padding and undergarments he had worn beneath the steel lay in a blood-soaked pile on the floor. Climbing off the cot, he searched among them to see if anything was wearable.

Sonia chose that moment to step into the tent, the freezing air from outside gusting against Killian's bare backside.

"By the Six, Sonia!" he snapped, snatching a blanket to make himself decent.

One of her eyebrows rose as she looked him up and down. Then she shrugged. "You're not my type."

"Noted." Finding his saddlebags, Killian dug out a pair of trousers and a wrinkled shirt, pulling them on. Then he rummaged about in the pile of armor and found his scabbard, empty.

"Looking for this?"

The pommel of a sword poked Killian in the back.

"Left it on the field along with most of your brains," Sonia added, handing the weapon over.

"I don't remember."

"Not surprised. You took a blade to the back of the head that split your helmet clean in two." Sonia nodded her head toward the cot, and when Killian turned he saw the pillow where his head had lain was drenched with blood. He raised his hand to the back of his head; his hair was matted with gore. "What happened?"

"High Lady Falorn arrived with five hundred horse, followed shortly by Malahi and the High Lords, as well as Quindor and a handful of healers. It was short, bloody work, but we got them pushed back to their side of the river."

"And our losses?"

Sonia sighed. "We have maybe three hundred left standing."

Three hundred out of two thousand. Panic abruptly burned through his chest. "Finn?"

"Who do you think found you? It's thanks to him you're alive. I set him to taking care of your horse in order to keep him out of trouble."

Thank the Six.

"There's more news. The Royal Army is marching up on the heels of the Derin forces."

Killian started to exhale a breath of relief when Sonia added, "They've got the enemy hemmed in with no avenue of escape. Their only way out is through us."

Killian clenched his teeth, then let loose a string of profanities, seeing exactly how this would go.

"They're rallying for an attack. High Lady Falorn expects it within the hour."

And the Derin army was desperate. They were trapped between two forces, and they had to know that they'd be granted
no mercy. So they'd strike against the force they perceived as
weaker, and that was undoubtedly Killian's. And if the Derin
army gained the eastern bank, they had the numbers to hold
the Royal Army in check while still sending soldiers to sack
Mudaire.

"Serrick needs to back off. Give them a route of escape and
then pursue."

"The High Lady has sent up signals, but he shows no incli-
nation to listen."

"Shit." Fastening his belt, Killian shoved his sword into the
scabbard. "Where's Malahi now?"

"Command tent."

Killian strode through the camp toward the command tent,
which was easily distinguishable by the dozen Rowenes banners flapping in the breeze, though the men standing guard
bore the white horse of House Calorian. They saluted at the
sight of him, moving aside so that he could enter.

"Thank the gods you're alive." A small form slammed into
him before his eyes could adjust to the dimness, and his nose
filled with the familiar scent of Malahi's perfume. Beyond, Dareena, Hacken, and the rest of the High Lords stood next to a
table covered with paper.

"How's the skull?" Dareena's armor still bore splatters from
the battle; her inky hair was pulled high into a topknot, the
base of her head shaved to reveal the black falcon tattoo of her
house. She looked tired, the war paint around her green eyes
smeared, but that was no surprise given that she must have
ridden day and night to get here in time.

"Still attached. I understand we have a surprise guest at our
party."

Dareena nodded. "The Derin army always wanted this side
of the river, but now they need it. Every single soldier in that
army knows that it's take this bank or die. Unless Serrick

gives them another option, they're going to hit us hard and we won't be able to hold."

Killian didn't question her. If Dareena said it was so, then it was so. He pushed Malahi back, noting the tense lines of her jaw. Gwen, Lena, and several other of her bodyguard stood watchfully, though Bercola's absence made his hackles rise, as did the fact that none of the women were meeting his gaze. "You have a plan, I take it? And an explanation for why you are all standing five hundred feet from a battle we're about to lose?"

"The plan is to remove Serrick from authority, and this time for good," Hacken replied. "Now, all in favor of crowning Princess Malahi as Queen of Mudamora let it be known."

All the men in the room lifted their hands. Then their eyes shifted to Dareena. "Allow me to remind you," the High Lady said, "that my presence is not by command, request, or"—she gave Malahi a flat stare—"invitation. You willfully excluded me from your plans, Malahi. Risked a good many lives in order to ensure it would be your head the crown sat upon, not mine."

"You had your chance, Dareena," Malahi answered. "The Twelve chose not to stand behind you. But they have chosen to stand behind me."

"Behind your gold, girl. Not you." Dareena squared her shoulders and lifted her chin. "But your father is a problem that needs to be remedied, and for that reason alone, I'll stand behind you. For now."

"Good," Hacken replied, dipping a pen in a bottle of ink and scrawling his name on a sheet of paper. "Now everyone sign. We need to get a copy of this to the Royal Army with instructions that Her Majesty is ordering them to stand down until we are properly fortified. Killian—"

"I'll go." If he could get there in time, it might be possible to save what remained of his forces. It might be possible to end this war today.

"No!" Malahi blurted out, then took a measured breath. "No.

You need to stay with me. One of the High Lady's soldiers can go."

Irritation flashed through Killian. "I'm not hiding behind the lines, Malahi. Not today. This is my fight."

"Which is why you need to be in command." The muscles of her jaw stood out against her skin, and her eyes flicked to Hacken.

Because even now, even in this moment when all their lives were in jeopardy, he was playing politics. Malahi needed Hacken's support to retain her crown, and that meant Killian marrying her. Though for the life of him, Killian couldn't understand what Hacken stood to gain from him on the throne. "No."

Dareena snorted with obvious irritation. "I'll send two of my best. We don't have time for this."

"I'll go myself," Killian said. "You can spout all the orders you want, Your Majesty. But *you* need to get on a horse with the rest of the High Lords and ride hard for Mudaire. Then you need to get on ships and sail to somewhere safe."

"He's right about that, my lady," Hacken said. "Even if the Royal Army stands down, we still might lose the ford. And when the enemy discovers you were here, you can bet they'll be in pursuit. But Killian, you are the commander. You've no business trying to cross enemy lines when you are needed here."

Killian crossed his arms. "High Lady Falorn is just as capable as I am." More so, if he was being honest.

"You aren't thinking this through, Killian." Hacken's jaw tightened. "You're too important to waste as a messenger."

He knew why Hacken and Malahi were pushing this. They wanted the victory to be Killian's, not Dareena's, and they were willing to risk it not being a victory at all in order to have their way. "Not with a message this important." Picking up the letter, he shoved it deep in one of his pockets.

"Killian—"

"Enough, both of you," Malahi interrupted. "I need to speak with Lord Calorian in *private*. Everyone out!"

"Be quick about it," Dareena said to him as she headed outside. "We're running out of time."

Killian waited until they were gone before rounding on Malahi. "Do you understand what's going to happen if we don't get word to the Royal Army to back off their advance? We're going to be overrun and slaughtered. Then the Derin army will hold this bank against your father while the rest of their force moves on to sack Mudaire and down to Abenharrow to attack all those undefended civilians. Those are the stakes. Are you still willing to risk someone else carrying that message?"

Malahi's face was white as a sheet. "I understand the stakes. But we are so close to achieving everything we wanted, Killian. So close. Please don't mess things up now because you're unwilling to *delegate*."

"So close to achieving what *we* want or what *you* want, Malahi?" He stared at her, anger rising in his chest. "What I want is to win this battle. To defeat Rufina and her army and drive them out of Mudamora. But it seems to me that you only care about winning this battle if it's on your terms."

"That's not true." Her eyes searched his. "You know that everything I've done has been to save this kingdom."

"I used to think that. Now I wonder if you care more about putting the crown on your head than you do for the people you claim to serve," he said. "I wonder if you're no better than the rest of the High Lords after all."

His cheek stung as the palm of her hand cracked against it. Killian had seen it coming and could have moved. But he'd chosen not to, watching now as she curled her hand against her chest. "I'm sorry," she whispered, lowering her head. "I should not have done that."

Killian didn't answer, only watched as she pulled herself together, smoothing both the wrinkles from her skirts and the emotion from her face.

"Please stay on this side of the wall," she finally said. "Send someone else. Send ten men. A hundred men. Send Dareena; just please don't go yourself."

His skin prickled with the sense an attack was coming, but it had nothing to do with the enemy on the other side of that wall.

"Let me go!" Lena's voice tore his attention from Malahi's face, and he turned to find the girl struggling with Gwen, who was trying to haul her out of the tent entrance while hissing, "You can't! She'll fire you and you'll have to go back to turning tricks," underneath her breath.

"What is the meaning of this?" Malahi demanded. "Have you two forgotten what the word *private* means?"

Shaking Gwen off her arm, Lena straightened. "Respectfully, Your Grace, I can't stay silent. He needs to know what you've done."

Malahi blanched, and Killian's skin crawled with apprehension. "What's she talking about, Malahi?"

"Nothing. It's nothing. She doesn't know what she's talking about."

It wasn't nothing. Even if Malahi didn't look ready to vomit on his boots, he would've known it wasn't *nothing*.

"I know I'm fired or worse for this," Lena said. "But what you did to Lydia wasn't right."

Lydia. Killian's pulse roared and it was all he could do not to grab Malahi by the shoulders and shake her. "Did you hurt her?"

"No! I—" She broke off, her chin trembling.

"Either you tell him or I do, Your Grace," Lena said. "Your choice."

Malahi closed her eyes for a long moment, then nodded. "Get out. I don't need you listening in."

"Where is Lydia?" Killian demanded, not noticing or caring if Lena complied. "What have you done to her?"

Silence.

"I didn't think Dareena would vote for me," she finally

answered. "I thought killing my father was the only way to take the crown away from him. I . . . I discovered that Lydia was a healer, and I used the information to convince her to help me."

It was the worst sort of betrayal. Even if Killian hadn't been truthful about Lydia's identity, she'd still risked her life to protect Malahi's. "You mean you threatened her until she agreed to be your assassin?"

"Yes."

Killian stepped back, needing distance from her. Not knowing how he could ever stand to be close to her again. "You're telling me that she's with the Royal Army planning to kill the King?"

"Yes, but she's supposed to have done it already. Something's gone wrong."

Lydia—Lydia who could barely manage to swing a sword without tripping over her own feet—was going to attempt to murder the most important man in the kingdom. A thousand things could've gone wrong.

"I'm sorry." Malahi reached for him, but he batted her hands away. "Please understand that I only did it to save our people."

"Why her?" he demanded. "You could've chosen anyone. Or is this all jealousy? All a result of you falling for my brother's manipulations rather than asking me for the truth?"

"Would you have given it?"

No.

She gave a slow shake of her head. "It doesn't matter. This isn't jealousy. I know she's the healer who saved your life and that you were helping her out of obligation."

If only that was the entire truth.

"Then why her?"

"You don't know her as well as you seem to think you do, Killian."

"I know she's innocent. I know she doesn't deserve this!"

"She's not innocent!" Malahi shouted the words in his face before checking herself. "If you knew the truth about her, you might not be so quick to defend her!"

He stared at his queen. "You more than anyone should understand why she'd be trying to evade Quindor's net."

"That's the least of it." Malahi's hands balled into fists. "She's corrupted."

"Bullshit!" he snarled. "I've seen her heal dozens of people with my own eyes."

"And I saw her almost kill one with her bare hands. The corrupted you beheaded in the tunnels? He tried to take her life and she took it back. And more. She can do what *they* do."

His mind raced back to that moment. Of running through the tunnels. Of seeing the corrupted kneeling above Lydia, her eyes wide in what he'd believed was fear. But had it been something else? "It was dark. You were seeing things."

"Not that dark."

"It doesn't make her corrupted. She was desperate."

Except it did. That was exactly what it meant.

There was pity in Malahi's eyes. "I sent her to kill my father with her touch so that everyone would believe he was assassinated by Rufina. He'd be a martyr and there would be no chance the Royal Army wouldn't want to take their revenge. I sent her because she was a life I was willing to sacrifice. If she succeeds, thousands will be saved."

And potentially thousands more lost. Teriana. Her crew. All the Maarin in captivity in the Celendor Empire. And gods, but he was certain the stakes were even higher than that. "She's more important than you know. What you've done . . ." Words failed him.

She reached for him again. "She's one life, Killian. And a tainted one at that."

"She's not just one life," he screamed. "Not to those who are counting on her. And not to me. I'm not allowing her to throw her life away."

Malahi's face hardened. "You're sworn to protect *me*, Killian Calorian. Not her. You swore to stay by *my* side."

The worst decision of his life. It would've been better to have let the executioner take his head, because then Lydia would never have met him. Would never have been marked. Would probably be on her way back to Celendor already instead of risking her life, her soul, because of Malahi's threats.

You swore an oath.

"Fine," he hissed. "Make me stay with you, Malahi. Make me *marry* you. And I will be loyal to you and protect your neck for as long as I live, but know that I will *hate* you every waking minute of it. And that on my dying breath, I'll curse your gods-damned soul to the underworld for this."

Malahi's face blanched; then slowly, she took a step back. "If my father dies, I'll be High Lady. I'll have a vote and it won't matter if Hacken retracts his. You wouldn't need to marry me and I . . . I could release you from your oath."

He'd have his freedom back. But at what cost? Lydia not just a murderer, but *corrupted*. "I'll suffer any amount of misery if it means sparing her from the fate *you* forced upon her."

"Misery." She whispered the word.

Neither of them spoke, but outside, shouts filled the air. The enemy was attacking again, but his mark was screaming that something else was wrong. That there was something he was missing. Then it struck him. "Where. Is. Bercola?"

Malahi bit her bottom lip. "She's on the other side of the Tarn behind the Derin lines. I couldn't risk Lydia failing and my father arriving at the head of—" She broke off, clenching her teeth hard.

Killian stared at her. Because it would've taken hours for Bercola to get into that position undetected. "Until an hour ago, we all believed the Royal Army was marching to Abenharrow. How is it that you had cause to believe otherwise?"

"I . . ."

"Lied." The memory of the King's message arriving flashed through Killian's mind. Of Malahi being alone in her rooms when she received it. Of him being distracted by the infection of High Lord Torrington. Of the smeared ink on the tiny roll of paper, as though the message had been written in great haste.

Written by her. "You forged a new message. You deceived everyone. You risked the lives of everyone."

"Can't you see that I didn't have a choice?" She clenched handfuls of her own hair, her face twisting. "Everything my father touches turns to rot. There is something *wrong* with him. I couldn't risk him arriving and losing this battle like he's lost *every single one of them*. So I did what the rest of you were too gods-damned afraid to do."

"And yet for all your plotting, here he is." Killian gestured west. "And it's too late for us to do anything about."

"It's not too late. Bercola—"

"No." He started to the front of the tent. "I'm going, Malahi. And you'd best pray to all the gods that I can undo the damage that you've done."

"Go, then," Malahi called after him, her voice bitter. "But know this, Killian. If you don't come back to me victorious and I lose the crown, everything that happens will be because of *you*. Because of the decision you made in *this* moment. And any blood that is shed will be on your hands."

"Have a look at your own hands, Your Majesty," Killian answered. "Because I assure you, they are far from clean."

The camp was chaos as soldiers ran to their posts, shouts and screams filling the air as the Derin army assaulted the wall, Falorn archers picking them off by the hundreds. To try to go through the ford would be throwing himself into a deathtrap, which meant he needed to find another way across.

Sonia was outside. "They're trying to scale the cliffs. They've got lines across both north and south. The High Lady has sent archers to pick them off, but we're spread too thin. Won't be long until they have enough men across to flank us."

"That's Dareena's problem," Killian said, motioning for the woman to follow him. "I need to get across."

"Are you insane?"

"Quite possibly." Leading her at a sprint, he tracked the lip of the ravine, keeping far enough back to avoid being shot by enemy archers. Derin soldiers climbed over the edge, some engaging with Mudamorians even as others secured lines their archers had shot across. The ravine was crisscrossed with ropes heavy with men, but Killian ignored them until he found a spot that suited his fancy.

Cutting down the men guarding the secured line, he sheathed his sword in favor of a sturdy branch, which he placed over the taut rope. Gripping it firmly on both sides, he shouted, "Cover me!," then jumped.

The eastern bank was higher, and he slid down the rope with speed, using his feet to knock loose climbers coming across. He lost momentum in the middle, grabbing hold of the rope with one hand even as he grappled with another man, elbowing him in the face until he fell screaming into the river.

Arrows whizzed past, one scoring a fiery line across his shoulder, another knocking against the heel of his boot as he slid toward the western bank.

"Shoot him! Shoot him!" the Derin soldiers screamed, and sweat dripped down Killian's brow as another arrow glanced off the hilt of his sword. "Shit!"

"Killian, hold on tight," he heard Sonia scream; then he was falling. His shoulders snapped and he swung toward the ravine wall, twisting to get his legs in place. The impact nearly jarred him loose. Dangling from one arm and breathing hard, he reached up to catch hold of the rope and then began to climb.

"Cover him!"

Arrows flew from Falorn bows, sinking into the enemy above. Reaching the top, Killian rolled over the edge and to his feet, sword in hand. He cut into the ranks of Derin soldiers, forcing his way past them and into the trees. The Derin army reeked of terror and desperation, black-clad corrupted driving them toward the ravine, killing those who attempted to flee.

Vaulting onto a loose horse, he kicked the animal into a gallop until he was clear of the enemy lines. In the distance, the

Royal Army was spread in a long line, rushing forward like a massive hammer intent on crushing the enemy against an anvil. Except it would be the anvil that shattered.

He lay low across the neck of the horse, riding hard, searching for the striking scorpion of House Rowenes even as he combed the trees for any sign of Bercola, but there was no sign of either of them. And no sign of Lydia, either. *Please be all right,* he prayed. *Please be alive.*

But it couldn't be Lydia he focused on. His first priority needed to be to wrest control from Serrick and reroute the Royal Army before it was too late. This would be done right, or not at all.

There.

In the center ranks, a group of cavalry surrounded a man in gilded armor, his head bare but for the golden circlet on his brow. *Serrick.* And next to him rode . . . Lydia?

But where the hell was Bercola?

He looked backward, seeking her large form among the trees and chaos, only to be forced to pull up his mount as archers trained their weapons on him. "I'm Lord Killian Calorian," he shouted. "I need to see the King."

Several of them lowered their weapons as they recognized him, but before he could proceed, motion in the tree line caught his attention. Turning his head, he saw a figure standing in the shadows of the trees, face obscured by a hood, a spear held in one hand.

"No!" he shouted, but Bercola either didn't hear him or chose not to listen.

Killian dug his heels into the sides of his horse and plunged forward.

65

LYDIA

The cavalry massed around Lydia shifted uneasily, the harsh tang of unwashed bodies rising to fill her nostrils as they pushed steadily toward the ravine containing both the river Tarn and most of the Derin forces.

Without her spectacles and through the falling snow, she could make out little detail, only that on the far side of the ravine the sheer cliff was broken in one spot with a steep incline that led up to a wall made of wood and rocks. Beneath it, the slope churned with motion, and though she knew it was the Derin army trying to break through the wall, it looked for all the world to her like a swarm of insects climbing only to be knocked back.

She rode at the King of Mudamora's left, under strict orders from the moment she'd told him Malahi's plans that she wasn't to leave his side. Sweat drenched her skin and the horse beneath her pranced sideways, picking up on her anxiety.

All her life, she'd been exposed to war. To strategies of deployment, the discussion of battles past and battles to come. Her ears had been filled with the costs of victories, the numbers of soldiers lost to death or injury tossed about as though they were nothing more than toys misplaced through careless play. The distance had made it palatable, but now she was about to see the reality.

She was terrified.

Horns sounded through the air from the opposite bank— signals, she guessed, though what they meant Lydia couldn't begin to guess.

High Lord Damashere wove through the lines toward her and the King, horse foaming at the bit as the man reined it in hard. "They're signaling again for us to back down, Your Grace. Their wall and lines are at risk of breach."

"I'm not deaf, Damashere; I can hear the horns," the King snapped, his breath forming clouds of mist in the cold air. "Ignore them. They are lies. All lies. Get back to your position."

Unease filled Lydia's chest. Malahi might be a liar, but it would be Killian and his soldiers who were sending those signals. She opened her mouth to say as much, but before she could, the King's healer, Cyntha, leaned in close.

"Her Highness wants this victory for herself. She'll risk the lives of everyone to ensure it. You must not let her have her way."

"But it's not the Princess who is giving orders," Lydia argued. "It's Lord Calorian."

"Who well you know has failed this kingdom in the past." Despite her words being directed at the King, Cyntha's eyes were latched on Lydia, her gaze searing. "Tremon turned his back on Lord Calorian. We've seen proof of it. Never mind that he's Malahi's tool. He cannot be trusted."

Lydia's skin was crawling. Bringing the Royal Army here was supposed to be delivering Killian from certain death, but now it felt like she'd damned him. "He's not a tool. He knows nothing about the Princess's intentions."

"That seems unlikely given that he's planning to marry her," Serrick growled. "He stands to gain as much as she does."

"He didn't ask for any of this." Terror was clawing at Lydia's insides now. "It was forced upon him."

"You are the true protector of Mudamora, Your Grace," Cyntha said. "Chosen by the gods to lead us. But part of that means bringing the Marked who go astray back to heel."

"Some are beyond redemption."

"Even so, Your Grace."

Lydia stared at the woman, expecting to see fanaticism burning in the woman's eyes, but there was only cunning. She *wanted* this.

"The armies of the Seventh stand before you." Cyntha's voice rose, loud enough for those around to hear. "None must be left alive!"

The King lifted his hand, but before he could speak, a commotion ahead caught his attention. Lydia squinted, catching sight of a rider just ahead of the front lines shouting at those whose arrows were trained at him. His face was too blurry for her to make out, but instinct told her who it was. "Killian?"

He wheeled his horse around, eyes scanning the snow-covered trees.

Another assassin. Of course Malahi wouldn't have banked everything on Lydia's success.

Then Killian dug his heels into the sides of his horse, the animal leaping forward. Not galloping toward the King, but in the path of—

"No!" Lydia screamed, but she was helpless to stop the spear that punched into Killian's unarmored side.

Lydia lashed her reins against her horse's neck, driving the animal through the soldiers surrounding the King, barely hearing the shouts of those around her.

Killian was swaying in the saddle, his shirt already drenched with blood, and then slowly he toppled off the horse.

A howl tore from her throat, and Lydia flung herself off the side of her own mount, falling to the ground and crawling to his side.

There was blood everywhere.

"No, no, no!" She reached for him, but he caught her wrists.

"Don't." The word was strangled, but his grip was strong. "They'll see. They'll know."

He was right. She could sense the soldiers who'd gathered around them, hear the faint drone of their voices. But she didn't care. "You'll die if I don't."

"Doesn't. Matter."

His grip on her was weakening. Marked or not, he was dying, and she refused to lose him.

Not like this.

Turning to the watching soldiers, she said, "On my count, I need you to pull the spear out."

"It will kill him," one of them said.

"It won't," she answered. "Because I'm going to save him."

"Lydia . . ."

"One," she said, seeing the soldier take hold of the spear. "Two." He braced his heels.

"Don't." Killian's eyes were pleading.

Bending over, she pressed her lips to his, silencing him even as their fingers interlaced. "Three."

66

KILLIAN

Agony tore through him, like his insides were being twisted and torn out of his body.

Everything went black. For a heartbeat. A moment. A lifetime.

Then with a gasp, Killian jerked upright, the pain gone. All of it. Not just from Bercola's spear, but every cut and bruise and torn muscle vanquished.

Lydia.

She was slumped next to him, fragile and ancient, her hair totally white.

Please, no. With a shaking hand, he pressed fingers against her throat, relief filling his chest at the faint pulse he found there.

"Eastern bank is signaling that they've been breached," someone shouted, cutting through the noise building around him.

"You have to go."

Her voice was little more than a whisper, but her green eyes were steady.

"I'm not leaving you." He'd left her too many times. He wouldn't do it again.

"You have to. They need you." Her hand found his, gripping it hard. "This was the chance you wanted."

It was, but not like this.

"Go."

It wasn't a request, but a command, and Killian's skin prickled. "Get somewhere safe," he said. "I'll find you."

Accepting the reins of a horse, he mounted, riding out among the cavalry of the Royal Army, pulling the blood-smeared page full of the High Lords' signatures out of his pocket. "Seven of the Twelve Houses of Mudamora have spoken," he shouted. "It is their will that Serrick Rowenes be removed from the throne, and in his place, Malahi Rowenes to be crowned Queen of Mudamora."

From across the masses of soldiers, he saw Serrick's glare, but Killian found his gaze drawn to the older woman in white robes at his side. She met Killian's stare, then reined her mount away from the King's, riding hard in the opposite direction. Killian's skin burned like fire ants marched across it, but whatever she was up to, he didn't have time to deal with it now.

"On the far side of that river," he shouted to the mounted men, "stand not only soldiers, but your mothers. Your wives. Your sisters. All who have fought day and night to hold back our enemy so that your children have a chance to flee to safety. They have bled and died so those you love might live another day. Will you leave them to fight alone? Or will you ride with me now and send these bastards to the underworld?"

The army roared their answer, the sound growing as his words passed back through the ranks, his name repeated on a dozen lips. Then on hundreds. Then on thousands. And when it reached the fevered pitch he was waiting for, Killian pulled his sword and held it in the air.

"For Mudamora and the Six," he shouted, then led the charge toward the battle.

67

LYDIA

Lydia awoke to the feel of a hand gripping her own, and she blinked in the faint light of a glowing lamp. She was in a tent, a pillow beneath her head and a heavy blanket pulled up to her throat. Beneath, her clothes were sticking to her skin and reeking of blood, but that all fell away as she turned her head to see who was next to her.

Killian sat on a stool, half-asleep with his chin resting on the palm of one hand, his elbow balanced next to her. There were dark shadows beneath his eyes, his clothes marked with mud, blood, and worse, but he was there.

"Killian," she whispered, and he blinked, focusing on her face.

"Thank the gods," he breathed. "I was afraid you'd never wake. That you'd . . ." His throat convulsed as he swallowed down the rest of his words, and she gripped his hand to prove she was alive and well.

Or at least as well as she could be. "What happened?"

"After the battle, I went in search of you. Found you passed out beneath a wagon and I brought you here. Camp is still in chaos, so no one paid me much attention, thank the Six."

He straightened, his back popping with the motion. "Army's flushing out the last pockets of resistance, but the war is done. What remains of the Derin forces are fleeing back to the wall, presumably with Rufina, as she hasn't been found among the dead. We've received word from Mudaire that the city is nearly evacuated. Everyone is safe."

"You won the war."

He shrugged a shoulder and looked away. "I wouldn't go that far."

But he had. The last thing she remembered was him galloping toward the enemy army, the Mudamorian cavalry rallying behind him, unblinking and unhesitating, as though they knew without a doubt that Killian would lead them to victory.

"Malahi lied to everyone," she said. "I discovered what she was up to and told the King that she wanted him dead. There was no other way for me to get him to march to your aid, but then it made everything worse."

Killian was silent for a moment. "Who knows what Malahi sent you to do besides Serrick?"

"His personal healer, Cyntha. He made me swear to tell no one else." It had been the reason Serrick had kept her next to him from the moment she'd confessed—he hadn't trusted her to keep her mouth shut.

"This is dire," Killian said. "I need to get you out of here. There were too many witnesses to you healing me and Serrick himself knows your face. Your description is being circulated and it's only a matter of time until someone finds you. And with the High Lords having voted to crown Malahi as queen, Serrick needs you as proof that Malahi tried to have him killed. It's the only chance he has at keeping his crown."

A chill ran down Lydia's spine knowing that she was being hunted.

"You need to get back to Celendor to help Teriana."

"Teriana's not in Celendor," she said, watching the color drain from his face as she told him what she'd learned from Bait. "I can't help her."

"Maybe not. But that doesn't mean I'm allowing Quindor to cage you up." Killian extracted a cloak from beneath the cot. "Put this on. Sonia has horses waiting. I'll sneak you out of camp and she'll get you to a small port and on a ship. If you ride fast, they won't be able to catch you, and they don't have the pigeons to warn every harbor on the coast. Sonia has connections and Gamdesh is the safest place for you to go. You won't need to hide your mark."

She held the clothing in her hands, staring at the fabric. "What about you?"

He looked away. "What about me?"

"They'll know it was you who helped me escape."

"They'll *suspect* it was me, but I'll lie through my teeth if they ask. And besides"—he hesitated—"without you, Malahi's rule is uncontested. And it's not in her best interest for me to be charged with a crime against the Crown."

Because he was betrothed to her. Was going to become Malahi's king or prince consort or whatever sort of nonsense title she forced upon him. Anger and grief abruptly rose in Lydia's chest, and she blurted out, "Do you want to be with her?"

Killian went still, his eyes fixed and unblinking on the ground. "I'm sworn to her."

"To protect her, not to marry her!"

"I . . ." He gave the slightest shake of his head as though to clear it. "I have to believe that Malahi will make a better ruler for Mudamora than any of the High Lords. Better than her father. If my marrying her is what it takes to get the crown on her head, and to keep it there, then I'll do it."

Lydia's chest throbbed in the way it did when she'd healed too much and it was threatening to give out. Like it was too tired to keep beating. "You didn't answer my question."

"I answered it well enough." He turned away, his back to her. "For all that she's done, Malahi is my queen and my future wife, and I'll not speak against her."

Of course he wouldn't. Not even if Malahi deserved it. He was too honorable. Too gods-damned loyal. "Do you love her?"

"Lydia . . ." His voice was hoarse. "Don't ask me that."

"Do you love her?" she demanded, rising to her feet, her knees wobbly.

"Please don't push this."

Let it go, a voice whispered in her head. *Nothing good will come of this.* But she couldn't. Not this time.

"Tell me that you love her, and I'll let you be." Hot tears

were rolling down her cheeks. "Say it. Just say it. Say that she's the one you want."

The silence was interminable. The worst she'd ever endured. Lydia was on the verge of speaking again just to break it when Killian turned around, voice low as he said, "Don't make me lie to you."

Lydia took one step toward him. Then another. Her foot rose to close the distance between them when he reached up, catching her shoulders. She could feel the heat of his hands through her clothes, his arms trembling, fingers flexing.

"You can't." He said the words under his breath, barely loud enough for her to hear. Not speaking to her, but to himself. "You can't do this."

Why can't you? Why does it have to be this way? The thoughts circled wildly in her head, demanding to be voiced, but Lydia shut them down. Because to ask him to betray his word to Malahi would be like asking him to betray who he was.

She squeezed her eyes shut, trying to hold back the flood of tears even as she felt the heat of his breath against her face, heard his soft inhale and exhale in her ears. *This* was what her heart wanted. *He* was what she wanted. But neither of them took that next step, only stood and breathed and thought of what might have been. Because it would never be more than that. Never more than a dream that taunted the mind in the darkest hour of the night.

"Lord Calorian?" a voice called from outside the tent, both of them jerking away from each other with a start.

"What?" Killian demanded. "I'm trying to get some sleep."

The individual coughed uncomfortably. "You've been summoned by the King."

"Malahi is queen."

A hesitation, then, "I'm just conveying the message."

Hissing between his teeth, Killian shook his head. "Keep the lamp down and your head covered. I'll be back as soon as I can."

68

KILLIAN

He strode through the muck of the Royal Army camp, barely noticing the soldiers who inclined their heads to him as he passed.

There was only one thing that Serrick could possibly want: Lydia.

Without her, he had no proof that Malahi had tried to kill him, and without that proof, the crown was no longer his.

If Serrick got his hands on her and forced her to testify, Malahi would be executed for treason and then Lydia would be given over to the healing temple, and Killian refused to allow that to happen to either of them. Which meant he was going to have to lie. Lie, and then get Lydia free of this camp and, in doing so, save both her and Malahi.

Guards opened the flaps to Serrick's tent and Killian stepped instead, making his way through the series of antechambers, following the sound of voices. The first face he saw as he stepped into the receiving chamber was Hacken's, and Killian froze in his tracks.

His brother was splattered with mud and a long red scrape marred one cheek. The rest of the High Lords who'd been with him were also present, equally filthy and battered, but alive. Serrick sat in a chair, hands folded, face grim, flanked by the High Lords who'd accompanied him on the campaign. Only Malahi was absent. "Where is the Queen?"

Serrick's face soured, but he gestured a hand to Hacken.

"We were attacked as dusk fell," he answered. "By Rufina. She was alone, but mounted on a deimos."

Killian couldn't breathe. "Malahi?"

"Rufina took her."

Gods, no. The room faded in and out of focus, Malahi's last words echoing through his head like a prophecy: *If you don't come back to me victorious and I lose the crown, everything that happens will be because of you. Because of the decision you made in this moment. And any blood that is shed will be on your hands.*

"You should've been with her," Hacken hissed. "You were supposed to protect her."

He'd sworn to protect her.

"And yet we cannot fault Lord Calorian's decision to do otherwise," Serrick said, rising to his feet. "We have him to thank for Mudamora's victory over our enemy. And I have him to thank for my life."

Rufina has Malahi.

"Whereas it was you worms"—Serrick gestured at the High Lords—"who put the target on my daughter's back. Setting her up as your paper queen. And you—" He glared at Hacken. "Don't for a heartbeat think that I don't see what you hoped to gain with your brother on the throne, you greedy little creature. You are *disgusting* to have used her so. And at what cost?" He looked away, grief painting his face. "My girl is gone and I should hang the lot of you for your meddling."

Vaguely, Killian realized that Serrick hadn't told anyone about Malahi's plot to assassinate him, but his mind couldn't focus. Couldn't move past that he'd left her alone and now she was gone.

"You have no authority over us, Serrick," Hacken growled. "You are no longer king."

"No?" Serrick spit the word. "Then who rules Mudamora? Your would-be queen is dead."

Malahi is dead.

"We have enough here for a majority vote, so why not do so? Crown a new king." Serrick laughed. "It need not be me. It could be any of us. It could be you, Hacken, who sits on the throne."

All the High Lords shifted uneasily.

"Of course." Serrick sat back down. "If you grasping fools

were capable of choosing among yourselves, Malahi would be alive."

Malahi would be alive if you hadn't left her.

"All of you get out," Serrick said, motioning for a servant to refill his cup. "Debate among yourselves somewhere out of my sight. Until you make a decision otherwise, I am King of Mudamora."

"Don't get comfortable on your throne, Serrick," Hacken said. "You won't be sitting on it for much longer." Then he and the other High Lords left the room.

Killian blindly followed them until Serrick called out, "Not you, Killian. You and I have much to discuss."

Freezing in his tracks, Killian fought to regain composure. Lydia was still at risk. He wouldn't fail her, too.

Serrick picked up the decanter sitting on the table and poured two glasses, handing Killian one. "Where's the girl? Lydia, I believe her name is."

"I don't know. The last time I saw her was moments before I rode into battle."

Taking a mouthful of his drink, Serrick eyed him. "I doubt that's the case, Lord Calorian, but given the circumstances, I'll not press that issue just yet."

Killian only crossed his arms, saying nothing.

"Lydia was adamant that you were unaware of Malahi's plot to kill me, but I did not believe her." Serrick shook his finger at Killian. "Did not believe her, that is, until you came galloping across that field to foil the second assassin, nearly losing your own life in the process. Seems unlikely you would've done so if you were complicit in the plotting."

Malahi was dead. What was the point in trying to protect her now? "She confessed what she'd sent Lydia to do. I took issue with it."

"I've no doubt you did." The King's eyes were too knowing for Killian's comfort. As if he saw quite clearly that the issue was not with Serrick being murdered but with Lydia being the one to do it.

"If that spear had been intended for me, would you still have ridden into its path?"

"It *was* intended for you."

Serrick gave a soft smile. "Oh, I think we both know it wasn't. Malahi had the crown in her hands—my death was hardly necessary. But killing the girl who knew her plans most certainly was. Malahi sent an assassin to kill Lydia, not me, and you knew it."

Had he? Killian wasn't certain. Wasn't even certain now if that had been Malahi's intent, and the only person who could confirm it was Bercola, who was nowhere to be found. Either she was dead or had fled, but even given the circumstances, Killian struggled to believe Bercola's honor would allow for the latter.

"I know it is your instinct to grieve for her death," Serrick continued. "Even though she conspired against me, she was still my daughter and her loss pains me more than you can know. But she was a conniving, wicked thing who manipulated everyone around her to achieve her own ends, caring not who she hurt in the process."

Malahi had made some unforgivable choices, but—

"She used you, Killian. She knew what you cared about. What you wanted. And she exploited that information in her quest for the crown. Surely you see that now?"

In hindsight, it was impossible *not* to see how he'd been manipulated. How little what he had wanted really mattered. How easily Malahi had risked everything and everyone Killian cared about in order to achieve her own ends.

"Yet despite my daughter's machinations, you have proven yourself, Killian Calorian. Proven that Tremon still values your service. And Mudamora needs you now more than it ever has." Serrick took a step back. "I would have you take command of my armies and see our kingdom put to rights."

It was what he'd wanted. What he'd always wanted. But not . . . Not like this. Not with this man as king.

"You were marked to protect the realm." Serrick inclined

his head. "And I intend to bestow upon you every resource in order to ensure that you can do so."

"I . . ."

"Remind me your age, Killian? I've forgotten."

He blinked. "Nineteen, Your Grace."

Serrick chuckled. "Such an enormous honor, especially for someone as young as yourself. But Tremon clearly believes you're ready."

Maybe this wasn't how he envisioned it, but this was his chance to atone. To give his people back their kingdom. To allow them to thrive.

Is that even possible with Serrick as king? Killian didn't know.

This was what you wanted, a voice screamed inside his head. *The only thing you've ever wanted.*

Except that wasn't true anymore. There was something—someone—else, and she was waiting for him. And for the first time since he'd met Lydia, he was free to do something about the way he felt.

A freedom that came at the expense of Malahi's life!

Guilt rose up in his core like bile. He had no right to be thinking such thoughts. Not now. Not ever. With Malahi gone, his duty needed to be to his country, and that meant serving whoever wore the crown. "I accept."

69

LYDIA

Lydia paced back and forth through the tent, her heart racing.

What had the King wanted from Killian? *Not the King,* she reminded herself. *Malahi is Queen now.*

But that didn't mean Killian was beyond punishment. There were people in the camp searching for her—and given their connection, he could be in a great deal of trouble.

You should go, she told herself. *You should run.*

He'd said Sonia had horses waiting. All she needed to do was track down the young woman and she could be on her way.

On your way where?

The thought stopped her in her tracks, because she didn't have an answer. Part of her wanted to go to Teriana, but her friend had a plan and she didn't need Lydia interfering, especially given Marcus would probably kill her on sight—she knew far too much for him to leave alive. Bait could deliver the truth to Teriana with much less risk to either of them.

Another part of her wanted to go back to Celendor. To see if her father was still alive and if her mark would still be with her, allowing her to heal him. Then together, they could pull Lucius from power.

But another part of her, growing stronger and more insistent, was pushing her in an entirely different direction.

A draft struck her in her back, and Lydia whirled around—

To find herself face-to-face with Hacken Calorian. "Now what do we have here?" he said, and she took several steps back at the fury burning in his eyes. His clothes were muddy and torn, a livid scrape marring one of his lovely cheeks.

"I've always had a knack for finding things that Killian

doesn't want found," the High Lord said, coming fully into the tent. "For a boy who is supposed to be such a strategic genius, he's never been very good at hiding things."

"What do you want?"

He barked out a humorless laugh. "What I want is Malahi alive, but not even a *healer* can bring back the dead. Especially when one doesn't even have a corpse to work with."

Lydia pressed a hand to her stomach, her core hollowing despite everything the other girl had done to her. "Malahi is dead? How?"

"Rufina attacked us on the road and took her. Killian no doubt would've been able to fight her off, but he wasn't with Malahi like he was supposed to have been. He was busy chasing after *you*."

Guilt flooded Lydia's veins, along with fear.

Reaching up, Hacken caught hold of Lydia's face, his fingers snagging in her hair. And though she knew that she should fight him off, that she was strong and capable, her entire body froze.

"This is your fault as much as his," he hissed. "Malahi is dead because of *you*. Don't think for a heartbeat that there won't be consequences."

Another draft struck Lydia, and Hacken dropped his hand from her face, turning. A rail-thin man stepped inside and Lydia's stomach plummeted as she recognized him from the day she'd brought Gwen to Hegeria's temple.

"This is her, Grand Master," Hacken said to the healer. "The girl who saved my brother's life."

"Thank you, High Lord. You've done us a great service in finding her for us."

"I serve the Six," Hacken said, but the look he cast Lydia before he left the tent was vicious in its triumph.

"We meet again," the Grand Master said, his eyes full of recognition.

Lydia found herself barely able to breathe, much less answer. This was the moment she'd been trying to avoid almost from the moment she'd arrived on the Dark Shores. And despite everything she'd done—everything Killian had done—here she stood. Like fate, unavoidable and unchangeable.

"I long suspected Lord Calorian had you hidden away. We heard the rumors that Hegeria herself walked the sewers at night healing the orphan children with a god-marked swordsman standing guard at her side. And stories, I find, always have some basis in truth."

"If you knew, why didn't you come for me?" The question slipped out from between her teeth.

The healer smoothed his white robes, which were spotted with blood. "Always, we are accused of hunting down those with Hegeria marks. Of stealing them away. But that is rarely the truth of it, because most often, the Marked come to us."

Lydia's skin prickled.

"Our goddess is not random in her choices—she knows who are suited to dedicating their life to the well-being of others, and it is those she marks." He eyed her for a long moment. "When I heard you were using your gift—likely because you couldn't help yourself—I knew it would only be a matter of time until you accepted your destiny and came to us willingly."

"Except I didn't come to you." Her voice was shaky. "High Lord Calorian turned me in."

"True. But even if he hadn't, I think you would have arrived on our doorstep, one way or another. It's where you are needed. Where you are wanted. Where you belong. You knew that the moment you stepped through the temple doors that day."

A shiver stole along her spine, his words the answer to the question that had haunted her since she'd spoken to Bait on the beach. Still she said, "And what if I don't agree? What if I resist? What if I run?"

Quindor sighed. "Don't make me resort to threats, Lydia." Gesturing outwards, he said, "Lord Calorian won a great victory today, and the King intends to reward him. To put him in command of Mudamora's armies and to give him the opportunity to use his mark as Tremon intended. But if Serrick were to learn that Lord Calorian had been knowingly harboring you? Breaking his most sacrosanct law? Things might go in a different direction."

"And who is to say it won't go in that direction even if I do go with you?"

Shaking his head, Quindor replied, "I cannot predict the future, but rest assured that Lord Calorian's downfall will not come by way of me. We might have won the battle today, but the war is not over. Mudamora had need of its Marked."

It wasn't over. Rufina was alive, her kingdom still a threat, and on the Southern Continent another shadow lurked.

This is where I'm meant to be.

As if hearing the words inside her head, Quindor straightened. "We ride for Mudaire immediately. The blight continues its spread, and the city is infested with those who've been infected. We must find a way to stop it, and I want you to be a part of that. I need your help in our war against the Seventh."

This is what I'm meant to do.

She allowed him to take her arm, and they stepped outside, where another pair of healers waited, along with a handful of soldiers. "Ready the horses," Quindor ordered.

They were leaving now.

"May I say good-bye?" she asked, her chest aching.

"Best not," Quindor said under his breath. "I doubt he'll take this well."

Men led horses toward them, and Lydia allowed one of them to boost her into the saddle. Instead of handing her the reins, he gave them to another mounted soldier as though she couldn't be trusted to follow.

"Quickly now," Quindor ordered. "We must be away."

"Lydia!"

Her name echoed through the camp and, taking a deep breath, she turned.

Killian was striding toward them, sword in hand, and she

knew that he'd fight to free her. That he might succeed. And that in doing so, he'd lose everything. That they both might lose everything. So she shook her head.

He froze.

"I choose this," she whispered to him, and the wind blew, seeming to catch her voice. "Don't try to stop me."

He lowered his sword and gave a faint, almost imperceptible nod.

She twisted back around, eyes on the snow and the mud. "Ride," she said, digging her heels into her horse's sides. Quindor gave her a long look, then nodded, and the group picked up the pace.

The long road stretched out ahead of them, and as her horse broke into a gallop, Lydia allowed the sob she'd been holding in to tear out of her chest, the tears to flood down her cheeks.

She cried for all that she'd gained. All that she'd lost. And all that would never be.

But not once did she look back.

ACKNOWLEDGMENTS

Seeing Lydia's and Killian's story to bookshelves has been a long, long journey. There are scenes in this novel that I first envisioned and wrote back in 2007, and while the story itself has undergone considerable change, some of my favorite parts have been with me for over a decade.

Endless thanks must go to my parents, Carol and Steve, and to my brother, Nick, who have all read countless versions of this novel and remained enthusiastic about the characters despite multiple name and personality changes. Thanks to Spencer for being supportive despite the challenges my career brings to our family and to our two daughters for putting up with a workaholic mother. To Pat for always being there to pick up my slack and to Steff and Kris for endless hours of driving into the city to entertain my children while I banged away at my keyboard.

I am eternally grateful to my agent extraordinaire, Tamar Rydzinski, for believing in this series and advocating so strongly for it. I've been on the higher maintenance side of things this year, and there are no words for how much I appreciate everything you've done and continue to do. Also thanks to Laura Dail and Samantha Fabien for your continued support!

To the team at Tor Teen, I am so grateful for all that you have done for this series and its characters. Special thanks to Melissa Frain for helping me make that rough mess full of endless NTD comments into the story it is now. Thanks to Devi Pillai, Saraciea Fennell, Isa Caban, and Elizabeth Vaziri. Thank you to the team at Macmillan Audio, most especially Thomas Mis for your enthusiasm and for involving me with the casting process.

Because I've been with this story for so long, I often struggled to see the forest through the trees, but I've had the good fortune to have several amazing early readers help me find my path. Huge thanks to Melissa, Shimrit, Eileen, and Amy, not only for helping me past my hurdles with this novel, but for your passion for ~~Killian~~ the Dark Shores world.

Biggest thanks of all to my loyal readers—those who've been with me for years and those who've only recently ventured into my worlds—thank you for your endless support and eagerness to read more of my words. Your reviews and blog posts and Instagram photos and fan art and cosplays featuring my stories are what keep me going through the tough times. I've so much love for you all and thank you for sticking with me on this journey.